ARABELLA

Arabella, daughter of an impoverished country parson, dreams of a new life in London. But her beauty and charm will only get her so far — and when she embarks on her first London season armed with nothing but a benevolent godmother, she quickly runs afoul of Robert Beaumaris. He's the most eligible bachelor of the day, with a personality as strong and combative as hers. Arabella cannot abide him thinking of her as just another pretty girl after his wealth, so she allows herself to be provoked into a game of deception — one that could have unexpected consequences . . .

Books *by Georgette Heyer*
Published in Ulverscroft Collections:

SPRIG MUSLIN

SPECIAL MESSAGE TO READERS

THE ULVERSCROFT FOUNDATION
(registered UK charity number 264873)
was established in 1972 to provide funds for
research, diagnosis and treatment of eye diseases.
Examples of major projects funded by
the Ulverscroft Foundation are:-

- The Children's Eye Unit at Moorfields Eye
Hospital, London
- The Ulverscroft Children's Eye Unit at Great
Ormond Street Hospital for Sick Children
- Funding research into eye diseases and
treatment at the Department of Ophthalmology,
University of Leicester
- The Ulverscroft Vision Research Group,
Institute of Child Health
- Twin operating theatres at the Western
Ophthalmic Hospital, London
- The Chair of Ophthalmology at the Royal
Australian College of Ophthalmologists

You can help further the work of the Foundation
by making a donation or leaving a legacy.
Every contribution is gratefully received. If you
would like to help support the Foundation or
require further information, please contact:

THE ULVERSCROFT FOUNDATION
**The Green, Bradgate Road, Anstey
Leicester LE7 7FU, England
Tel: (0116) 236 4325**

website: www.foundation.ulverscroft.com

GEORGETTE HEYER

ARABELLA

Complete and Unabridged

ULVERSCROFT
Leicester

First published in Great Britain in 1949

This Ulverscroft Edition
published 2019
by arrangement with
Penguin Random House UK
London

A catalogue record for this book is available
from the British Library.

ISBN 978–1–4448–4127–5

Published by
F. A. Thorpe (Publishing)
Anstey, Leicestershire

Set by Words & Graphics Ltd.
Anstey, Leicestershire
Printed and bound in Great Britain by
T. J. International Ltd., Padstow, Cornwall

This book is printed on acid-free paper

1

The schoolroom in the Parsonage at Heythram was not a large apartment, but on a bleak January day, in a household where the consumption of coals was a consideration, this was not felt by its occupants to be a disadvantage. Quite a modest fire in the high, barred grate made it unnecessary for all but one of the four young ladies present to huddle shawls round their shoulders. But Elizabeth, the youngest of the Reverend Henry Tallant's handsome daughters, was suffering from the ear-ache, and, besides stuffing a roasted onion into the afflicted orifice, had swathed her head and neck in an old Cashmere shawl. She lay curled up on an aged sofa, with her head on a worn red cushion, and from time to time uttered a long-suffering sigh, to which none of her sisters paid any heed. Betsy was known to be sickly. It was thought that the climate of Yorkshire did not agree with her constitution, and since she spent the greater part of the winter suffering from a variety of minor ills her delicacy was regarded by all but her Mama as a commonplace.

There were abundant signs, littered over the table in the centre of the room, that the young ladies had retired to this cosy, shabby apartment to hem shirts, but only one of them, the eldest, was thus engaged. In a chair on one side of the fireplace, Miss Margaret Tallant, a buxom fifteen-year old, was devouring the serial story in a bound volume of *The Ladies' Monthly Museum*, with her fingers stuffed in her ears; and seated opposite to Miss Arabella, her stitchery lying neglected on the table before her, sat Miss Sophia, reading aloud from another volume of this instructive periodical.

'I must say, Bella,' she remarked, momentarily lowering the book, 'I find this most perplexing! Only listen to what it says here! *We have presented our subscribers with fashions of the newest pattern, not such as shall violate the laws of propriety and decorum, but such as shall assist the smile of good humour, and give an additional charm to the carriage of benevolence. Economy ought to be the order of the day* — And then, if you please, there is a picture of the most ravishing evening-gown — Do but look at it, Bella! — and it says that the Russian bodice is of blue satin, fastened in front with diamonds! *Well!*'

Her sister obediently raised her eyes from the wristband she was hemming, and critically scanned the willowy giantess depicted amongst the Fashion Notes. Then she sighed, and once more bent her dark head over her work. 'Well, if that is their notion of economy, I am sure I couldn't go to London, even if my godmother invited me. And I know she won't,' she said fatalistically.

'You must and you shall go!' declared Sophy, in accents of strong resolution. 'Only think what it may mean to all of us if you do!'

'Yes, but I won't go looking like a dowd,'

objected Arabella, 'and if I am obliged to have diamond fastenings to my bodices, you know very well — '

'Oh, stuff! I daresay that is the extreme of fashion, or perhaps they are made of paste! And in any event this is one of the older numbers. I know I saw in one of them that jewelry is no longer worn in the mornings, so very likely — Where is that volume? Margaret, you have it! Do, pray, give it to me! You are by far too young to be interested in such things!'

Margaret uncorked her ears to snatch the book out of her sister's reach. 'No! I'm reading the serial story!'

'Well, you should not. You know Papa does not like us to read romances.'

'If it comes to that,' retorted Margaret, 'he would be excessively grieved to find you reading nothing better than the latest modes!'

They looked at one another; Sophy's lip quivered. 'Dear Meg, do pray give it to me, only for a *moment*!'

'Well, I will when I have finished the *Narrative of Augustus Waldstein*,' said Margaret. 'But *only* for a moment, mind!'

'Wait, I know there is something here to the purpose!' said Arabella, dropping her work to flick over the pages of the volume abandoned by Sophia. '*Method of Preserving Milk by Horse-Radish . . . White Wax for the Nails . . . Human Teeth placed to Stumps . . .* Yes, here it is! Now, listen, Meg! *Where a Female has in early life dedicated her attention to novel-reading she is unfit to become the companion of a man of* sense, or to conduct a family with propriety and decorum. There!' She looked up, the prim pursing of her lips enchantingly belied by her dancing eyes.

'I am sure Mama is not unfit to be the companion of a man of sense!' cried Margaret indignantly. 'And she reads novels! And even Papa does not find The Wanderer objectionable, or Mrs. Edgeworth's Tales!'

'No, but he did not like it when he found Bella reading The Hungarian Brothers, or The Children of the Abbey,' said Sophia, seizing the opportunity to twitch The Ladies' Monthly Museum out of her sister's slackened grasp. 'He said there was a great deal of nonsense in such books, and that the moral tone was sadly lacking.'

'Moral tone is not lacking in the serial I am reading!' declared Margaret, quite ruffled. 'Look what it says there, near the bottom of the page! 'Albert! be purity of character your duty!' I am sure he could not dislike that!'

Arabella rubbed the tip of her nose. 'Well, I think he would say it was fustian,' she remarked candidly. 'But do give the book back to her, Sophy.'

'I will, when I have found what I'm looking for. Besides, it was I who had the happy notion to borrow the volumes from Mrs Caterham, so — Yes, here it is! It says that only jewelry of very plain workmanship is worn in the mornings nowadays.' She added, on a note of doubt: 'I daresay the fashions don't change so very fast, even in London. This number is only three years old.'

The sufferer on the sofa sat up cautiously. 'But Bella hasn't got any jewelry, has she?'

This observation, delivered with all the bluntness natural in a damsel of only nine summers, threw a blight over the company.

'I have the gold locket and chain with the locks of Papa's and Mama's hair in it,' said Arabella defensively.

'If you had a tiara, and a — a cestus, and an armlet to match it, it might answer,' said Sophy. 'There is a toilet described here with just those ornaments.'

Her three sisters gazed at her in astonishment. 'What is a cestus?' they demanded.

Sophy shook her head. 'I don't know,' she confessed.

'Well, Bella hasn't got one at all events,' said the Job's comforter on the sofa.

'If she were so poor-spirited as to refuse to go to London for such a trifling reason as that, I would never forgive her!' declared Sophy.

'Of course I would not!' exclaimed Arabella scornfully. 'But I have not the least expectation that Lady Bridlington will invite me, for why should she, only because I am her goddaughter? I never saw her in my life!'

'She sent a very handsome shawl for your christening gift,' said Margaret hopefully.

'Besides being Mama's dearest friend,' added Sophy.

'But Mama has not seen her either — at least, not for years and years!'

'And she never sent Bella anything else, not even when she was confirmed,' pointed out

Betsy, gingerly removing the onion from her ear, and throwing it into the fire.

'If your ear-ache is better,' said Sophia, eyeing her with disfavour, 'you may hem this seam for me! I want to draw a pattern for a new flounce.'

'Mama said I was to sit quietly by the fire,' replied the invalid, disposing herself more comfortably. 'Are there any acrostics in those fusty old books?'

'No, and if there were I would not give them to anyone so disobliging as you, Betsy!' said Sophy roundly.

Betsy began to cry, in an unconvincing way, but as Margaret was once more absorbed in her serial, and Arabella had drawn Sophia's attention to the picture of a velvet pelisse trimmed lavishly with ermine, no one paid any heed to her, and she presently relapsed into silence, merely sniffing from time to time, and staring resentfully at her two eldest sisters.

They presented a charming picture, as they sat poring over their book, their dark ringlets intermingled, and their arms round each other's waists. They were very plainly dressed, in gowns of blue kerseymere, made high to the throat, and with long tight sleeves; and they wore no other ornaments than a knot or two of ribbons; but the Vicar's numerous offspring were all remarkable for their good-looks and had very little need of embellishment. Although Arabella was unquestionably the Beauty of the family, it was pretty generally agreed in the neighbourhood that once Sophia had outgrown the over-plumpness of her sixteen years she might reasonably hope to rival her senior. Each had large, dark, and expressive eyes, little straight noses, and delicately moulded lips; each had complexions which were the envy of less fortunate young ladies, and which owed nothing to Denmark Lotion, Olympian Dew, Bloom of Ninon, or any other aid to beauty advertised in the society journals. Sophia was the taller of the two; Arabella had by far the better figure, and the neater ankle. Sophia looked to be the more robust; Arabella enchanted her admirers by a deceptive air of fragility, which inspired one romantically-minded young gentleman to liken her to a leaf blown by the wind; and another to address a very bad set of verses to her, apostrophizing her as the New Titania. Unfortunately, Harry had found this effusion, and had shown it to Bertram, and until Papa had said, with his gentle austerity, that he considered the jest to be outworn, they had insisted on hailing their sister by this exquisitely humorous appellation.

Betsy, brooding over her wrongs, found nothing to admire in either sister, and was weighing the advantage of cosseting from old Nurse against the possibility of being called upon to amuse Baby Jack, were she to remove herself to the nursery, when the door burst open, and a stout boy of eleven years, in nankeens and a frilled shirt, and with a mop of curly hair, precipitated himself into the room, exclaiming loudly: 'Hallo! Such a kick-up! Mama is with Papa in the study, but *I* know what it's all about!'

'Why, what has happened?' exclaimed Sophia.

'Don't you wish you knew!' said Harry,

drawing a piece of twine from his pocket, and beginning to tie it into a complicated knot. 'Watch me tie this one, Meg! I know six of the chief knots now, and if Uncle James does not get Captain Bolton to take me on his next commission it will be the most infamous, swindling thing I ever heard of!'

'But you didn't come to tell us that!' said Arabella. 'What is it?'

'Nothing but one of Harry's hums!' said Margaret.

'No such thing!' retorted her brother. 'Joseph Eccles has been down to the White Hart, and brought back the post with him.' He perceived that he had succeeded in riveting his sisters' attention on himself, and grinned at them. 'Ay, you may stare! There's a letter from London, for Mama. Franked by some lord, too: I saw it.'

Margaret's book slipped from her fingers to the floor; Sophia gave a gasp; and Arabella flew up out of her chair. 'Harry! Not — oh, not from my godmother?'

'Oh, ain't it?' said Harry.

'If it comes from London, it must be from Lady Bridlington!' declared Sophia. 'Arabella, I do believe our fortunes are in a way to being made!'

'I *dare* not suppose it to be possible!' said Arabella, quite faintly. 'Depend upon it, she has written to say she cannot invite me!'

'Nonsense!' replied her practical sister. 'If that were all, pray why should Mama take the letter to my father? I regard the matter as settled already. You are going to London for the Season.'

'Oh, if it could be so indeed!' said Arabella, trembling.

Harry, who had abandoned knot-making in favour of trying to stand on his head, overbalanced at this moment, and fell in a heap on the floor, together with a chair, Sophia's work-box, and a hand-screen, which Margaret had been painting before succumbing to the superior attraction of *The Ladies' Monthly Museum*. Beyond begging him not to be such an ape, none of his sisters censured his clumsiness. He picked himself up, remarking scornfully that only a girl would make such a fuss about a mere visit to London. 'The slowest thing!' he said. 'I should like to know what you think you would do there!'

'Oh, Harry, how can you be so stupid? The balls! the theatres! Assemblies!' uttered Arabella, in choked accents.

'*I* thought you were going there to form an eligible connection,' said Betsy. 'That is what Mama said, for I heard her.'

'Then you had no business to be listening!' said Sophia tartly.

'What's an eligible connection?' demanded Harry, beginning to juggle with several reels of sewing-silk, which had spilled out of the work-box on to the floor.

'I'm sure I don't know!'

'I do,' offered the invalid. 'It's a splendid marriage, of course. And *then* Bella will invite Sophy and Meg and me to stay with her in London, and we shall *all* find rich husbands!'

'That I shall certainly not do, miss!' declared

9

Arabella. 'Let me tell you that no one will invite you anywhere until you have a little more conduct!'

'Well, Mama *did* say it,' argued Betsy, in a whining voice. 'And you need not think I do not know about such things, because —'

Sophia interrupted her ruthlessly. 'If, Betsy, you do not desire me to tell Papa of your shocking lack of delicacy, I advise you to take yourself off to the nursery — where you belong!'

This terrible threat did not fail of its object. Complaining that her sisters were disagreeable cats, Betsy, went as slowly from the room as she dared, trailing her shawl behind her.

'She is very sickly,' said Arabella, in an excusing tone.

'She is a precocious brat!' retorted Sophia. 'One would have thought that she would have had more elegance of mind than to be thinking of such things! Oh, Bella, if only you were to be so fortunate as to make a Splendid Marriage! And if Lady Bridlington is to bring you out I am sure I do not see how you can fail to! For,' she added nobly, 'you are by far the prettiest girl *I* have ever seen!'

'Hoo!' interpolated Harry, adding his mite to the conversation.

'Yes,' agreed Margaret, 'but if she must have diamond buttons, and tiaras, and — and those things you spoke of, I don't see how it can be done!'

A damped silence greeted her words. Sophie was the first to recover herself. 'Something,' she announced resolutely, 'will be contrived!'

No one answered her. Arabella and Margaret appeared to be dubiously weighing her pronouncement; and Harry, having discovered a pair of scissors, was pleasurably engaged in snipping short lengths off a skein of darning-wool. Into this pensive silence walked a young gentleman just emerging from adolescence into manhood. He was a handsome youth, fairer than his elder sister, but with something of her cast of countenance; and it was manifest, from the alarming height of his shirt collar, and the disorder of his chestnut locks, that he affected a certain modishness that bordered on dandyism. The Knaresborough tailor who enjoyed his patronage could not aspire to the height of art achieved by Weston or Stultz, but he had done his best, and had indeed been greatly assisted by the admirable proportions of his client. Mr Bertram Tallant set off a coat to advantage, and was blessed with a most elegant pair of legs. These were at the moment encased in a pair of buckskin breeches, but their owner cherished in one of his chests of drawers a pair of yellow pantaloons which he had not yet dared to display to his Papa, but which, he rather fancied, turned him into a veritable Tulip of Fashion. His top-boots, on which he expended much thought and labour, were as refulgent as could be expected of boots belonging to a gentleman whose parents were unhappily unable to supply their second son with the champagne indispensible for a really good blacking; and the points of his shirt-collars, thanks to the loving hands of his sisters, were so stiffly starched that it was only

11

with great difficulty that he could turn his head. Like his elder brother James, at present up at Oxford, prior to taking Orders, he had been educated at Harrow, but he was at present domiciled at home, working under his father's guidance with a view to passing Smalls during the Easter Vacation. This task he had embarked on without enthusiasm, his whole ambition being to obtain a cornetcy in a Hussar regiment. But as this would cost not a penny less than eight hundred pounds, and the termination of the long war with Bonaparte had made promotion unlikely, unless by expensive purchase, Mr Tallant had decided, not unreasonably, that a civil occupation would prove less ruinous than a military career. He intended that Bertram, once provided with a respectable degree, should adorn the Home Office; and any doubts which the volatile disposition of his offspring might have engendered in his mind of his eligibility for that service, he was nearly able to allay by the reflection that Bertram was, after all, not yet eighteen, and that Oxford University, where he himself had passed three scholarly years, would exert a stabilizing influence on his character.

The future candidate for Parliament heralded his entrance into the schoolroom with a muted hunting-cry, followed immediately by the announcement that some people were unfairly favoured by fortune.

Arabella clasped both her hands at her breast, and raised a pair of speaking eyes to his face. 'Bertram, is it *indeed* true? Now, don't try to roast me — pray don't!'

'Lord, yes! But who told you?'

'Harry, of course,' replied Sophia. 'The children know everything in this house!'

Mr Bertram Tallant nodded gloomily, and pulled up his sleeves a trifle. 'You don't want him in here: shall I turn him out?' he enquired.

'Ho!' cried Harry, leaping to his feet, and squaring up to his senior in great good-humour. 'A mill!'

'Not in here!' shrieked his sisters, with one accustomed voice.

But as they had no expectation of being attended to, each damsel made a dive to snatch her own particular property out of harm's way. This was just as well, since the room, besides being small, was crowded with knick-knacks. The brothers struggled and swayed together for a brief minute or two, but since Harry, though a lusty lad, was no match for Bertram, he was very soon thrust outside the room, and the door slammed against him. After dealing the scarred panels a few kicks, and threatening his senior with gruesome reprisals, he took himself off, whistling loudly through the convenient gap occasioned by the loss of one of his front teeth; and Bertram was able to remove his shoulders from the door, and to straighten his cravat.

'Well, you are to go,' he informed Arabella. 'I wish I had a rich godmother, that's all! Much old Mrs Calne ever did for me, except to give me a devilish book called the *Christian Comforter*, or some such thing, which was enough to send a fellow to the dogs directly!'

'I must say, I think it was excessively shabby of

her,' agreed Margaret. 'Even Papa said that if she had thought you had a taste for such literature, she might have supposed that you would find it upon his shelves.'

'Well, my father knows I have no turn in that direction, and this I will say for him, he don't expect it of me,' said Bertram handsomely. 'He may be devilish straitlaced, and full of old-fashioned notions, but he's a right one at heart, and don't plague one with a pack of humbug.'

'Yes, yes!' said Arabella impatiently, 'but does he know of this letter? Will he let me go?'

'I fancy he don't like it above half, but he said he could not stand in your way, and must trust to your conducting yourself in Society with propriety, and not allowing your head to be turned by frivolity and admiration. And as to that,' Bertram added, with brotherly candour, 'I don't suppose they will think you anything out of the way amongst all the nobs, so there's precious little chance of its happening.'

'No, I am sure they will not,' said Arabella. 'But tell me the whole! What did Lady Bridlington say in her letter?'

'Lord, I don't know! I was trying to make sense of a whole rigmarole of Greek when Mama came in, and I wasn't listening with more than half an ear. I daresay she'll tell it all to you. She sent me to say she wants you in her dressing-room.'

'Good gracious, why could you not have told me that before?' cried Arabella, stuffing the half-finished shirt into a work-bag and flitting out of the room.

The Parsonage, although built on two storeys only, was a large, old-fashioned house, and to reach Mrs Tallant's dressing-room Arabella was obliged to traverse several corridors, all carpeted with a worn drugget, and all equally draughty.

The living of Heythram was respectable, being worth some three hundred pounds a year, in addition to which the present incumbent was possessed of a small independence; but the claims of a numerous family made the recarpeting of passages more a thing to be dreamed of than an allowable expense. The Vicar, himself the son of a landed gentleman, had married the beautiful Miss Theale, who might have been expected to have done better for herself than to have thrown her cap over the windmill for a mere younger son, however handsome he might be. Indeed, it had been commonly said at the time that she had married to disoblige her family, and might, if she had chosen, have caught a baronet on her hook. Instead she had fallen in love with Henry Tallant at first sight. Since his birth was genteel, and her parents had other daughters to dispose of, she had been permitted to have her way; and apart from wishing sometimes that the living were worth more, or that Henry would not put his hand in his pocket for every beggar who crossed his path, she had never given anyone reason to suppose that she regretted her choice. To be sure, she would have liked to have installed into the Parsonage one of the new water-closets, and a Patent Kitchen Range; or, like her brother-in-law up at the Hall, have been able, without

15

feeling the pinch, to have burnt wax candles in all the rooms; but she was a sensible woman, and even when the open fire in the kitchen smoked, and the weather made a visit to the existing water-closet particularly disagreeable, she realized that she was a great deal happier with her Henry than ever she could have been with that almost forgotten baronet. She naturally concurred in his decision that whatever became of their daughters their sons at least must receive every advantage of education; but even while employing every shift of economy to ensure the respectable maintenance of James and Bertram at Harrow she was gradually building her ambitions more and more on the future of her eldest and most beautiful daughter. Without precisely regretting the circumstances which had made it impossible for herself to shine farther afield than York and Scarborough, she was determined that Arabella should not be similarly circumscribed. Perhaps it had been with this hope already at the back of her mind that she had invited her school-friend, Arabella Haverhill, who had contracted such a brilliant match, to stand as godmother to her infant daughter. Certainly her resolve to send the younger Arabella to make her début into society under the ægis of Lady Bridlington was of no very recent date. She had maintained throughout the years an infrequent but regular correspondence with her old friend, and was tolerably certain that fashionable life had in no way impaired the easy good-nature which had characterized the plump and cheerful Miss Haverhill. Lady

16

Bridlington was not herself blessed with daughters — she was, in fact, the mother of only one child, a son, some seven or eight years older than Mrs Tallant's daughter — but from her friend's point of view this was a decided advantage. The mother of a family of hopeful girls, however goodnatured, would not be in the least likely to take under her wing yet another young female in search of an eligible husband. But a widow in comfortable circumstances, with a strong inclination for all the amusements of fashion, and no daughters to launch upon the world, might reasonably be supposed to welcome the opportunity of chaperoning a young protégée to the balls, routs, and Assemblies she herself delighted in. Mrs Tallant could not conceive it to be otherwise. Nor was she disappointed. Lady Bridlington, crossing several sheets of gilt-edged notepaper with her sprawling pen, could not imagine why she should not have hit upon the notion herself. She was excessively dull, and liked nothing in the world so much as having young persons about her. It had long been a grief to her, she wrote, that she had no daughter of her own; and as she had no doubt that she would love her dearest Sophia's girl on sight she should await her arrival in the greatest impatience. Mrs Tallant had had no need to mention her object in sending Arabella to town: Henry Tallant might consider that Lady Bridlington's letters betrayed little but folly and frivolity, but her ladyship, however lacking in mental profundity, had plenty of worldly sense. Sophia might rest assured, she wrote, that she would leave no stone unturned to provide Arabella with a suitable husband. Already, she hinted, she had several eligible bachelors in her eye.

It was small wonder, then, that Arabella, peeping into her mother's dressing-room, should have found that admirable lady lost in a pleasant daydream.

'Mama?'

'Arabella! Come in, my love, and close the door! Your godmother has written, and in the kindest way! Dear, dear creature, I knew I might depend upon her!'

'It's true then? I am to go?' Arabella breathed.

'Yes, and she begs I will send you to her as soon as may be contrived, for it seems that Bridlington is travelling on the Continent, and she is quite moped to death, living in that great house all alone. I knew how it must be! She will treat you as her own daughter. And, oh, my dearest child, I never asked it of her, but she has offered to present you at one of the Drawing-rooms!'

This dizzy prospect took from Arabella all power of speech. She could only gaze at her mother, while that lady poured out a list of the delights in store for her.

'Everything I could wish for you! Almack's — I am sure she will be able to procure you a voucher, for she knows all the patronesses! Concerts! The theatre! All the *ton* parties — breakfasts, Assemblies, balls — my love, you will have such opportunities! you can have no notion! Why, she writes that — but never mind that!'

Arabella found her voice. 'But Mama, how shall we contrive? The expense! I cannot — I *cannot* go to London without any clothes to wear!'

'No, indeed!' said Mrs Tallant, laughing. 'That would present a very odd appearance, my love!'

'Yes, Mama, but you know what I mean! I have only two ball dresses, and though they do very well for the Assemblies in Harrowgate, and country parties, I *know* they are not modish enough for Almack's! And Sophy has borrowed all Mrs Caterham's *Monthly Museums*, and I have been looking at the fashions in them, and it is too lowering, ma'am! Everything must be trimmed with diamonds, or ermine, or point-lace!'

'My dear Arabella, don't put yourself in a taking! *That* has all been thought of, I assure you. You must know that I have had this scheme in my mind for many a long day.' She saw her daughter's face of mystification, and laughed again. 'Why, did you think I would send you into society looking like a rustic? I am not quite such a zany, I hope! I have been putting by for this very occasion since I don't know when.'

'Mama!'

'I have a little money of my own, you know,' explained Mrs Tallant. 'Your dear Papa would never use it, but desired me to spend it only as I liked, because I used to be very fond of pretty things, and he never could bear to think I might not have them when I married him. That was all nonsense, of course, and I'm sure I very soon gave up thinking of such fripperies. But I was very glad to have it to spend on my children. And in spite of Margaret's drawing-lessons, and Sophy's music-master, and dearest Bertram's new coat, and those yellow pantaloons which he dare not let Papa see — my love, was there ever such a foolish boy? As though Papa did not know all along! — and having to take poor Betsy to the doctor three times this year, I have quite a little nest-egg saved for you!'

'Oh, mama, no, no!' cried Arabella, distressed. 'I would rather not go to London at all than that you should be put to such dreadful expense!'

'That is because you are sadly shatterbrained, my dear,' replied her mother calmly. 'I regard it as an investment, and I shall own myself extremely astonished if a great deal of good does not come of it.' She hesitated, looked a little conscious, and said, picking her words: 'I am sure I do not have to tell you that Papa is a Saint. Indeed, I don't suppose there is a better husband or father alive! But he is not at all practical, and when one has eight children to provide for, one must have a little worldly sense, or I don't know how one is to go on. One need have no anxiety about dear James, to be sure; and since Harry is set on going to sea, and his uncle is so obliging as to use his influence in his behalf, *his* future is settled. But I own I cannot be happy about poor Bertram; and where I am to find suitable husbands for all you girls in this restricted neighbourhood, I have not the least notion! Now, that is speaking more plainly than perhaps Papa would like, but you are a sensible puss, Arabella, and I have no scruple in being open with you. If I can but contrive to establish you respectably, you may bring out your sisters, and perhaps, even, if you should be so fortunate as to marry a gentleman of position, you might be able to help Bertram to buy his commission. I do not mean, of course, that your husband should purchase it precisely, but he might very likely have an interest at the Horse Guards, or — or something of the sort!'

Arabella nodded, for it was no news to her that she, as the eldest of four sisters, was expected to marry advantageously. She knew it to be her duty to do so. 'Mama, I will *try* not to disappoint you!' she said earnestly.

2

It was the candidly expressed opinion of the
Vicar's children that Mama must have had a
great work to prevail upon Papa to consent to
Arabella's going to London. Few things were
more reprehensible in his eyes than vanity and
pleasure-seeking; and although he never raised
any objection to Mama's chaperoning Arabella
and Sophia to the Assemblies at Harrowgate, and
had even been known to comment favourably
upon their gowns, he always impressed upon
them that such diversions, innocent in themselves, would, if indulged in to excess, inevitably
ruin the character of the most virtuous female.
He had himself no taste for society, and had
frequently been heard to animadvert severely on
the useless and frivolous lives led by ladies of
fashion. Moreover, although he was not in the
least above enjoying a good joke, he had the
greatest dislike of levity, could never be brought
to tolerate idle chatter, and if the conversation
turned upon worldly trifles would never fail to
give it a more proper direction.

But Lady Bridlington's invitation to Arabella
did not take the Vicar by surprise. He knew that
Mrs Tallant had written to her old friend, and
however little he approved of the chief motive
behind her resolve to launch her daughter into
society, certain of the arguments she employed
to persuade him could not but carry weight.

'My dear Mr Tallant,' said his lady, 'do not let us dispute about the merits of an advantageous match! But even you will allow that Arabella is an uncommonly handsome girl!'

Mr Tallant allowed it, adding reflectively that Arabella put him forcibly in mind of what her Mama was at the same age. Mrs Tallant was not impervious to this flattery: she blushed, and looked a little roguishly, but said that he need not try to bamboozle her (an expression she had picked up from her sons).

'All I wish to point out to you, Mr Tallant, is that Arabella is fit to move in the first circles!' she announced.

'My love,' responded the Vicar, with one of his humorous looks, 'if I believed you, I should perhaps consider it my duty to show you that an ambition to move in the first circles, as you call them, could never be an ideal I could wish any of my daughters to aspire to. But as I am persuaded that you have a great many other arguments to advance, I will hold my peace, and merely beg you to continue!'

'Well,' said Mrs Tallant seriously, 'I fancy — but you must tell me if I am mistaken — that you would not regard with any degree of complaisance an alliance with the Draytons of Knaresborough!'

The Vicar was plainly startled, and directed an enquiring look at his spouse.

'Young Joseph Drayton is growing extremely particular in his attentions,' pronounced Mrs Tallant, in a voice of doom. She observed the effect of this, and continued in the blandest way:

'Of course, I am aware that he is considered to be a great catch, for he will inherit all his father's wealth.'

The Vicar was betrayed into an unchristian utterance. 'I could not consent to it! He smells of the shop!'

'Exactly so!' agreed Mrs Tallant, well-satisfied. 'But he has been dangling after Arabella these past six months.'

'Do you tell me,' demanded the Vicar, 'that a daughter of mine encourages his attentions?'

'By no means!' promptly responded the lady. 'Any more than she encourages the attentions of the curate, young Dewsbury, Alfred Hitchin, Humphrey Finchley, or a dozen others! Arabella, my dear sir, is by far the most sought-after belle of these parts!'

'Dear me!' said the Vicar, shaking his head in wonderment. 'I must confess, my love, that none of these young gentlemen would be welcome to me as a son-in-law.'

'Then, perhaps, Mr Tallant, you cherish hopes of seeing Arabella married to her cousin Tom?'

'Nothing,' said the Vicar forcibly, 'could be farther from my wishes!' He recollected himself, and added in a more moderate tone: 'My brother is a very worthy man, according to his lights, and I wish his children nothing but good; but on several counts, which I need not enumerate, I should not desire to see any of my daughters marry their cousins. And, what is more, I am very sure that he has quite other designs for Tom and Algernon!'

'Indeed he has!' corroborated Mrs Tallant

cordially. 'He means them to marry heiresses.'

The Vicar bent an incredulous gaze upon her. 'Does my daughter affect any of these young men?' he demanded.

'I fancy not,' replied Mrs Tallant. 'That is to say, she does not show any marked preference for any one of them. But when a girl sees no other gentlemen than those who have been dangling after her ever since she left the schoolroom, what, my dear Mr Tallant, must be the end of it? And young Drayton,' she added musingly, 'is possessed of a considerable fortune. I do not mean that Arabella would consider *that*, but there is no denying that the man who drives a smart curricle, and can afford to be begging a female's acceptance of all the most elegant trifles imaginable, has a decided advantage over his rivals.'

There was a pregnant silence, while all the implications of this speech sank into the Vicar's brain. He said at length, rather wistfully: 'I had hoped that one day a suitable *parti* would present himself, to whom I might have given Arabella with a thankful heart.'

Mrs Tallant threw him an indulgent glance. 'Very likely, my dear, but it would be a great piece of nonsense to pretend that such things happen when one has made not the least push to bring them about! Eligible *partis* do not commonly appear as by magic in country villages: one must go out into the world to find them!' She saw that the Vicar was looking a little pained, and laughed. 'Now, do not tell me that it was otherwise with us, Mr Tallant, for you know very well I met you first at a party in York! I own it was not in the expectation of my falling in love with *you* that my Mama took me there, but in your turn *you* will own that we should never have met if I had sat at home waiting for you!'

He smiled. 'Your arguments are always unanswerable, my love. Yet I cannot entirely like it. I believe Arabella to be a well-behaved girl enough, but she is very young, after all, and I have thought sometimes that her spirits might, lacking wiser guidance, betray her into unbecoming conduct. Under Lady Bridlington's roof, she would, I fear, lead a life gay to dissipation, such as must make her unfit afterwards for rational society.'

'Depend upon it,' said Mrs Tallant soothingly, 'she is by far too well-behaved a girl to occasion us a moment's anxiety. I am sure, too, that her principles are too sound to allow her to lose her head. To be sure, she can be a sad romp, and *that*, my dear sir, is because she has not yet enjoyed the advantages of town polish. I am hopeful of seeing her much improved by a season spent with Bella Bridlington. And if — mind, I only say if! — she were to contract a suitable alliance I am sure you would be as thankful as anyone could be!'

'Yes,' agreed the Vicar, sighing. 'I should certainly be glad to see her comfortably established, the wife of a respectable man.'

'And *not* the wife of young Dewsbury!' interpolated Mrs Tallant.

'Indeed, no! I cannot suppose that any child of mine could attain happiness with a man whom I must — with reluctance — think a very vulgar fellow!'

'In that case, my dear,' said Mrs Tallant, rising briskly to her feet, 'I will write to accept Lady Bridlington's most obliging invitation.'

'You must do as you think right,' he said. 'I have never interfered with what you considered proper for your daughters.'

Thus it was that, at four o'clock on this momentous day, when the Vicar joined his family at the dinner-table, he surprised them by making a humorous reference to Arabella's projected trip. Not even Betsy would have ventured to have mentioned the scheme, for it was generally supposed that he must disapprove of it. But after grace had been said, and the family had disposed themselves about the long table, Arabella began, not very expeditiously, to carve one of the side-dishes, and the Vicar, looking up from his own labours in time to see her place a slightly mangled wing of chicken on a plate, remarked, with a twinkle: 'I think Arabella must take lessons in carving before she goes into society, or she will disgrace us all by her unhandiness. It will not do, you know, my dear, to precipitate a dish into your neighbour's lap, as you seem to be in danger of doing at this moment!'

Arabella blushed, and protested. Sophia, the first to recover from the shock of hearing Papa speak with such good-humour of the London scheme, said: 'Oh, but, Papa, I am sure it will not signify, for ten to one all the dishes are served by the footmen in grand houses!'

'I stand corrected, Sophia,' said the Vicar, with dry meekness.

'Will Lady Bridlington have many footmen?'

asked Betsy, dazzled by this vision of opulence.

'One to stand behind every chair,' promptly replied Bertram. 'And one to talk behind Arabella everytime she desires to take the air; and two to stand up behind my lady's carriage; and a round dozen, I daresay, to form an avenue in the front hall anytime her ladyship increases her covers for guests. When Arabella returns to us she will have forgotten how to pick up her own handkerchief, mark my words!'

'Well, I don't know how she will go on in such a house!' said Betsy, half-believing him.

'Nor I, indeed!' murmured Arabella.

'I trust she will go on, as you not very elegantly phrase it, my child, exactly as she would in her own home,' said the Vicar.

Silence followed this rebuke. Bertram made a grimace at Arabella across the table, and Harry dug her surreptitiously in the ribs with his elbow. Margaret, who had been wrinkling her brow over her father's words, ventured at last to say: 'Yes, Papa, but I do not precisely see how she can do so! It must be so very different to what we are accustomed to! I should not be surprised, for instance, if she found herself obliged to wear her party-gowns every evening, and I am sure she will not help with the baking, or starch shirts, or feed the chickens, or — or anything of that nature!'

'That was not quite what I meant, my dear,' responded the Vicar repressively.

'Will she not be made to do any work at all?' exclaimed Betsy. 'Oh, how much I wish *I* had a rich godmother!'

This ill-timed remark brought an expression of grave displeasure to the Vicar's face. It was evident to his family that the picture thus conjured up, of a daughter given over wholly to pleasure, was not one he could contemplate with anything but misgiving. Several darkling looks were cast at Betsy, which boded ill for one tactless enough to call down upon her sisters a lecture on the evils of idleness; but before the Vicar could speak, Mrs Tallant had intervened, calling Betsy to order for chattering, and saying cheerfully: 'Well, and I think Papa will agree that Arabella is a good girl, and deserves this indulgence more than any of you. I am sure I do not know how I shall manage without her, for whenever I want a task performed I know I may rely upon her to do it. And, what is a great deal to the point, let me tell you all! — she never shows me a pouting face, or complains that she is bored, or falls into a fit of the sullens because she is obliged to mend her old gown instead of purchasing a new one.'

It could scarcely be expected that this masterly speech would please the three damsels to whom it was pointedly addressed, but it had the happy effect of softening the Vicar's countenance. He glanced at Arabella, who was furiously blushing and holding her head bent over her plate, and said gently: 'Indeed, I am disposed to think that her character is well-established amongst us as one who wants neither sense nor feeling.' Arabella looked up quickly, her eyes brightened by tears. He smiled at her, and said in a teasing voice: 'If she will not let her tongue run like a fiddle-stick, nor express herself in terms which I might almost suppose she learns from her brothers, nor play pranks like a hoyden, I really believe I may indulge the hope that we shall not hear from Lady Bridlington that she is sunk quite beyond reproach in London!'

Such was the relief of his children at escaping one of Papa's homilies that this mild jest was received with a flattering degree of appreciation. Bertram seized the opportunity afforded by the general outcry of laughing protests to inform Betsy in a savage under-voice that if she opened her lips again he would most faithfully drop her in the middle of the duck-pond on the morrow, which promise so terrified her that she sat mumchance throughout the rest of the meal. Sophia, with real nobility of character, then asked Papa to explain something she had read in Sir John Malcolm's *History of Persia*, which the Vicar, whose only personal extravagance was his purchase of books, had lately added to his library. This was a happy inspiration: while her contemporaries gazed at Sophia in stupefaction, the Vicar, becoming quite animated, expounded at length on the subject, quite forgetting the immediate problems of the hour, and reducing his other offspring to a state of speechless indignation by saying, as he rose from the table, that he was glad to find that he had one daughter at least of a scholarly turn of mind.

'And Sophy never read a word of the book!' Bertram said bitterly, when, after enduring an evening in the parlour under the scourge of having passages from Sir John Malcolm's memorable work read aloud to them, he and his two elder sisters had escaped to the sanctuary of the girls' bedchamber.

'Oh, yes, I had!' retorted Sophia, sitting down on the end of her bed, and curling her legs under her in a way that, could her Mama but have seen it, would certainly have called down reproof upon her head.

Margaret, who was always sent up to bed before the appearance of the tea-tray, and thus had been spared the greater part of the evening's infliction, sat up, hugging her knees, and asked simply: 'Why?'

'Well, it was that day that Mama was obliged to go out, and desired me to remain in the parlour in case old Mrs Farnham should call,' explained Sophia. 'I had nothing else to do!'

After regarding her fixedly for several moments, her brother and sisters apparently decided that the excuse was reasonable, for they abandoned the subject.

'I declare I was ready to sink when Papa said *that* about me!' remarked Arabella.

'Yes, but you know, Bella, he is very absent-minded,' said Sophia, 'and I fancy he had forgotten what you and Bertram did on Boxing Day, and what he said about your inclination for finery, when you pulled the feathers out of Uncle's peacocks to furbish up your old bonnet.'

'Yes, perhaps he had,' agreed Arabella, in a dampened tone. 'But all the same,' she added, her spirits reviving, 'he never said I had no delicacy of principle, which he said to you when he discovered it was you, Sophy, who put one of

Harry's trousers-buttons into the bag in Church that Sunday!'

This was so unanswerable that Sophia could think of no retort to make. Bertram said suddenly: 'Well, since it is decided that you are to go to London, Bella, I'll tell you something!'

Seventeen years' intimate knowledge of her younger brother was not enough to restrain Arabella from demanding eagerly: 'Oh, what, pray?'

'You may get a surprise when you are there!' said Bertram, in a voice of mystery. 'Mind, I don't say you will, but you *may*!'

'What can you possibly mean? Tell me, Bertram! — *dearest* Bertram!'

'I'm not such a saphead! Girls always blab everything!'

'I would not! You know I would not! Oh, Bertram!'

'Don't heed him!' recommended Margaret, sinking back on to her pillow. 'It's all humbug!'

'Well, it's not, miss!' said her brother, nettled. 'But you needn't think I mean to tell you, for I don't! But don't be surprised, Bella, if you get a surprise before you have been in London very long!'

This ineptitude naturally threw his sisters into whoops. Unfortunately their mirth reached the ears of old Nurse, who promptly sailed into the room, and delivered herself of a shrill homily on the general impropriety of young gentlemen who sat on the ends of their sisters' beds. Since she was quite capable of reporting this shocking conduct to Mama, Bertram thought it prudent to remove himself, and the symposium came to an abrupt end. Nurse, blowing out the candles, said that if this came to Mama's ears there would be no London for Miss Arabella; but apparently it did not come to Mama's ears, for on the morrow, and indeed on all the succeeding days, nothing was talked of in the Parsonage (except in Papa's presence) but Arabella's entrance into the Polite World.

The first and most pressing consideration was the getting together of a wardrobe suitable for a young lady hopeful of making a successful début. Earnest perusal of the fashion journals had cast Arabella into a mood of despair, but Mama took a more cheerful view of the matter. She commanded the houseboy to summon the ubiquitous Joseph Eccles up to the Parsonage, and desired the pair of them to fetch down from one of the attics two formidable trunks. Joseph, who had been employed by the Vicar since the first year of his marriage as the farm-hand, considered himself the mainstay of the establishment, and was only too ready to oblige the ladies; and he lingered in the dressing-room, proffering counsel and encouragement in the broadest of Yorkshire dialects until kindly but firmly dismissed.

A pleasing aroma of camphor pervaded the air as soon as the lids were raised from the trunks, and the removal of a covering of silver paper disclosed treasures innumerable. The trunks contained the finery which Mama had worn (she said) when she was just such a giddy puss as Arabella. When she had married Papa she had

had no occasion for such fripperies, but she had not been able to bring herself to give them away, and had packed them up and well-nigh forgotten all about them.

Three ecstatic gasps shuddered on the air as three rapt young ladies dropped down on their knees beside the trunks, and prepared to rummage to their hearts' content.

There were unimagined delights in the trunks: curled ostrich plumes of various colours; branches of artificial flowers; an ermine tippet (alas, turned sadly yellow with age, but it would serve to trim Sophy's old pelisse!); a loo-mask; a whole package of finest thread-lace; a tiffany cloak, which set Margaret peacocking round the room; several ells of ribbon of a shade which Mama said was called in her young days *opéra brulé*, and quite the rage; scarves of gauze, lace, and blonde, spangled and plain; a box containing intriguing knots of ribbon, whose names Mama could not quite remember, though she rather thought that that pale blue bunch was A Sign of Hope, and the pink bow A Sigh of Venus; point-lace tuckers, and lappet-heads; a feather muff; innumerable fans; sashes; a scarlet-flowered damask mantua petticoat — what a figure Mama must have looked in it! — and a velvet cloak, miraculously lined with sable, which had been a wedding-gift to Mama, but which she had scarcely worn, 'because, my loves, it was finer than anything your aunt possessed, and, after all, she was the Squire's wife, and dreadfully inclined to take a pet, so that I always took care never to give her the least cause to be offended. But it is a beautiful fur, and will make a muff for Arabella, besides trimming a pelisse!'

It was fortunate that Mama was an indulgent parent, and so very fond of a joke, for the trunks contained, besides these treasures, such old-fashioned garments that the three Misses Tallant were obliged to laugh. Fashions had changed a great deal since Mama was a girl, and to a generation accustomed to high-waisted gowns of muslin and crape, with little puff-sleeves, and demure flounces round the hems, the stiff, voluminous silks and brocades Mama had worn, with their elaborate undergowns, and their pads, and their wired bodices, seemed not only archaic, but very ugly too. What was this funny jacket, with all the whalebone? A Caraco? Gracious! And this striped thing, for all the world like a dressing-gown? A lustring sack — well, it was certainly very little a sack, to be sure! Did Mama wear it in *company*? What was in this elegant box? Poudre à la Maréchale! But did Mama then powder her hair, like the picture of Grandmama Tallant, up at the Hall? Oh, *not* quite like that! A *gray* powder? Oh, Mama, no! and you without a gray hair to your head! How did you dress it? Not cut *at all*? Curls to the waist at the back? And all those rolls and puffs over the ears! How could Mama have had the patience to do it? So odd as it must have looked, too!

But Mama, turning over half-forgotten dresses, grew quite sentimental, remembering that she had been wearing this very gown of green Italian taffeta, over a petticoat of satin, *soupir d'étouffe* (unaccountably missing), when she had first met

35

Papa; remembering the pretty compliment paid to her by that rejected baronet when he had seen her in the white silk waist Sophia was holding up (it had had a book-muslin train, and there should be somewhere a pink silk coat, very smart, which she had worn with it); remembering how shocked her Mama had been when she had seen that rose-coloured Indian muslin underwear which Eliza — your Aunt Eliza, my loves — had brought her from London.

The girls did not know where to look when Mama sighed over a cherry-striped gown, and said how pretty it had been, for really it was quite hideous, and it made them feel almost uncomfortable to think of Mama's being seen abroad in such a garment. It was beyond laughter, so they sat respectfully silent, and were profoundly relieved when suddenly she shook off this unaccustomed mood, and smiled, and said in her own brisk way: 'Well, I daresay you think I must have looked like a dowd, but I assure you I did not! However, none of these brocades is of any use to Arabella, so we will put them up again. But that straw-coloured satin will do famously for a ball-dress, and we may trim it with some of the point-lace.'

There was a dressmaker in High Harrowgate, an elderly Frenchwoman, who had originally come to England as an émigrée from the Revolution. She had very often made dresses for Mrs Tallant and her daughters, and since she had excellent taste, and did not charge extortionate prices, except during the short season, it was decided that she should be entrusted with the task of making all Arabella's gowns. On the first day that the horses could be spared from the farm, Mrs Tallant and her two elder daughters drove to High Harrowgate, taking with them three bandboxes full of the silks, velvets, and laces which had finally been selected from Mrs Tallant's hoard.

Harrowgate, which was situated between Heythram and the large town of Knaresborough, was a watering-place renowned more for the excellent properties of its medicinal springs than for the modishness of its visitors. It consisted of two straggling villages, more than a mile apart, and enjoyed a summer season only. Since upwards of a thousand persons, mostly of valetudinarian habits, visited it then to drink the waters, both villages and their environs boasted more hotels and boarding-houses than private residences. From May till Michaelmas, public balls were held twice a week at the new Assembly Rooms; there was a Promenade, standing in the middle of an agreeable garden; a theatre; and a lending library, much patronized by Mrs Tallant and her daughters.

Mme Dupont was delighted to receive a client in the middle of January, and no sooner learned the reason for the bespeaking of such an extensive wardrobe than she entered into the spirit of the adventure with Gallic enthusiasm, fell into raptures over the silks and satins in the three bandboxes, and spread fashion-plates, and rolls of cambric and muslin and crape before the ladies' eyes. It would be a pleasure, she said, to make for a *demoiselle* with such a *taille* as

Mademoiselle Tallant's; already she perceived how Madame's satin polonaise could be transformed into a ball-dress of the most ravishing, while as for the taffeta over-dress — alas, that the elegant toilettes of the last century were no longer in vogue! — she could assure Madame that nothing could be more *comme il faut* than an opera cloak fashioned out of its ample widths, and trimmed with ruched velvet ribbon. As for the cost, that would be a matter for arrangement of the most amicable.

Arabella, who in general had a decided will of her own, as well as very definite ideas on the colour and style of her dresses, was so much shocked by the number of gowns Mama and Mme Dupont seemed to think indispensable for a sojourn in London that she scarcely opened her lips, except to agree in a faint voice with whatever was suggested to her. Even Sophia, who so often earned reproofs from Papa for chattering like a magpie, was awed into comparative silence. Not all her study of the fashion-plates in *The Ladies' Monthly Museum* had prepared her for the dazzling creations sketched in *La Belle Assemblée*. But Mama and Mme Dupont were agreed that only the simplest of these would be *convenable* for such a young lady. One or two ball-dresses of satin, or orange-blossom sarsnet, would be needed for grand occasions, but nothing could be prettier, said Madame, than crape or fine jaconet muslin for the Assemblies at Almack's. Some silver net drapery, perhaps — she had the very thing laid by — or a Norwich shawl, carried negligently across the elbows, would lend a *cachet* to the plainest gown. Then, for a morning half-dress, might she suggest a figured French muslin, with a demi-train? Or perhaps Mademoiselle would prefer a Berlin silk, trimmed with silk floss? For carriage dresses, she would recommend fine cambric, worn with a velvet mantle, and a Waterloo hat, or even a fur bonnet, ornamented — Mademoiselle's colouring made it permissible, even imperative! — with a bunch of cherries.

Morning dresses, afternoon dresses, carriage dresses, walking dresses, ball dresses — it seemed to Arabella and Sophia that the list would never come to an end. 'I cannot imagine how you will find time to wear the half of them!' whispered Sophia.

'Shoes, half-boots, reticules, gloves, stockings,' murmured Mrs Tallant, conning her list. 'Those will do for another day. You must take the greatest care of your silk stockings, my love, for I cannot afford to buy you many pairs! Hats — h'm, yes! What a fortunate thing it was that I kept all my old ostrich feathers! We shall see what we can contrive. I think that will do for today.'

'Mama, what will Bella wear when she goes to the Drawing-room?' asked Sophia.

'*Ah, pour ça, alors, la grande parure!*' cried Madame, her eyes brightening.

Mrs. Tallant crushed these budding hopes. 'Full dress, to be sure, my dear: satin, I daresay. Feathers, of course. I do not know if hoops are still worn at Court. Lady Bridlington is to make your sister a present of the dress, and I know I may depend upon her to choose just what is right. Come, my dears! If we are to call upon your uncle on our way home it is high time we were off!'

'Call upon my uncle?' repeated Sophia, surprised.

Mrs Tallant coloured slightly, but replied in an airy way: 'Certainly, my love: why should we not? Besides, one should never neglect the observances of civility, and I am sure he would think it very odd in me not to apprise him of Arabella's going to London.'

Sophia knitted her brows a little over this, for although there had always been a good deal of coming and going between the two boys at the Hall, and their young cousins at the Vicarage, visits between their respective parents were rare. The Squire and his brother, while remaining on perfectly amicable terms, scarcely possessed a thought in common, each regarding the other with affectionate contempt; while the late Lady Tallant, besides labouring under all the disadvantages of a jealous temper, had been, even in her charitable brother-in-law's estimation, a very under-bred woman. There were two children of the marriage: Thomas, a bucolic young man of twenty-seven; and Algernon, who held a commission in the — th Regiment, stationed at present in Belgium.

The Hall, which was situated in a pretty little park, about a mile from the village of Heythram, was a commodious, unpretentious house built of the prevailing gray stone of the district. Comfort rather than elegance was the predominant note struck by its furniture and decorations, and it bore, in despite of the ministrations of an excellent housekeeper, the indefinable air of a residence that lacked a mistress. The Squire was more interested in his stables than in his house. He was generally thought to be a warm man, but careful; and although he was fond of his nephews and nieces, and always goodnaturedly mounted Bertram during the hunting-season, it was rarely that his affection led him to do more for them than to give them a guinea apiece every Christmas. But he was a hospitable man, and always seemed pleased to welcome his brother's family to his board.

He came bustling out of the house as soon as the Parsonage carriage drew up at his door, and exclaimed in a loud voice: 'Well, well, if it's not Sophia, and the girls! Well, this is a pleasant circumstance! What, only the two of you? Never mind! Come in, and take a glass of wine! Bitter cold, ain't it? Ground's like iron: don't know when we shall get out again, damme if I do!'

Talking all the time, he led the ladies into a square parlour in the front of the house, breaking off his conversation only to shout to someone to bring refreshments into the parlour, and to be quick about it. He then ran his eye over his nieces, and said that they were prettier than ever, and demanded to be told how many beaux they could boast between them. They were spared the necessity of answering this jocular question by his instantly turning to Mrs Tallant, and saying: 'Can't hold a candle to their Mama, though, I swear! I declare, it's an age since I've clapped eyes on you, Sophia! Can't think why you and poor Henry don't come up more often to eat your mutton with me! And how is Henry? Still poring over his books, I dare swear! I never knew such a fellow! But you shouldn't let him keep young Bertram's nose glued to 'em, my dear: that's a good lad — regular devil to go, nothing bookish about him!'

'Bertram is reading for Oxford, Sir John. You know he must do so!'

'Mark my words, he'll do no good there!' said the Squire. 'Better make a soldier of him, as I did with my young rascal. But tell him to come up to the stables here, if he wants to see a rare piece of horseflesh: great rumps and hocks, grand shoulders! Don't mind the boy's trying him, if he likes to, but he's young yet: needs schooling. Does Bertram mean to come out when this frost breaks? Tell him the bay has a splint forming, or you may call me a Dutchman, but he may ride Thunderer, if he chooses.'

'I think,' said Mrs Tallant, with a faint sigh, 'that his Papa does not wish him to hunt any more this season. It quite takes his mind off his book, poor boy!'

'Henry's an old woman,' replied the Squire. 'Ain't it enough for him to have James as bookish as he is himself? Where is that lad? Up at Oxford, eh? Ah well, each man to his taste! Now, that other young rascal of yours — what's his name? Harry! I like the cut of his jib, as he'd say himself. Going to sea, he tells me. How shall you manage it?'

Mrs Tallant explained that one of her brothers was to use his interest in Harry's favour. The Squire seemed satisfied with this, asked jovially after the health of his godson and namesake, and set about pressing cold meat and wine upon his guests. It was some time before any opportunity offered of breaking to him the reason of the visit, but when the spate of his conversation abated a little, Sophia, who could scarcely contain herself for impatience, said abruptly: 'Sir, do you know that Arabella is going to London?'

He stared, first at her, and then at Arabella. 'Eh? What's that you say? How comes this about?'

Mrs Tallant, frowning reprovingly at Sophia, explained the matter. He listened very intently, nodding, and pursing up his lips, as his habit was when he was interested; and after turning it over in his mind for several moments, began to perceive what an excellent thing it was, and to congratulate Arabella upon her good fortune. After he had wished her a great many town-beaux, envied the lucky one who should win her, and prophesied that she would shine down all the London beauties, Mrs Tallant brought his gallantry to an end by suggesting that her daughters would like to go to the housekeeper's room to visit good Mrs Paignton, who was always so kind to them. The style of the Squire's pleasantries was not just to her taste; moreover, she wished to have some private talk with him.

He had a great many questions to ask her, and comments to make. The more he thought about

43

the scheme the better he liked it, for although he was fond of his niece, and considered her a remarkably handsome girl, he did not wish her to become his daughter-in-law. His understanding was not quick, nor had he much power of perception, but it had lately been borne in upon him that his heir had begun to dangle after his cousin in a marked manner. He did not suppose that Tom's affections were deeply engaged, and he was hopeful that if Arabella were removed from the neighbourhood he would soon recover from his mild infatuation, and make some more eligible lady the object of his gallantry. He had a suitable girl in his eye for Tom, but being a fairminded man he was obliged to own that Miss Maria was cast very much in the shade by Arabella. Nothing, therefore, that Mrs Tallant could have told him would have met with more approval from him. He gave the scheme his warmest approbation, and told her that she was a sensible woman.

'Ay, you need not tell me! this is your doing, Sophia! Poor Henry never had a particle of sense! A dear, good fellow, of course, but when a man has a quiverful of children he needs to be a little sharper than Henry. But you have all your wits about you, my dear sister! You are doing just as you should: the girl's uncommon handsome, and should do well for herself. Ay, ay, you will be setting about the wedding preparations before the cat has time to lick her ear! Lady Bridlington, eh? One of the London nobs, I daresay: couldn't be better! But it will cost a great deal!'

'Indeed, you are right, Sir John,' said Mrs Tallant. 'It will cost a very great deal, but when such an opportunity is offered every effort should be made to take advantage of it, I believe.'

'Ay, ay, you will be laying your money out to good purpose!' he nodded. 'But can you trust this fine lady of yours to keep half-pay officers, and such-like, out of the girl's way? It won't do to have her running off with some penniless fellow, you know, and all your trouble wasted!'

The fact that the same thought had more than once crossed her mind did not make this piece of plain-speaking any more agreeable to Mrs Tallant. She considered it extremely vulgar, and replied in a repressive tone that she believed she might depend on Arabella's good sense.

'You had better drop a word of warning in your friend's ear,' said Sir John bluntly. 'You know, Sophia, if that girl of yours were to catch a man of property, and, damme, I don't see why she shouldn't! — it would be a great thing for her sisters! Ay, the more I think on it the better I like it! It is worth all the expense. When does she go? How do you mean to send her?'

'As to that, it is not yet decided, Sir John, but if Mrs Caterham holds by her original scheme, and lets Miss Blackburn go next month — you must know that she is the governess, I daresay — she could travel with Arabella. I believe her home is in Surrey, so she must go to London.'

'But you won't send little Bella on the stage-coach!'

Mrs Tallant sighed. 'My dear sir, the cost of

posting is too great to be even thought of! I own, I do not like it, but beggars, you know, cannot be choosers!'

The Squire began to look very thoughtful. 'Well, that won't do,' he said presently. 'No, no, we can't have that! Driving up to your grand friend's house in a hackney! We shall have to contrive a little, Sophia. Now, let me see!'

He sat staring into the fire for some minutes, while his sister-in-law pensively gazed out of the window, and tried not to let her mind dwell on what her sensitive husband's feelings must be, could he but have had the least idea of what she was doing.

'I'll tell you what, sister!' said the Squire suddenly. 'I'll send Bella to London in my travelling-carriage, that's what I'll do! No sense in wasting money on posting: it don't matter to the girl if she spends some time on the road. What's more, those post-chaises can't take up all the baggage I'll be bound Bella will have with her. Ay, and this governess of yours will have a box as well, I daresay.'

'Your travelling carriage!' exclaimed Mrs Tallant, rather startled.

'That's it. Never use it myself: it hasn't been out of the coachhouse since my poor Eliza died. I'll set the men on to furbish it up: it ain't one of these smart, newfangled barouches, but it's a handsome carriage — I bought it for Eliza, when we were first married, and it has my crest on the panel. You would not be comfortable, sending the girl off with strange post-boys, you know: much better to let my old coachman drive her, and I'll send one of the grooms along to sit up beside him, with a pistol in his pocket in case of highwaymen.' He rubbed his hands together, well-pleased with the scheme, and began to estimate how many days it would take a strong pair of horses — or, at a pinch, even four — to reach London without getting knocked-up. He was inclined to think the plan would answer very well, and that Arabella would not at all object to resting the nags a day here or there upon the road. 'Or she might travel by easy stages, you know!' he said.

Upon reflection, Mrs Tallant perceived that this plan had much to recommend it. Against the evils of lingering in the various posting-houses along the route, must be set the advantages of being driven by a steady, trustworthy coachman, and of being able, as the Squire had pointed out, to carry all the trunks and bandboxes in the carriage, instead of having to send them to town by carrier. She thanked him, therefore, and was still expressing the sense of her obligation to him when the young ladies came back into the room.

The Squire greeted Arabella with great joviality, pinching her cheek, and saying: 'Well, puss, this is a new come-out for you, eh? I'll swear you're in high gig! Now, here's your mother and I have been putting our heads together, and the long and the short of it is you are to go to London in prime style, in your poor aunt's carriage, and Timothy-coachman to drive you. How will that be, my lass?'

Arabella, who had very pretty manners, thanked him, and said everything that was

47

proper. He appeared pleased, told her she might give him a kiss, and he would be satisfied, and suddenly walked out of the room, adjuring her to wait, for he had a little something for her. When he came back, he found his visitors ready to take their leave of him. He shook hands warmly with them all, and pressed into Arabella's a folded banknote, saying: 'There! that is to buy yourself some fripperies with, puss!'

She was quite overcome, for she had not expected anything of the sort; coloured, and stammered that he was by far too kind. He liked to be thanked, and beamed at her, and pinched her cheek again, very well satisfied with himself and her.

'But, Mama,' said Sophia, when they were driving away from the Hall, 'you will never let poor Arabella go to town in that antiquated carriage of my uncle's!'

'Nonsense!' replied her mother. 'It is a very respectable carriage, and if it is oldfashioned I daresay it is none the worse for that. No doubt you would rather see her dash off in a chaise-and-four, but it would cost as much as fifty or sixty pounds, besides what one must give the postilions, and is not to be thought of. Why, even a pair of horses, so far as we are from London, would mean thirty pounds, and all for what? To be sure, it will be a little slow, but Miss Blackburn will be with your sister, and if they are obliged to stay a day in an inn — to rest the horses, you know — she will be able to look after her, and I may be comfortable in my mind.'

'Mama!' said Arabella faintly. '*Mama!*'

'Good gracious, my love, what is it?'

Arabella dumbly proffered the Squire's bank-note. Mrs Tallant took it from her, saying: 'You would like me to take care of it for you, would you? Very well, I will do so, my dear, or you would be squandering it on presents for your brothers and sisters, perhaps!'

'Mama, it is a bill for *fifty pounds*!'

'No!' gasped Sophia.

'Well, that is certainly very generous of your uncle,' said Mrs Tallant. 'If I were you, Arabella, I would embroider a pair of slippers for him before you go away, for you will not like to be backward in any little attention.'

'Oh, no! But I never dreamed — I am sure I did not thank him half enough! Mama, will you take it for my dresses, please?'

'Certainly not. *That* is all provided for. You will find it very much more comfortable in London to have this money by you — indeed, I had hoped your uncle might give you something to spend! There will be little things you may want to purchase, and vails to the servants, you know, and so on. And although your Papa would not like you to *gamble* precisely, there may be loo-parties, and naturally you would wish to play. In fact, it would be awkward if you did not.'

Sophia opened her eyes at this. 'Papa does not like any of us to play gambling games, ma'am, does he? He says that cards are to blame for many of the evils —'

'Yes, my dear, very likely! But a loo-party is quite a different thing!' said Mrs Tallant, somewhat obscurely. She fidgeted with her reticule for a moment, and then added, a little consciously: 'I should not tease Papa with telling him the whole history of our doings today, girls. Gentlemen do not take the same interest in such things as we do, and I am sure he has very much more important things to think of.'

Her daughters did not pretend to misunderstand her. 'Oh, I would not breathe a word to him!' said Sophia.

'No,' agreed Arabella. 'And *particularly* not about the fifty pounds, for I am sure he would say it was too much, and I must give it back to my uncle! And I don't think I *could*!'

3

In the end, it was not until after the middle of February that Arabella set out to accomplish the long journey to London. Not only had Mme Dupont taken more time to make the necessary gowns than had been anticipated, but there had been many details to arrange besides; and Betsy had not failed to delay preparations by contracting a putrid sore throat, and low fever. It was felt to be typical of her. While Mrs Tallant still had her hands full, nursing her, Bertram, succumbing to temptation, took French leave of his books and his Papa, and enjoyed a splendid day with the hounds, which culminated in his return to the Parsonage on a farm wagon, with a broken collar-bone. A gloom was thrown over the house for quite a week by this mishap, because the Vicar was not only vexed, but deeply grieved as well. It was not the accident which upset him, for although he did not hunt himself now he had done so regularly in his youth, but (he said) the want of openness in Bertram which had led him to go off without asking permission, or, indeed, even telling his father what he meant to do. The Vicar could not understand such conduct at all, for surely he was not a harsh parent, and surely his sons must know that he did not wish to deprive them of rational enjoyment? He was bewildered, and disturbed, and begged Bertram to explain why he had behaved in such a manner. But it was quite impossible to explain to Papa why one chose rather to play truant, and afterwards take the consequences, than to ask his leave to do something of which one knew well he would not approve.

'How *can* you explain anything to my father?' Bertram demanded of his sisters, in a despairing tone. 'He would only be more hurt than ever, and give one a thundering jaw, and make one feel like the greatest beast in nature!'

'I know,' said Arabella feelingly. 'I think what makes him look so displeased and sad is that he believes you must be afraid of him, and so dared not ask his leave to go. And, of course, one *can't* explain that it isn't *that*!'

'He wouldn't understand if you did,' remarked Sophia.

'Well, exactly so!' said Bertram. 'Besides, you couldn't do it! A pretty botch I should make of telling him that I didn't ask leave because I knew he would look grave, and say I must decide for myself, but did I feel it to be right to go pleasuring when I have examinations to pass — oh, you know the way he talks! The end of it would be that I shouldn't have gone at all! I hate moralizing!'

'Yes,' agreed Sophia, 'but the worst of it is that whenever one of us vexes him he very likely falls into the most dreadful dejection, and worries himself with thinking that we are all of us heedless and spoilt, and himself much to blame. I wish he may not forbid you to go to London because of Bertram's wretched folly, Bella!'

'What a bag of moonshine!' exclaimed Bertram scornfully. 'Why the deuce should he, pray?'

It certainly seemed a trifle unreasonable, but when his children next encountered the Vicar, which was at the dinner-table, his countenance wore an expression of settled melancholy, and it was plain that he derived no comfort from the young people's cheerful conversation. A somewhat thoughtless enquiry from Margaret about the exact colour of the ribbons chosen for Arabella's second-best ball dress provoked him to say that it seemed to him that amongst all his children only James was not wholly given over to levity and frivolity. Unsteadiness of character was what he perceived about him; when he considered that the mere prospect of a visit to London sent all his daughters fashion-mad he must ask himself whether he was not doing very wrong to permit Arabella to go.

A moment's reflection would have convinced Arabella that this was the merest irritation of nerves, but her besetting sin, as her Mama had frequently told her, was the impetuosity which led her into so many scrapes. Alarm at the Vicar's words for an instant suspended every faculty; then she exclaimed hotly: 'Papa! You are unjust! It is too bad!'

The Vicar had never been a severe parent; indeed, he was thought by some to allow his children a shocking degree of licence: but such a speech as this went beyond the bounds of what he would tolerate. His face stiffened to an expression of quelling austerity; he replied in a voice of ice: 'The unwarrantable language you have used, Arabella; the uncontrolled violence of your manner; the want of respect you have shown me — all these betray clearly how unfit you are to be sent into the world!'

Under the table, Sophia's foot kicked Arabella's ankle; across it, Mama's eyes met hers in a warning, reproving look. The colour surged up into her cheeks; her eyes filled; and she stammered: 'I beg your p-pardon, P-papa!'

He returned no answer. Mama broke the uneasy silence by calmly desiring Harry not to eat so fast; and then, just as though nothing untoward had occurred, began to talk to the Vicar about some parish business.

'What a dust you made!' Harry said presently, when the young people had fled to Mama's dressing-room, and poured out the whole story to Bertram, who had had his dinner brought to him there, on the sofa.

'I am *sick* with apprehension!' Arabella said tragically. 'He means to forbid me!'

'Fudge! It was only one of his scolds! Girls are such fools!'

'Ought I to go down and beg his pardon? Oh, no, I dare not! He has shut himself up in the study! What shall I do?'

'Leave it to Mama!' said Bertram, yawning. 'She's as shrewd as she can hold together, and if she means you to go to London, go you will!'

'I would not go to him now, if I were you,' said Sophia. 'You are in such an agitation of spirits that you would be bound to say something unbecoming, or start to cry. And you know how much he dislikes an excess of sensibility! Speak to him in the morning, after prayers!'

This course was decided on. And then, as Arabella afterwards confided to Bertram, it was more dreadful than all the rest! Mama had done her work too well: before the Vicar's erring daughter could utter a word of her carefully rehearsed apology, he had taken her hand, and said with his sweet, wistful smile: 'My child, you must forgive your father. Indeed, I spoke to you with grave injustice yesterday! Alas, that I, who preach moderation to my children, should have so little control over my own temper!'

'Bertram, I had rather by far he had *beaten* me!' said Arabella earnestly.

'Lord, yes!' agreed Bertram, shuddering. 'What a shocking thing! I'm glad I wasn't downstairs! It makes me feel like the devil when he gets to blaming himself. What did you say?'

'I could not utter a word! My voice was *wholly* suspended by tears, as you may imagine, and I was so afraid that he would be vexed with me for not being able to contain my feelings better! But he was not. Only fancy! he took me in his arms, and kissed me, and said I was his dear, good daughter, and oh, Bertram, I'm *not*!'

'Well, you need not put yourself in a pucker for that,' recommended her matter-of-fact brother. 'He won't think it above a day or two. The thing is that his dejected fit is at an end.'

'Oh, yes! But it was much, much worse at breakfast! He would keep on talking to me about the London scheme — teasing me, you know, about the giddy life I should lead there, and saying that I must be sure to write very long letters home, even if I cannot get a frank for them, for he would be so much interested to hear of all my doings!'

Bertram stared at her in undisguised horror. 'He did not!'

'But he did! And in the kindest way, only with that sad look in his eyes — *you* know! until I was ready to give up the whole scheme!'

'My God, I don't wonder at it!'

'No, and to crown all — as though I had not borne enough!' disclosed Arabella, hunting wildly for her handkerchief, 'he said I should want something pretty to wear in London, and he would have a pearl pin he wore when he was a young man made into a ring for me!'

This staggering intelligence made Bertram's jaw drop. After a moment's stupefaction, he said resolutely: 'That settles it! I shan't come downstairs today after all. Ten to one, if he saw me he would start to blame himself for my frisk, and I should be driven into running away to enlist, or something, because, you know, a fellow can't stand that kind of thing!'

'No, indeed! I am sure all *my* pleasure has been quite cut up!'

Since Papa's tender mood of forbearance showed every sign of continuance, Arabella fell into such an abyss of despondency that she was only saved from renouncing the London scheme by the timely intervention of Mama, who gave her thoughts a more cheerful direction by calling her into her bedroom one morning, and saying with a smile: 'I have something to show you, my love, which I think you will like.'

There was a box lying open upon Mama's dressing-table. Arabella blinked at the flash of diamonds, and uttered a long-drawn: 'Oh-h!'

'My father gave them to me,' said Mrs Tallant, sighing faintly. 'Of course I have never worn them of late years, for I have no occasion to. Besides, they are scarcely suitable for a clergyman's wife. But I have had them cleaned, and I mean to lend them to you to take with you to London. And I have asked Papa if he thinks I might give you Grandmama Tallant's pearl necklet, and he sees no objection to it. Your Papa has never cared for sparkling stones, you know, but he thinks pearls both modest and becoming to a female. However, if Lady Bridlington takes you to any dress-parties, which I am sure she will, the diamond set would be just the thing. You see, there is the crescent to set in your hair, and a brooch, and the bracelet as well. Nothing pretentious or vulgar, such as Papa would dislike, but I know the stones are of the finest water.'

It was impossible to be dejected after this, or even to contemplate abandoning the London scheme. What with the trimming of hats, hemming of handkerchiefs, embroidering of slippers for the Squire, the arrival of her gowns from Harrowgate, and the knitting of a new purse for Papa, together with all the ordinary duties which fell to her lot, Arabella had no time to indulge in morbid reflections. Everything went on prosperously: the Caterhams' retiring govern-ess expressed herself all willingness to chaperon

57

Arabella on the journey; the Squire discovered that by driving only a few miles out of the way she could spend a day or two with her Aunt Emma, at Arksey, and so rest the horses; Bertram's collar-bone knit itself again; and even Betsy recovered from her sore throat. Not until the Squire's carriage actually stood at the Parsonage gate, waiting to take up the travellers, with all the trunks strapped securely behind it, and Mama's dressing-case (also lent for the occasion) placed tenderly within the vehicle, did the mood of depression again descend upon Arabella. Whether it was Mama's embrace, or Papa's blessing, or Baby Jack's fat little hand waving farewell which overcame her, it would have been hard to say, but her feelings were quite overset, and it was a lady dissolved in tears whom Bertram thrust forcibly into the carriage. It was long before she could be composed again, nor was her companion of much support to her, since an excessive sympathy, coupled, perhaps, with the natural melancholy of a female obliged by circumstances to seek a new post, caused her to weep quite as bitterly in her corner of the capacious carriage.

While familiar landmarks were still to be observed out of the windows, Arabella's tears continued to flow, but by the time the carriage had reached an unknown countryside they had ceased, and after sniffing cautiously at the vinaigrette, proffered in a trembling hand by Miss Blackburn, she was able to dry her wet cheeks, and even to derive a sensible degree of comfort from the opulence of the huge sealskin pillow-muff lying on her lap. This, with the tippet round her throat, had been sent to her with her Aunt Eliza's love — the same who had once given Mama a set of pink Indian muslin underwear. Even though one had never left one's home before, one could not be wholly given over to wretchedness when one's hands were tucked into a muff as large as any depicted in *La Belle Assemblée*. So large, indeed, was it, that Papa — But it would be wiser not to think of Papa, or any of the dear ones at home, perhaps. Better to fix one's attention on the countryside, and one's thoughts on the delights ahead.

To a young lady who had never been farther afield than to York — and that only when Papa had taken her and Sophia to be confirmed in the Minster — every new thing seen on the road was a matter for eager interest and exclamation. To those accustomed to the rapid mode of travel achieved by post-chaises, a journey in a somewhat ponderous carriage drawn by two horses, chosen more for their stamina than their speed, would have seemed slow beyond all bearing. To Arabella it was adventure, while to Miss Blackburn, inured by long custom to the horrors of the stage, it was unlooked-for comfort. Both ladies, therefore, soon settled down to enjoy themselves, thought the refreshments they were offered at the various halts excellent, found nothing to complain of in the beds at the posting-houses, and could not conceive of a more delightful way of undertaking a long journey. They were made very welcome at Arksey, where Aunt Emma received them with the greatest kindness, and the exclamation that Arabella was so like her dear Mama that she had nearly fainted away at the sight of her.

They spent two days at Arksey before taking the road again, and Arabella was quite sorry to leave the large, untidy house, so kind had Aunt Emma been, and so jolly all her cheerful cousins. But Timothy-coachman reported the horses to be quite fresh and ready for the road again, so there could be no lingering. They set forth once more, followed by the shouted good wishes and many hand-wavings of Aunt Emma's family.

After all the fun and the hospitality at Arksey, it did seem to be a little tedious to be sitting all day in a carriage, and once or twice, when a post-chaise-and-four dashed by, or some sporting curricle, with a pair of quick-goers harnessed to it, was encountered, Arabella found herself wishing that the Squire's carriage were not quite so large and unwieldy, and his horses less strengthy and rather more speedy beasts. It would have been pleasant, too, to have been able to have had a fresh pair poled-up when one of Uncle John's cast a shoe, instead of having to wait in a stuffy inn parlour while it was reshod; and Arabella, eating her dinner in the coffee-room of some posting-house, could not quite forbear a look of envy when some smart chaise drove into the courtyard, with horses sweating, and ostlers running out with a fresh team for the impatient traveller. Nor could she help wishing, once she had watched the mail-coach sweep through a turnpike, that Uncle John had provided the groom not with a horse-pistol, for

60

which there did not seem to be the slightest occasion, but with a yard of tin, that he might have blown up for the pike in that same lordly style.

The weather, which had been cold but bright in Yorkshire, worsened as they drove farther south. It was raining in Lincolnshire, and the landscape looked sodden. Not many people were to be seen on the road, and the prospect was so uninviting that Miss Blackburn said that it was a pity they had not had the forethought to provide themselves with a travelling chessboard, with which, in default of looking out of the windows, they might have whiled away the time. At Tuxford they were unlucky enough to find the New Castle Arms without a bed to spare, and were obliged to put up at a smaller and by far less genteel inn, where the sheets had been so ill-aired that Miss Blackburn not only lay and shivered in her bed all night, but arose in the morning with a sore throat, and a tickling at the back of her nose which presaged a cold in the head. Arabella, who, for all her air of fragility, rarely succumbed to minor ailments, was not a penny the worse for the experience, but her north-country soul had been offended by the dust she had seen under her bed, and she was beginning to think that it would be a relief to reach her journey's end. It was vexing to discover, just as she had packed Mama's dressing-case, and was ready to leave the inn, that one of the traces needed repair, for it had been arranged that they should spend the following night at Grantham, which, the guide-book informed her, lay some twenty-nine or thirty miles on from Tuxford. She hoped very much that the coachman would not decide that his horses could go no farther than to Newark, but since he was something of a despot, and had no opinion of fast travelling, it seemed more than likely that he would. However, the trace was mended in fairly good time, and they reached Newark in time to eat a late luncheon. Here, while he baited his horses, the coachman fell out with one of the ostlers, who asked him whether it was the King's state coach he had there; and this so much affronted him that he was quite as anxious as Arabella to reach Grantham that evening.

It was raining again when they left Newark, and the atmosphere was dank and chilly. Miss Blackburn wrapped herself up in a large shawl, and sniffed unhappily, as her cold gained on her. Even Arabella, who was largely impervious to climatic conditions, suffered a little from the many draughts that crept into the carriage, and wriggled numbed toes inside her half-boots of crimson jean.

The carriage bowled along at a sedate pace for several miles, the tedium being enlivened only at the Balderton turnpike, where, recognizing a Johnny Raw in the coachman, the pike-keeper made a spirited attempt to extort a fee from him. But although Timothy-coachman might never have set foot beyond the boundaries of Yorkshire before, he was harder-headed than any of these soft southern folk whom he despised so profoundly, and he knew very well that the ticket bought as the last toll-gate opened all the pikes to him until the next, south of Grantham, was reached. After an exchange of personalities which made Miss Blackburn utter little moans of dismay, and Arabella — regrettably — giggle, he won a signal victory over the pike-keeper, and drove through with a triumphant flourish of his whip.

'Oh, dear, I am becoming so tired of this journey!' confided Arabella. 'I could almost wish to be held up by a highwayman!'

'My dear Miss Tallant, pray do not *think* of such a thing!' shuddered her companion. 'I only hope we may be spared any sort of accident!'

Neither lady's wish was destined to be granted her. No such excitement as a hold-up awaited them, but a little way short of the Marston turnpike the perch of the carriage broke, and the body fell forward upon the box. The Squire's travelling carriage had stood too long in his coach-house.

After the coachman had delivered himself of a long, self-exculpatory monologue, the groom was sent off to take counsel of the pike-keeper, half a mile down the road. When he returned, it was with the pleasing intelligence that no adequate assistance was to be hoped for in the next village: it must be sought in Grantham, five or six miles farther on, where a conveyance could no doubt be hired to fetch the ladies in while the perch was mended, or replaced. The coachman then suggested that his passengers, both of whom were standing by the roadside, should climb up into the carriage again to await deliverance, while the groom took one of the

63

horses and rode on to Grantham. Miss Black-burn was meekly ready to follow this advice, but her charge thought poorly of it.

'What! Sit in that horrid, draughty carriage all that time? I won't do it!' she declared.

'But we cannot continue to stand in the rain, dear Miss Tallant!' said Miss Blackburn.

'Of course we cannot! Either way I am persuaded you would catch your death! There must be a house hereabouts which would lend us shelter! What are those lights over there?'

They plainly shone from the windows of a residence set a little back from the road. The groom volunteered the information that he had noticed some lodge gates a few steps back.

'Good!' said Arabella briskly. 'We will walk up to it, ma'am, and beg them to give us shelter for a little while.'

Miss Blackburn, a timorous soul, protested feebly. 'They would think it so strange of us!'

'No, why should they?' returned Arabella. 'Why, when a carriage had an accident outside *our* gates last year, Papa sent Harry out at once to offer shelter to the travellers! We cannot shiver for an hour or more in that horrid carriage, ma'am, with nothing to do! Besides, I am shockingly hungry, and I should think they would be bound to offer us refreshment, would not you? I am sure it is dinner-time, and past!'

'Oh, I do not think we should!' was all Miss Blackburn had to say, and it seemed so stupid to Arabella that she paid no heed to it, but desired the groom to escort them to the lodge gates before riding off to Grantham. This he did, and the ladies, dismissing him there, trod up the short drive to the house, one of them murmuring disjointed protests, the other perceiving no reason in the world why she should not claim a hospitality anyone in Yorkshire would have been eager to offer.

4

It was at about this moment that that erratic young sprig of fashion, Lord Fleetwood, fixed his friend, and host, Mr Beaumaris, with a laughing eye, and demanded in a rallying tone: 'Well! You promise me a rare day with the hounds tomorrow — by the by, where do we meet? — but what — *what*, Robert, do you offer me for my entertainment this evening?'

'My cook,' said Mr Beaumaris, 'is generally thought to be an artist in his own line. A Frenchman: I think you will like his way of dressing a Davenport chicken, while some trick he has of flavouring a Benton sauce — '

'What, did you send Alphonse down, then, from London?' interrupted Lord Fleetwood, momentarily diverted.

'Alphonse?' repeated Mr Beaumaris, his finely chiselled brows lifting a little. 'Oh, no! this is another. I don't think I know his name. But I like his way with fish.'

Lord Fleetwood burst out laughing. 'I expect if you discovered a cook with a way of serving game which you liked, you would send him off to that shooting-box of yours, and pay him a king's ransom, only to kick his heels for three parts of the year!'

'I expect I should,' agreed Mr Beaumaris imperturbably.

'*But*,' said his lordship severely, 'I am not to be

put off with a cook! I came here in the expectation of finding fair Paphians, let me tell you, and all manner of shocking orgies — wine out of skulls, y'know, and —'

'The lamentable influence of Lord Byron upon society!' interpolated Mr Beaumaris, with a faint, contemptuous smile.

'What? Oh, that poet-fellow that set up such a dust! Myself, I thought him devilish underbred, but of course it don't do to say so. But that's it! Where, Robert, are the fair Paphians?'

'If I had any Paphians in keeping here, you don't imagine, do you, Charles, that I would run the risk of being cut-out by a man of *your* address?' retorted Mr Beaumaris.

Lord Fleetwood grinned at him, but replied: 'None of your gammon to me! It would take ten times my address to cut-out a — a — dash it, a Midas like you!'

'If my memory does not err, all that Midas touched turned to gold,' said Mr Beaumaris. 'I think you mean Crœsus.'

'No, I don't! Never heard of the fellow!'

'Well, most of the things I touch have a disheartening way of turning to dross,' said Mr Beaumaris, lightly, but with a note of bitter self-mockery in his languid voice.

This was going a little too deep for his friend. 'Humdudgeon, Robert! You can't bamboozle me! If there are to be no Paphians — '

'I can't conceive why you should have supposed there would be,' interrupted his host.

'Well, I didn't, but I can tell you this, my boy! — that's the latest *on-dit!*'

'Good God! Why?'

'Lord, how should I know? Daresay it's because you won't throw your glove at any of the beauties who have been setting their caps at you any time these five years. What's more, your *chères-amies* are always such devilish high-flyers, dear boy, it puts notions into the heads of all the old tabbies! Think of the Faraglini!'

'I had rather not. The most rapacious female of my acquaintance.'

'But what a face! what a figure!'

'And what a temper!'

'What became of her?' asked his lordship. 'I haven't laid eyes on her since she left your protection.'

'I think she went to Paris. Why? Had you a fancy to succeed me?'

'No, by Jove, I couldn't have stood the nonsense!' said his lordship frankly. 'She'd have had me rolled-up within a month! What did you have to give for those match-grays she used to drive all over town?'

'I can't remember.'

'To tell you the truth,' confided Lord Fleetwood, 'I shouldn't have thought it worth it myself — though I'm not denying she was a curst fine woman!'

'It wasn't.'

Lord Fleetwood regarded him, half-curious, half-amused. 'Is anything worth while to you, Robert?' he asked quizzically.

'Yes, my horses!' retorted Mr Beaumaris. 'And, talking of horses, Charles, what the devil possessed you to buy one of Lichfield's breakdowns?'

'That bay? Now, there's a horse that fairly took my fancy!' said his lordship, his simple countenance lighting up with enthusiasm. 'What a piece of blood and bone! No, really, Robert — !'

'If ever I find myself with a thoroughly unsound animal in my stables,' said Mr Beaumaris ruthlessly, 'I shall offer him to you in the happy certainty that he will take your fancy!'

Lord Fleetwood was still protesting with indignation and vehemence when the butler entered the room to inform his master, rather apologetically, that, a carriage had broken down outside his gates, and the two ladies it bore were desirous of sheltering for a short time under his roof.

Mr Beaumaris's cool gray eyes betrayed no emotion, but his mouth seemed for an instant to harden. He said calmly: 'Certainly. There should be a fire in the saloon. Tell Mrs. Mersey to wait upon the ladies there.'

The butler bowed, and would have withdrawn, but Lord Fleetwood checked him, exclaiming: 'No, no, too shabby by half, Robert! I won't be fobbed off so! What do they look like, Brough? Old? Young? Pretty?'

The butler, inured to his lordship's free and easy ways, replied with unimpaired solemnity that one of the ladies was both young, and — he ventured to think — very pretty.

'I insist on your receiving these females with a proper degree of civility, Robert!' said his lordship firmly. 'Saloon, indeed! Show 'em in, Brough!'

The butler glanced for guidance towards his master, as though he doubted whether the command would be endorsed, but Mr Beaumaris merely said with his usual indifference: 'As you please, Charles.'

'What an ungrateful dog you are!' said Lord Fleetwood, when Brough had left the room. 'You don't deserve your fortune! This is the hand of Providence!'

'I should doubt of their being Paphians,' was all Mr Beaumaris found to say. 'I thought that was what you wanted?'

'Any diversion is better than none!' replied Lord Fleetwood.

'What a singularly infelicitous remark! I wonder why I invited you.'

Lord Fleetwood grinned at him. 'Now, Robert, did you think — *did* you think — to come Tip Street over me? There may be plenty of toadies ready to jump out of their skins at the very thought of being invited to the Nonpareil's house — and no better entertainment offered than a rubber of piquet, I dare swear — '

'You are forgetting the cook.'

'*But,*' continued his lordship inexorably, 'I ain't amongst 'em!'

Mr Beaumaris's habitual aspect was one of coldness, and reserve, but sometimes he could smile in a way that not only softened the austerity of his countenance but lit his eyes with a gleam of the purest amusement. It was not the smile he kept for social occasions — a faintly sardonic curl of the lips, that one — but those who were honoured by a glimpse of it generally revised their first impressions of him. Those who had never seen it were inclined to think him a proud, disagreeable sort of a man, though only the most daring would ever have uttered aloud such a criticism of one who, besides possessing all the advantages of birth and fortune, was an acknowledged leader of society. Lord Fleetwood, no stranger to that smile, saw it dawn now, and grinned more broadly than ever.

'How can you, Charles? When you must know that almost your only claim to fashion is being noticed by me!'

Arabella entered the room to find both its occupants laughing, and thus had the felicity of seeing Mr Beaumaris at his best. That she herself was looking remarkably pretty, with her dusky curls and charming complexion admirably set off by a high-crowned bonnet, with curled ostrich-feather tips, and crimson ribbons tied into a bow under one ear, never entered her head, since Mr Tallant's daughters had always been discouraged from thinking much about their appearance. She paused on the threshold, while the butler murmured her name and Miss Blackburn's, quite unselfconscious, but looking about her with a kind of wide-eyed, innocent interest. She was very much impressed by what she saw. The house was not a large one, but she perceived that it was furnished with a good taste which was as quiet as it was expensive. Her quick scrutiny took in Lord Fleetwood, who had put up an instinctive hand to straighten the Belcher necktie he affected, and passed on to Mr. Beaumaris.

Arabella had one brother who aspired to

dandyism, and she had thought that she had seen in Harrowgate gentlemen of decided fashion. She now perceived that she had much mistaken the matter. No one she had ever seen approached the elegance of Mr Beaumaris.

Lord Fleetwood, or any of his cronies, could have recognized the tailoring of that coat of olive-green superfine at a glance; Arabella, to whom the magic name of Weston was unknown, was merely aware of a garment so exquisitely cut that it presented all the appearance of having been moulded to its wearer's form. A very good form, too, she noted, with approval. No need of buckram wadding, such as that Knaresborough tailor had inserted into Bertram's new coat, to fill out those shoulders! And how envious Bertram would have been of Mr Beaumaris's fine legs, sheathed in tight pantaloons, with gleaming Hessian boots pulled over them! Mr Beaumaris's shirt-points were not as high as Bertram's, but his necktie commanded the respect of one who had more than once watched her brother's struggles with a far less complicated arrangement. Arabella was not perfectly sure that she admired his style of hairdressing — he affected a Stanhope crop — but she did think him a remarkably handsome man, as he stood there, laughter dying on his lips, and out of his gray eyes.

It was only a moment that he stood thus. She had the impression that he was scanning her critically; then he moved forward, and bowed slightly, and begged, in a rather colourless tone, to know in what way he could be of service to her.

'How do you do?' said Arabella politely. 'I beg your pardon, but the thing is that there has been an accident to my carriage, and — and it is raining, and horridly cold! The groom has rid in to Grantham, and I daresay will bring another carriage out directly, but — but Miss Blackburn has taken a chill, and we should be very much obliged if we might wait here in the warm!'

She was stammering and blushing by the time she came to the end of this speech. Outside, it had seemed the simplest thing in the world to solicit shelter; under Mr Beaumaris's eye, it all at once seemed as though the request were outrageous. To be sure, he was smiling, but it was a very different smile from the one his face had worn when she had entered the room. It was such a very slight curl of the lips, yet there was some quality in it which made her feel ruffled and uncomfortable.

But he said with perfect civility: 'An unfortunate mishap. You must permit me to send you to Grantham in one of my carriages, ma'am.'

Lord Fleetwood, who had been standing staring in the frankest admiration at Arabella, was jerked into action by this speech. Pulling a chair invitingly close to the fire, he exclaimed: 'No, no, come and sit down, ma'am! I can see you are chilled to the bone! Shocking weather for travelling! You will have got your feet wet, I daresay, and *that* will never do, you know! Robert, where have your wits gone a-begging? Why don't you desire Brough to fetch some refreshment for Miss — er — Miss — for the ladies?'

With a look which Arabella was strongly inclined to construe as one of resignation, Mr. Beaumaris replied: 'I trust he may be doing so. I beg you will be seated, ma'am!'

But it was Lord Fleetwood who handed Arabella to the chair he had placed, saying solicitously: 'I am sure you are hungry, and will be glad of something to eat!'

'Well, yes, sir,' confessed Arabella, who was very hungry indeed. 'I own, I have been thinking of my dinner for several miles! And no wonder, for I see it is already past five o'clock!'

This naïve speech made his lordship, who never sat down to his dinner before half-past seven at the very earliest, swallow convulsively, but he recovered himself in an instant, and replied without a blink: 'So it is, by Jupiter! You are famished, then! But never mind! Mr Beaumaris here was just saying that dinner would be served in a trice. Weren't you, Robert?'

'Was I?' said Mr Beaumaris. 'I have the wretchedest of memories, but I am sure you are right. I beg you will do me the honour of dining with me, ma'am.'

Arabella hesitated. She could see from her anguished expression that Miss Blackburn thought she should rather accept Mr Beaumaris's first offer; and not the most inveterate of optimists could have read into that languid gentleman's voice anything more than a reluctant civility. But this warm, comfortably furnished room was a most welcome change from the travelling carriage, and the aroma of cooking which had assailed her nostrils as she

74

had crossed the hall had considerably whetted her appetite. She looked a little doubtfully at her host. Again it was Lord Fleetwood who, with his friendly smile and easy manners, clinched the matter. 'Of course they will dine with us! Now, won't you, ma'am?'

'It would be giving too much trouble, sir!' said Miss Blackburn, in a sort of gasp.

'No trouble in the world, ma'am, I assure you! In fact, we are very much obliged to you, for we had been wishing that we were to have company, eh, Robert?'

'Certainly,' agreed Mr Beaumaris. 'Was I not just saying so?'

Miss Blackburn, having undergone a life-time of slights and snubs, was quick to catch the satirical inflexion. She cast him a scared, deprecating look, and coloured. His eyes met hers; he stood looking down at her for a moment, and then said in a much kinder tone: 'I am afraid you are not quite comfortable there, ma'am. Will you not draw nearer to the fire?'

She was thrown into a flutter, and assured him rather disjointedly that she was perfectly comfortable, and himself too good, too obliging! Brough had come into the room with a tray of glasses and decanters, which he set down on a table, and Mr Beaumaris moved towards it, saying: 'You will like to go upstairs with my housekeeper, I daresay, to take off your wet coat, but first you must let me give you a glass of wine.' He began to pour out some Madeira. 'Two extra covers for dinner, Brough — which you will serve immediately.'

Brough thought of the Davenport fowls roasting on the spits in the kitchen, and of the artist in charge of them, and was visibly shaken. 'Immediately, sir?' he said, in a failing voice.

'Let us say, within half-an-hour,' amended Mr Beaumaris, carrying a glass of wine over to Miss Blackburn.

'Yes, sir,' said Brough, and tottered from the room, a broken man.

Miss Blackburn accepted the wine gratefully, but when it was offered to Arabella she declined it. Papa did not like his daughters to taste anything stronger than porter, or the very mild claret cup served at the Harrowgate Assembly Rooms, and she was a little doubtful of its possible effect on her. Mr Beaumaris did not press her in any way, but set the glass down again, poured out some sherry for himself and his friend, and returned to sit beside Miss Blackburn on the sofa.

Lord Fleetwood, meanwhile, had ensconced himself beside Arabella, and was chatting to her in his inconsequent, cheerful way, which set her quite at her ease. He was delighted to hear that she was on her way to London, hoped to have the pleasure of meeting her there — in the Park, possibly, or at Almack's. He had plenty of anecdotes of *ton* with which to entertain her, and rattled on in an agreeable fashion until the housekeeper came to escort the ladies upstairs.

They were taken to a guest-chamber on the first floor, and handed over there to a housemaid, who brought up hot water for them, and bore their damp coats away to be dried in the kitchen.

'Everything in the first style of elegance!' breathed Miss Blackburn. 'But we should not be dining here! I feel sure we ought not, my dear Miss Tallant!'

Arabella was a little doubtful on this score herself, but as it was now too late to draw back she stifled her misgivings, and said stoutly that she was persuaded there could be no objection. Finding a brush and comb laid out on the dressing-table, she began to tidy her rather tumbled locks.

'They are *most* gentlemanlike,' said Miss Blackburn, deriving comfort from this circumstance. 'Of the first rank of fashion, I daresay. They will be here for the hunting, depend upon it: I collect this is a hunting-box.'

'A hunting-box!' exclaimed Arabella, awed. 'Is it not very large and grand, ma'am, to be that?'

'Oh, no, my dear! Quite a small house! The Tewkesburys, whose sweet children I was engaged to instruct before I removed to Mrs Caterham's establishment, had one much larger, I assure you. This is the Melton country, you must know.'

'Good heavens, are they Melton men, then? Oh, how much I wish Bertram could be here! What I shall have to tell him! I think it is Mr Beaumaris who owns the house: I wonder who the other is? I thought when I first saw him he could not be quite the thing, for that striped waistcoat, you know, and that spotted handkerchief he wears instead of a cravat makes him look like a groom, or some such thing. But when he spoke, of course I knew he was not a vulgar person at all.'

Miss Blackburn, feeling for once in her life pleasantly superior, gave a titter of laughter, and said pityingly: 'Oh, dear me no, Miss Tallant! You will find a great many young gentlemen of fashion wearing much odder clothes than *that*! It is what Mr Geoffrey Tewkesbury — a very modish young man! — used to call *all the crack*!' She added pensively: 'But I must confess that I do not care for it myself, and nor did dear Mrs Tewkesbury. My notion of a true gentleman is someone like Mr Beaumaris!'

Arabella dragged the comb ruthlessly through a tangle. '*I* thought him a very proud, reserved man!' she declared. 'And not at all hospitable!' she added.

'Oh, no, how can you say so? How very kind and obliging it was of him to place me in the best place, so near the fire! Delightful manners! nothing high in them at all! I was quite overcome by his condescension!'

It was evident to Arabella that she and Miss Blackburn regarded their host through two very different pairs of spectacles. She preserved an unconvinced silence, and as soon as Miss Blackburn had finished prinking her crimped gray locks at the mirror, suggested that they should go downstairs again. Accordingly they left the room, and crossed the upper hall to the head of the stairway. Mr Beaumaris's fancy had led him to carpet his stairs, a luxury which Miss Blackburn indicated to her charge with one pointing finger and a most expressive glance.

Across the lower hall, the door into the library stood ajar. Lord Fleetwood's voice, speaking in rallying tones, assailed the ladies' ears. 'I swear you are incorrigible!' said his lordship. 'The loveliest of creatures drops into your lap, like a veritable honey-fall, and you behave as though a gull-groper had forced his way into your house!'

Mr Beaumaris replied with disastrous clarity: 'My dear Charles, when you have been hunted by every trick known to the ingenuity of the female mind, you may more readily partake of my sentiments upon this occasion! I have had beauties hopeful of wedding my fortune swoon in my arms, break their bootlaces outside my London house, sprain their ankles when my arm is there to support them, and now it appears that I am to be pursued even into Leicestershire! An accident to her coach! Famous! What a green-horn she must believe me to be!'

A small hand closed like a vice about Miss Blackburn's wrist. Herself bridling indignantly, she saw Arabella's eyes sparkling, and her cheeks most becomingly flushed. Had she been better acquainted with Miss Tallant she might have taken fright at these signs. Arabella breathed into her ear: 'Miss Blackburn, can I *trust* you?'

Miss Blackburn would have vigorously assured her that she could, but the hand released her wrist, and flew up to cover her mouth. Slightly startled, she nodded. To her amazement, Arabella then picked up her skirts, and fled lightly back to the top of the stairs. Turning there, she began to come slowly down again, saying in a clear, carrying voice: 'Yes, indeed! I am sure I have said the same, dear ma'am, times out of mind! But do, pray, go before me!'

Miss Blackburn, turning to stare at her, with her mouth at half-cock, found a firm young hand in the small of her back, and was thrust irresistibly onward.

'But in spite of all,' said Arabella, 'I prefer to travel with my own horses!'

The awful scowl that accompanied these light words quite bewildered the poor little governess, but she understood that she was expected to reply in kind, and said in a quavering voice: 'Very true, my dear!'

The scowl gave place to an encouraging smile. Any one of Arabella's brothers or sisters would have begged her at this point to consider all the consequences of impetuosity; Miss Blackburn, unaware of the eldest Miss Tallant's besetting fault, was merely glad that she had not disappointed her. Arabella tripped across the hall to that half-open door, and entered the library again.

It was Lord Fleetwood who came forward to receive her. He eyed her with undisguised appreciation, and said: 'Now you will be more comfortable! Devilish dangerous to sit about in a wet coat, y'know! But we are yet unacquainted, ma'am! The stupidest thing! — never can catch a name when it is spoken! That man of Beaumaris's mumbles so that no one can hear him! You must let me make myself known to you, too — Lord Fleetwood, very much at your service!'

'I,' said Arabella, a most dangerous glitter in her eye, 'am Miss Tallant!'

His lordship, murmuring polite gratification at

being made the recipient of this information, was surprised to find his inanities quite misunderstood. Arabella fetched a world-weary sigh, and enunciated with a scornful curl of her lip: 'Oh, yes! *The* Miss Tallant!'

'Th — *the* Miss Tallant?' stammered his lordship, all at sea.

'The rich Miss Tallant!' said Arabella.

His lordship rolled an anguished and an enquiring eye at his host, but Mr Beaumaris was not looking at him. Mr Beaumaris, his attention arrested, was regarding the rich Miss Tallant with a distinct gleam of curiosity, not unmixed with amusement, in his face.

'I had hoped that here at least I might be unknown!' said Arabella, seating herself in a chair a little withdrawn from the fire. 'Ah, you must let me make you known to Miss Blackburn, my — my *dame de compagnie*!'

Lord Fleetwood sketched a bow; Miss Blackburn, her countenance wooden, dropped him a slight curtsy, and sat down on the nearest chair.

'Miss Tallant!' repeated Lord Fleetwood, searching his memory in vain for enlightenment. 'Ah, yes! Of course! Er — I don't think I have ever had the honour of meeting you in town, have I, ma'am?'

Arabella directed an innocent look from him to Mr Beaumaris, and back again, and clapped her hands together with an assumption of mingled delight and dismay. 'Oh, you *did* not know!' she exclaimed. 'I need never have told you! But when you looked *so*, I made sure you

81

were as bad as all the rest! Was anything ever so vexatious? I most particularly desire to be quite unknown in London!'

'My dear ma'am, you may rely on me!' promptly replied his lordship, who, like most rattles, thought himself the model of discretion. 'And Mr Beaumaris, you know, is in the same case as yourself, and able to sympathize with you!'

Arabella glanced at her host, and found that he had raised his quizzing-glass, which hung round his neck on a long black riband, and was surveying her through it. She put up her chin a little, for she was by no means sure that she cared for this scrutiny. 'Indeed?' she said.

It was not the practice of young ladies to put up their chins in just that style if Mr Beaumaris levelled his glass at them: they were more in the habit of simpering, or of trying to appear unconscious of his regard. But Mr Beaumaris saw that there was a decidedly militant sparkle in this lady's eye, and his interest, at first tickled, was now fairly caught. He let his glass fall, and said gravely: 'Indeed! And you?'

'Alas!' said Arabella, 'I am fabulously wealthy! It is the greatest mortification to me! You can have no notion!'

His lips twitched. 'I have always found, however, that a large fortune carries with it certain advantages.'

'Oh, you are a man! I shall not allow you to know anything of the matter!' she cried. 'You cannot know what it means to be the object of every fortune-hunter, courted and odiously flattered only for your wealth, until you are ready to wish that you had not a penny in the world!'

Miss Blackburn, who had hitherto supposed her charge to be a modest, well-behaved girl, barely repressed a shudder. Mr Beaumaris, however, said: 'I feel sure that you underrate yourself, ma'am.'

'Oh, dear me, no!' said Arabella. 'I have too often heard myself pointed out as the rich Miss Tallant to be under any illusion, sir! And it is for this reason that I wish to be quite unknown in London.'

Mr Beaumaris smiled, but as the butler came in just then to announce dinner, he said nothing, but merely offered his arm to Arabella.

The dinner, which consisted of two courses, seemed to Arabella sumptuous beyond her wildest imaginings. No suspicion crossed her mind that her host, after one swift glance at his board, had resigned himself to the knowledge that the reputations of himself and his cook had been placed in jeopardy; or that that artist in the kitchen, having, with strange Gallic imprecations which made his various assistants quake, rent limb from limb two half-roasted Davenport fowls, and flung them into a pan with a béchamel sauce and some tarragons, was even now, as he arranged a basket of pastry on a dish, undecided whether to leave this dishonoured house on the instant, or to cut his throat with the larger carving-knife. Soup à la Reine was removed with fillets of turbot with an Italian sauce; and the chickens à la Tarragon were flanked by a dish of spinach and croûtons, a glazed ham, two cold partridges, some broiled mushrooms, and a raised mutton pie. The second course presented Arabella with an even more bewildering choice, for there was, besides the baskets of pastry, a Rhenish cream, a jelly, a Savoy cake, a dish of salsify fried in butter, an omelette, and some anchovy toast. Mrs Tallant had always prided herself on her housekeeping, but such a repast as this, embellished as it was by elegant garnitures, and subtle sauces, was quite beyond the range of the Vicarage cook. Arabella could not help opening her eyes a little at the array of viands spread before her, but she managed to conceal her awe, and to partake of what was offered to her with a very creditable assumption of unconsciousness. Mr Beaumaris, perhaps loth to degrade his burgundy, or perhaps with a faint, despairing hope of adding piquancy to this commonplace meal, had instructed Brough to serve champagne. Arabella, having already cast discretion to the winds, allowed her glass to be filled, and sipped her way distastefully through it. It had a pleasantly exhilarating effect upon her. She informed Mr Beaumaris that she was bound for the town residence of Lady Bridlington; created several uncles for the simple purpose of endowing herself with their fortunes; and at one blow disposed of four brothers and three sisters who might have been supposed to have laid a claim to a share of all this wealth. She contrived, without precisely making so vulgar a boast, to convey the impression that she was escaping from courtships so persistent as to amount to persecution; and Mr Beaumaris,

84

listening with intense pleasure, said that London was the very place for anyone desirous of escaping attention.

Arabella, embarking recklessly on her second glass of champagne, said that in a crowd one could more easily pass unnoticed than in the restricted society of the country.

'Very true,' agreed Mr Beaumaris.

'*You* never did so!' remarked Lord Fleetwood, helping himself from the dish of mushrooms which Brough presented at his elbow. 'You must know, ma'am, that you are in the presence of the Nonpareil — none other! quite the most noted figure in society since poor Brummell was done-up!'

'Indeed!' Arabella looked from him to Mr Beaumaris with a pretty air of innocent enquiry. 'I did not know — I might not have heard the name quite correctly, perhaps?'

'My dear Miss Tallant!' exclaimed his lordship, in mock horror. 'Not know the great Beaumaris! the Arbiter of Fashion! Robert, you are quite set down!'

Mr Beaumaris, whose almost imperceptibly lifted finger had brought the watchful Brough to his side, was murmuring some command into that attentive but astonished ear, and paid no heed. His command was passed on to the footman hovering by the side-table, who, being quite a young man, and as yet imperfectly in control of his emotions, betrayed in his startled look some measure of the incredulity which shook his trained soul. The coldly quelling eye of his superior recalled him speedily to a sense of his position, however, and he left the room to carry the stupefying command still farther.

Miss Tallant, meanwhile, had perceived an opportunity to gratify her most pressing desire, which was to snub her host beyond possibility of his recovery. 'Arbiter of Fashion?' she said, in a blank voice. 'You cannot, surely, mean one of the *dandy-set*? I had thought — Oh, I beg your pardon! I expect that in London that is quite as important as being a great soldier, or a statesman, or — or some such thing!'

Even Lord Fleetwood could scarcely mistake the tenor of this artless speech. He gave an audible gasp. Miss Blackburn, whose enjoyment of dinner had already been seriously impaired, refused the partridge, and tried unavailingly to catch her charge's eye. Only Mr Beaumaris, hugely enjoying himself, appeared unmoved. He replied coolly: 'Oh, decidedly! One's influence is so far-reaching!'

'Oh?' said Arabella politely.

'Why, certainly, ma'am! One may blight a whole career by the mere raising of an eyebrow, or elevate a social aspirant to the ranks of the highest *ton* only by leaning on his arm for the length of a street.'

Miss Tallant suspected that she was being quizzed, but the strange exhilaration had her in its grip, and she did not hesitate to cross swords with this expert fencer. 'No doubt, sir, if *I* had ambitions to cut a figure in society *your* approval would be a necessity?'

Mr Beaumaris, famed for his sword-play, slipped under her guard with an unexpected thrust. 'My dear Miss Tallant, *you* need no passport to admit you to the ranks of the most sought-after! Even I could not depress the claims of one endowed with — may I say it? — your face, your figure, and your fortune!'

The colour flamed up into Arabella's cheeks; she choked over the last of her wine, tried to look arch, and only succeeded in looking adorably confused. Lord Fleetwood, realizing that his friend had embarked on yet another of his practised flirtations, directed an indignant glance at him, and did his best to engage the heiress's attention himself. He was succeeding quite well when he was thrown off his balance by the unprecedented behaviour of Brough, who, as the second course made its appearance, removed his champagne-glass, replacing it with a goblet, which he proceeded to fill with something out of a tall flagon which his lordship strongly suspected was iced lemonade. One sip was enough alike to confirm this hideous fear and to deprive his lordship momentarily of the power of speech. Mr Beaumaris, blandly swallowing some of the innocuous mixture, seized the opportunity to re-engage Miss Tallant in conversation.

Arabella had been rather relieved to see her wine-glass removed, for although she would have died rather than have owned to it she thought the champagne decidedly nasty, besides making her want to sneeze. She took a revivifying draught of lemonade, glad to discover that in really fashionable circles this mild beverage was apparently served with the second course. Miss Blackburn, better versed in the ways of the *haut ton*, now found herself unable to form a correct judgment of her host. To be plunged from a conviction that he was truly gentlemanlike to a shocked realization that he was nothing but a coxcomb, and then back again, quite overset the poor little lady. She knew not what to think, but could not forbear casting him a glance eloquent of the warmest gratitude. His eyes encountered hers, but for such a fleeting instant that she could never afterwards be sure whether she had caught the glimmer of an amused smile in them, or whether she had imagined it.

Brough, receiving a message at the door, announced that madam's groom had brought a hired coach to the house, and desired to know when she would wish to resume her journey to Grantham.

'It can wait,' said Mr Beaumaris, replenishing Arabella's glass. 'A little of the Rhenish cream, Miss Tallant?'

'How long,' demanded Arabella, recalling Mr Beaumaris's odious words to his friend, 'will it take them to mend my own carriage?'

'I understand, miss, that a new pole will be needed. I could not say how long it will be.'

A faint clucking from Miss Blackburn indicated dismay at this intelligence. Mr Beaumaris said: 'A tiresome accident, but I beg you will not distress yourselves! I will send my chaise to pick you up in Grantham at whatever hour tomorrow should be agreeable to you.'

Arabella thanked him, but was resolute in refusing his offer, for which, she assured him, there was not the slightest occasion. If the wheelwright proved too dilatory for her patience she would finish her journey post. 'It will be quite an experience!' she declared truthfully. 'My friends assure me that I am a great deal too old-fashioned in my notions — that quite a respectable degree of comfort is to be found in hired chaises!'

'I perceive,' said Mr Beaumaris, 'that we have much in common, ma'am. But I shall not allow a distaste for hired vehicles to be oldfashioned. Let us rather say that we have a little more nicety than the general run of our fellow-creatures!' He turned his head towards the butler. 'Let a message be conveyed to the wheelwright, Brough, that he will oblige me by repairing Miss Tallant's carriage with all possible expedition.'

Miss Tallant had nothing to do but thank him for his kind offices, and finish her Rhenish cream. That done, she rose from the table, saying that she had trespassed too long on her host's hospitality, and must now take her leave of him, with renewed thanks for his kindness.

'The obligation, Miss Tallant, is all on my side,' he replied. 'I am grateful for the chance which has made us acquainted, and shall hope to have the pleasure of calling upon you in town before many days.'

This promise threw Miss Blackburn into agitation. As she accompanied Arabella upstairs, she whispered: 'My dear Miss Tallant, how *could* you? And now he means to call on you, and you have told him — oh dear, oh dear, what would your Mama say?'

'Pooh!' returned Arabella, brazening it out. 'If

he is indeed a rich man, he will not care a fig, or think of it again!'

'*If* he is — Good gracious, Miss Tallant, he must be one of the wealthiest men in the country! When I collected that he was in very truth Mr Beaumaris I nearly swooned where I stood!'

'Well,' said the pot-valiant Arabella, 'if he is so very grand and important you may depend upon it he has not the least intention of calling on me in town. And I am sure I hope he will not, for he is an odious person!'

She refused to be moved from this standpoint, or even to acknowledge that in Mr Beaumaris's person at least no fault could be found. She said that she did not think him handsome, and that she held dandies in abhorrence. Miss Blackburn, terrified that she might, in this alarming mood, betray her dislike of Mr Beaumaris at parting, begged her not to forget what the barest civility rendered obligatory. She added that one slighting word uttered by him would be sufficient to wither any young lady's career at the outset, and then wished that she had held her tongue, since this warning had the effect of bringing the militant sparkle back into Arabella's eyes. But when Mr Beaumaris handed her into the coach, and, with quite his most attractive smile, lightly kissed the tips of her fingers before letting her hand go, she bade him farewell in a shy little voice that gave no hint of her loathing of him.

The coach set off down the drive; Mr Beaumaris turned, and in a leisurely way walked back into his house. He was pounced on in the hall by his injured friend, who demanded to know what the devil he meant by inflicting lemonade upon his guests.

'I don't think Miss Tallant cared for my champagne,' he replied imperturbably.

'Well, if she didn't, she could have refused it, couldn't she?' protested Lord Fleetwood. 'Besides, it was no such thing! She drank two glasses of it!'

'Never mind, Charles, there is still the port,' said Mr Beaumaris.

'Yes, by God!' said his lordship, brightening. 'And, mind, now! I expect the very best in your cellar! A couple of bottles of that '75 of yours, or — '

'Bring it to the library, Brough — something off the wood!' said Mr Beaumaris.

Lord Fleetwood, always the easiest of preys, rose to the bait without a moment's hesitation. 'Here, no, I say!' he cried, turning quite pale with horror. 'Robert! No, really, Robert!'

Mr Beaumaris lifted his brows in the blandest astonishment, but Brough, taking pity on his lordship, said in a soothing tone: 'We have nothing like that in our cellars, I assure your lordship!'

Lord Fleetwood, perceiving that he had once more been gulled, said with strong feeling: 'You deserve I should plant you a facer for that, Robert!'

'Well, if you think you can —!' said Mr Beaumaris.

'I don't,' replied his lordship frankly, accompanying him into the library. 'But that lemonade was a dog's trick to serve me, you know!' His brow puckered in an effort of thought. 'Tallant! . . . Did you ever hear the name before, for I'll swear I never did?'

Mr Beaumaris looked at him for a moment. Then his eyes fell to the snuff-box he had drawn from his pocket. He flicked open the box, and took a delicate pinch between finger and thumb. 'You have never heard of the Tallant fortune?' he said. 'My *dear* Charles — !'

5

Thanks to Mr Beaumaris's message, which worked so powerfully on the wheelwright as to cause him to ignore the prior claims of three other owners of damaged vehicles, Arabella was only kept waiting for one day in Grantham. Since the Quorn met there on the morning following her encounter with Mr Beaumaris, she was able, from the window of a private parlour at the Angel and Royal Inn, to see just how he looked on horseback. She could have seen how Lord Fleetwood looked too, had she cared, but curiously enough she never even thought of his lordship. Mr Beaumaris looked remarkably well, astride a beautiful thoroughbred, with long, sloping pasterns, and shoulders well laid back. She decided that Mr Beaumaris's seat was as good as any she had ever seen. The tops to his hunting-boots were certainly whiter than a mere provincial would have deemed possible.

The Hunt having moved off, there was nothing for two delayed travellers to do for the rest of the day but stroll about the town, eat their meals, and yawn over the only books to be found in the inn. But by the following morning the Squire's carriage was brought round to the Angel, with a new pole affixed, and the horses well-rested, and the ladies were able to set forward betimes on the last half of their long journey.

Even Miss Blackburn was heartily sick of the road by the time the muddied carriage at last drew up outside Lady Bridlington's house in Park Street. She was sufficiently well acquainted with the metropolis to feel no interest in the various sounds and sights which had made Arabella forget her boredom and her fidgets from the moment that the carriage reached Islington. These, to a young lady who had never seen a larger town than York in her life, were at once enthralling and bewildering. The traffic made her feel giddy, and the noise of post-bells, of wheels on the cobbled streets, and the shrill cries of itinerant vendors of coals, brick-dust, door-mats, and rat-traps quite deafened her. All passed before her wide gaze in a whirl; she wondered how anyone could live in such a place and still retain her sanity. But as the carriage, stopping once or twice for the coachman to enquire the way of nasal and not always polite Cockneys, wound its ponderous way into the more modish part of the town, the din abated till Arabella began even to entertain hopes of being able to sleep in London.

The house in Park Street seemed overpoweringly tall to one accustomed to a rambling two-storeyed country-house; and the butler who admitted the ladies into a lofty hall, whence rose an imposing flight of stairs, was so majestic that Arabella felt almost inclined to apologize for putting him to the trouble of announcing her to her godmother. But she was relieved to find that he was supported by only one footman, and so was able to follow him up with tolerable composure to the drawing-room on the first floor.

Here her qualms were put to flight by the welcome she received. Lady Bridlington, whose plump, pink cheeks were wreathed in smiles, clasped her to an ample bosom, kissed her repeatedly, exclaimed, just as Aunt Emma had, on her likeness to her Mama, and seemed so unaffectedly glad to see her that all constraint was at an end. Lady Bridlington's good-nature extended even to the governess, to whom she spoke with kindness, and perfect civility.

When Mama had known Lady Bridlington, she had been a pretty girl, without more than commonsense, but with such a respectable portion, and with so much vivacity and good-humour, that it was no surprise to her friends when she contracted a very eligible match. Time had done more to enlarge her figure than her mind, and it was not many days before her young charge had discovered that under a superficial worldly wisdom there was little but a vast amount of silliness. Her ladyship read whatever new work of prose or verse was in fashion, understood one word in ten of it, and prattled of the whole; doted on the most admired singers at the Opera, but secretly preferred the ballet; vowed there had never been anything to equal Kean's *Hamlet* on the English stage, but derived considerably more enjoyment from the farce which followed this soul-stirring performance. She was incapable of humming a tune correctly, but never failed to patronize the Concerts of Ancient Music during the season, just as she never failed to visit the Royal Academy every year, at Somerset House, where, although her notion of a good picture was a painting that reminded her forcibly of some person or place with which she was familiar, she unerringly detected the hand of a master in all the most distinguished artists' canvasses. Her life seemed to a slightly shocked Arabella to consist wholly of pleasure; and the greatest exertion she ever put her mind to was the securing of her own comfort. But it would have been unjust to have called her a selfish woman. Her disposition was kindly; she liked the people round her to be as happy as she was herself, for that made them cheerful, and she disliked long faces; she paid her servants well, and always remembered to thank them for any extraordinary service they per- formed for her, such as walking her horses up and down Bond Street in the rain for an hour while she shopped, or sitting up till four or five in the morning to put her to bed after an evening-party; and, provided she was not expected to put herself out for them, or to do anything disagreeable, she was both kind and generous to her friends.

She expected nothing but pleasure from Arabella's visit, and although she knew that in launching the girl into society she was behaving in a very handsome way, she never dwelled on the reflection, except once or twice a day in the privacy of her dressing-room, and then not in any grudging spirit, but merely for the gratifying sensation it gave her of being a benevolent person. She was very fond of visiting, shopping, and spectacles; liked entertaining large gatherings in her own house; and was seldom bored by even the dullest Assembly. Naturally, since every woman of fashion did so, she complained of dreadful squeezes or sadly insipid evenings, but no one who had seen her at these functions, greeting a multitude of acquaintances, exchanging the latest *on-dits*, closely scanning the newest fashions, or taking eager part in a rubber of whist, could have doubted her real and simple enjoyment of them.

To be obliged, then, to chaperon a young lady making her début to a succession of balls, routs, Assemblies, Military Reviews, balloon ascensions, and every other diversion likely to be offered to society during the season, exactly suited her disposition. She spent the better part of Arabella's first evening in Park Street in describing to her all the delightful plans she had been making for her amusement, and could scarcely wait for Miss Blackburn's departure next day before ordering her carriage to be sent round, and taking Arabella on a tour of all the smartest shops in London.

These cast the shops of High Harrowgate into the shade. Arabella was obliged to exercise great self-restraint when she saw the alluring wares displayed in the windows. She was helped a little by her north-country shrewdness, which recoiled from trifles priced at five times their worth, and not at all by her cicerone who, having been blessed all her life with sufficient means to enable her to purchase whatever took her fancy, could not understand why Arabella would not buy a bronze-green velvet hat, trimmed with feathers and a broad fall of lace, and priced at a figure which would have covered the cost of all the hats so cleverly contrived by Mama's and Sophia's neat fingers. Lady Bridlington owned that it was an expensive hat, but she held that to buy what became one so admirably could not be termed an extravagance. But Arabella put it resolutely aside, saying that she had as many hats as she required, and explaining frankly that she must not spend her money too freely, since Papa and Mama could not afford to send her any more. Lady Bridlington was quite distressed to think that such a pretty girl should not be able to set her beauty off to the best advantage. It seemed so sad that she was moved to purchase a net stocking-purse, and a branch of artificial flowers, and to bestow them on Arabella. She hesitated for a few minutes over a handsome shawl of Norwich silk, but it was priced at twenty guineas, and although this could not be said to be a high price, she remembered that she had one herself, a much better one, for which she had paid fifty guineas, which she could very well lend to Arabella whenever she did not wish to wear it herself. Besides, there would be all the expense of Arabella's Court dress to be borne later in the season, and even though a great deal might be found in her own wardrobe which could be converted to Arabella's needs, the cost was still certain to be heavy. A further inspection of the shawl convinced her that it was of poor quality, not at all the sort of thing she would like to give her young charge, so they left the shop without buying it. Arabella was profoundly relieved, for although she would naturally have liked to have possessed the shawl, it made her very uncomfortable to be in danger of costing her hostess so much money.

Her frankness in speaking of her circumstances made Lady Bridlington a little thoughtful. She did not immediately mention the matter, but when the two ladies sat before the fire in the small saloon that evening, drinking tea, she ventured to put into words some at least of the thoughts which were revolving in her head.

'You know, my dear,' she said, 'I have been considering the best way to set to work, and I have made up my mind to it that as soon as you have grown more used to London — and I am sure it will not be long, for you are such a bright, clever little puss! — I should introduce you, quietly, you know! The season has not yet begun, and London is still very thin of company. And I think that will suit us very well, for you are not used to the way we go on here, and a small Assembly — no dancing, just an evening-party, with music, perhaps, and cards — is the very thing for your first appearance! I mean to invite only a few of my friends, the very people who may be useful to you. You will become acquainted with some other young ladies, and of course with some gentlemen, and that will make it more comfortable, I assure you, when I take you to Almack's, or to some large ball. Nothing can be more disagreeable than to find oneself in a gathering where one does not recognize a single face!'

Arabella could readily believe it, and had

nothing but approbation for this excellent scheme. 'Oh, yes, if you please, ma'am! It is of all things what I should like, for I know I shall not know how to go on at first, though I mean to learn as fast as I can!'

'Exactly so!' beamed her ladyship. 'You are a sensible girl, Arabella, and I am very hopeful of settling you respectably, just as I promised your Mama I would!' She saw that Arabella was blushing, and added: 'You won't object to my speaking plain, my love, for I daresay you know how important it is that you should be creditably established. Eight children! I do not know how your poor Mama will ever contrive to get good husbands for your sisters! And boys are such a charge on one's purse! I am sure I do not care to think of what my dear Frederick cost his father and me from first to last! First it was one thing, and then another!'

A serious look came into Arabella's face, as she thought of the many and varied needs of her brothers and sisters. She said earnestly: 'Indeed, ma'am, what you say is very just, and I mean to do my best not to disappoint Mama!'

Lady Bridlington leaned forward to lay her pudgy little hand over Arabella's, and to squeeze it fondly. 'I knew you would feel just as you ought!' she said. 'Which brings me to what I had in mind to say to you!' She sat back again in her chair, fidgeted for a moment with the fringe of her shawl, and then said without looking at Arabella: 'You know, my love, everything depends on first impressions — at least, a great deal does! In society, with everyone trying to find eligible husbands for their daughters, and so many beautiful girls for the gentlemen to choose from, it is in the highest degree important that you should do and say exactly what is right. That is why I mean to bring you out quietly, and not at all until you feel yourself at home in London. For you must know, my dear, that only rustics appear amazed. I am sure I do not know why it should be so, but you may believe that innocent girls from the country are not at all what the gentlemen like!'

Arabella was surprised, for her reading had taught her otherwise. She ventured to say as much, but Lady Bridlington shook her head. 'No, my love, it is not so at all! That sort of thing may do very well in a novel, and I am very fond of novels myself, but they have nothing to do with life, depend upon it! But that was not what I wished to say!' Again she played with the shawl-fringe, saying in a little burst of eloquence: 'I would not, if I were you, my dear, be for ever talking about Heythram, and the Vicarage! You must remember that nothing is more wearisome than to be obliged to listen to stories about a set of persons one has never seen. And though of course you would not prevaricate in any way, it is quite unnecessary to tell everyone — or, indeed, anyone! — of your dear Papa's situation! *I* have said nothing to lead anyone to suppose that he is not in affluent circumstances, for nothing, I do assure you, Arabella, could be more fatal to your chances than to have it known that your expectations are very small!'

Arabella was about to reply rather more hotly

than was civil when the recollection of her own conduct in Mr Beaumaris's house came into her mind with stunning effect. She hung her head, and sat silent, wondering whether she ought to make a clean breast of the regrettable affair to Lady Bridlington, and deciding that it was too bad to be spoken of.

Lady Bridlington, misunderstanding the reason for her evident confusion, said hastily: 'If you should be fortunate enough to engage some gentleman's affection, dear Arabella, of course you will tell him just how you are placed, or I shall, and — and, depend upon it, he will not care a button! You must not be thinking that I wish you to practise the least deception, for it is no such thing! Merely, it would be foolish, and quite unnecessary, for you to be talking of your circumstances to every chance-met acquaintance!'

'Very well, ma'am,' said Arabella, in a subdued tone.

'I knew you would be sensible! Well, now, I am sure there is no need for me to say anything more to you on this head, and we must decide whom I shall invite to my evening-party. I wonder, my love, if you would see if my tablets are on that little table. And a pencil, if you will be so good!'

These commodities having been found, the good lady settled down happily to plan her forthcoming party. Since the names she recited were all of them unknown to Arabella, the discussion resolved itself into a gentle monologue. Lady Bridlington ran through the greater part of her acquaintance, murmuring that it would be useless to invite the Farnworths, since they had no children; that Lady Kirkmichael gave the shabbiest entertainments, and could not be depended on to invite Arabella, even if she did decide to give a ball for that lanky daughter of hers; that the Accringtons must of course be sent a card, and also the Buxtons — delightful families, both, and bound to entertain largely this season! 'And I mean to invite Lord Dewsbury, and Sir Geoffrey Morecambe, my dear, for there is no saying but what one of them might — And I am sure Mr Pocklington has been hanging out for a wife these two years, not but what he is perhaps a little old — However, we will ask him to come, for there can be no harm in that! Then, I must certainly prevail upon dear Lady Sefton to come, for she is one of the patronesses of Almack's, you know; and perhaps Emily Cowper might — And the Charnwoods, and Mr Catwick; and, if they are in town, the Garthorpes . . .'

She rambled on in this style, while Arabella tried to appear interested. But as she could do no more than agree with her hostess when she was appealed to, her attention soon wandered, to be recalled with a jerk when Lady Bridlington mentioned a name she did know.

'And I shall send Mr Beaumaris a card, because it would be such a splendid thing for you, my love, if it were known that he came to your début — for such we may call it! Why, if he were to come, and perhaps talk to you for a few minutes, and seem pleased with you, you would be *made*, my dear! Everyone follows his lead!

And perhaps, as there are so few parties yet, he *might* come! I am sure I have been acquainted with him for years, and I knew his mother quite well! She was Lady Mary Caldicot, you know: a daughter of the late Duke of Wigan, and such a beautiful creature! And it is not as though Mr Beaumaris has never been to my house, for he once came to an Assembly here, and stayed for quite half-an-hour! Mind, we must not build upon his accepting, but we need not despair!'

She paused for breath, and Arabella, colouring in spite of herself, was able at last to say: 'I — I am myself a little acquainted with Mr Beaumaris, ma'am.'

Lady Bridlington was so much astonished that she dropped her pencil. 'Acquainted with Mr Beaumaris?' she repeated. 'My love, what *can* you be thinking about? When can you possibly have met him?'

'I — I quite forgot to tell you, ma'am,' faltered Arabella unhappily, 'that when the pole broke — I told you *that*! — Miss Blackburn and I sought shelter in his hunting-box, and — and he had Lord Fleetwood with him, and we stayed to dine!'

Lady Bridlington gasped. 'Good God, Arabella, and you never told me! Mr Beaumaris's house! He actually asked you to dine, and you never breathed a word of it to me!'

Arabella found herself quite incapable of explaining why she had been shy of mentioning this episode. She stammered that it had slipped out of her mind in all the excitement of coming to London.

'Slipped out of your mind?' exclaimed Lady Bridlington. 'You dine with Mr Beaumaris, and at his hunting-box, too, and then talk to me about the excitement of coming to London? Good gracious, child — But, there, you are such a country-mouse, my love, I daresay you did not know all it might mean to you! Did he seem pleased? Did he like you?'

This was a little too much, even for a young lady determind to be on her best behaviour. 'I daresay he disliked me excessively, ma'am, for I thought *him* very proud and disagreeable, and I hope you won't ask him to your party on *my* account!'

'Not ask him to my party, when, if he came to it, everyone would say it was a success! You must be mad, Arabella, to talk so! And do let me beg of you, my dear, never to say such a thing of Mr Beaumaris in public! I daresay he may be a little stiff, but what is that to the purpose, pray? There is no one who counts for more in society, for setting aside his fortune, which is immense, my love, he is related to half the houses in England! The Beaumarises are one of the oldest of our families, while on his mother's side he is a grandson of the Duchess of Wigan — the Dowager Duchess, I mean, which of course makes him cousin to the present Duke, besides the Wainfleets, and — But you would not know!' she ended despairingly.

'I thought Lord Fleetwood most amiable, and gentleman — like,' offered Arabella, by way of palliative.

'Fleetwood! I can tell you this, Arabella: there

is no use in your setting your cap at *him*, for all the world knows that he *must* marry money!'

'I hope, ma'am,' cried Arabella, flaring up, 'that you do not mean to suggest that I should *set my cap* at Mr Beaumaris, for nothing would prevail upon me to do so!'

'My love,' responded Lady Bridlington frankly, 'it would be quite useless for you to do so! Robert Beaumaris may have his pick of all the beauties in England, I daresay! And, what is more, he is the most accomplished flirt in London! But I do most earnestly implore you not to set him against you by treating him with the least incivility! You may think him what you please, but, believe me, Arabella, he could ruin your whole career — and mine, too, if it came to that!' she added feelingly.

Arabella propped her chin in her hand, pondering an agreeable thought. 'Or he could make everything easy for me, ma'am?' she enquired.

'Of course he could — if he chose to do it! He is the most unpredictable creature! It might amuse him to make you the rage of town — or he might take it into his head to say you were not quite in his style — and if once he says *that*, my dear, what man will look twice at you, unless he has already fallen in love with you, which, after all, we *cannot* expect?'

'My dear ma'am,' said Arabella, in dulcet accents, 'I hope I should not be so ill-bred as to be uncivil to *anyone* — even Mr Beaumaris!'

'Well, my dear, I hope not, indeed!' said her ladyship doubtfully.

'I promise I will not be in the least degree uncivil to Mr Beaumaris, if he should come to your party,' said Arabella.

'I am happy to hear you say so, my love, but ten to one he won't come,' responded her ladyship pessimistically.

'He said to me at parting that he hoped to have the pleasure of calling on me in town before many days,' said Arabella disinterestedly.

Lady Bridlington considered this, but in the end shook her head. 'I do not think we should set any store by that,' she said. 'Very likely he said it for politeness' sake.'

'Very likely,' agreed Arabella. 'But if you are acquainted with him, I wish you will send Lord Fleetwood a card for your party, ma'am, for he was excessively kind, and I liked him!'

'Of course I am acquainted with him!' declared Lady Bridlington, quite affronted. 'But do not be setting your heart on him, Arabella, I beg of you! A delightful rattle, but the Fleetwoods are all to pieces, by what I hear, and however much he may flirt with you, I am persuaded he will never make you an offer!'

'Must every man I meet make me an offer?' asked Arabella, controlling her voice with an effort.

'No, my love, and you may depend upon it that they won't!' replied her ladyship candidly. 'In fact, I have had it in mind to warn you against setting your ambitions *too* high! I mean to do all I can for you, but there is no denying that suitable husbands do not grow upon every bush! Particularly, my dear — and I know you

107

will not fly into a miff with me for saying it!
— when you have no portion to recommend
you!'

In face of her ladyship's conviction, Arabella
hardly liked to betray her feelings, so she bit her
lip, and was silent. Fortunately, Lady Bridlington's mind was not of a tenacious nature, and as
she just then recollected a very important lady
whose name must be included amongst the list
of invited persons, she forgot about Arabella's
matrimonial chances in explaining why it would
be folly to omit Lady Terrington from that list.
Nothing more was said about Mr Beaumaris, her
ladyship having been diverted, by some chance
reference of her own, into describing to Arabella
the various social treats she had in store for her.
In spite of the fact that the season had not yet
begun, these were so numerous that Arabella felt
almost giddy, and wondered whether, in this
round of gaiety, her hostess would find the time
to accompany her to Church on Sunday. But in
doubting whether Lady Bridlington would go to
Church she wronged her: Lady Bridlington
would have thought it a very odd thing not to be
seen in her pew every Sunday morning, unless,
as was very often the case, she chose to attend
the service at the Chapel Royal, where, in
addition to listening to an excellent sermon, she
could be sure of seeing all her more distinguished friends, and even, very often, some
member of the Royal Family. This good fortune
was hers on Arabella's first Sunday in London,
and the circumstance made fine reading for the
interested brothers and sisters in Yorkshire,

following, as it did (most artistically), descriptions of Hyde Park, and St. Paul's Cathedral, and a lively account of the racket and bustle of the London Streets.

'*We attended Morning Service at the Chapel Royal, St James's on Sunday,*' wrote Arabella, in a fine, small hand, and on very thin paper, crossing her lines. '*We heard a very good sermon on a text from the Second Epistle to the Corinthians, pray tell dear Papa: He that had gathered much had nothing over; and he that had gathered little had no lack. London is still very thin of company*' — not for nothing had Arabella dutifully attended to her godmother's conversation! — '*but there were a great many fashionables present, and also the Duke of Clarence, who came up to us afterwards, and was very affable, with nothing high in his manner at all.*' Arabella paused, nibbling the end of her pen, and considering the Duke of Clarence. Papa might not care to have his Royal Highness described, but Mama, and Sophy, and Margaret would most certainly wish to know just what he was like, and what he had said. She bent again over her page. '*I do not think one would say that he is precisely handsome,*' she wrote temperately, '*but his countenance is benevolent. His head is a queer shape, and he is inclined to corpulence. He made me think of my uncle, for he talks in just that way, and very loud, and he laughs a great deal. He did me the honour to say that I wore a vastly fetching hat: I hope Mama will be pleased, for it was the one with her pink feathers, which she made for me.*' There did not seem to be anything more to be said about the Duke of Clarence, except that he talked quite audibly in Church, and that was information scarcely likely to please the inhabitants of the Vicarage. She read over what she had written, and felt that it might disappoint Mama and the girls. She added a line. '*Lady Bridlington says that he is not near as fat as the Prince Regent, or the Duke of York.*' On this heartening note she ended her paragraph, and embarked on a fresh one.

'*I am growing quite accustomed to London, and begin to know my way about the streets, though of course I do not walk out by myself yet. Lady Bridlington sends a footman with me, just as Bertram said she would, but I see that young females do go alone nowadays, only perhaps they are not of the* haut ton. *This is very important, and I am in constant dread that I shall do something improper, such as walking down St James's Street, where all the gentlemen's clubs are, and very fast, which of course I do not wish to be thought. Lady Bridlington gives an evening-party, to introduce me to her friends. I shall be all of a quake, for everyone is so grand and fashionable, though perfectly civil, and much kinder than I had looked for. Sophy will like to know that Lord Fleetwood, whom I met on the road, as I wrote to you from Grantham, paid us a morning-visit, to see how I did, which was very amiable and obliging of him. Also Mr Beaumaris, but we were out driving in the Park. He left his card. Lady Bridlington was in transports, and has placed it above all the rest, which I think nonsensical, but I find that that is*

110

the way of the World, and makes me reflect on all Papa has said on the subject of Folly, and the Hollowness of Fashionable Life.' That seemed to dispose satisfactorily of Mr Beaumaris. Arabella dipped her pen in the standish again. *'Lady Bridlington is everything that is kind, and I am persuaded that Lord Bridlington is a very respectable young man, and not at all abandoned to the Pursuit of Pleasure, as Papa feared. His name is Frederick. He is travelling in Germany, and has visited a great many of the battlefields. He writes very interesting letters to his Mama, with which I am sure Papa would be pleased, for he seems to feel just as he ought, and moralizes on all he sees in a truly elevating way, though rather long.'* Arabella perceived that there was little room left on her sheet, and added in a cramped fist: *'I would write more only that I cannot get a frank for this, and do not wish to put Papa to the expense of paying some sixpences for the second sheet. With my love to my brothers and sisters, and my affectionate duty to dear Papa, I remain your loving daughter Arabella.'*

Plenty of promising matter there for Mama and the girls to pore over, and to discuss, even though so much remained unwritten! One could not resist boasting a very little about the compliments paid to one by a Royal Duke, or just mentioning that a fashionable peer of the realm had called to see how one did — not to mention the great Mr Beaumaris, if one had happened to care a fig for that — but one felt quite shy of disclosing even to Mama how very gracious — how amazingly kind — everyone was being to an insignificant girl from Yorkshire.

For so it was. Shopping in Bond Street, driving on clement afternoons in Hyde Park, attending the service at the Chapel Royal, Lady Bridlington naturally encountered friends, and never failed to present Arabella to their notice. Some really forbidding dowagers who might have been expected to have paid scant heed to Arabella unbent in the most gratifying way, quite overpowering her by the kindness of their enquiries, and their insistence that Lady Bridlington should bring her to see them one day. Several introduced their daughters to Arabella, suggesting that she and they might walk in the Green Park some fine morning, so that in less than no time it seemed as though she had a host of acquaintances in London. The gentlemen were not more backward: it was quite a commonplace thing for some stroller in the Park to come up to Lady Bridlington's barouche, and stand chatting to her, and to her pretty protégée; while more than one sprig of fashion, with whom her ladyship was barely acquainted, paid her a morning-visit on what seemed even to one so little given to speculation as Lady Bridlington the slenderest of excuses.

She was a little surprised, but after thinking about it for a few minutes she was as easily able to account for the ladies' civility as the gentlemen's. They were anxious to oblige her. This led her by natural stages to the reflection that she deserved a great deal of credit for having so well advertised Arabella's visit to town. As for the gentlemen, she had never doubted, from the moment of setting eyes on her goddaughter, that that fairy figure and charming countenance could fail to attract instant admiration. Arabella had, moreover, the most enchanting smile, which brought dimples leaping to her cheeks, and was at once mischievous and appealing. Any but the most case-hardened of men, thought Lady Bridlington enviously, would be more than likely, under its intoxicating influence, to behave in a rash manner, however much he might afterwards regret it.

But none of these conclusions quite explained the morning-visits of several high-nosed ladies of fashion, whose civilities towards Lady Bridlington had hitherto consisted of invitations to their larger Assemblies, and bows exchanged from their respective carriages. Lady Somercote was particularly puzzling. She called in Park Street when Arabella was out walking with the three charming daughters of Sir James and Lady Hornsea, and she sat for over an hour with her gratified hostess. She expressed the greatest admiration of Arabella, whom she had met at the theatre with her godmother. 'A delightful girl!' she said graciously. 'Very pretty-behaved, and without the least hint of pretension in her dress or bearing!'

Lady Bridlington agreed to it, and since her mind did not move rapidly it was not until her guest was well into her next observation that she wondered why Arabella should be supposed to show pretension.

'Of good family, I apprehend?' said Lady

Somercote, carelessly, but looking rather searchingly at her hostess.

'Of course!' replied Lady Bridlington, with dignity. 'A most respected Yorkshire family!'

Lady Somercote nodded. 'I thought as much. Excellent manners, and conducts herself with perfect propriety! I was particularly pleased with the modesty of her bearing: not the least sign of wishing to put herself forward! And her dress too! Just what I like to see in a young female! Nothing vulgar, such as one too often sees nowadays! When every miss out of the schoolroom is decked out with jewelry, it is refreshing to see one with a simple wreath of flowers in her hair. Somercote was much struck. Indeed, he quite took one of his fancies to her! You must bring her to Grosvenor Square next week, dear Lady Bridlington! Nothing formal, you know: a few friends only, and perhaps the young people may find themselves with enough couples to get up a little dance.'

She waited only for Lady Bridlington's acceptance of this flattering invitation before taking her leave. Lady Bridlington was left with her mind in a whirl. She was shrewd enough to know that more than a compliment to herself must lie behind this unexpected honour, and was at a loss to discover the lady's motive. She was the mother of five hopeful and expensive sons, and it was well known that the Somercote estates were heavily mortgaged. Advantageous marriages were a necessity to the Somercotes' progeny, and no one was more purposeful in her pursuit of a likely heiress than their Mama. For a dismayed instant Lady Bridlington wondered whether, in her anxiety to assist Arabella, she had concealed her circumstances too well. But she could not recall that she had ever so much as mentioned them: indeed, her recollection was that she had taken care never to do so.

The Honourable Mrs Penkridge, calling on her dear friend for the express purpose of bidding her and her protégée to a select Musical Soirée, and explaining, with apologies, how it was due to the stupidity of a secretary that her card of invitation had not reached her long since, spoke in even warmer terms of Arabella. 'Charming! quite charming!' she declared, bestowing her frosted smile upon Lady Bridlington. 'She will throw all our beauties into the shade! That simplicity is so particularly pleasing! You are to be congratulated!'

However perplexed Lady Bridlington might be by this speech, issuing, as it did, from the lips of one famed as much for her haughtiness as for her acid tongue, it seemed at least to dispose of the suspicion roused in her mind by Lady Somercote's visit. The Penkridges were a childless couple. Lady Bridlington, on whom Mrs Penkridge had more than once passed some contemptuous criticism, was not well-enough acquainted with her to know that almost the only sign of human emotion she had ever been seen to betray was her doting fondness for her nephew, Mr Horace Epworth.

This elegant gentleman, complete to a point as regards side-whiskers, fobs, seals, quizzing-glass, and scented handkerchief, had lately honoured his aunt with one of his infrequent visits. Surprised and delighted, she had begged to know in what way she could be of service to him. Mr Epworth had no hesitation in telling her. 'You might put me in the way of meeting the new heiress, ma'am,' he said frankly. 'Dev'lish fine gal — regular Crœsus, too!'

She had pricked up her ears at that, and exclaimed: 'Whom can you be thinking of, my dear Horace? If you mean the Flint chit, I have it for a fact that — '

'Pooh! nothing of the sort!' interrupted Mr Epworth, waving the Flint chit away with one white and languid hand. 'I daresay *she* has no more than thirty thousand pounds! This gal is so rich she puts 'em all in the shade. They call her the Lady Dives.'

'Who calls her so?' demanded his incredulous relative.

Mr Epworth again waved his hand, this time in the direction which he vaguely judged to be northward. 'Oh, up there somewhere, ma'am! Yorkshire, or some other of those dev'lish remote counties! Daresay she's a merchant's daughter: wool, or cotton, or some such thing. Pity, but I shan't regard it: they tell me she's charming!'

'I have heard nothing of this! Who is she? Who told you she was charming?'

'Had it from Fleetwood last night, at the Great-Go,' explained Mr Epworth negligently.

'That rattle! I wish you will not go so often to Watier's, Horace! I warn you, it is useless to apply to me! I have not a guinea left in the world, and I dare not ask Mr Penkridge to assist

116

you again, until he has forgotten the last time!'

'Put me in the way of meeting this gal, and I'll kiss my fingers to Penkridge, ma'am,' responded Mr Epworth, gracefully suiting the action to the word. 'Acquainted with Lady Bridlington, ain't you? The gal's staying with her.'

She stared at him. 'If Arabella Bridlington had an heiress staying with her she would have boasted of it all over town!'

'No, she wouldn't. Fleetwood particularly told me the gal don't want it known. Don't like being courted for her fortune. Pretty gal, too, by what Fleetwood says. Name of Tallant.'

'I never heard of a Tallant in my life!'

'Lord, ma'am, why should you? Keep telling you she comes from some dev'lish outlandish place in the north!'

'I would not set the least store by anything Fleetwood told me!'

'Oh, it ain't him!' said Mr Epworth cheerfully. 'He don't know the gal's name either. It's the Nonpareil. Knows all about the family. Vouches for the gal.'

Her expression changed; a still sharper look entered her eyes. She said quickly: 'Beaumaris?' He nodded. 'If *he* vouches for her — Is she presentable?'

He looked shocked, and answered in protesting accents: ' 'Pon my soul, ma'am, you can't be in your senses to ask me such a demned silly question! Now, I put it to you, *would* Beaumaris vouch for a gal that wasn't slap up to the echo?'

'No. No, he would not,' she said decidedly. 'If it's true, and she has no vulgar connections, it would be the very thing for you, my dear Horace!'

'Just what I was thinking myself, ma'am,' said her nephew.

'I will pay Lady Bridlington a morning-visit,' said Mrs Penkridge.

'That's it: do the pretty!' Mr Epworth encouraged her.

'It is tiresome, for I have never been upon intimate terms with her! However, this alters the circumstances! Leave it to me!'

Thus it was that Lady Bridlington found herself the object of Mrs Penkridge's attentions. Since she had never before been honoured with an invitation to one of that lady's more exclusive parties, she was considerably elated, and at once seized the opportunity to invite Mrs Penkridge to her own evening-party. Mrs Penkridge accepted with another of her thin smiles, saying that she knew she could answer for her husband's pleasure in attending the party, and departed, thinking out rapidly some form of engagement for him which would at once spare him an insipid evening, and render it necessary for her to claim her nephew's escort.

6

Lady Bridlington did not expect Arabella's first party to be a failure, since she was a good hostess, and never offered her guests any but the best wines and refreshments, but that it should prove to be a wild success had not even entered her head. She had planned it more with the idea of bringing Arabella to the notice of other hostesses than as a brilliant social event; and although she had certainly invited a good many unattached gentlemen she had not held out the lure of dancing, or of cards, and so had little hope of seeing more than half of them in her spacious rooms. Her main preoccupation was lest Arabella should not be looking her best, or should jeopardize her future by some unconventional action, or some unlucky reference to that regrettable Yorkshire Vicarage. In general, the child behaved very prettily, but once or twice she had seriously alarmed her patroness, either by a remark which betrayed all too clearly the modesty of her circumstances — as when she had asked, in front of the butler, whether she should help to prepare the rooms for the party, for all the world as though she expected to be given an apron and a duster! — or by some impulsive action so odd as to be positively outrageous. Not readily would Lady Bridlington forget the scene outside the Soho Bazaar, when she and Arabella, emerging from this mart,

119

found a heavy wagon stationary in the road, with the one scraggy horse between its shafts straining under an unsparing lash to set it in motion. At one instant a demure young lady had been at Lady Bridlington's side; at the next a flaming fury was confronting the astonished wagoner, commanding him, with a stamp of one little foot to get down from the wagon at once — *at once!* — and not to *dare* to raise his whip again! He got down, quite bemused, and stood in front of the small fury, an ox of a man, towering above her while she berated him. When he had recovered his wits he attempted to justify himself, but failed signally to pacify the lady. He was a cruel wretch, unfit to be in charge of a horse, and a dolt, besides, not to perceive that one of the wheels was jammed, and through his own bad driving, no doubt! He began to be angry, and to shout Arabella down, but by this time a couple of chairmen, abandoning their empty vehicle, came across the square, expressing, in strong Hibernian accents, their willingness to champion the lady, and their desire to know whether the wagoner wanted to have his cork drawn. Lady Bridlington, all this time, had stood frozen with horror in the doorway of the Bazaar, unable to think of anything else to do than to be thankful that none of her acquaintances was present to witness this shocking affair. Arabella told the chairmen briskly that she would have no fighting, bade the wagoner observe the obstruction against which one of his rear wheels was jammed, herself went to the horse's head, and began to back him. The chairmen promptly lent their aid; Arabella addressed a short, pithy lecture to the wagoner on the folly and injustice of losing one's temper with animals, and rejoined her godmother, saying calmly: 'It is mostly ignorance, you know!'

And although she did, when shown the impropriety of her behaviour, say she was sorry to have made a scene in public, it was evident that she was not in the least penitent. She said that Papa would have told her it was her duty to interfere in such a cause.

But no representations could induce her to say she was sorry for her quite unbecoming conduct two days later, when she entered her bedchamber to find a very junior housemaid, with a swollen face, lighting the fire. It appeared that the girl had the toothache. Now, Lady Bridlington had no desire that any of her servants should suffer the agonies of toothache, and had she been asked she would unquestionably have said that at the first convenient moment the girl should be sent off to have the tooth drawn. The mistress of a large household naturally had a duty to oversee the general well-being of her staff. Indeed, some years previously, when inoculation against cowpox had been all the rage, she had with her own hands inoculated all the servants at Bridlington, and most of the tenants on the estate. Nearly every great lady had done so: it had been the accepted order of the day. But to bid the sufferer seat herself in the armchair in the best guest-chamber, to give her an Indian silk shawl to wrap round her head; and to disturb one's hostess during the sacred hour of her afternoon-nap by bursting in upon her with a demand for laudanum,

121

was carrying benevolence to quite undesirable lengths. Lady Bridlington did her best to convey the sense of this to Arabella, but she spoke to deaf ears. 'The poor girl is in the most dreadful pain, ma'am!'

'Nonsense, my love! You must not let yourself be imposed upon. Persons of her class always made a to-do about nothing. She had better have the tooth drawn tomorrow, if she can be spared from her work, and — '

'Dear madam, I assure you she is in no case to be toiling up and down all these stairs with coal-scuttles!' said Arabella earnestly. 'She should take some drops of laudanum, and lie down on her bed.'

'Oh, very well!' said her ladyship, yielding to the stronger will. 'But there is no occasion for you to be putting yourself into this state, my dear! And to be asking one of the under-housemaids to sit down in your bedroom, and giving her one of your best shawls — '

'No, no, I have only lent it to her!' Arabella said. 'She is from the country, you know, ma'am, and I think the other servants have not used her as they ought. She was homesick, and so unhappy! And the toothache made it worse, of course. I do believe she wanted someone to be kind to her more than anything else! She has been telling me about her home, and her little sisters and brothers, and — '

'Arabella!' uttered Lady Bridlington. 'Surely you have not been *gossiping with the servants?*' She saw her young guest stiffen, and added hastily: 'You should never encourage persons of her sort to pour out the history of their lives into your ears. I expect you meant it for the best, my dear, but you have no notion how encroach-ing — '

'I hope, ma'am — indeed, I *know!*' said Arabella, her eyes very bright, and her small figure alarmingly rigid, 'that not one of Papa's children would pass by a fellow-creature in distress!'

It was fast being borne in upon Lady Bridlington that the Reverend Henry Tallant was not only a grave handicap to his daughter's social advancement, but a growing menace to her own comfort. She was naturally unable to express this conviction to Arabella, so she sank back on her pillows, saying feebly: 'Oh, very well, but if people were to hear of it they would think it excessively odd in you, my dear!'

Whatever anyone else might think, it soon became plain that the episode had given her ladyship's upper servants the poorest idea of Arabella's social standing. Her ladyship's per-sonal maid, a sharp-faced spinster who had grown to middle-age in her service, and bullied her without compunction, ventured to hint, while she was dressing her mistress's hair that evening, that it was easy to see Miss was not accustomed to living in large and genteel households.

Lady Bridlington allowed Miss Clara Crowle a good deal of licence, but this was going too far. A pretty thing it would be if the servants, in that odious way they all had of talking about their betters, were to spread such a thing abroad! It would reach the ears of their employers in less than no time, and then the fat would indeed be in the fire! In a few dignified, well-chosen words Lady Bridlington gave her henchwoman to understand that Miss Tallant came from a mansion of awe-inspiring gentility, and was quite above considering appearances. She added, to clinch the matter, that very different customs obtained in the north from those common in London. Miss Crowle, a little cowed, but with a sting yet left in her tongue, sniffed, and said: 'So I have always understood, my lady!' She then encountered her mistress's eyes in the mirror, and added obsequiously: 'Not but what I am sure no one would ever suspicion Miss came from the north, my lady, so prettily as she speaks!'

'Certainly not,' said Lady Bridlington coldly, and quite forgetful of the fact that she had experienced considerable relief, when Arabella had greeted her on her arrival, at finding that no ugly accent marred her soft voice. The dreadful possibility that she might speak with a Yorkshire burr had more than once occurred to her. Had she but known it, she had the Reverend Henry Tallant to thank for his daughter's pure accent. Papa was far too fastidious and cultured a man to permit his children to be slipshod in their speech, even frowning upon the excellent imitations of the farm-hand's conversation, achieved by Bertram and Harry in funning humour.

Miss Clara Crowle might be silenced, but Arabella's reprehensible conduct gave her hostess some serious qualms, and caused her to anticipate her evening-party with less than her usual placidity.

But nothing could have gone off better. To ensure that in appearance at least Arabella should do her credit, Lady Bridlington sent no less a personage than Miss Crowle herself to put the finishing touches to her toilet, rounding off the efforts of the housemaid detailed to wait on her. Miss Crowle was not best pleased when sent off to offer her services to Arabella, but it was many years since she had dressed a young and beautiful lady, and in spite of herself her enthusiasm awoke when she saw how delightfully Arabella's gown of jonquil crape became her, and how tasteful was the spangled scarf hanging over her arms. She saw at a glance that she could scarcely better the simple arrangement of those dark curls, twisted into a high knot on the top of her head, and with the short ringlets allowed to fall over her ears, but she begged Miss to permit her to place her flowers more becomingly. Her cunning hands deftly placed the faggot of artificial roses at just the right angle, and she was so well-satisfied with the result that she said Miss would be quite the belle of the evening, being as she was dark, and the fashion for fair beauties quite outdated.

Arabella, unaware of how greatly Miss Crowle was condescending to her, only laughed, a piece of unconcern that did her no harm in that critical maiden's eyes. Arabella was embarking on her first London party enormously heartened by the arrival, not an hour earlier, of her first

London posy of flowers. The exciting box had been carried up to her room immediately, and, when opened, had been found to contain a charming bouquet, tied up — so fortunately! — with long yellow ribbons. Lord Fleetwood's card accompanied the tribute, and was even now propped up against the mirror. Miss Crowle saw it, and was impressed.

Lady Bridlington, presently setting eyes on Arabella just before dinner was announced, was delighted, and reflected that Sophia Theale had always had exquisite taste. Nothing could have set Arabella off to greater advantage than that delicate yellow robe, open down the front over a slip of white satin, and ornamented with clasps of tiny roses to match those in her hair. The only jewelry she wore was the ring Papa had had made for her, and Grandmama's necklet of pearls. Lady Bridlington was half inclined to ring for Clara to fetch down from her own jewel-case two bracelets of gold and pearls, and then decided that Arabella's pretty arms needed no embellishment. Besides, she would be wearing long gloves, so that the bracelets would be wasted.

'Very nice, my love!' she said approvingly. 'I am glad I sent Clara to you. Dear me, where had you those flowers?'

'Lord Fleetwood sent them, ma'am,' replied Arabella proudly.

Lady Bridlington received this information with disappointing composure. 'Did he so? Then at all events we may be sure of seeing *him* here tonight. You know, my love, you must not be expecting a squeeze! I am sure I hope to see my drawing-rooms respectably filled, but it is early in the year still, so you must not be cast-down if you do not see as many people as you might have supposed you would.'

She might have spared her breath. By half-past ten her drawing-rooms were crowded to overflowing, and she was still standing at the head of the stairs receiving late-comers. Nothing, she thought dizzily, had ever been like it! Even the Wainfleets, whom really she had not expected to see, were there; while the haughty Mrs Penkridge, escorted by her dandified nephew, had been amongst the earliest arrivals, unbending amazingly to Arabella, and begging leave to introduce Mr Epworth. Lord Fleetwood, and his crony, Mr Oswald Warkworth, were there, both hovering assiduously near Arabella, very full of gallantry and good spirits; Lady Somercote had brought two of her sons, and the Kirkmichaels their lanky daughter; Lord Dewsbury had failed, but Sir Geoffrey Morecambe was much in evidence, as were also the Accringtons, the Charnwoods, and the Seftons. Lady Sefton, dear creature that she was, had spoken with the greatest kindness to Arabella, and had promised later on to send her a voucher admitting her to Almack's Assembly Rooms. Lady Bridlington felt that her cup was full. It was to overflow. Last of all the guests, arriving after eleven o'clock, when her ladyship, having long since released Arabella from her place at her side, was on the point of abandoning her post and joining her guests in the drawing-rooms, Mr Beaumaris arrived, and came unhurriedly up the stairs. Her ladyship awaited him with a bosom swelling beneath its rich covering of purple satin, and her hand, clasping her fan, trembling slightly under the influence of the accumulated triumphs of this night. He greeted her with his cool civility, and she replied with tolerable composure, thanking him for his kind offices, in Leicestershire, towards her goddaughter.

'A pleasure, ma'am,' said Mr. Beaumaris. 'I trust Miss Tallant reached town without further mishap?'

'Oh, yes, indeed! So obliging of you to have called to enquire after her! We were sorry to have been out. You will find Miss Tallant in one of the rooms. Your cousin, Lady Wainfleet, too, is here.'

He bowed, and followed her into the front drawing-room. A minute later, Arabella, enjoying the attentions of Lord Fleetwood, Mr Warkworth, and Mr Epworth, saw him coming towards her across the room, pausing once or twice on his way to exchange salutations with his friends. Until that moment she had thought Mr Epworth quite the best-dressed man present: indeed, she had been quite dazzled by the exquisite nature of his raiment, and the profusion of rings, pins, fobs, chains, and seals which he wore; but no sooner had she clapped eyes on Mr Beaumaris's tall, manly figure than she realized that Mr Epworth's wadded shoulders, wasp-waist, and startling waistcoat were perfectly ridiculous. Nothing could have been in greater contrast to the extravagance of his attire than Mr Beaumaris's black coat and pantaloons, his plain white waistcoat, the single fob that hung to one side of it, the single pearl set chastely in the intricate folds of his necktie. Nothing he wore was designed to attract attention, but he made every other man in the room look either a trifle overdressed or a trifle shabby.

He reached her side, and smiled, and when she put out her hand raised it fleetingly to his lips. 'How do you do, Miss Tallant?' he said. 'I am happy indeed to have been granted this opportunity of renewing my acquaintance with you.'

'Oh, it is too bad — a great deal too bad!' fluted Mr Epworth, rolling an arch eye at Arabella. 'You and Fleetwood have stolen a march on the rest of us, you know — a shameful thing, 'pon my soul!'

Mr Beaumaris glanced down at him from his superior height, seemed to debate within himself whether this sally was worth the trouble of a reply, to decide that it was not, and turned back to Arabella. 'You must tell me how you like London,' he said. 'It is abundantly plain that London likes you! May I procure you a glass of lemonade?'

This offer brought Arabella's chin up, and made her look at him with a distinct challenge in her eyes. She had had plenty of time to discover that it was not the common practice of hosts to sweep the wine from their tables at the end of the first course, and she strongly suspected Mr Beaumaris of quizzing her. He was looking perfectly grave, however, and met her eyes without a shadow of mockery in his own. Before she could answer him, Lord Fleetwood committed a strategical error, and exclaimed: 'Of course! I'll swear you are parched with thirst, ma'am! I will get you a glass immediately!'

'Splendid, Charles!' said Mr Beaumaris cordially. 'Do let me take you a little out of this crush, Miss Tallant!'

He seemed to take her acquiescence for granted, for he did not await a reply, but led her to where a sofa standing against one wall was momentarily unoccupied. How he contrived to find a way through the crowd of chattering guests was a mystery to Arabella, for he certainly did not force a passage. A touch on a man's shoulder, a bow and a smile to a lady, and the thing was done. He sat down beside her on the sofa, seated a little sideways, so that he could watch her face, one hand on the back of the sofa, the other playing idly with his quizzing-glass. 'Does it come up to your expectations, ma'am?' he asked smilingly.

'London? Yes, indeed!' she responded. 'I am sure I was never so happy in my life!'

'I am glad,' he said.

Arabella remembered that Lady Bridlington had warned her against betraying too much enthusiasm: it was unfashionable to appear pleased. She remembered also that she had promised not to make a bad impression on Mr Beaumaris, so she added in a languid tone: 'It is a shocking squeeze, of course, but it is always diverting to meet new people.'

He looked amused, and said with a laugh in

his voice: 'No, don't spoil it! Your first answer was charming.'

She eyed him doubtfully for a moment; then her irrepressible dimples peeped out. 'But it is only rustics who own to enjoyment, sir!'

'Is it?' he returned.

'*You*, I am persuaded, do not enjoy such an Assembly as this!'

'You are mistaken: my enjoyment depends on the company in which I find myself.'

'That,' said Arabella naïvely, having thought it over, 'is quite the prettiest thing that has been said to me tonight!'

'Then I can only suppose, Miss Tallant, that Fleetwood and Warkworth were unable to find words to express their appreciation of the exquisite picture you present. Strange! I formed the opinion that they were paying you all manner of compliments.'

She laughed out at that. 'Yes, but it was nonsense! I did not believe a word they said!'

'I hope you believe what *I* say, however, for I am very much in earnest.'

The light tone he used seemed to belie his words. Arabella found him baffling, and directed another of her speculative glances at him. She decided that he must be answered in kind, and said daringly: 'Are you being so obliging as to bring me into fashion, Mr Beaumaris?'

He let his eyes travel round the crowded room, his brows a little raised. 'You do not appear to me to stand in any need of my assistance, ma'am.' He perceived that Lord Fleetwood was edging his way past a knot of people, a glass in his hand, and waited for him to reach the sofa. 'Thank you, Charles,' he said coolly, taking the glass from his lordship, and presenting it to Arabella.

'You,' said Lord Fleetwood, with deep feeling, 'will receive a message from me in the morning, Robert! This is the most barefaced piracy I ever beheld in my life! Miss Tallant, I wish you will send this fellow about his business: his effrontery goes beyond what is allowable!'

'You must learn not to act on impulse,' said Mr Beaumaris kindly. 'A moment's reflection, the least touch of adroitness, and it would have been I who fetched the lemonade and you who had the privilege of sitting beside Miss Tallant on this sofa!'

'But it is Lord Fleetwood who earns my gratitude, for he was the more chivalrous!' said Arabella.

'Miss Tallant, I thank you!'

'You have certainly been amply rewarded, and have now nothing to do but to take yourself off,' said Mr Beaumaris.

'Not for the world!' declared his lordship.

Mr Beaumaris sighed. 'How often I have had to deplore your lack of tact!' he said.

Arabella, sparkling under the influence of all this exciting banter, raised her posy to her nose, and said, with a grateful look cast up at Fleetwood: 'I stand *doubly* in Lord Fleetwood's debt!'

'No, no, it is I who stand in yours, ma'am, since you deigned to accept my poor tribute!'

Mr Beaumaris glanced at the posy, and smiled

slightly, but said nothing. Arabella, catching sight of Mr Epworth, who was hovering hopefully in the vicinity, suddenly said: 'Mr Beaumaris, who *is* that oddly dressed man?'

He looked round, but said: 'There are so many oddly dressed men present, Miss Tallant, that I fear I am at a loss. You do not mean poor Fleetwood here?'

'Of course I do not!' exclaimed Arabella indignantly.

'Well, I am sure it would be difficult to find anything odder than that waistcoat he wears. It is very disheartening, for I have really expended a great deal of time in trying to reform his taste. Ah, I think I see whom you must mean! That, Miss Tallant, is Horace Epworth. In his own estimation, he undoubtedly personifies a set of creatures whom I have reason to believe you despise.'

Blushing hotly, Arabella asked: 'Is he a — a dandy?'

'He would certainly like you to think so.'

'Well, if he is,' said Arabella frankly, 'I am sure you are no such thing, and I beg your pardon for saying it that evening!'

'Don't apologize to him, ma'am!' said Lord Fleetwood gaily. 'It is time someone gave him a set-down, and *that*, I assure you, smote him with stunning effect! You must know that he thinks himself a notable Corinthian!'

'What is that, pray?' enquired Arabella.

'A Corinthian, ma'am, besides being a very Tulip of Fashion, is an amateur of sport, a master of sword-play, a deadly fellow with a pistol, a

Nonpareil amongst whips, a —'

Mr Beaumaris interrupted this mock-solemn catalogue. 'If you will be such a dead bore, Charles, you will provoke me to explain to Miss Tallant what the world means when it calls you a sad rattle.'

'Well?' demanded Arabella mischievously.

'A fribble, ma'am, not worth your attention!' he replied, rising to his feet. 'I see my cousin over there, and must pay my respects to her.' He smiled, bowed, and moved away; stayed for a minute or two, talking to Lady Wainfleet; drank a glass of wine with Mr Warkworth; complimented his hostess on the success of her party; and departed, having done precisely what he had set out to do, which was to place Miss Tallant's feet securely on the ladder of fashion. The news would be all over town within twenty-four hours that the rich Miss Tallant was the Nonpareil's latest flirt.

'Did you see Beaumaris paying court to that dashed pretty girl?' asked Lord Wainfleet of his wife, as they drove away from Lady Bridlington's house.

'Of course I did!' replied his wife.

'Seemed very taken with her, didn't he? Not in his usual style, was she? I wonder if he means anything?'

'Robert?' said his wife, with something very like a snort. 'If you knew him as well as I do, Wainfleet, you would have seen at one glance that he was amusing himself! *I* know how he looks in just that humour! Someone ought to warn the child to have nothing to do with him! It

134

is too bad of him, for she is nothing but a baby, I'll swear!'

'They're saying in the clubs that she's as rich as a Nabob.'

'So I have heard, but what that has to say to anything I don't know! Robert is quite odiously wealthy, and if ever he marries, which I begin to doubt, it will not be for a fortune, I can assure you!'

'No, I don't suppose it will,' agreed his lordship. 'Why did we go there tonight, Louisa? Devilish flat, that kind of an affair.'

'Oh, shocking! Robert asked me to go. I own I was curious to see his heiress. He said he was going to make her the most sought-after female in London.'

'Sounds like a hum to me,' said his lordship. 'Why should he do so?'

'Exactly what I asked him! He said it might be amusing. There are times, Wainfleet, when I would like to box Robert's ears!'

7

Not only in his cousin's bosom were vengeful thoughts nourished against Mr Beaumaris. Lady Somercote, not so doting a mother that she supposed any of her sons would be likely to prove more attractive to the heiress than the Nonpareil, could with pleasure have driven the long diamond pin she wore in her hair between his ribs; Mrs Kirkmichael thought bitterly that he might, considering the number of times she had gone out of her way to be agreeable to him, have bestowed a little of his attention upon her lanky daughter, a gesture which would have cost him nothing, and might have given poor Maria a start in the world; Mr Epworth, uneasily aware that for some inscrutable reason he was consistently cast in the shade by the Nonpareil, went the round of the clubs, saying that he had a very good mind to give Beaumaris a set-down at no very distant date; his aunt recalled that she had once quarrelled violently with Lady Mary Beaumaris, and said that it was from his mother Beaumaris had inherited his flirtatious disposition, adding that she was sorry for the woman he eventually married. Even Mr Warkworth and Lord Fleetwood said that it was rather too bad of the Nonpareil to trifle with the season's biggest catch; while several gentlemen who slavishly copied every detail of Mr Beaumaris's attire wished him safely underground.

There was one voice which was not raised to swell this chorus of disapprobation: Lady Bridlington was in raptures over Mr Beaumaris. She could talk of nothing else throughout the following day. While he sat beside Arabella, not a smile, not a gesture had escaped the good lady's anxious eye. He had paid no heed to any other girl in the room; he had plainly advertised to his world that he found Miss Tallant charming: there was no one in London more amiable, more truly polite, more condescending, or more in her ladyship's good graces! Over and over again she told Arabella that her success was now assured; it was not until her first transports had somewhat abated that she could be rational enough to drop a word of warning in Arabella's ear. But the more she thought of Mr Beaumaris's pronounced attentions to the girl, the more she remembered how many innocent maidens had fallen victims to his spear, the more she became convinced that it was necessary to put Arabella on her guard. So she said in an earnest voice, and with a slightly anxious look in her eye: 'I am persuaded, my love, that you are too sensible a girl to be taken-in! But, you know, I stand to you in place of your Mama, and I think I should tell you that Mr Beaumaris is a most accomplished flirt! No one could be more delighted than I am that he should have singled you out, but it will never do, my dear, if you were to develop a *tendre* in *that* direction! I know I have only to drop a word in your ear, and you will not be offended by it! He is a confirmed bachelor. I could not tell you the number of hearts he has broken! Poor Theresa

137

Howden — she married Lord Congleton some years later — went into a decline, and was the despair of her afflicted parents! They *did* think — and I am sure that nothing could have been more pronounced for all one season than — But no! Nothing came of it!'

Arabella had not been the reigning belle for twenty miles round Heythram without learning to distinguish between the flirt and the man who was in earnest, and she replied instantly: 'I know very well that Mr Beaumaris means nothing by his compliments. Indeed, I am in no danger of being taken-in like a goose!'

'Well, my love, I *hope* you are not!'

'You may be sure I am not. If you do not see any objection, ma'am, I mean to encourage Mr Beaumaris's attentions, and make the best use I may of them! *He* believes himself to be amusing himself at my expense; *I* mean to turn him to very good account! But as for losing my heart — No, indeed!'

'Mind, we cannot depend upon his continuing to single you out!' said Lady Bridlington, with unwonted caution. 'If he did, it would be beyond anything great, but there is no saying, after all! However, last night's work was enough to launch you, my dear, and I am *deeply* thankful!' She heaved an ecstatic sigh. 'You will be invited everywhere, I daresay!'

She was quite right. Within one fortnight, she was in the happy position of finding herself with five engagements for the same evening, and Arabella had had to break into Sir John's fifty-pound bill to replenish her wardrobe. She had been seen at the fashionable hour of the Prom-enade in the Park, sitting beside the Nonpareil, in his high-perch phæton; she had been almost mobbed at the theatre; she was on nodding terms with all manner of exalted persons; she had received two proposals of marriage; Lord Fleetwood, Mr Warkworth, Mr Epworth, Sir Geoffrey Morecambe, and Mr Alfred Somercote (to mention only the most notable of her suitors) had all entered the lists against Mr Beaumaris; and Lord Bridlington, travelling by fast post all the way, had returned from the Continent to discover what his mother meant by filling his house with unknown females in his absence.

He expressed himself, in measured terms, as being most dissatisfied with Lady Bridlington's explanation. He was a stocky, somewhat ponder-ous young man, with more sobriety than properly belonged to his twenty-six years. His understand-ing was not powerful, but he was bookish, and had early formed the habit of acquiring informa-tion by the perusal of authoritative tomes, so that by the time he had attained his present age his retentive memory was stocked with a quantity of facts which he was perhaps a little too ready to impart to his less well-read contemporaries. His father's death, while he was still at Eton, coupled with a conviction that his mother stood in constant need of superior male guidance, had added disas-trously to his self-consequence. He prided himself on his judgment; was a careful steward of his fortune; had the greatest dislike of anything bor-dering on the unusual; and deplored the frivolity of those who might have been expected to have been his cronies. His mother's elation at not having spent one evening at home in ten days found no echo in his heart. He could neither understand why she should want to waste her time at social functions, nor why she should have been foolish enough to have invited a giddy girl to stay with her. He was afraid that the cost of all this mummery would be shocking; had Lady Bridlington asked for his counsel, which she might easily have done, he would have advised most strongly against Arabella's visit.

Lady Bridlington was a trifle cast-down by this severity, but since her late husband had left her to the enjoyment of a handsome jointure, out of which she always shared the expenses of the house in Park Street with Frederick, she was able to point out to him that the charge of entertaining Arabella fell upon her, and not upon him. He said that the wish to dictate to his Mama was far from him, but that he must persist in thinking the affair most ill-advised. Lady Bridlington was fond of her only son, but Arabella's success had quite gone to her head, and she was in no mood to listen to sober counsels. She retorted that he was talking a great deal of nonsense; upon which he bowed, compressed his lips, and bade her afterwards remember his words. He added that he washed his hands of the whole business. Lady Bridlington, who had no desire to see him fall a victim to Arabella's charms, was torn between exasperation, and relief that he showed no sign of succumbing to them.

'I will allow her to be a pretty-enough young

female,' said Frederick fairmindedly, 'but there is a levity in her bearing which I cannot like, and all this gadding-about which she has led you into is not at all to my taste.'

'Well, I can't conceive why you should have come running home in this foolish way!' retorted his mother.

'I thought it my duty, ma'am,' said Frederick.

'It is a great piece of folly, and people will think it excessively odd in you! No one looked to see you in England again until July at the earliest!'

She was mistaken. No one thought it in the least odd of Lord Bridlington to have curtailed his tour. The opinion of society was pithily summed up by Mrs Penkridge, who said that she had guessed all along that that scheming Bridlington woman meant to marry the heiress to her own son. 'Anyone could have seen how it would be!' she declared, with her mirthless jangle of laughter. 'Such odious hypocrisy, too, to hold to it that she did not expect to see Bridlington in England until the summer! Mark my words, Horace, they will be married before the season is over!'

'Good gad, ma'am, I don't fear Bridlington's rivalry!' said her nephew, affronted.

'Then you are a goose!' said Mrs Penkridge. 'Everything is in his favour! He is the possessor of an honoured name, and a title, which you may depend upon it the girl wants, and — what is a great deal to the point, let me tell you! — he has all the advantage of living in the same house, of being always at hand to minister to her wishes, squire her to parties, and — Oh, it puts me out of all patience!'

But Miss Tallant and Lord Bridlington, from the very moment of exchanging their first polite greetings, had conceived a mutual antipathy which was in no way mitigated by the necessity each was under to behave towards the other with complaisance and civility. Arabella would not for the fortune she was believed to possess have grieved her kind hostess by betraying dislike of her son; Frederick's sense of propriety, which was extremely nice, forbade him to neglect the performance of any attention due to his mother's guest. He could appreciate, and, indeed, since he had a provident mind, applaud Mrs Tallant's ambition to dispose of her daughters creditably; and since his own mother had undertaken the task of finding a husband for Arabella, he was prepared to lend his countenance to her schemes. What shocked and disturbed him profoundly was the discovery, within a week of his homecoming, that every gazetted fortune-hunter in London was dangling after Arabella.

'I am at a loss, ma'am, to guess what you can possibly have said to lead anyone to suppose that Miss Tallant is an heiress!' he announced.

Lady Bridlington, who had several times wondered much the same thing, replied uneasily: 'I never said a word, Frederick! There is not the least reason why anyone should suppose such an absurdity! I own, I was a trifle surprised when — But she is a very pretty girl, you know, and Mr Beaumaris took one of his fancies to her!'

'I have never been intimate with Beaumaris,'

said Frederick. 'I do not care for the set he leads, and must deplore his making any modest female the object of his gallantry. The influence he exerts, moreover, over persons whom I should have supposed to have had more — '

'Never mind that!' begged his mother hastily. 'You told me yesterday, Frederick! You may think Beaumaris what you please, but even you will not deny that it lies in his power to bring whom he will into fashion!'

'Very likely, ma'am, but I have yet to learn that it lies in his power to prevail upon such men as Epworth, Morecambe, Carnaby, and — I — must add! — Fleetwood, to offer marriage to a female with nothing but her face to recommend her!'

'Not Fleetwood!' protested Lady Bridlington feebly.

'Fleetwood!' repeated Frederick in an inexorable tone. 'I do not mean to say that he is precisely hanging out for a rich wife, but that he cannot afford to marry a penniless girl is common knowledge. Yet his attentions towards Miss Tallant are more marked even than those of Horace Epworth. And this is not all! From hints dropped in my presence, from remarks actually made to me, I am persuaded that the greater part of our acquaintance believes her to be in the possession of a handsome fortune! I repeat, ma'am: what can you have said to have given rise to this folly?'

'But I didn't!' cried poor Lady Bridlington almost tearfully. 'Indeed, I took the greatest pains not to touch on the question of her expectations! It is false to call her penniless, because she is no such thing! With all those children, of course the Tallants can do very little for her upon her marriage, but when her father dies — and Sophia, too, for she has some money as well — '

'A thousand or so!' interrupted Frederick contemptuously. 'I beg your pardon, ma'am, but nothing could be more plain to me than that something you have said — inadvertently, I daresay! — has done all this mischief. For mischief I must deem it! A pretty state of affairs it will be if we are to have the world saying — as it will say, once the truth is known! — that you have foisted an impostress upon society!'

This terrible forecast temporarily outweighed in Lady Bridlington's mind the sense of strong injustice the rest of her son's remarks had aroused. She turned quite pale, and exclaimed: 'What is to be done?'

'You may rely upon me, ma'am, to do what is necessary,' replied Frederick. 'Whenever the opportunity offers, I shall say that I have no notion how such a rumour came to be spread about.'

'I suppose you must do so,' agreed his mother dubiously. 'But I do beg of you, Frederick, not to take the whole world into your confidence on the subject! There is not the least need for you to enter into all the details of the poor child's circumstances!'

'It would be quite improper for me to do so, ma'am,' replied Frederick crushingly. '*I* am not responsible for her visit to London! I must point out to you, Mama, that it is *you* who have engaged yourself — unwisely, I consider — to establish her suitably. I am sure I have no desire to prejudice her chances of matrimony. Indeed, since I understand that you mean to keep her with you until some man offers for her, I shall be happy to see her married as soon as possible!'

'I think you are very disagreeable!' said Lady Bridlington, dissolving into tears.

Her peace of mind was quite cut up. When Arabella came into the room presently, she found her still dabbing at her eyes, and giving little sniffs. Quite dismayed, Arabella begged to be told the cause of this unhappiness. Lady Bridlington, glad of a sympathetic audience, squeezed her hand gratefully, and without reflection poured forth the sum of her grievances.

Kneeling beside her chair, Arabella listened in stricken silence, her hand lying slackly within Lady Bridlington's. 'It is so unkind of Frederick!' Lady Bridlington complained. 'And so unjust, for I assure you, my dear, I never said such a thing to a soul! How could he think I would do so? It would have been quite wicked to have told such lies, besides being so foolish, and vulgar, and everything that is dreadful! And why Frederick should think I could be so lost to all sense of propriety I am sure I don't know!'

Arabella's head sank; guilt and shame almost overpowered her; she could not speak. Lady Bridlington, misreading her confusion, felt a qualm of conscience at having so unguardedly taken her into her confidence, and said: 'I should

145

not have told you! It is all Frederick's fault, and I daresay he has exaggerated everything, just as he so often does! You must not let it distress you, my love, for even if it were true it would be absurd to suppose such a man as Mr Beaumaris, or young Charnwood, or a great many others I could name, care a button whether you are a rich woman or a pauper! And Frederick will make everything right!'

'How can he do so, ma'am?' Arabella managed to ask.

'Oh, when he sees the opportunity, he will say something to damp such ridiculous notions! Nothing very much, you know, but making light of the story! We need not concern ourselves, and I am sorry I spoke of it to you.'

With all her heart Arabella longed for the courage to confess the whole. She could not. Already Lady Bridlington was rambling on, complaining fretfully of Frederick's unkindness, wondering what cause he had to suppose his mother ill-bred enough to have spread a false tale abroad, and wishing that his father were alive to give him one of his famous scolds. She said instead, in a subdued tone: 'Is that why — why everyone has been so very polite to me, ma'am?'

'Certainly not!' said Lady Bridlington emphatically. 'You must have perceived, my love, how many, many friends I have in London, and you may believe they accepted you out of compliment to me! Not that I mean to say — But before you were at all known, naturally it was my sponsorship that started you in the right way.' She patted Arabella's hand consolingly. 'Then, you know, you are so bright, and pretty, that I am sure it is no wonder that you are so much sought-after. And above all, Arabella, we must remember that the world always follows what is seen to be the mode, and Mr Beaumaris has made you the fashion by singling you out, even driving you in his phæton, which is an honour indeed, I can tell you!'

Arabella's head was still bowed. 'Does — does Lord Bridlington mean to tell everyone that I — that I have no fortune at all, ma'am?'

'Good gracious, no, child! That would be a fatal thing to do, and I hope he would have more sense! He will merely say it has been greatly exaggerated — enough to frighten away the fortune-hunters, but what will not weigh with an honest man! Do not give it another thought!'

Arabella was unable to obey this injunction. It was long before she could think of anything else. Her impulse was to fly from London, back to Heythram, but hardly had she reached the stage of calculating whether she still possessed enough money to pay her fare on the first coach than all the difficulties attached to such a precipitate retreat presented themselves to her. They were insuperable. She could not bring herself to confess to Lady Bridlington that her own was the wicked, ill-bred tongue accountable for the rumour, nor could she think of any excuse for returning to Yorkshire. Still less could she face the necessity of telling Papa and Mama of her shocking behaviour. She must remain in Park Street until the season came to an end, and if

Mama was sadly disappointed at the failure of her schemes, at least Papa would never blame his daughter for returning to her home unbetrothed. She perceived clearly that unless something very wonderful were to happen this must be so, and felt herself guilty indeed.

Not for several hours did her mind recover its tone, but she was both young and optimistic, and after a hearty burst of tears, followed by a period of quiet reflection, she began insensibly to be more hopeful. Something would happen to unravel her difficulties; the odious Frederick would scotch the rumour; people would gradually grow to realize that they had been mistaken. Mr Beaumaris and Lord Fleetwood would no doubt write her down as a vulgar, boasting miss, but she must hope that they had not actually told everyone that it was she who had been responsible for the rumour. Meanwhile there was nothing to be done but to behave as though nothing were the matter. This, to a naturally buoyant spirit was not so hard a task as might have been supposed: London was offering too much to Arabella for her to be long cast-down. She might fancy all her pleasure destroyed, but she would have been a very extraordinary young woman who could have remembered her difficulties while cards and floral offerings were left every day at the house; while invitations poured in to every form of entertainment known to ingenious hostesses; while every gentleman was eager to claim her hand for the dance; while Mr Beaumaris took her driving in the Park behind his match-grays, and every other young lady gazed enviously after her. Whatever the cause, social success was sweet; and since Arabella was a very human girl she could not help enjoying every moment of it.

She expected to see some considerable diminution in her court once Lord Bridlington had let it be known that her fortune had been grossly exaggerated, and braced herself to bear this humiliation. But although she knew from Lady Bridlington that Frederick had faithfully performed his part, still the invitations came in, and still the unattached gentlemen clustered round her. She took fresh heart, glad to find that fashionable people were not, after all, so mercenary as she had been led to think. Neither she nor Frederick had the smallest inkling of the true state of affairs: she because she was too unsophisticated; Frederick because it had never yet occurred to him that anyone could doubt what he said. But he might as well have spared his breath on this occasion. Even Mr Warkworth, a charitably-minded gentleman, shook his head over it, and remarked to Sir Geoffrey Morecambe that Bridlington was doing it rather too brown.

'Just what I was thinking myself,' agreed Sir Geoffrey, scrutinizing his neck-tie in the mirror with a dissatisfied eye. 'Shabby, I call it. Do you think this way I have tied my cravat has something of the look of the Nonpareil's new style?'

Mr Warkworth directed a long, dispassionate stare at it. 'No,' he said simply.

'No, no more do I,' said Sir Geoffrey, sad but

unsurprised. 'I wonder what he calls it? It ain't precisely a Mail-coach, and it certainly ain't an Osbaldeston, and though I did think it had something of the look of a *Trône d'amour*, it ain't that either. I can tie every one of *them*.'

Mr Warkworth, whose mind had wandered from this vital subject, said, with a frown: 'Damn it, it *is* shabby! You're right!'

Sir Geoffrey was a little hurt. 'Would you say it was as bad as that, Oswald?'

'I would,' stated Mr Warkworth. 'In fact, the more I think of it the worse it appears to me!'

Sir Geoffrey looked intently at his own image, and sighed. 'Yes, it does. I shall have to go home and change it.'

'Eh?' said Mr. Warkworth, puzzled. 'Change what? Good God, dear boy, I wasn't talking about your neck-tie! Wouldn't dream of saying such a thing to my worst enemy! Bridlington!'

'Oh, him!' said Sir Geoffrey, relieved. 'He's a gudgeon!'

'Oughtn't to be gudgeon enough to think every-one else is one. Tell you what: wouldn't do him any good if he did hoax everybody with that bag of moonshine! She's a devilish fine girl, the little Tallant, and if you ask me she wouldn't have him if he were the only man to offer for her.'

'You can't expect him to know that,' said Sir Geoffrey. 'I shouldn't wonder if he hasn't a suspicion he's a dead bore: in fact, he can't have! Stands to reason: wouldn't prose on as he does, if he knew it!'

Mr Warkworth thought this over. 'No,' he pronounced at last. 'You're wrong. If he don't

150

know he's a dead bore, why does he want to frighten off everyone else? Havey-cavey sort of a business: don't like it! a man ought to fight fair.'

'It ain't that,' replied Sir Geoffrey. 'Just remembered something: the little Tallant don't want it to be known she's as rich as a Nabob. Fleetwood told me: tired of being courted for her money. They were all after her in the north.'

'Oh!' said Mr Warkworth. He asked with vague interest: 'Where does she come from?'

'Somewhere up north: Yorkshire, I believe,' said Sir Geoffrey, inserting a cautious finger into one of the folds of his neck-tie, and easing it a trifle. 'I wonder if that's better?'

'Well, that's a queer thing. Saw Clayton the other day. *He* comes from Yorkshire, and he don't know the Tallant.'

'No, and Withernsea don't either. Mind you, I won't swear it was Yorkshire! Might have been one of those other devilish rural places — Northumberland, or something. Know what I think?'

'No,' said Mr. Warkworth.

'Shouldn't be surprised if she's the daughter of some merchant or other, which would account for it.'

Mr Warkworth looked shocked. 'No, really, dear old boy! Nothing of that sort about the girl! Never heard her utter a word that smelled of the shop!'

'Granddaughter, then,' said Sir Geoffrey, stretching a point. 'Pity, if I'm right, but I'll tell you one thing, Oswald! I wouldn't let it weigh with me.'

Upon consideration, Mr Warkworth decided that he would not either.

Since these views were fairly representative, Arabella was not destined to suffer the mortification of seeing her usual gallants hang back when next she attended the Assembly at Almack's. Lord Bridlington was escorting his mother and her guest, for besides being very correct in such matters, he liked Almack's, and approved of the severity of the rules imposed on the club by its imperious hostesses. A number of his contemporaries said openly that an evening spent at Almack's was the flattest thing in town, but these were frippery fellows with whom Lord Bridlington had little to do.

His politeness led him to engage Miss Tallant for the first country-dance, a circumstance which made the unsuccessful applicants for her hand exchange significant glances. They saw to it that he should have no further opportunity of standing up with her. Not one of them would have believed that he had no desire to do so, much preferring to stroll about the rooms, telling as many people as could be got to listen to him all about his travels abroad.

The waltz, which was still looked at askance by old-fashioned persons, had long since forced its way into Almack's, but it was still the unwritten law that no lady might venture to take part in it unless one of the patronesses had clearly indicated her approval. Lady Bridlington had taken care to impress this important convention upon Arabella's mind, so she refused all solicitations to take the floor when the fiddles struck up for the waltz. Papa would certainly not approve of the dance, she knew: she had never dared to tell him that she and Sophia had learnt the steps from their friends the Misses Caterham, a very dashing pair. So she retired to a chair against the wall, beside Lady Bridlington's, and sat fanning herself, and trying not to look as though she longed to be whirling round the floor. One or two more fortunate damsels, who had watched with disfavour her swift rise to popularity, cast her glances of such pitying superiority that she had to recollect a great many of Papa's maxims before she could subdue the very improper sentiments which entered her breast.

Mr Beaumaris, who had looked in midway through the evening — in fact, a bare ten minutes before the doors were relentlessly shut against late-comers — apparently for no other purpose than to entertain the wife of the Austrian Ambassador, saw Arabella, and was amused, guessing her emotions correctly. Suddenly he cast one of his quizzical looks at Princess Esterhazy, and said: 'Shall I ask that chit to dance?'

She raised her delicate black brows, a faint smile flickering on her lips. '*Here*, my friend, you are not supreme! I think you dare not.'

'I know I dare not,' said Mr Beaumaris, disarming her promptly. 'That is why I ask you, Princess, to present me to the lady as a desirable partner.'

She hesitated, glancing from him to Arabella, and then laughed, and shrugged. 'Well! She does not put herself forward, after all, and I find her style excellent. Come, then!'

Arabella, startled to find herself suddenly confronted by one of the most formidable patronesses, rose quickly.

'You do not dance, Miss Tallant. May I present Mr Beaumaris to you as a very desirable partner?' said the Princess, with a slightly malicious smile cast at Mr Beaumaris.

Arabella could only curtsy, and blush, and be sorry to find that she was so ill-natured as to be conscious of feelings of ignoble triumph over the ladies who had been kind enough to look pityingly at her.

Mr Beaumaris led her on to the floor, and encircled her waist with one arm, taking her right hand in a light clasp. Arabella was naturally a good dancer, but she felt extremely nervous, partly because she had never attempted the waltz, except in the Misses Caterham's old schoolroom, and partly because it was so strange to be held in such close proximity to a man. For several turns she answered Mr Beaumaris very much at random, being preoccupied with her feet. She was so much shorter than he that her head only just reached his shoulder, and since she felt shy she did not look up, but steadfastly regarded the top of his waistcoat. Mr Beaumaris, who was not in the habit of devoting himself to such very young ladies, found this bashfulness amusing, and not unattractive. After he thought she had had time to recover from it a little, he said: 'It *is* a nice waistcoat, isn't it, Miss Tallant?'

That did make her look up, and quickly too,

her face breaking into laughter. She looked so lovely, and her big eyes met his with such a frank, ingenuous expression in them, that he was aware of a stir of something in his heart that was not mere amusement. But he had no intention of going to dangerous lengths with this or any other pretty chit, and he said, in a bantering tone: 'It is customary, you know, to exchange polite conversation during the dance. I have now addressed no fewer than three unexceptionable remarks to you without winning one answer!'

'You see, I am minding my steps,' she confided seriously.

Decidedly this absurd child was a refreshing change from the generality of damsels! Had he been a younger man, he reflected, he might easily have succumbed to her charm. It was fortunate that he was thirty, and no longer to be caught by a pretty face and naïve ways, for he knew well that these would pall on him, and that he wanted something more in the lady whom he would one day marry. He had never yet found just what he was looking for, did not even know what it might prove to be, and was perfectly resigned to his bachelordom.

'It is not at all necessary,' he said. 'You dance delightfully. You do not mean to tell me that this is the first time you have waltzed?'

Miss Tallant certainly did not mean to tell him anything of the sort, and was already regretting her impulsive confidence. 'Good gracious, no!' she said. 'The first time at Almack's, however.'

'I am happy to think, then, that mine was the honour of first leading you on to the floor. You will certainly be besieged by every man present now it is seen that you have no objection to the waltz.'

She said nothing, but fell to studying his waistcoat again. He glanced down at her, a hint of mockery in the smile that hovered about his mouth. 'How does it feel, Miss Tallant, to be the rage of town? Do you enjoy it, or have your northern triumphs given you a distaste for this sort of thing?'

She raised her eyes, and her chin too. 'I am afraid, Mr Beaumaris, that you betrayed what I — what I begged you not to speak of!'

There was a distinctly sardonic look in his eye, but he replied coolly: 'I assure you, ma'am, I have mentioned your circumstances to one person only: Lord Fleetwood.'

'Then it is he who — ' She broke off, flushing.

'Very probably,' he agreed. 'You must not blame him, however. Such things are bound to leak out.'

Her lips parted, and then closed again. He wondered what she had so nearly said: whether he was to have been treated to her society manners, or whether she had been about to tell him the truth. On the whole, he was glad that she had thought better of it. If she took him into her confidence, he supposed he would be obliged, in mercy, to bring this game to a close, which would be a pity, since it was providing him with a great deal of entertainment. To have elevated an unknown provincial to the heights of society was an achievement which only one who had no illusions about the world he led could properly appreciate. He was deriving much enjoyment too from observing the efforts of his devoted copyists to win the provincial's hand. As for Arabella herself, Mr Beaumaris shrugged off a momentary compunction. She would no doubt retire in due course to her northern wilds, marry some red-faced squire, and talk for the rest of her life of her brilliant London season. He glanced down at her again, and thought that it would be a pity if she were to retire too soon. Probably, by the end of the London season he would be only too thankful to see her go, but for the present he was very well satisfied to gratify her by a little flirtation.

The music ceased, and he led her off the floor, to one of the adjoining rooms, where refreshments were served. These were of a very simple nature, the strongest drink offered being a mild claret-cup. Mr Beaumaris procured a glass of lemonade for Arabella, and said, 'You must let me thank you for a delightful few minutes, Miss Tallant: I have seldom enjoyed a dance more.' He received only a slight smile, and an inclination of the head in answer to this which were both so eloquent of incredulity that he was delighted. No fool, then, the little Tallant! He would have pursued this new form of sport, in the hope of teasing her into retort, but at that moment two purposeful gentlemen bore down upon them. Arabella yielded to the solicitations of Mr Warkworth, and went off on his arm. Sir Geoffrey Morecambe sighed in a languishing way, but turned his rebuff to good account by seizing the opportunity to ask Mr Beaumaris what he called the arrangement of his neck-cloth. He had to repeat the question, for Mr Beaumaris, watching Arabella walk away with Mr Warkworth, was not attending. He brought his gaze to bear on Sir Geoffrey's face, however, at the second time of asking, and raised his brows enquiringly.

'That style you have of tying your cravat!' said Sir Geoffrey. 'I don't perfectly recognize it. Is it something new? Should you object to telling me what you call it?'

'Not in the least,' replied Mr Beaumaris blandly. 'I call it Variation on an Original Theme.'

8

Mr Beaumaris's sudden realization that the little Tallant was no fool underwent no modification during the following days. It began to be borne in upon him that, charm he never so wisely, she was never within danger of losing her head over him. She treated him in the friendliest fashion, accepted his homage, and — he suspected — was bent upon making the fullest use of him. If he paid her compliments, she listened to them with the most innocent air in the world, but with a look in her candid gaze which gave him pause. The little Tallant valued his compliments not at all. Instead of being thrown into a flutter by the attentions of the biggest matrimonial prize in London, she plainly considered herself to be taking part in an agreeable game. If he flirted with her, she would generally respond in kind, but with so much the manner of one willing to indulge him that the hunter woke in him, and he was quite as much piqued as amused. He began to toy with the notion of making her fall in love with him in good earnest, just to teach her that the Nonpareil was not to be so treated with impunity. Once, when she was apparently not in the humour for gallantry, she actually had the effrontery to cut him short, saying: 'Oh, never mind that! Who was that odd-looking man who waved to you just now? Why does he walk in that ridiculous way, and screw up his mouth so? Is he in pain?'

He was taken aback, for really he had paid her a compliment calculated to cast her into exquisite confusion. His lips twitched, for he had as few illusions about himself as had, to all appearances the lady beside him. 'That,' he replied, 'is Golden Ball, Miss Tallant, one of our dandies, as no doubt you have been told. He is not in pain. That walk denotes his consequence.'

'Good gracious! He looks as though he went upon stilts! Why does he think himself of such consequence?'

'He has never accustomed himself to the thought that he is worth not a penny less than forty thousand pounds a year,' replied Mr Beaumaris gravely.

'What an odious person he must be!' she said scornfully. 'To be consequential for such a reason as that is what I have no patience with!'

'Naturally you have not,' he agreed smoothly.

Her colour rushed up. She said quickly: 'Fortune cannot make the man: I am persuaded you agree with me, for they tell me you are even more wealthy, Mr Beaumaris, and I *will* say this! — you do not give yourself such airs as that!'

'Thank you,' said Mr Beaumaris meekly. 'I scarcely dared to hope to earn so great an encomium from you, ma'am.'

'Was it rude of me to say it? I beg your pardon!'

'Not at all.' He glanced down at her. 'Tell me, Miss Tallant! — Just why do you grant me the pleasure of driving you out in my curricle?'

She responded with perfect composure, but with that sparkle in her eye which he had encountered several times before: 'You must know that it does me a great deal of good socially to be seen in your company, sir!'

He was so much surprised that momentarily he let his hands drop. The grays broke into a canter, and Miss Tallant kindly advised him to mind his horses. The most notable whip in the country thanked her for her reminder, and steadied his pair. Miss Tallant consoled him for the chagrin he might have been supposed to feel by saying that she thought he drove very well. After a stunned moment, laughter welled up within him. His voice shook perceptibly as he answered: 'You are too good, Miss Tallant!'

'Oh, no!' she said politely. 'Shall you be at the masquerade at the Argyll Rooms tonight?'

'I never attend such affairs, ma'am!' he retorted, putting her in her place.

'Oh, then I shall not see you there!' remarked Miss Tallant, with unimpaired cheerfulness.

She did not see him there, but, little though she might have known it, he was obliged to exercise considerable restraint not to cast to the four winds his famed fastidiousness, and to minister to her vanity by appearing at the ball. He did not do it, and hoped that she had missed him. She had, but this was something she would not acknowledge even to herself. Arabella, who had liked the Nonpareil on sight, was setting a strong guard over her sensibilities. He had seemed to her, when first her eyes had alighted on his handsome person, to be almost the embodiment of a dream. Then he had uttered such words to his friend as must shatter for ever

161

her esteem, and had wickedly led her into vulgar prevarication. Now it pleased his fancy to single her out from all the beauties in town, for reasons better known to himself than to her, but which she darkly suspected to be mischievous. No fool, the little Tallant! Not for one moment would she permit herself to indulge the absurd fancy that his court was serious. He might intrude into her meditations, but whenever she was aware of his having done so she was resolute in banishing his image. Sometimes she was strongly of the opinion that he had not believed a word of her boasts on that never to be sufficiently regretted evening in Leicestershire; at others, it seemed as though she had deceived him as completely as she had deceived Lord Fleetwood. It was impossible to fathom the intricacies of his mind, but one thing was certain: the great Mr Beaumaris and the Vicar of Heythram's daughter could have nothing to do with one another, so that the less the Vicar's daughter thought about him the better it would be for her. One could not deny his address, or his handsome face, but one could — and one did — dwell on the many imperfections of his character. He was demonstrably indolent, a spoilt darling of society, with no thought for anything but his fleeting pleasure: a heartless, heedless leader of fashion, given over to selfishness, and every other vice which Papa's daughter had been taught to think reprehensible.

If she missed him at the masquerade, no one would have guessed it. She danced indefatigably the whole night through, refused an offer of marriage from a slightly intoxicated Mr Epworth, tumbled into bed at an advanced hour in the morning, and dropped instantly into untroubled sleep.

She was awakened at a most unseasonable hour by the sudden clatter of fire-irons in the cold hearth. Since the menial who crept into her chamber each morning to sweep the grate, and kindle a new fire there, performed her task with trained stealth, this noise was unusual enough to rouse Arabella with a start. A gasp and a whimper, proceeding from the direction of the fireplace, made her sit up with a jerk, blinking at the unexpected vision of a small, dirty, and tearstained little boy, almost cowering on the hearth-rug, and regarding her out of scared, dilating eyes.

'Good gracious!' gasped Arabella, staring at him. 'Who are you?'

The child cringed at the sound of her voice, and returned no answer. The mists of sleep curled away from Arabella's brain; her eyes took in the soot lying on the floor, the grimed appearance of her strange visitant, and enlightenment dawned on her. 'You must be a climbing-boy!' she exclaimed. 'But what are you doing in my room?' Then she perceived the terror in the pinched, and grimed small face, and she said quickly: 'Don't be afraid! Did you lose your way in those horrid chimneys?'

The urchin nodded, knuckling his eyes. He further volunteered the information that ole Grimsby would bash him for it. Arabella, who had had leisure to observe that one side of his face was swollen and discoloured, demanded: 'Is that your master? Does he beat you?'

The urchin nodded again, and shivered.

'Well, he shan't beat you for this!' said Arabella, stretching out her hand for the dressing-gown that was chastely disposed across the chair beside her bed. 'Wait! I am going to get up!'

The urchin looked very much alarmed by this intelligence, and shrank back against the wall, watching her defensively. She slid out of bed, thrust her feet into her slippers, fastened her dressing-gown, and advanced kindly upon her visitor. He flung up an instinctive arm, cringing before her. He was clad in disgraceful rags, and Arabella now saw that the ends of his frieze nether-garments were much charred, and that his skinny legs and his bare feet were badly burnt. She dropped to her knees, crying out pitifully: 'Oh, poor little fellow! You have burnt yourself so dreadfully!'

He slightly lowered his protective arm, looking suspiciously at her over it. 'Ole Grimsby done it,' he said.

She caught her breath. 'What!'

'I'm afeard of going up the chimbley,' explained the urchin. 'Sometimes there's rats — big, fierce 'uns!'

She shuddered. 'And he forces you to do so — like that?'

'They most of 'em does,' said the urchin, accepting life as he found it.

She held out her hand. 'Let me see! I will not hurt you.'

He looked wary, but after a moment appeared to consider that she might be speaking the truth, for he allowed her to take one of his feet in her hand. He was surprised when he saw that tears stood in her eyes, for in his experience the gentler sex was more apt to beat one with a broom-handle than to weep over one.

'Poor child, poor child!' Arabella said, a break in her voice. 'You are so thin, too! I am sure you are half-starved! Are you hungry?'

'I'm allus hungry,' he replied simply.

'And cold too!' she said. 'No wonder, in those rags! It is wicked, *wicked*!' She jumped up, and, grasping the bell pull that hung beside the fireplace, tugged it violently.

The urchin uttered another of his frightened whimpers, and said: 'Ole Grimsby 'll beat the daylights out of me! Lemme go!'

'He shan't lay a finger on you!' promised Arabella, her cheeks flushed, and her eyes sparkling through the tears they held.

The urchin came to the conclusion that she was soft in her head. 'Ho!' he remarked bitterly, 'you don' know ole Grimsby! Nor you don' know his ole woman! Broke one of me ribs he did, once!'

'He shall never do so again, my dear,' Arabella said, turning aside to pull open a drawer in one of the chests. She dragged out the soft shawl which had not so long since been swathed round the head of the sufferer from toothache, and put it round the boy, saying coaxingly: 'There, let me wrap you up till we have had a fire lit! Is that more comfortable, my little man? Now sit down in this chair, and you shall have something to eat directly!'

165

He allowed himself to be lifted into the armchair, but his expression was so eloquent of suspicion and terror that it wrung Arabella's tender heart. She smoothed his cropped, sandy hair with one gentle hand, and said soothingly: 'You must not be afraid of me: I promise you I will not hurt you, nor let your master either. What is your name, my dear?'

'Jemmy,' he replied, clutching the shawl about him, and fixing her with a frightened stare.

'And how old are you?'

This he was unable to answer, being uninstructed in the matter. She judged him to be perhaps seven or eight years old, but he was so undernourished that he might have been older. While she waited for the summons of the bell to bring her maid to the room, she put more questions to the child. He seemed to have no knowledge of the existence of any parents, volunteering that he was an orphing, on the Parish. When he saw that this seemed to distress her, he tried to comfort her by stating that one Mrs Balham said he was love-begotten. It appeared that this lady had brought him up until the moment when he had passed into the hands of his present owner. An enquiry into Mrs Balham's disposition elicited the information that she was a rare one for jackey, and could half-murder anyone when under the influence of this stimulant. Arabella had no idea what jackey might be, but she gathered that Jemmy's foster-mother was much addicted to strong drink. She questioned Jemmy more closely, and he, gaining confidence, imparted to her, in the most matter-of-fact way, some details of a climbing-boy's life which drove the blood from her cheeks. He told her, with a certain distorted pride, of the violence of one of ole Grimsby's associates, Mr Molys, a master-sweep, who, only a year before, had been sentenced to two years imprisonment for causing the death of his six-year old slave.

'Two years!' cried Arabella, sickened by the tale of cruelty so casually unfolded. 'If he had stolen a yard of silk from a mercer's factory they would have deported him!'

Jemmy was not in a position to deny or to corroborate this statement, and preserved a wary silence. He saw that the young lady was very angry, and although her wrath did not seem to be directed against himself his experience had taught him to run no unnecessary risks of being suddenly knocked flying against the wall. He shrank into the corner of the chair therefore, and clutched the shawl more tightly round his person.

A discreet knock fell on the door, and a slightly flustered and considerably startled housemaid entered the room. 'Was it you rang, miss?' she asked, in astonished accents. Then her eye alighted on Arabella's visitor, and she uttered a genteel shriek. 'Oh, miss! What a turn it gave me! The young varmint to give you such a fright! It's the chimney-sweep's boy, miss, and him looking for him all over! You come with me this instant, you wicked boy, you!'

Jemmy, recognizing a language he understood, whined that he had not meant to do it.

'Hush!' Arabella said, dropping her hand on one bony little shoulder. 'I know very well it is the sweep's boy, Maria, and if you look at him you will see how he has been used! Go downstairs, if you please, and fetch me some food for him directly — and send someone up to kindle the fire here!'

Maria stared at her as though she thought she had taken leave of her senses. 'Miss!' she managed to ejaculate. 'A dirty little *climbing-boy*?'

'When he has been bathed,' said Arabella quietly, 'he will not be dirty. I shall need plenty of warm water, and the bath, if you please. But first a fire, and some milk and food for the poor child!'

The affronted handmaid bridled. 'I hope, miss, you do not expect *me* to wash that nasty little creature! I'm sure I don't know what her ladyship would say to such goings-on!'

'No,' said Arabella, 'I expect nothing from you that I might expect from a girl with a more feeling heart than yours! Go and do what I have asked you to do, and desire Becky to come upstairs to me!'

'Becky?' gasped Maria.

'Yes, the girl who had the toothache. And when you have brought up food — some bread-and-butter, and some meat will do very well, but do not forget the milk! — you may send someone to tell Lord Bridlington that I wish to see him at once.'

Maria gulped, and stammered: 'But, miss, his lordship is abed and asleep!'

'Well, let him be wakened!' said Arabella impatiently.

'Miss, I dare not for my life! His orders were no one wasn't to disturb him till nine o'clock, and he won't come, not till he has shaved himself, and dressed, not his lordship!'

Arabella considered the question, and finally came to the conclusion that it might be wiser to dispense with his lordship's assistance for the time being. 'Very well,' she said. 'I will dress immediately, then, and see the sweep myself. Tell him to wait!'

'See the sweep — dress — Miss, you won't never! With that boy watching you!' exclaimed the scandalized Maria.

'Don't be such a fool, girl!' snapped Arabella, stamping her foot. 'He's scarcely older than my little brother at home! Go away before you put me out of all patience with you!'

This, however, Maria could not be persuaded to do until she had arranged a prim screen between the wondering Jemmy and his hostess. She then tottered away to spread the news through the house that Miss was raving mad, and likely to be taken off to Bedlam that very day. But since she did not dare to thwart a guest so much petted by her mistress, she delivered Arabella's message to Becky, and condescended to carry up a tray of food to her room.

Jemmy, still huddled in the big chair, was bewildered by the unprecedented turn of events, and understood nothing of what was intended towards him. But he perfectly understood the significance of a plate of cold beef, and half a

169

loaf of bread, and his sharp eyes glistened. Arabella, who had flung on her clothes at random, and done up her hair in a careless knot, settled him down to the enjoyment of his meal, and sallied forth to do battle with the redoubtable Mr Grimsby, uneasily awaiting her in the front hall.

The scene, conducted under the open-mouthed stare of a footman in his shirt-sleeves, two astonished and giggling maids, and the kitchen-boy, was worthy of a better audience. Mr Beaumaris, for instance, would have enjoyed it immensely. Mr Grimsby, knowing that the sympathies of those members of the household he had so far encountered were with him, and seeing that his assailant was only a chit of a girl, tried at the outset to take a high line, rapidly cataloguing Jemmy's many vices, and adjuring Arabella not to believe a word the varmint uttered. He soon discovered that what Arabella lacked in inches she more than made up for in spirit. She tore his character to shreds, and warned him of his ultimate fate; she flung Jemmy's burns and bruises in his face, and bade him answer her if he dared. He did not dare. She assured him that never would she permit Jemmy to go back to him, and when he tried to point out his undoubted rights over the boy she looked so fierce that he backed before her. She said that if he wished to talk of his rights he might do so before a magistrate, and at these ominous words all vestige of fight went out of him. The misfortune which had overtaken his friend, Mr Molys, was still fresh in his mind, and he desired to have no dealings with an unjust Law. There was no doubt that a young lady living in a house of this style would have those at her back who could, if she urged them to it, make things very unpleasant for a poor chimney-sweep. The course for a prudent man to follow was retreat: climbing-boys were easily come by, and Jemmy had never been a success. Mr Grimsby, his back bent nearly double, edged himself out of the house, trying to assure Arabella in one breath that she might keep Jemmy and welcome, and that, whatever the ungrateful brat might say, he had been like a father to him.

Flushed with her triumph, Arabella returned to her room, where she found Jemmy, the plate of meat long since disposed of, eyeing with a good deal of apprehension the preparations for his ablutions. A capacious hip-bath stood before the fire, into which Becky was emptying the last of three large brass cans of hot water. Whatever Becky might think of climbing-boys, she had conceived a slavish adoration of Arabella, and she declared her willingness to do anything Miss might require of her.

'First,' said Arabella briskly, 'I must wash him, and put basilicum ointment on his poor little feet and legs. Then I must get him some clothes to wear. Becky, do you know where to procure suitable clothes for a child in London?'

Becky nodded vigorously, twisting her apron between her fingers. She ventured to say that she had sent home a suit for her brother Ben which Mother had been ever so pleased with.

'Have you little brothers? Then you will know

just what to buy for this child!' Arabella said. 'A warm jacket, and some smalls, and a shirt — oh, and some shoes and stockings! Wait! I will give you the money, and you shall go and procure the things immediately!'

'If you please, miss,' said Becky firmly, 'I think I ought to help you wash him first.' She added sapiently: 'Likely he'll struggle, miss — not being used to it.'

She was quite right. Jemmy fought like a tiger to defend his person from the intended rape, and was deaf alike to coaxings and to reassurances. But the two damsels before him had not helped to bring up their respective young brothers for nothing. They stripped Jemmy of his rags, heedless of his sobs and his protests, and they dumped him, wildly kicking, in the bath, and ruthlessly washed every inch of his emaciated small person.

It was not to be expected that Jemmy's howls would not be heard beyond the confines of the room. They were lusty, and they penetrated to Lady Bridlington's ears. It was inconceivable to the good lady that they could really be emanating from within her house, as they seemed to be, and she was just about to ring her bell, and desire Clara Crowle to send away whatever child it was who was screaming in the street, when the howls ceased (Jemmy had been lifted out of the bath, and wrapped in a warm towel), and she sank back again in her bed. Not long after this, Miss Crowle came softly in with her breakfast-tray, and the pleasing intelligence that Miss Arabella was out of her mind, and had

172

got a dirty little boy in her room, and wouldn't let him go, not whatever anyone said. Hardly had her ladyship grasped the essential points of the story poured into her bemused ears than Arabella herself came in. Her visit made it necessary for Miss Crowle to revive her mistress with hartshorn-and-water, and to burn pastilles, for it brought on a nervous spasm of alarming intensity. Lady Bridlington now understood that she was expected not only to house a boy picked out of the gutter, but to pursue his late master by every means in her power. Arabella talked of the Law, and of magistrates; of cruelties which made it almost impossible for Lady Bridlington even to swallow her coffee; and of what Papa would say must be done in so shocking a case. Lady Bridlington moaned, and said faintly: 'But you cannot! The boy must be given back to his master! You don't understand these things!'

'Cannot?' cried Arabella, her eyes flashing. '*Cannot* ma'am? I beg your pardon, but it is you who have not understood! When you have seen the dreadful marks on the poor little soul's back — and his ribs almost breaking through his skin! — you will not talk so!'

'No, no, Arabella, for heaven's sake — !' begged her godmother. 'I won't have you bring him in here! Where is Frederick? My dear, of course it is all very dreadful, and we will see what can be done, but do, pray, wait until I am dressed! Clara, where is his lordship?'

'His lordship, my lady,' responded Clara with relish, 'having partaken of his breakfast, has gone riding in the Park, as is his custom. His

173

lordship's gentleman happening to mention that Miss had a climbing-boy in her room, his lordship said as how he must be sent off at once.'

'Well, he will not be!' said Arabella, not mincing matters.

Lady Bridlington, reflecting that it was just like Frederick to issue orders in this foolish style, and leave others to see them carried out, decided to postpone any further discussion until he should be present to lend her his support. She persuaded Arabella to go away, looked with distaste at her breakfast-tray, and begged Clara, in a failing voice, to give her her smelling-salts.

When Lord Bridlington returned from his morning exercise, he was displeased to learn that nothing had so far been done about the climbing-boy, except that Miss had sent one of the under-servants out to buy him a suit of clothes. He was still frowning over this when his Mama came downstairs, and almost fell upon his neck. 'Thank heaven you are come at last!' she uttered. 'What can have induced you to go out with the house in this uproar? I am driven nearly distracted! She wants me to employ the boy as a page!'

Frederick led her firmly into the saloon on the ground-floor, and shut the door upon the interested butler. He then demanded an explanation of an affair which he said he was at a loss to understand. His mother was in the middle of giving him one when Arabella came into the room, leading the washed and clothed Jemmy by the hand.

'Good-morning, Lord Bridlington!' she said

calmly. 'I am glad you are come home, for you will best be able to help me to decide what I ought to do with Jemmy here.'

'I can certainly do so, Miss Tallant,' he answered. 'The boy must of course go back where he belongs. It was most improper of you, if you will permit me to say so, to interfere between him and his master.'

He encountered a look which surprised him. 'I do not permit anyone, Lord Bridlington, to tell me that in rescuing a helpless child from the brutality of a monster I am doing what is improper!' said Arabella.

'No, no, my dear, of course not!' hastily interposed Lady Bridlington. 'Frederick did not mean — But, you see, there is nothing one can do in these sad cases! That is — I am sure Frederick will speak to the man — give him a good fright, you know!'

'Really, Mama — '

'And Jemmy?' demanded Arabella. 'What will you do with him?'

His lordship looked distastefully at the candidate for his protection. Jemmy had been well scrubbed, but not the most thorough application of soap and water could turn him into a well-favoured child. He had a sharp little face, a wide mouth, from which a front tooth was missing, and a very snub nose. His short, ragged hair was perfectly straight, and his ears showed a tendency to stick out from his head.

'I do not know what you expect me to do!' said his lordship fretfully. 'If you had any knowledge of the laws governing apprentices, my dear Miss Tallant, you would know that it is quite impossible to steal this boy away from his master!'

'When the master of an apprentice misuses a boy as this child has been misused,' retorted Papa's daughter, 'he renders himself liable to prosecution! What is more, this man knows it, and I assure you he does not expect to have Jemmy returned to him!'

'I suppose you think I should adopt the boy!' said Frederick, goaded.

'No, I do not think that,' replied Arabella, her voice a little unsteady. 'I only think that you might — show some compassion for one so wretchedly circumstanced!'

Frederick coloured hotly. 'Well, of course I am excessively sorry, but — '

'Do you know that his master lights a fire in the grate beneath him, to force him up the chimney?' interrupted Arabella.

'Well, I don't suppose he would go up if — Yes, yes, shocking, I know, but chimneys must be swept, after all, or what would become of us all?'

'Oh, that Papa were here!' Arabella cried. 'I see that it is useless to talk to you, for you are selfish and heartless, and you care for nothing but your own comfort!'

It was at this inopportune moment that the door was opened, and the butler announced two morning-callers. He afterwards explained this lapse, which he felt quite as acutely as his mistress, by saying that he had supposed Miss to be still upstairs with That Boy. Frederick made a

176

hasty gesture indicative of his desire that the visitors should be excluded, but it was too late. Lord Fleetwood and Mr Beaumaris walked into the room.

Their reception was unusual. Lady Bridlington gave vent to an audible moan; her son stood rooted to the floor in the middle of the room, his face flushed, and his whole appearance that of a man who had been stuffed; and Miss Tallant, also very much flushed, bit her lip, and turned on her heel, leading a small urchin over to a chair by the wall, and bidding him gently to sit down on it, and to be a good boy.

Lord Fleetwood blinked upon this scene; Mr Beaumaris's brows went up, but he gave no other sign of surprise, merely bowing over Lady Bridlington's nerveless hand, and saying: 'How do you do? I trust we don't intrude? I called in the hope of persuading Miss Tallant to drive to the Botanical Gardens with me. They tell me the spring flowers are quite a sight there.'

'You are very obliging, sir,' said Arabella curtly, 'but I have more important affairs to attend to this morning.'

Lady Bridlington pulled herself together. 'My love, we can discuss all that later! I am sure it would do you good to take the air! Do but send that — that child down to the kitchen, and — '

'Thank you, ma'am, but I do not stir from the house until I have settled what is to be done with Jemmy.'

Lord Fleetwood, who had been regarding Jemmy with frank curiosity, said: 'Jemmy, eh? Er — friend of yours, Miss Tallant?'

177

'No. He is a climbing-boy who came by mistake down the chimney of my bedchamber,' Arabella replied. 'He has been most shamefully used, and he is only a child, as you may see — I daresay not more than seven or eight years old!'

The warmth of her feelings brought a distinct tremor into her voice. Mr Beaumaris looked curiously at her.

'No, really?' said Lord Fleetwood, with easy sympathy. 'Well, that's a great deal too bad! Shocking brutes, some of these chimney-sweeps! Ought to be sent to gaol!'

She said impulsively: 'Yes, that is what I have been telling Lord Bridlington, only he seems not to have the least understanding!'

'Arabella!' implored Lady Bridlington. 'Lord Fleetwood can have no interest in such matters!'

'Oh, I assure you, ma'am!' said his lordship. 'I am interested in anything that interests Miss Tallant! Rescued the child, did you? Well, upon my soul, I call it a devilish fine thing to do! Not as though he was a taking brat, either!'

'What does that signify?' said Arabella contemptuously. 'I wonder how taking, my lord, you or I should be had we been brought up from infancy by a drunken foster-mother, sold while still only babies to a brutal master, and forced into a hateful trade!'

Mr Beaumaris moved quietly to a chair a little removed from the group in the centre of the room, and stood leaning his hands on the back of it, his eyes still fixed on Arabella's face.

'No, no! Exactly so!' hastily said Lord Fleetwood.

Lord Bridlington chose, unwisely, to intervene at this point. 'No doubt it is just as you say, ma'am, but this is hardly a topic for my mother's sitting-room! Let me beg of you — '

Arabella turned on him like a flash, her eyes bright with tears, her voice unsteady with indignation. 'I will not be silenced! It is a topic that should be discussed in every Christian lady's sitting-room! Oh, I mean no disrespect, ma'am! You have not thought — you cannot have thought! Had you seen the wounds on this child's body you could not refuse to help him! I wish I had made you come into my room when I had him naked in the bath! Your heart must have been touched!'

'Yes, but, Arabella, my heart *is* touched!' protested her afflicted godmother. 'Only I don't want a page, and he is much too young, and such an ugly little thing! Besides, the sweep will very likely claim him, because, whatever you may think, if the boy is apprenticed to him, which he must be — '

'You may make your mind easy on that score, ma'am! His master will never dare to lay claim to him. He knows very well that he is in danger of being taken before a magistrate, for I told him so, and he did not doubt me! Why, he cringed at the very word, and backed himself out of the house as fast as he could!'

Mr Beaumaris spoke at last. 'Did you confront the sweep, Miss Tallant?' he asked, an odd little smile flickering on his lips.

'Certainly I did!' she replied, her glance resting on him for an indifferent moment.

Lady Bridlington was suddenly inspired. 'He must go to the Parish, of course! Frederick, *you* will know how to set about it!'

'No, no, he must not!' Arabella declared. 'That would be worse than anything, for what will they do with him, do you suppose, but set him to the only trade he knows? And he is afraid of those dreadful chimneys! If it were not so far away, I would send him to Papa, but how could such a little boy go all that way alone?'

'No, certainly not!' said Lord Fleetwood. 'Not to be thought of!'

'Lord Bridlington, surely, surely you would not condemn a child to such a life as he has endured?' Arabella begged, her hands going out in a pleading gesture. 'You have so *much!*'

'Of course he wouldn't!' declared Fleetwood rashly. 'Now, come, Bridlington!'

'But why should I?' demanded Frederick. 'Besides, what could I do with the brat? It is the greatest piece of nonsense I ever had to listen to!'

'Lord Fleetwood, will *you* take Jemmy?' asked Arabella, turning to him beseechingly.

His lordship was thrown into disorder. 'Well, I don't think — You see, ma'am — Fact of the matter is — Dash it, Lady Bridlington's right! The Parish! That's the thing!'

'Unworthy, Charles!' said Mr Beaumaris.

The much goaded Lord Bridlington rounded on him. 'Then, if that is what you think, Beaumaris, perhaps *you* will take the wretched brat!'

Then it was that Mr Beaumaris, looking across

the room at Arabella, all flushed cheeks and heaving bosom, astonished the company, and himself as well. 'Yes,' he said. 'I will.'

9

These simple words struck the ears of his audience with stunning effect. Lord Fleetwood's jaw dropped; Lady Bridlington's and her son's rather protruberant eyes started at Mr Beaumaris; and Arabella stared at him in amazement. It was she who broke the silence. '*You?*' she said, the incredulity in her tone leaving him in no doubt of her opinion of his character.

A rather rueful smile twisted his lips. 'Why not?' he said.

Her eyes searched his face. 'What would you do with him?' she demanded.

'I haven't the smallest notion,' he confessed. 'I hope you may be going to tell me what I am to do with him, Miss Tallant.'

'If I let you take him, you would throw him on the Parish, like Lord Fleetwood!' she said bitterly.

His lordship uttered an inarticulate protest.

'I have a great many faults,' replied Mr Beaumaris, 'but, believe me, you may trust my pledged word! I will neither throw him on the Parish, nor restore him to his master.'

'You must be mad!' exclaimed Frederick.

'You would naturally think so,' said Mr Beaumaris, flicking him with one of his disdainful glances.

'Have you considered what people would be bound to say?' Frederick said.

182

'No, nor do I propose to burden my head with anything that interests me so little!' retorted Mr Beaumaris.

Arabella said in a softened voice: 'If you mean it indeed, sir, you will be doing the very kindest thing — perhaps the best thing you have ever done, and, oh, I *thank* you!'

'Certainly the best thing I have ever done, Miss Tallant,' he said, with that wry smile.

'What will you do with him?' she asked again. 'You must not be thinking that I mean you to adopt him as your own, or anything of that nature! He must be brought up to a respectable trade, only I do not know what would be the best for him!'

'Perhaps,' suggested Mr Beaumaris, 'he has views of his own on the subject. What, Jemmy, would you choose to do?'

'Yes, what would you like to do when you are a man?' said Arabella, turning to kneel beside Jemmy's chair, and speaking in a coaxing tone. 'Tell me!'

Jemmy, who had been following all this with an intent look in his face, had no very clear idea of what it was about, but his quick, cockney mind had grasped that none of these swells, not even the stout, cross one, intended any harm to him. The scared expression in his eyes had given place to one of considerable acuteness. He answered his protectress without hesitation. 'Give ole Grimsby a leveller!' he said.

'Yes, my dear, and so you shall, and I hope you will do the same by everyone like him!' said Arabella warmly. 'But how would you choose to earn your living?'

Mr Beaumaris's lips twitched appreciatively. So the little Tallant had brothers, had she?

Lady Bridlington was looking bewildered, and her son disgusted. Lord Fleetwood, accepting Arabella's unconsciously betrayed knowledge of boxing-cant without question, looked Jemmy over critically, and gave it as his opinion that the boy was not the right build for a bruiser.

'Of course not!' said Arabella. 'Think, Jemmy! What could you do, do you suppose?'

The urchin reflected, while the company awaited his pleasure. 'Sweep a crossing,' he pronounced at last. 'I could 'old the gen'lemen's 'orses, then.'

'Hold the gentlemen's horses?' repeated Arabella. Her eye brightened. 'Are you fond of horses, Jemmy?'

Jemmy nodded vigorously. Arabella looked round in triumph. 'Then I know the very thing!' she said. 'Particularly since it is you who are to take charge of him, Mr Beaumaris!'

Mr Beaumaris waited in deep foreboding for the blow to fall.

'He must learn to look after horses, and then, as soon as he is a little older, you may employ him as your Tiger!' said Arabella radiantly.

Mr Beaumaris, whose views on the folly of entrusting blood-cattle to the guardianship of small boys were as unequivocal as they were well-known, replied without a tremor: 'To be sure I may. The future now being provided for — '

'But you never drive with a Tiger up behind you!' exclaimed Lord Bridlington. 'You have said

184

I know not how many times — '

'I do wish, Bridlington, that you would refrain from interrupting with these senseless comments,' said Mr Beaumaris.

'But that child is far too young to be a Tiger!' pointed out Lady Bridlington.

Arabella's face fell. 'Yes, he is,' she said regretfully. 'Yet it would be the very thing for him, if only we knew what to do with him in the meantime!'

'I think,' said Mr Beaumaris, 'that in the meantime I had better convey him to my own house, and place him in the charge of my housekeeper, pending further discussion between us, Miss Tallant.'

He was rewarded with a glowing look. 'I did not know you would be so kind!' said Arabella. 'It is a splendid notion, for the poor little fellow needs plenty of good food, and I am sure he must get it in your house! Listen, Jemmy, you are to go with this gentleman, who is to be your new master, and be a good boy, and do as he bids you!'

Jemmy, clutching a fold of her dress was understood to say that he preferred to remain with her. She bent over him, patting his shoulder. 'No, you cannot stay with me, my dear, and I am sure you would not like it half so well if you could, for you must know that he has a great many horses, and will very likely let you see them. Did you come here in your curricle, sir?' Mr Beaumaris bowed. 'Well, there, do you hear that, Jemmy?' said Arabella, in a heartening tone. 'You are to drive away in a carriage, behind a pair of beautiful gray horses!'

'I am driving my chestnuts today,' said Mr Beaumaris apologetically. 'I am so sorry, but I feel I should perhaps mention it!'

'You did very right,' said Arabella approvingly. 'One should never tell untruths to children! Chestnuts, Jemmy, glossy brown horses! How grand you will feel sitting up behind them!'

Apparently the urchin felt that there was much in what she said. He released her gown, and directed his sharp gaze upon his new owner. 'Proper good 'uns?' he asked suspiciously.

'Proper good 'uns,' corroborated Mr Beaumaris gravely.

Jemmy slid from the chair. 'You ain't slumming me? You won't go a-givin' of me back to ole Grimsby?'

'No, I won't do that. Come and take a look at my horses!'

Jemmy hesitated, glancing up at Arabella, who at once took his hand, and said: 'Yes, let us go and see them!'

When Jemmy beheld the equipage being led up and down the street, his eyes widened, and he drew a shuddering breath of ecstasy. 'That's a bang-up set-out, that is!' he said. 'Will I drive them 'orses, guv'nor?'

'You will not,' said Mr Beaumaris. 'You may sit up beside me, however.'

'Yessir!' said Jemmy, recognizing the voice of authority.

'Up with you, then!' Mr Beaumaris said, lifting him into the curricle. He turned, and found that Arabella was holding her hand out to him. He took it in his, and held it for a moment.

'I wish I might find the words to thank you!' she said. 'You will let me know how he goes on.'

'You may rest easy on that head, Miss Tallant,' he said, bowing. He took the reins in his hand, and mounted into the carriage, and looked down maliciously at Lord Fleetwood, who had accompanied them out of the house, and was just taking his leave of Arabella. 'Come, Charles!'

Lord Fleetwood started, and said hurriedly: 'No, no, I'll walk! No need to worry about me, my dear fellow!'

'Come, Charles!' repeated Mr Beaumaris gently.

Lord Fleetwood, aware of Arabella's eyes upon him, sighed, and said: 'Oh, very well!' and climbed into the curricle, wedging Jemmy between himself and Mr. Beaumaris.

Mr Beaumaris nodded to his gaping groom, and steadied the chestnuts as they sprang forward. 'Coward,' he remarked.

'It ain't that I'm a coward!' protested his lordship. 'But we shall have all the fools in London staring after us! I can't think what's come over you, Robert! You're never going to keep this brat in Mount Street! If it leaks out, and it's bound to, I suppose you know everyone will think it's a by-blow of yours?'

'The possibility had crossed my mind,' agreed Mr Beaumaris. 'I am sure I ought not to let it weigh with me: Miss Tallant certainly would not.'

'Well, damn it, I think that prosy fool, Bridlington, was right for once in his life! You've gone stark, staring mad!'

'Very true: I have known it this half-hour and more.'

Lord Fleetwood looked at him in some concern. 'You know, Robert, if you're not careful you'll find yourself walking to the altar before you're much older!' he said.

'No, she has the poorest opinion of me,' replied Mr Beaumaris. 'I perceive that my next step must be to pursue the individual known to us as 'ole Grimsby'.'

'What?' gasped Fleetwood. 'She never asked that of you!'

'No, but I feel she expects it of me.' He saw that the mention of the sweep's name had made Jemmy look up at him in quick alarm, and said reassuringly: 'No, I am not going to give you to him.'

'Robert, never in all the years I've known you have I seen you make such a cake of yourself!' said his friend, with brutal frankness. 'First you let the little Tallant bamboozle you into saddling yourself with this horrid brat, and now you talk of meddling with a chimney-sweep! *You!* Why, it's unheard of!'

'Yes, and, what is more, I have a shrewd suspicion that a benevolent career is going to prove extremely wearing,' said Mr Beaumaris thoughtfully.

'I see what it is,' said Fleetwood, after regarding his profile for a few moments. 'You're so piqued she don't favour you you'll go to any lengths to fix your interest with the girl!'

'I will,' said Mr Beaumaris cordially.

'Well, you'd better take care what you are

about!' said his worldly-wise friend.

'I will,' said Mr Beaumaris again.

Lord Fleetwood occupied himself during the rest of the short drive in delivering a severe lecture on the perfidy of those who, without having any serious intentions, attempted to cut out their friends with the season's most notable catch, adding, for good measure, a lofty condemnation of hardened rakes who tried to deceive innocent country maidens.

Mr Beaumaris listened to him with the utmost amiability, only interrupting to applaud this last flight of eloquence. 'That's very good, Charles,' he said approvingly. 'Where did you pick it up?'

'Devil!' said his lordship, with feeling. 'Well, I wash my hands of you — and I hope she will lead you a pretty dance!'

'I have a strong premonition,' replied Mr Beaumaris, 'that your hope is likely to be realized.'

Lord Fleetwood gave it up, and as Mr Beaumaris saw no reason to take him into his confidence, what little time was left before Mount Street was reached was occupied in discussing the chances of the newest bruiser in his forthcoming fight with an acknowledged champion.

Mr Beaumaris, at this stage, would have been chary of confiding in anyone the precise nature of his intentions. He was by no means sure that he knew what they were himself, but that he had called in Park Street for precisely the reasons described by his friend, and, when confronted by the vision of Arabella fighting for the future of her unattractive protégé, had undergone an enlightenment so blinding as almost to deprive him of his senses, was certain. No consideration of the conduct to be expected of a delicately nurtured female had stopped her. She knew no discomfiture when two gentlemen of fashion had arrived to find her embroiled in the concerns of an urchin far beneath the notice of any aspirant to social heights. No, by God! thought Mr Beaumaris exultantly, she showed us what she thought of such frippery fellows as we are! We might have gone to the devil for all she cared. *I* might have made her a laughing-stock only by recounting the story — as I could! Lord, yes, as I *could!* Did she know it? Would she have cared? Not a farthing, the little Tallant! But I must stop Charles spreading this all over town.

Mr Beaumaris, hunting now in earnest, was by far too experienced a sportsman to pursue his quarry too closely. He let several days pass before making any attempt to approach Arabella. When next he encountered her it was at a ball given by the Charnwoods. He asked her to stand up with him for one of the country-dances, but when the moment for taking their places in the set came, led her to a sofa, saying: 'Shall you object to sitting down with me instead? One can never converse in comfort while dancing, and I must consult you about our urchin.'

'No, indeed!' she said warmly. 'I have been so anxious to know how he goes on!' She seated herself, holding her fan in her clasped hands, and raised her eyes to his face in an enquiring look. 'Is he well? Is he happy?'

'As far as I have been able to ascertain,' replied Mr Beaumaris carefully, 'he is not only fast recovering the enjoyment of excellent health, but is achieving no common degree of felicity by conduct likely to deprive me of the services of most of my existent staff.'

Arabella considered this. Mr Beaumaris watched appreciatively the wrinkling of her thoughtful brow. 'Is he very naughty?' she asked presently.

'According to the report of my housekeeper, Miss Tallant — but I daresay she is not to be at all believed! — he is the embodiment of too many vices for me to enumerate.'

She seemed to accept this with unimpaired calm, for she nodded understandingly.

'Pray do not think that I should dream of burdening you with anything so unimportant as the complaints of a mere housekeeper!' begged Mr Beaumaris. 'Nothing but the most urgent of exigencies could have prevailed upon me to open my lips to you upon this subject!' She looked startled, and enquiring: 'You see,' he said apologetically, 'it is Alphonse!'

'Alphonse?'

'My chef,' explained Mr Beaumaris. 'Of course, if you say so, ma'am, he shall go! But I must own that his departure would cause me grave concern. I do not mean to say that my life would be shattered, precisely, for no doubt there *are* other chefs who have his way with a soufflé, and who do not take such violent exception to the raids of small boys upon the larder!'

'But this is quite absurd, Mr Beaumaris!' said

191

Arabella severely. 'You must have been indulging Jemmy beyond what is right! I daresay he is excessively ill-behaved: it is always so, unless their spirits are utterly broken, and we must be thankful that his are not!'

'Very true!' agreed Mr Beaumaris, entranced by this wisdom. 'I will at once present this view of the matter to Alphonse.'

Arabella shook her head. 'Oh, no! it would not be of the least avail, I daresay! Foreigners,' she said largely, 'have no notion how to manage children! What is to be done?'

'I cannot help feeling,' said Mr Beaumaris, 'that Jemmy would benefit by country air.'

This suggestion found favour. 'Nothing could be better for him!' agreed Arabella. 'Besides, there is no reason why he should tease you, I am sure! Only how may it be contrived?'

Much relieved at having so easily cleared this fence, Mr Beaumaris said: 'The notion did just cross my mind, ma'am, that if I were to take him into Hampshire, where I have estates, no doubt some respectable household might be found for him.'

'One of your tenants! The very thing!' exclaimed Arabella. 'Quite a simple cottage, mind, and a sensible woman to take care of him! Only I am afraid she would have to be paid a small sum to do it.'

Mr Beaumaris, who felt that no sum could be too large for the ridding of his house of one small imp who threatened to disrupt it, bore up nobly under the warning, and said that he had envisaged this possibility, and was prepared to meet it. It then occurred to Arabella that he might reasonably expect so great an heiress as herself to bear the charge of her protégé; and she embarked on a tangled explanation of why she could not at present do so. Mr Beaumaris interrupted her speech when it showed signs of becoming ravelled beyond hope. 'No, no, Miss Tallant!' he said. 'Do not deny me this opportunity to perform a charitable action, I beg of you!'

So Arabella very kindly refrained from doing so, and bestowed so grateful a smile upon him that he felt himself to have been amply rewarded.

'Are you quite in disgrace with Lady Bridlington?' he asked quizzically.

She laughed, but looked a little guilty. 'I *was*,' she owned. 'But since she has seen that the story has not got about, she has forgiven me. She was persuaded that everyone would be laughing at me. As though I would care for such a thing as that, when I had but done my duty!'

'Certainly not!'

'Do you know, I had begun to believe that everyone in town — all the grand people, I mean — were quite heartless, and selfish?' she confided. 'I am afraid I was not quite civil to you — indeed, Lady Bridlington assures me that I was shockingly rude! — but then, you see, I had no notion that you were not like all the rest. I beg your pardon!'

Mr Beaumaris had the grace to acknowledge a twinge of conscience. It led him to say: 'Miss Tallant, I did it in the hope of pleasing you.'

Then he wished that he had curbed his

tongue, for her confiding air left her, and although she talked easily for a few more minutes he was fully aware that she had withdrawn from him again.

He was able to retrieve his position a few days later, and took care not to jeopardize it again. When he returned from a visit to his estates he called in Park Street to give Arabella comfortable tidings of Jemmy, whom he had foisted on to a retired servant of his own. She was a little concerned lest the town-bred waif should feel lost and unhappy in the country, but when he informed her that the last news he had of Jemmy, before leaving Hampshire, was that he had let a herd of bullocks out of the field where they were confined, pulled the feathers from the cock's tail, tried to ride an indignant pig round the yard, and eaten a whole batch of cakes newly baked by his kind hostess, she perceived that Jemmy was made of resilient stuff, and laughed, and said that he would soon settle down, and learn to be a good boy.

Mr Beaumaris agreed to it, and then played his trump card. He thought Miss Tallant would like to know that he had taken steps to ensure the well-being of Mr Grimsby's future apprentices.

Arabella was delighted. 'You have brought him to justice!'

'Well, not quite that,' confessed Mr Beaumaris. He saw the disappointed look in her eye, and added hastily: 'You know, I could not feel that to be appearing in a court of law was just what you would like. Then, too, when it is a question of apprentices one is apt to find oneself confronted with all manner of difficulties in the way of removing boys from their masters. It seemed best, therefore, to drop a word in Sir Nathaniel Conant's ear. He is the Chief Magistrate, and as I have some acquaintance with him the thing was easy. Mr Grimsby will take care how he disregards a warning from Bow Street, I assure you.'

Arabella was a little sorry to think that Mr Grimsby was not to be cast into gaol, but being a sensible girl she readily appreciated the force of Mr Beaumaris's arguments, and told him that she was very much obliged to him. She sat pondering deeply for some moments, while he watched her, wondering what now was in her head. 'It should be the business of people with interest and fortune to enquire into such things!' she said suddenly. 'No one seems to care a button in a great city like this! I have seen such dreadful sights since I came to London — such beggary, and misery, and such countless ragged children who seem to have no parents and no homes! Lady Bridlington does not care to have anything of that nature spoken about, but, oh, I would like so much to be able to help such children as poor Jemmy!'

'Why don't you?' he asked coolly.

Her eyes flew to his; he knew that he had been too blunt: she would not tell him the truth about herself. Nor did she. After a tiny pause, she said: 'Perhaps, one day, I shall.'

He wondered whether her godmother had warned her against him, and when she excused herself from dancing with him at the next Assembly was sure of it.

But the warning came from Lord Bridlington. Mr Beaumaris's marked attentions to Arabella, including, as they had, so extraordinary a gesture as the adoption of Jemmy, had aroused the wildest hopes in Lady Bridlington's shallow brain. If any of his previous amatory adventures had led him to perform a comparable deed, she at least had never heard of it. She began to indulge the fancy that his intentions were serious, and had almost written to give Mrs Tallant a hint of it when Lord Bridlington dashed her hopes.

'You would do well, ma'am, to put your young friend a little on her guard with Beaumaris,' he said weightily.

'My dear Frederick, and so I did, at the outset! But he has become so particular in his attentions, showing such a decided preference for her, and trying to fix his interest with her by every means in his power, that I really begin to think he has formed a lasting attachment! Only fancy if she were to form such a connexion, Frederick! I declare, I should feel it as much as if she were my own child! For it will be all due to me, you know!'

'You would be very unwise to put such a notion into the girl's head, Mama,' he said, cutting short these rhapsodies. 'I can tell you this: Beaumaris's intimates don't by any means regard his pursuit of Miss Tallant in that light!'

'No?' she said, in a faltering tone.

'Far otherwise, ma'am! They are saying that it

is all pique, because she does not appear to favour him above any other. I must say, I should not have expected her to have shown such good sense! You must know that men of his type, accustomed as he is to being courted and flattered, are put very much on their mettle by a rebuff from any female who has not been so foolish as to pick up the handkerchief he has carelessly tossed towards them. It puts me out of all patience to see anyone so spoiled and caressed! But be that as it may, you should know, Mama, that bets are being laid and taken at White's against Miss Tallant's holding out against this siege!'

'How odious men are!' exclaimed Lady Bridlington indignantly.

Odious they might be, but if they were laying bets of that nature at the clubs there was nothing for a conscientious chaperon to do but warn her charge once more against lending too credulous an ear to an accomplished flirt. Arabella assured her that she had no intention of doing so.

'No, my dear, very likely not,' replied her ladyship. 'But there is no denying that he is a very attractive man! I am conscious of it myself! Such an air! Such easy address! But it is of no use to think of that! I am sadly afraid that it is a kind of sport with him to make females fall in love with him.'

'I shall not do so!' declared Arabella. 'I like him very well, but, as I told you before, I am not such a goose as to be taken-in by him!'

Lady Bridlington looked at her rather doubtfully. 'No, my love, I hope not indeed. To be sure, you have so many admirers that we need not consider Mr Beaumaris. I suppose — you will not be offended at my asking, I know! — I suppose no eligible gentleman has proposed to you?'

Quite a number of gentlemen, eligible and ineligible, had proposed to Arabella, but she shook her head. She might acquit some of her suitors of having designs on her supposed wealth, but two among them at least would never have offered for her hand, she was very sure, had they known her to be penniless; and the courtships of several notorious fortune-hunters made it impossible for her to believe that Lord Bridlington's well-meaning efforts had in any way scotched that dreadful rumour. She felt her situation to be unhappy indeed. Easter was almost upon them, and there had been plenty of time for her, with the opportunities which had been granted to her, to have fulfilled her Mama's ambitions. She felt guilty, for it had cost Mama so much money, which she could ill-afford, to send her to London, so that the least a grateful daughter could have done would have been to have repaid her by accepting some respectable offer of marriage. She could not do it. She cared for none of those who had proposed to her, and although that, she supposed, ought not to weigh too heavily in the scales when balanced against the benefits that would accrue to the dear brothers and sisters, she was resolved to accept no offer from anyone ignorant of her true circumstances. Perhaps there was still to come into her life some suitor to whom it would be possible to confess the whole, but he had not yet appeared, and, pending his arrival, it was with relief that Arabella turned to Mr Beaumaris, who, whatever his intentions might be, certainly coveted no fortune.

Mr Beaumaris offered her every facility to turn to him, but he could scarcely congratulate himself on the outcome. The smallest attempt at gallantry had the effect of transforming her from the confiding child he found so engaging into the society damsel who was ready enough to fence lightly with him, but who showed him quite clearly that she wanted none of his practised love-making. And when Lady Bridlington had repeated much of her son's warning, not omitting to mention the fact that Mr Beaumaris's friends knew him to be merely trifling, Mr Beaumaris found Miss Tallant even more elusive. He was reduced to employing an ignoble stratagem, and, having been obliged to visit his estates on a matter of business, sought Arabella out upon his return, and told her that he wished to consult her again about Jemmy's future. In this manner, he lured her to drive out with him in his curricle. He drove her to Richmond Park, and she raised no objection to this, though he had not previously taken her farther afield than Chelsea. It was a fine, warm afternoon, with the sun so brightly shining that Arabella ventured to wear a very becoming straw hat, and to carry a small sunshade with a very long handle, which she had seen in the Pantheon Bazaar, and had not been able to resist purchasing. She said, as Mr Beaumaris handed her up into the curricle,

199

that it was very kind of him to drive her into the country, since she liked it of all things, and was able to think herself, while in that great park, many miles from town.

'Do you know Richmond Park, then?' he asked.

'Oh, yes!' replied Arabella cheerfully. 'Lord Fleetwood drove me there last week; and then, you know, the Charnwoods got up a party, and we all went in three barouches. And tomorrow, if it is fine, Sir Geoffrey Morecambe is to take me to see the Florida Gardens.'

'I must count myself fortunate, then, to have found you on a day when you had no other engagement,' remarked Mr Beaumaris.

'Yes, I am out a great deal,' agreed Arabella. She unfurled the sunshade, and said: 'What was it that you wished to tell me about Jemmy, sir?'

'Ah, yes, Jemmy!' he said. 'Subject to your consent, Miss Tallant, I am making — in fact, I have made — a trifling change in his upbringing. I fear he will never come to any good under Mrs Buxton's roof, and still more do I fear that if he remained there he would shortly be the death of her. At least, so she informed me when I went down to Hampshire the day before yesterday.'

She gave him one of her warm looks. 'How very kind that was of you! Did you go all that way on that naughty boy's account?'

Mr Beaumaris was sorely tempted. He glanced down at his companion, met her innocently enquiring gaze, hesitated, and then said: 'Well, no, Miss Tallant! I had business there.'

She laughed. 'I thought it had been that.'

'In that case,' said Mr Beaumaris, 'I am glad I did not lie to you.'

'How can you be so absurd? As though I should wish you to put yourself to so much trouble! What has Jemmy been doing?'

'It would sadden you to know: Mrs Buxton is persuaded that he is possessed of a fiend. The language he employs, too, is not such as she is accustomed to. I regret to say that he has also alienated my keepers, who have quite failed to impress upon him the impropriety of disturbing my birds, or, I may add, of stealing pheasants' eggs. I cannot imagine what he can want with them.'

'Of course he should be punished for doing so! I daresay he has not enough employment. One must remember that he has been used to work and should be made to do so now. It is not at all good for anyone to be perfectly idle.'

'Very true, ma'am,' agreed Mr Beaumaris meekly.

Miss Tallant was not deceived. She looked sharply up at him, and bit her lip, saying after a moment: 'We are speaking of *Jemmy*!'

'I hoped we were,' confessed Mr Beaumaris.

'You are being nonsensical,' said Arabella, with some severity. 'What is to be done with him?'

'I found, upon enquiry, that the only person who is inclined to regard him favourably is my head groom, who says that his way with the horses is quite remarkable. It appears that he has been for ever slipping off to the stables, where, for a wonder, he comports himself unexceptionably. Wrexham was so much impressed by

201

finding him — er — hobnobbing with a bay stallion generally thought to be extremely dangerous, that he came up to represent to me the propriety of handing the boy over to him to train. He is a childless man, and since he expressed his willingness to house Jemmy, I thought it better to fall in with his schemes. I hardly think Jemmy's language will shock him, and I am encouraged to hope, from what I know of Wrexham, that he will know how to keep the boy in order.'

Arabella approved so heartily of this arrangement, that he took the risk of saying in a melancholy tone: 'Yes, but if it succeeds, I shall be at a loss to think of a pretext for getting you to drive out with me.'

'Dear me, have I shown myself so reluctant?' said Arabella, raising her eyebrows. 'I wonder why you will talk so absurdly, Mr Beaumaris? You may depend upon it that I shall take care to be seen every now and then in your company, for I cannot be so sure of my credit as to run the risk of having it said that the Nonpareil has begun to find me a dead bore!'

'You stand in no such danger, Miss Tallant, believe me.' He drew in his horses for a sharp bend in the road, and did not speak again until the corner was negotiated. Then he said: 'I am afraid that you deem me a very worthless creature, ma'am. What am I to do to convince you that I can be perfectly sensible?'

'There is not the least need: I am sure that you can,' she replied amicably.

After that she became interested in the

countryside, and from that passed to her forthcoming presentation. This event was to take place in the following week, and already her dress had been sent home from the skilful costumier who had altered an old gown of Lady Bridlington's to the present mode. Miss Tallant did not tell Mr Beaumaris that, naturally, but she did describe its magnificence to him, and found him both sympathetic and knowledgeable. He asked her what jewels she would wear with it, and she replied, in a very grand way: 'Oh, nothing but diamonds!' and was promptly ashamed of herself for having said it, although it was perfectly true.

'Your taste is always excellent, Miss Tallant. Nothing could be more displeasing to a fastidious eye than a profusion of jewelry. I must congratulate you on having exerted so beneficial an influence over your contemporaries.'

'I?' she gasped, quite startled, and half-suspecting him of quizzing her.

'Certainly. The total lack of ostentation which characterizes your appearance is much admired, I assure you, and is beginning to be copied.'

'You cannot be serious!'

'But of course I am serious! Had you not noticed that Miss Accrington has left off that shocking collar of sapphires, and that Miss Kirkmichael no longer draws attention to the limitations of her figure by a profusion of chains, brooches, and necklaces which I should have supposed her to have chosen at random from an over-stocked jewel-box?'

There was something so irresistibly humorous

to Arabella in the thought that her straitened circumstances had been at the root of a new mode that she began to giggle. But she would not tell Mr Beaumaris why she sat chuckling beside him. He did not press her for an explanation, but as they had by this time reached the Park, suggested that she might like to walk on the grass for a little way, while the groom took charge of the curricle. She assented readily, and while they strolled about, Mr Beaumaris told her something of that home of his in Hampshire. The bait failed. Miss Tallant confined her remarks on her own home to descriptions of the Yorkshire scene, and would not be lured into exchanging family reminiscences.

'I collect that your father is still alive, ma'am? You mentioned him, as I remember, on the day that you adopted Jemmy.'

'Did I? Yes, indeed he is alive, and I wished for him very much that day, for he is the best man in the world, and he would have known just what was right to be done!'

'I shall hope to have the pleasure of making his acquaintance one day. Does he come to London at all?'

'No, never,' replied Arabella firmly. She could not imagine that Mr Beaumaris and Papa would have the least pleasure in one another's acquaintance, thought that the conversation was getting on to dangerous ground, and reverted to her society manner.

This was maintained during most of the drive back to London, but when the open country was left behind, and the curricle was passing once more between rows of houses, it deserted her abruptly. In the middle of a narrow street, the grays took high-bred exception to a wagon with a tattered and flapping canvas roof, which was drawn up to one side of the road. There was barely room for the curricle to slip past this obstruction, and Mr Beaumaris, his attention all on his horses, failed to take notice of a group of youths bending over some object on the flag-way, or to heed the anguished yelp which made Arabella, casting aside the light rug which covered her legs, cry out: 'Oh, stop!' and shut her sunshade with a snap.

The grays were mincing past the wagon; Mr Beaumaris did indeed pull them up, but Arabella did not wait for the curricle to come to a standstill, but sprang hazardously down from it. Mr Beaumaris holding his sidling, snorting pair in an iron hand, took one quick glance over his shoulder, saw that Arabella was dispersing the group on the flag-way by the vigorous use of her sunshade, and snapped: 'Go to their heads, fool!'

His groom, still perched up behind, and apparently dumbfounded by Miss Tallant's strange conduct, came to himself with a start, jumped down, and ran round to hold the grays. Mr Beaumaris sprang down, and descended swiftly upon the battleground. Having scientifically knocked two louts' heads together, picked up the third lout by his collar and the seat of his frieze breeches, and thrown him into the road, he was able to see what had aroused Miss Tallant's wrath. Crouched, shivering and whimpering, on the flag-way, was a small, sandy-coated mongrel, with a curly tail, and one ear disreputably flying.

'Those wicked, brutal, *fiends!*' panted Miss Tallant, cheeks and eyes in a glow. 'They were *torturing* the poor little thing!'

'Take care! He may snap at you!' Mr Beaumaris said quickly, seeing her about to kneel down beside the dog. 'Shall I thrash them all soundly?'

At these words, the two smaller boys departed precipitately, the two whose heads were still ringing drew circumspectly out of range of Mr Beaumaris's long-lashed whip, and the bruised youth in the road, whined that they weren't doing any harm, and that all his ribs were busted.

'How badly have they hurt him?' Miss Tallant asked anxiously. 'He cries when I touch him!'

Mr Beaumaris pulled off his gloves, and handed them to her, together with his whip, saying: 'Hold those for me, and I'll see.'

She obediently took them, and watched anxiously while he went over the mongrel. She saw with approval that he handled the little creature firmly and gently, in a way that showed he knew what he was about. The dog whined, and uttered little cries, and cowered, but he did not offer to snap. Indeed, he feebly wagged his disgraceful tail, and once licked Mr Beaumaris's hand.

'He is badly bruised, and has one or two nasty sores, but there are no bones broken,' Mr Beaumaris said, straightening himself. He turned to where the two remaining youths were standing, poised on the edge of flight, and said sternly: 'Whose dog is this?'

'It don't belong to no one,' he was sullenly informed. 'It goes all over, stealing things off of the rubbish-heaps: yes, *and* out of the butcher's shop!'

'I seen 'im in Chelsea once with 'alf a loaf of bread,' corroborated the other youth.

The accused crawled to Mr Beaumaris's elegantly shod feet, and pawed one gleaming Hessian appealingly.

'Oh, see how intelligent he is!' cried Arabella, stooping to fondle the animal. 'He knows he has you to thank for his rescue!'

'If he knows that, I think little of his intelligence, Miss Tallant,' said Mr Beaumaris, glancing down at the dog. 'He certainly owes his life to you!'

'Oh, no! I could never have managed without your help! Will you be so obliging as to hand him up to me, if you please?' said Arabella, prepared to climb into the curricle again.

Mr Beaumaris looked from her to the unkempt and filthy mongrel at his feet, and said: 'Are you quite sure that you want to take him with you, ma'am?'

'Why, of course! You do not suppose that I would leave him here, for those wretches to torment as soon as we were out of sight! Besides, you heard what they said! He has no master — no one to feed him, or to take care of him! Please give him to me!'

Mr Beaumaris's lips twitched, but he said with perfect gravity: 'Just as you wish, Miss Tallant!'

and picked up the dog by the scruff of his neck. He saw Miss Tallant's arms held out to receive her new protégé, and hesitated. 'He is very dirty, you know!'

'Oh, what does that signify? I have soiled my dress already, with kneeling on the flag-way!' said Arabella impatiently.

So Mr Beaumaris deposited the dog on her lap, received his whip and gloves from her again, and stood watching with a faint smile while she made the dog comfortable, and stroked its ears, and murmured soothingly to it. She looked up. 'What do we wait for, sir?' she asked, surprised.

'Nothing at all, Miss Tallant!' he said, and got into the curricle.

Miss Tallant, continuing to fondle the dog, spoke her mind with some force on the subject of persons who were cruel to animals, and thanked Mr Beaumaris earnestly for his kindness in knocking the horrid boys' heads together, a violent proceeding which seemed to have met with her unqualified approval. She then occupied herself with talking to the dog, and informing him of the splendid dinner he should presently be given, and the warm bath which he would (she said) so much enjoy. But after a time she became a little pensive, and relapsed into meditative silence.

'What is it, Miss Tallant?' asked Mr Beaumaris, when she showed no sign of breaking the silence.

'Do you know,' she said slowly, 'I have just thought — Mr Beaumaris, something tells me that Lady Bridlington may not like this dear little dog!'

Mr Beaumaris waited in patient resignation for his certain fate to descend upon him.

Arabella turned impulsively towards him. 'Mr Beaumaris, do you think — *would* you — ?'

He looked down into her anxious, pleading eyes, a most rueful twinkle in his own. 'Yes, Miss Tallant,' he said. 'I would.'

Her face broke into smiles. '*Thank* you!' she said. 'I knew I might depend upon you!' She turned the mongrel's head gently towards Mr Beaumaris. 'There, sir! that is your new master, who will be very kind to you! Only see how intelligently he looks, Mr Beaumaris! I am sure he understands. I daresay he will grow to be quite devoted to you!'

Mr Beaumaris looked at the animal, and repressed a shudder. 'Do you think so indeed?' he said.

'Oh, yes! He is not, perhaps, a very *beautiful* little dog, but mongrels are often the cleverest of all dogs.' She smoothed the creature's rough head, and added innocently: 'He will be company for you, you know. I wonder you do not have a dog already.'

'I do — in the country,' he replied.

'Oh, sporting dogs! They are not at all the same.'

Mr Beaumaris, after another look at his prospective companion, found himself able to agree with this remark with heartfelt sincerity.

'When he has been groomed, and has put some flesh on his bones,' pursued Arabella, serene in the conviction that her sentiments were being shared, 'he will look very different. I am quite anxious to see him in a week or two!'

Mr Beaumaris drew up his horses outside Lady Bridlington's house. Arabella gave the dog a last pat, and set him on the seat beside his new owner, bidding him stay there. He seemed a little undecided at first, but being too bruised and battered to leap down into the road, he did stay, whining loudly. However, when Mr Beaumaris, having handed Arabella up to the door, and seen her admitted into the house, returned to his curricle, the dog stopped whining, and welcomed him with every sign of relief and affection.

'Your instinct is at fault,' said Mr Beaumaris. 'Left to myself, I should abandon you to your fate. That, or tie a brick round your neck, and drown you.'

His canine admirer wagged a doubtful tail, and cocked an ear. 'You are a disgraceful object!' Mr Beaumaris told him. 'And what does she expect me to do with you?' A tentative paw was laid on his knee. 'Possibly, but let me tell you that I know your sort! You are a toadeater, and I abominate toadeaters. I suppose, if I sent you into the country my own dogs would kill you on sight.'

The severity in his tone made the dog cower a little, still looking up at him with the expression of a dog anxious to understand.

'Have no fear!' Mr Beaumaris assured him, laying a fleeting hand on his head. 'She clearly wishes me to keep you in town. Did it occur to her, I wonder, that your manners, I have no doubt at all, leave much to be desired? Do your wanderings include the slightest experience of the conduct expected of those admitted into a gentleman's house? Of course they do not!' A choking sound from his groom, made him say over his shoulder: 'I hope you like dogs, Clayton, for you are going to wash this specimen.'

'Yes, sir,' said his grinning attendant.

'Be very kind to him!' commanded Mr Beaumaris. 'Who knows? he may take a liking to you.'

But at ten o'clock that evening, Mr Beaumaris's butler, bearing a tray of suitable refreshments to the library, admitted into the room a washed, brushed, and fed mongrel, who came in with something as near a prance as could be expected of one in his emaciated condition. At sight of Mr Beaumaris, seeking solace from his favourite poet in a deep winged chair by the fire, he uttered a shrill bark of delight, and reared himself up on his hind legs, his paws on Mr Beaumaris's knees, his tail furiously wagging, and a look of beaming adoration in his eyes.

Mr. Beaumaris lowered his Horace. 'Now, what the devil — ?' he demanded.

'Clayton brought the little dog up, sir,' said Brough. 'He said as you would wish to see how he looked. It seems, sir, that the dog didn't take to Clayton, as you might say. Very restless, Clayton informs me, and whining all the evening.' He watched the dog thrust his muzzle under Mr Beaumaris's hand, and said: 'It's strange the way animals always go to you, sir. Quite happy now, isn't he?'

'Deplorable,' said Mr Beaumaris. 'Down, Ulysses! Learn that my pantaloons were not made to be pawed by such as you!'

'He'll learn quick enough, sir,' remarked Brough, setting a glass and a decanter down on the table at his master's elbow. 'You can see he's as sharp as he can stare. Would there be anything more, sir?'

'No, only give this animal back to Clayton, and tell him I am perfectly satisfied with his appearance.'

'Clayton's gone off, sir. I don't think he can have understood that you wished him to take charge of the little dog,' said Brough.

'I don't think he can have wanted to understand it,' said Mr Beaumaris grimly.

'As to that, sir, I'm sure I couldn't say. I doubt whether the dog will settle down with Clayton, him not having a way with dogs like he has with horses. I'm afraid he'll fret, sir.'

'Oh, my God!' groaned Mr Beaumaris. 'Then take him down to the kitchen!'

'Well, sir, of course — if you say so!' replied Brough doubtfully. 'Only there's Alphonse.' He met his master's eye, apparently had no difficulty in reading the question in it, and said: 'Yes, sir. Very French he has been on the subject. Quite shocking, I'm sure, but one has to remember that foreigners are queer, and don't like animals.'

'Very well,' said Mr Beaumaris, with a resigned sigh. 'Leave him, then!'

'Yes, sir,' said Brough, and departed.

Ulysses, who had been thoroughly, if a little timidly, inspecting the room during this

212

exchange, now advanced to the hearth-rug again, and paused there, suspiciously regarding the fire. He seemed to come to the conclusion that it was not actively hostile, for after a moment he curled himself up before it, heaved a sigh, laid his chin on Mr Beaumaris's crossed ankles, and disposed himself for sleep.

'I suppose you imagine you are being a companion to me,' said Mr Beaumaris.

Ulysses flattened his ears, and gently stirred his tail.

'You know,' said Mr Beaumaris, 'a prudent man would draw back at this stage.'

Ulysses raised his head to yawn, and then snuggled it back on Mr Beaumaris's ankles, and closed his eyes.

'You may be right,' admitted Mr Beaumaris. 'But I wonder what next she will saddle me with?'

10

When Arabella had parted from Mr Beaumaris at the door of Lady Bridlington's house, the butler who had admitted her informed her that two gentlemen had called to see her, and were even now awaiting her in the smaller saloon. This seemed to her a trifle unusual, and she looked surprised. The butler explained the matter by saying that one of the young gentlemen was particularly anxious to see her, since he came from Yorkshire, and would not be unknown to her. A horrid fear gripped Arabella that she was now to be exposed to the whole of London, and it was with an almost shaking hand that she picked up the visiting-card from the salver the butler was holding out to her. But the name elegantly inscribed upon it was unknown to her: she could not recall ever having heard of, much less met, a Mr Felix Scunthorpe.

'*Two* gentlemen?' she said.

'The other young gentleman, miss, did not disclose his name,' replied the butler.

'Well, I suppose I must see them,' Arabella decided. 'Pray tell them that I shall be downstairs directly! Or is her ladyship in?'

'Her ladyship has not yet returned, miss.'

Arabella hardly knew whether to be glad or sorry. She went up to her room to change her soiled gown, and came down again some few minutes later hoping that she had schooled her face not to betray her inward trepidation. She entered the saloon in a very stately way, and looked rather challengingly across it. There were, as the butler had warned her, two young gentlemen standing by the window. One was a slightly vacuous looking youth, dressed with extreme nicety, and holding, besides his tall hat, an ebony cane, and an elegant pair of gloves; the other was a tall, loose-limbed boy, with curly dark hair, and an aquiline cast of countenance. At sight of him, Arabella uttered a shriek, and ran across the room to cast herself upon his chest. '*Bertram!*'

'Here, I say, Bella!' expostulated Bertram, recoiling. 'Mind what you are about, for the lord's sake! My neck-cloth!'

'Oh, I beg your pardon, but I am so *glad* to see you! But how is this? Bertram, Papa is not in town?'

'Good God, no!'

'Thank heaven!' Arabella breathed, pressing her hands to her cheeks.

Her brother found nothing to wonder at in this exclamation. He looked her over critically, and said: 'Just as well he ain't, for he'd be bound to give you one of his scolds for dressing-up as fine as five pence! I must say, Bella, you're turned out in prime style! Slap up to the mark, ain't she, Felix?'

Mr Scunthorpe, much discomposed at being called upon to give an opinion, opened and shut his mouth once or twice, bowed, and looked despairing.

'He thinks you're complete to a shade,'

explained Bertram, interpreting these signs. 'He ain't much of a dab with the petticoats, but he's a great gun, I can tell you! Up to every rig and row in town!'

Arabella looked at Mr Scunthorpe with interest. He presented the appearance of a very mild young man; and although his fancy waistcoat bespoke the man of fashion, he seemed to her to lack address. She bowed politely, which made him blush very much, and fall into a fit of stuttering. Bertram, feeling that some further introduction might be considered desirable by his sister, said: 'You don't know him: he was at Harrow with me. He's older than I am, but he's got no brains, y'know: never could learn anything! I ran into him in the High.'

'The High?' repeated Arabella.

'Oxford, you know!' said Bertram loftily. 'Dash it, Bella, you can't have forgot I've been up to take my Smalls!'

'No, indeed!' she said. 'Sophy wrote that you were gone there, and that poor James was unable to accompany you, because of the jaundice. I was so sorry! But how did you go on, Bertram? Do you think you have passed?'

'Lord, I don't know! There was one devilish paper — but never mind that now! The thing is that I met old Felix here, the very man I wanted!'

'Oh, yes?' Arabella said, adding with a civil smile: 'Were you up for Smalls too, sir?'

Mr Scunthorpe appeared to shrink from such a suggestion, shaking his head, and making a sound in his throat which Arabella took to be a negative.

'Of course he wasn't!' said Bertram. 'Don't I keep telling you he can't learn anything? He was visiting some friends in Oxford! He found it pretty dull work, too, didn't you, Felix? They would take him to blue-parties, all professors, and Bagwigs, and the poor fellow couldn't follow the stuff they talked. Shabby thing to do to him, for he was bound to make a cake of himself in that sort of company! However, that's not what I want to talk about. The thing is, Bella, that Felix is going to show me all the sights, because he's at home to a peg in London — been on the town ever since they threw him out of Harrow.'

'And Papa gave his consent?' exclaimed Arabella.

'As a matter of fact,' said Bertram airily, 'he don't know I'm here.'

'Doesn't know you're here?' cried Arabella.

Mr Scunthorpe cleared his throat. 'Given him the bag,' he explained. He added: 'Only thing to do.'

Arabella turned her eyes wonderingly towards her brother. He looked a little guilty, but said: 'No, you can't say I've given him the bag!'

Mr Scunthorpe corrected himself. 'Hoaxed him.'

Bertram seemed to be about to take exception to this too, but after beginning to refute it he broke off, and said: 'Well, in a way I suppose I did.'

'Bertram, you must be mad!' cried Arabella, pale with dismay. 'When Papa knows you are in town, and without leave — '

'The thing is he won't know it,' interrupted

Bertram. 'I wrote a letter to Mama, telling her I had met my friend Felix, and he had invited me to stay with him. So they won't be in a fret when I don't go back immediately, and they won't know where I am, because I didn't give my direction. And that brings me to what I particularly want to warn you about, Bella! I'm going by the name of Anstey while I'm in town, and while I don't mind if you tell this godmother of yours that I'm a friend of yours, you are not to say I'm your brother! She'd be bound to write and tell my mother, and then the fat would be in the fire!'

'But, Bertram, how can you *dare?*' asked Arabella, in an awed voice. 'Papa will be so angry!'

'Yes, I know. I shall get a rare trimming, but I shall have had a bang-up time first, and I can stand a lick or two after,' said Bertram cheerfully. 'I made up my mind I'd do it, before you came to town. Do you remember my telling you that you might get a surprise? I'll swear you never thought *this* would be it!'

'No, indeed I did not!' Arabella said, sinking into a chair. 'Oh, Bertram, I am quite in a quake! I cannot understand any of it! How can you afford to be staying in London? Are you Mr Scunthorpe's guest?'

'No, no, poor old Felix ain't standing the huff! I won a ticket in a lottery! Only think of it, Bella! A hundred pounds!'

'A lottery! Good God, what would Papa say if he knew *that?*'

'Oh, he would kick up no end of a bobbery, of

course, but I shan't tell him. And, you know, once I had won it the only thing to be done was to spend it, because you must see I had to get rid of it before Papa found I had it!' He saw that his sister was looking horrified, and said indignantly: 'I must say, I don't see why you should grudge it to me! I daresay you are having a capital time yourself!'

'No, no, how could you think I would grudge you *anything*, Bertram? But to have you in town, and to be obliged to pretend I am not your sister, and to deceive Papa and Mama — ' She stopped, remembering her own situation. 'Oh, Bertram, how *wicked* we are!'

Mr Scunthorpe looked very much alarmed at this, but Bertram said: 'Fudge! It's not telling lies precisely just not to mention that you have seen me when you write to Mama!'

'You do not know! It is worse than that!' whispered Arabella. 'Bertram, I am in such a scrape!'

He stared at her. 'You are? How is this?' He saw her glance towards his friend, and said: 'You needn't mind Felix: he's no gabster!'

Arabella was easily able to believe this, but she not unnaturally felt reluctant to disclose her story to one who was a stranger to her, even though she had already realized that if he was not to betray her unwittingly he must be taken some way at least into her confidence. Mr Scunthorpe tweaked his friend's sleeve. 'Must help your sister out of the scrape, dear boy. Happy to be of service!'

'I am very much obliged to you, sir, but no

one can help me out of it!' said Arabella tragically. 'If only you will be so kind as not to betray me!'

'Of course he won't betray you!' declared Bertram. 'What in thunder have you been about, Bella?'

'Bertram, everyone believes me to be a great heiress!' disclosed Arabella, in a stricken tone.

He stared at her for a moment, and then burst out laughing. 'You goosecap! I'll wager they don't! Why, Lady Bridlington knows you are not! You don't mean that she put such a tale about?'

She shook her head. '*I* said it!' she confessed.

'*You* said it? What the devil made you do such a thing? However, I don't suppose anyone believed you!'

'They do believe it. Lord Bridlington says that every gazetted fortune-hunter in town is dangling after me — and, oh, Bertram, it is true! I have refused *five* offers already!'

The idea that there could be found five gentlemen ready to marry his sister struck Bertram as being exquisitely humorous, and he went off into another burst of laughter. Arabella was obliged to confess the whole, since he seemed so incredulous. Her narrative was rather disjointed, since he interpolated so many questions; and at one point a considerable digression was caused by Mr Scunthorpe, who, having regarded her fixedly for some moments, suddenly became loquacious, and said: 'Beg pardon, ma'am, but did you say Mr Beaumaris?'

'Yes. He and Lord Fleetwood.'

'The Nonpareil?'

'Yes.'

Mr Scunthorpe drew a breath, and turned to address his friend. 'You hear that, Bertram?'

'Well, of course I heard it!'

'Didn't think you could have. You see this coat of mine?'

Both Tallants stared at his coat in some bewilderment.

'Got my man to copy the lapels of one Weston made for the Nonpareil,' said Mr Scunthorpe, with simple pride.

'Good God, what has that to say to anything?' demanded Bertram.

'Thought you might be interested,' explained Mr Scunthorpe apologetically.

'Never mind him!' Bertram told his sister. 'If it wasn't just like you, Bella, to fly into a miff, and go off into one of your crazy starts! Mind, I don't say I blame you! Did he spread the story over London?'

'I think it was Lord Fleetwood who did that. Mr Beaumaris told me once that he had not discussed the matter with anyone but Lord Fleetwood. Sometimes I have wondered whether — whether he had guessed the truth, but I cannot believe that he has, for he would despise me dreadfully, I am sure, if he knew how odiously I behaved, and certainly not stand up with me at all the balls — for he very seldom dances! — or take me out driving in his curricle.'

Mr Scunthorpe looked very much impressed. 'He does that?'

'Oh, yes!'

Mr Scunthorpe nodded portentously at

Bertram. 'You know what, dear boy? All the crack, your sister! Not a doubt of it: Knows all the best people. Drives out with the Nonpareil. Good thing she said she was an heiress.'

'Oh, no, no, I wish I had never done so, for it has made everything so uncomfortable!'

'Now, Bella, that's gammon! I know you! Don't you try to tell me you don't like being all the go, because I wouldn't believe you if you did!' said Bertram, with brotherly candour.

Arabella thought it over. Then she gave a reluctant smile. 'Well, yes, perhaps I do like it, but when I remember the cause of it I do indeed wish I had never said such a thing! Only consider what a fix I am in! If the truth were known now I should be utterly discredited! No one would even *bow* to me, I daresay, and I have the greatest dread that Lady Bridlington would send me home in disgrace! And then Papa would know, and — Bertram, I had almost rather throw myself into the river than have him know such a thing of me!'

'Lord, yes!' he agreed, with a shudder. 'But it won't come to that! If anyone asks *me* any prying questions, I shall say you are well known to me, and so will Felix!'

'Yes, but that is not all!' Arabella pointed out. 'I can never, never accept any offer made to me, and what Mama will think of such selfishness I dare not consider! For she so much hoped that I should form an eligible connection, and Lady Bridlington is bound to tell her that — that quite a number of *very* eligible gentlemen have paid me the most marked attentions!'

222

Bertram knit his brows over this. 'Unless — No, you're right, Bella; devilish awkward fix! You would have to tell the truth, if you accepted an offer, and ten to one he'd cry off. What a tiresome girl you are, to be sure! Dashed if I see what's to be done! Do you, Felix?'

'Very difficult situation,' responded Mr Scunthorpe, shaking his head. 'Only one thing to be done.'

'What's that?'

Mr Scunthorpe gave a diffident cough. 'Just a little thing that occurred to me. Daresay you won't care about it: can't say I care about it myself, but can't hang back when a lady's in a fix.'

'But what *is* it?'

'Mind, only a notion I had!' Mr Scunthorpe warned him. 'You don't like it: you say so! *I* don't like it, but ought to offer.' He perceived that the Tallants were quite mystified, blushed darkly, and uttered in a strangled voice: 'Marriage!'

Arabella stared at him for a moment, and then went into a peal of mirth. Bertram said scornfully: 'Of all the cork-brained notions — ! *You* don't want to marry Bella!'

'No,' conceded Mr Scunthorpe. 'Promised I would help her out of the scrape, though!'

'What's more,' Bertram said severely, 'those trustees of yours would never let you! You're not of age.'

'Talk them over,' said Mr Scunthorpe hopefully.

However, Arabella, thanking him for his kind offer, said that she did not think they would suit. He seemed grateful, and relapsed into the silence which appeared to be natural to him.

'I daresay I shall hit upon something,' said Bertram. 'I'll think about it, at all events. Should I stay to do the pretty to this godmother of yours, do you think?'

Arabella urged him strongly to do so. She was inclined to grieve over his necessary incognito, but he told her frankly that it would not at all suit him to be for ever gallanting her to the *ton* parties. 'Very dull work!' he said. 'I know you are gone civility-mad since you came to town, but it's not in my line.' He then enumerated the sights he meant to see in London, and since these seemed to consist mostly of such innocuous entertainments as Astley's Amphitheatre, the Royal Menagerie at the Tower, Madame Tussaud's Waxworks, Napoleon's carriage, on view at Bullock's Museum, a look-in at Tattersall's, the departure of the Brighton coaches from the White Horse Cellar, and the forthcoming Military Review in Hyde Park, his anxious sister's worst qualms were allayed. At first sight he had seemed to her to have grown a great deal older, for he was wearing a sophisticated waistcoat, and had brushed his hair in a new style; but when he told her about the peep-show which had diverted him so much in Coventry Street, and expressed a purely youthful desire to witness that grand spectacle, *The Burning Of Moscow* (supported by Tight-rope Walking, and an Equestrian Display) she could feel that he was still boy enough not to hanker after the more sophisticated and by far more dangerous amusements to be found in London. But, then, as he confidentially informed Mr

224

Scunthorpe, when they presently left Park Street together, females took such foolish notions into their heads that it would have been ridiculous to have disclosed to her that he had an equally ardent desire to see a bout of fisticuffs at the Fives-court, to blow a cloud with all the Corinthians at the Daffy Club, to penetrate the mysteries of the Royal Saloon, and the Peerless Pool, and certainly to put in an appearance at the Opera — not, he hastened to assure his friend, because he wanted to listen to music, but because he was credibly informed that to stroll in the Fops' Alley was famous sport, and all the go. Since he had decided, very prudently, to put up at one of the City inns, where, if he chose, he could be sure of a tolerable dinner at the Ordinary, which was very moderately priced, he entertained reasonable hopes of being able to afford all these diversions. But first, he perceived, it was necessary to buy a much higher-crowned and more curly-brimmed beaver to set on his head; a pair of Hessians with tassels; a fob, and perhaps a seal; and certainly a pair of natty yellow gloves. Without these adjuncts to a gentleman's costume he would look like a Johnny Raw. Mr Scunthorpe agreed, and ventured to point out that a driving-coat with only two shoulder-capes was thought, in well-dressed circles, to be a paltry affair. He said he would take Bertram along to his own man, a devilish clever tailor, even though he had not acquired the fame of a Weston or a Stultz. However, as the great advantage of patronizing this rising man lay in the assurance that he

225

would be willing to rig out any friend of Mr Scunthorpe's on tick, Bertram raised no objection to jumping into a hackney at once, and telling the jarvey to drive with all speed to Clifford Street. Mr Scunthorpe vouched for it that Swindon's art would give his friend quite a new touch, and as this seemed extremely desirable to Bertram, he thought he could hardly lay out a substantial sum of money to better advantage. Mr Scunthorpe then imparted to him a few useful hints, particularly warning him against such extravagances of style as must give rise to the suspicion that he belonged to the extreme dandy-set frowned upon by the real Pinks of the *Ton*. Beyond question, the finest model for any aspiring gentleman to copy was the Nonpareil, that Go amongst the Goers. This put Bertram in mind of something which had been slightly troubling his mind, and he said: 'I say, Felix, do you think my sister should be driving about the town with him? I don't mind telling you I don't like it above half!'

Here Mr Scunthorpe was able at once to allay his qualms: for a lady to drive in a curricle or a phæton, with a groom riding behind, was unexceptionable. 'Mind, it would not do for a female to go in a tilbury!' he said.

His brotherly concern relieved, Bertram abandoned the question, merely remarking that he would give a monkey to see his father's face if he knew how racketty Bella had become.

Arrived in Clifford Street, they obtained instant audience of Mr Swindon, who was so obliging as to bring out his pattern-card immediately, and to advise his new client on the respective merits of Superfine and Bath Suiting. He thought six capes would be sufficient for a light drab driving-coat, an opinion in which Mr Scunthorpe gravely concurred, explaining to Bertram that it would never do for him to ape the Goldfinches, with their row upon row of capes. Unless one was an acknowledged Nonesuch, capable of driving to an inch, or one of the Melton men, it was wiser, he said, to aim at neatness and propriety rather than the very height of fashion. He then bent his mind to the selection of a cloth for a coat, and although Bertram had not intended to order a new coat, he was persuaded to do so, as much by the assertion of Mr Swindon that a single-breasted garment of corbeau-coloured cloth, with wide lapels, and silver buttons, would set his person off to advantage, as by the whispered assurance of his friend that the snyder always gave his clients long credit. Indeed, Mr Scunthorpe was rarely troubled with his tailor's account, since that astute man of business was well aware that being a fatherless minor Mr Scunthorpe's considerable fortune was held in trust by tight-fisted guardians, who doled him out a beggarly allowance. Nothing so ungenteel as cost or payment was mentioned during the session in Clifford Street, so that Bertram left the premises torn between relief and a fear that he might have pledged his credit for a larger sum than he could afford to pay. But the novelty and excitement of a first visit to the Metropolis soon put such untimely thoughts to rout, while a lucky bet at

227

the Fives-court clearly showed the novice the easiest way of raising the wind.

A close inspection of such sprigs of fashion as were to be seen at the Fives-court made Bertram very glad to think he had bespoken a new coat, and he confided to Mr Scunthorpe that he would not visit the haunts of fashion until his clothes had been sent home. Mr Scunthorpe thought this a wise decision, and, as it was of course absurd to suppose that Bertram should kick his heels at the City inn which enjoyed his patronage, he volunteered to show him how an evening full of fun and gig could be spent in less exalted circles. This entertainment, beginning as it did in the Westminster Pit, where it seemed to the staring Bertram that representatives of every class of society, from the Corinthian to the dustman, had assembled to watch a contest between two dogs; and proceeding by way of the shops of Tothill Fields, where adventurous bucks tossed off noggins of Blue Ruin, or bumpers of heavy wet, in company with bruisers, prigs, coal-heavers, Nuns, Abbesses, and apple-women, to a coffee-shop, ended in the watch-house, Mr Scunthorpe having become bellicose under the influence of his potations. Bertram, quite unused to such quantities of liquor as he had imbibed, was too much fuddled to have any very clear notion of what circumstance it was that had excited his friend's wrath, though he had a vague idea that it was in some way connected with the advances being made by a gentleman in Petersham trousers towards a lady who had terrified him earlier in the proceedings by laying

228

a palpable lure for him. But when a mill was in progress it was not his part to enquire into the cause of it, but to enter into the fray in support of his cicerone. Since he was by no means unlearned in the noble art of self-defence, he was able to render yeoman service to Mr Scunthorpe, no proficient, and was in a fair way to milling his way out of the shop when the watch, in the shape of several Charleys, all springing their rattles, burst in upon them and, after a spirited set-to, overpowered the two peacebreakers, and hailed them off to the watch-house. Here, after considerable parley, conducted for the defence by the experienced Mr Scunthorpe, they were admitted to bail, and warned to present themselves next day in Bow Street, not a moment later than twelve o'clock. The night-constable then packed them both into a hackney, and they drove to Mr Scunthorpe's lodging in Clarges Street, where Bertram passed what little was left of the night on the sofa in his friend's sitting-room. He awoke later with a splitting headache, no very clear recollection of the late happenings, but a lively dread of the possible consequences of what he feared had been a very bosky evening. However, when Mr Scunthorpe's man had revived his master, and he emerged from his bedchamber, he was soon able to allay any such misgivings. 'Nothing to be in a fret for, dear boy!' he said. 'Been piloted to the lighthouse scores of times! Watchman will produce broken lantern in evidence — they always do it! — you give false name, pay fine, and all's right!'

So, indeed, it proved, but the experience a

little shocked the Vicar's son. This, coupled with the extremely unpleasant after-effects of drinking innumerable flashes of lightning, made him determine to be more circumspect in future. He spent several days in pursuing such harmless amusements as witnessing a badger drawn in a menagerie in Holborn, losing his heart to Miss O'Neill from a safe position in the pit, and being introduced by Mr Scunthorpe into Gentleman Jackson's exclusive Boxing School in Bond Street. Here he was much impressed by the manners and dignity of the proprietor (whose decision in all matters of sport, Mr Scunthorpe informed him, was accepted as final by patrician and plebeian alike), and was gratified by a glimpse of such notable amateurs as Mr Beaumaris, Lord Fleetwood, young Mr Terrington, and Lord Withernsea. He had a little practise with the single-stick with one of Jackson's assistants, felt himself honoured by receiving a smiling word of encouragement from the great Jackson himself, and envied the assurance of the Goes who strolled in, exchanged jests with Jackson, who treated them with the same degree of civility as he showed to his less exalted pupils, and actually enjoyed bouts with the ex-champion himself. He was quick to see that no consideration of rank or consequence was enough to induce Jackson to allow a client to plant a hit upon his person, unless his prowess deserved such a reward; and from having entered the saloon with a feeling of superiority he swiftly reached the realization that in the Corinthian world excellence counted for more than lineage. He heard Jackson say chidingly to the great Nonpareil himself (who stripped to remarkable advantage, he noticed) that he was out of training; and from that moment his highest ambition was to put on the gloves with this peerless master of the art.

At the end of a week, Mr Swindon, urged thereto by Mr Scunthorpe, delivered the new clothes, and, after purchasing such embellishments to his costume as a tall cane, a fob, and a Marseilles waistcoat, Bertram ventured to show himself in the Park, at the fashionable hour of five o'clock. Here he had the felicity of seeing Lord Coleraine, Georgy à Cock-horse, prancing down Rotten Row on his mettlesome steed; Lord Morton, on his long-tailed gray; and, amongst the carriages, Tommy Onslow's curricle; a number of dashing gigs and tilburies; the elegant barouches of the ladies; and Mr Beaumaris's yellow-winged phæton-and-four, which he appeared to be able to turn within a space so small as to seem impossible to any mere whipster. Nothing would do for Bertram after that but to repair to the nearest jobmaster's stables, and to arrange for the hire of a showy chestnut hack. Whatever imperfections might attach to the bearing and style of a young gentleman from the country, Bertram knew himself to be a bruising rider, and in this guise determined to show himself to the society which his sister already adorned.

As luck would have it, he encountered her on the day when he first sallied forth, mounted upon his hired hack. She was sitting up beside Mr Beaumaris in his famous phæton, animatedly

231

describing to him the scene of the Drawing-room in which she had taken humble part. This event had necessarily occupied her thoughts so much during the past week that she had been able to spare very few for the activities of her adventurous brother. But when she caught sight of him, trotting along on his chestnut hack, she exclaimed, and said impulsively: 'Oh, it is — Mr Anstey! Do pray stop, Mr Beaumaris!'

He drew up his team obediently, while she waved to Bertram. He brought his hack up to the phæton, and bowed politely, only slightly quizzing her with his eyes. Mr Beaumaris, glancing indifferently at him, caught this arch look, became aware of a slight tension in the trim figure beside him, and looked under his lazy eyelids from one to the other.

'How do you do? How do you go on?' said Arabella, stretching out her hand in its glove of white kid.

Bertram bowed over it very creditably, and replied: 'Famously! I mean to come — I mean to visit you some morning, Miss Tallant!'

'Oh, yes, please do!' Arabella looked up at her escort, blushed, and stammered: 'May I p-present Mr Anstey to you, Mr Beaumaris? He — he is a friend of mine!'

'How do you do?' responded Mr Beaumaris politely. 'From Yorkshire, Mr Anstey?'

'Oh, yes! I have known Miss Tallant since I was in short coats!' grinned Bertram.

'You will certainly be much envied by Miss Tallant's numerous admirers,' responded Mr Beaumaris. 'Are you staying in town?'

232

'Just a short visit, you know!' Bertram's gaze reverted to the team harnessed to the phæton, all four of them on the fret. 'I say, sir, that's a bang-up team you have in hand!' he said, with all his sister's impulsiveness. 'Oh, don't look at this hack of mine — showy, but I never crossed a greater slug in my life!'

'You hunt, Mr Anstey?'

'Yes, with my uncle's pack, in Yorkshire. Of course, it is not like the Quorn country, or the Pytchley, but we get some pretty good runs, I can tell you!' Bertram confided.

'Mr Anstey,' interrupted Arabella, fixing him with a very compelling look, 'I think Lady Bridlington has sent you a card for her ball: I hope you mean to come!'

'Well, you know, Bel — Miss Tallant!' said Bertram, with disastrous lack of gallantry, 'that sort of mummery is not much in my line!' He perceived an anguished expression in her eyes, and added hastily: 'That is, delighted, I am sure! Yes, yes, I shall be there! And I shall hope to have the honour of standing up with you!' he ended punctiliously.

Mr Beaumaris was obliged to pay attention to his team, but he did not miss the minatory note in Arabella's voice as she said: 'I collect we are to have the pleasure of receiving a visit from you *tomorrow*, sir!'

'Oh!' said Bertram. 'Yes, of course! As a matter of fact, I shall be taking a look-in at Tattersall's, but — Yes, to be sure! I'll come to visit you all right and tight!'

He then doffed his new hat, and bowed, and

rode off at an easy canter. Arabella appeared to be conscious that some explanation was called for. She said airily: 'You must know, sir, that we have been brought up almost as — as brother and sister!'

'I thought perhaps you had,' responded Mr Beaumaris gravely.

She glanced sharply up at his profile. He seemed to be wholly absorbed in the task of manœuvring the phæton through a gap between a dowager's landaulet and a smart barouche with a crest on the panel. She reassured herself with the reflection that whereas she favoured her Mama, Bertram was said to be the image of what the Vicar had been at the same age, and said, 'But I was telling you about the Drawing-room, and how graciously the Princess Mary smiled at me! She was wearing the most magnificent toilet I ever saw in my life! Lady Bridlington tells me that when she was young she was thought to be the most handsome of all the princesses. I thought she looked to be very good-natured.'

Mr Beaumaris agreed to it, reserving to himself his enjoyment in hearing this innocent description of the Regent's most admired sister. Miss Tallant, entrancing him with one of her unguarded moments of naivety, then told him of the elegant, gilt-edged card of invitation which had arrived that very day in Park Street from no less a personage than the Lord Chamberlain, who informed Lady Bridlington that he was commanded by his Royal Highness the Prince Regent to invite her, and Miss Tallant, to a Dress-party at Carlton House on Thursday next, to have the honour of meeting (in large capitals) Her Majesty The Queen. He said that he should be on the look-out for her at Carlton House, and refrained from observing that the Regent's parties, planned as they were on a magnificent scale which offended the taste of such arbiters of true elegance as himself, were amongst the worst squeezes in town, and had even been known to include such vulgarities as a fountain playing in the middle of the dinner-table to which he had himself been bidden.

He entered into her feelings upon this event with far more sympathy than did Bertram, when he presented himself in Park Street on the following afternoon. Lady Bridlington having retired, as she always did, to her couch, to recruit her energies for an evening to be spent at no fewer than four different parties, Arabella was able to enjoy the luxury of a tête-à-tête with her favourite brother. While acknowledging handsomely that he was glad to think of her being invited to Carlton House, he said that he supposed there would be a vast rout of fashionables present, and that for himself he preferred to spend his evenings in a simpler style. He further begged her not to favour him with a description of the gown she meant to wear. She perceived that he was not much interested in her social triumphs, and turned willingly enough to his own chosen amusements. He was slightly evasive on this subject, replying to her questions in general terms. His experience of the female sex had not led him to indulge his imagination with the belief that even an adoring sister would regard with favour such delights as a visit to Cribb's Parlour, where he had actually handled the Champion's famous silver cup, presented to him after his last fight, some years previously, against Molyneux, the Black; the blowing of a cloud at the Daffy Club, surrounded by young Bloods of the Fancy, veterans of the Ring, promising novices, and an array of portraits hanging round the walls of past champions whose very names filled him with awe; or a lounge through the famous Saloon at Covent Garden, where the bold, ogling glances of the Cyprians who made this haunt their hunting-ground both shocked and terrified him. Nor did he tell her of an assignation he had made with a new acquaintance, encountered at Tattersall's that very morning. He had seen at a glance that Mr Jack Carnaby was quite the thing — almost a Tulip of Fashion, in fact, if dress and air were anything to judge by — but something warned him that Arabella would regard with horror his approaching introduction into a snug little gaming-house under the auspices of this gentleman. It would be of very little use to assure her that he was going merely for the experience, and had not the least intention of gaming away his precious blunt; even his knowledgeable cicerone had shaken his head over this new scheme, and had uttered cryptic warnings against ivory-turners and Greek banditti, adding that his uncle and principal trustee held that it was a good flat that was never down. He said that he had himself proved the truth of this excellent maxim, but since he owned, upon

236

enquiry, that nothing was known to Mr Carnaby's discredit, Bertram paid scant heed to his advice. Mr Carnaby led him to a discreet house in Pall Mall, where, upon knocking in a certain fashion on the door, they were inspected through a grille, and finally admitted. Nothing could have been further removed from Bertram's expectations of what a gaming-hell would be like than the decorous house in which he found himself. The various servants were all very respectable men, with quiet manners, and it would have been hard to have found a more civil or obliging host than the proprietor. Never having indulged in any game more dashing than whist, Bertram spent some time in looking-on, but when he thought he had mastered the rules governing hazard, he ventured to join that table, armed with a modest rouleau. He soon perceived that Mr Scunthorpe had been quite at fault in his talk of Fulhams, and up-hills, for he enjoyed a run of astonishing luck, and came away at last with his pocket so full of guineas that he had no longer any need to worry over his growing expenses. A lucky bet at Tattersall's on the following day put him in a fair way to thinking himself at home on the Turf and at the Table, and it was not to be expected that he would lend any but an impatient ear to Mr. Scunthorpe's dark prophecy that having got into Tow Street he would end up in the clutch of a Bum-trap.

'Know what my uncle says?' Mr Scunthorpe demanded. 'They always let a flat win the first time he goes to a hell. Hedge off, dear boy! they'll queer you on that suit!'

'Oh, fudge!' retorted Bertram. 'I hope I'm not such a gudgeon as to dip too deeply! I'll tell you what, Felix, I *would* like to play just once at Watier's, if you could contrive it for me!'

'What?' gasped Mr Scunthorpe. 'Dear old boy, they would never let you set foot inside the Great-Go, upon my honour they would not! Why, I've never played there myself! Much better go to Vauxhall! Might meet your sister there! See the Grand Cascade! Listen to the Pandean band! All the crack, you know!'

'Oh, dull work, when I might be trying my luck at faro!' said Bertram.

11

From the Daffy Club to Limmer's Hotel in
Conduit Street was an inevitable step for any
young gentleman interested in the Fancy to take.
Here were to be found all the Pets of the Ring,
and the Corinthians who patronized them.
Bertram went there under the auspices of Mr
Scunthorpe, who was anxious to turn his friend's
thoughts away from more dangerous haunts. He
had begun to acquire acquaintances in London,
and was thus in the proud position of
exchanging greetings with several of the men
present. He and Mr Scunthorpe sat down in one
of the boxes, and Mr Scunthorpe painstakingly
pointed out to him all the notabilities he could
see, including a very down-the-road looking man
who, he whispered, could be trusted to tip a man
the office what to back in any race. He then
excused himself, and bore down upon this
knowledgeable person, and became absorbed in
conversation with him. While he was thus
engaged, Bertram saw Mr Beaumaris stroll in
with a party of friends, but as he had by this time
fully grasped the exalted position occupied by
the Nonpareil he was flattered beyond measure
when, after raising his glass and regarding him
through it for a moment, Mr Beaumaris walked
across the sanded floor, and sat down at his
table, saying with a slight smile: 'Did I not meet
you in the Park the other day? Mr — er

— Anstey, I believe?'

Bertram acknowledged it, flushing shyly; but when Mr Beaumaris added casually: 'You are related to Miss Tallant, I collect?' he made haste to deny any relationship, adding that Miss Tallant was quite above his touch. Mr Beaumaris accepted this without comment, and asked him where he was putting up in town. Bertram saw no harm in disclosing his direction, or even in telling Mr Beaumaris that this was his first visit to the Metropolis.

It was the expressed opinion of Mr Jack Carnaby that the Nonpareil was a haughty, disagreeable kind of man, but Bertram was unable to trace the least sign of haughtiness, or of reserve, in his manners. Mr Beaumaris's intimates could have informed Mr Tallant that while no one could be more snubbing, no one, on the other hand, could be — when he chose — more sympathetic. In less than no time, Bertram, forgetting his bashfulness, was confiding far more to his grand new acquaintance than he had the least idea of. Mr Beaumaris, himself a Melton man, complimented him on his seat on a horse, and any barrier Bertram might have raised between himself and the author of his sister's predicament crumbled at this touch. He was led on to describe the country over which he hunted, the exact locality of Heythram, and his own impossible ambitions, without having the smallest suspicion that all this information was being skilfully extracted from him. He told Mr Beaumaris about Smalls, and his hopes of adorning the Home Office, and when Mr

Beaumaris said, with a humorous lift to one eyebrow, that he should not have supposed him to have had parliamentary ambitions, he blurted out his real ambition, ending by saying wistfully: 'But it can't be, of course. Only I would have liked of all things to have been able to have joined a cavalry regiment!'

'I think you would do very well in a cavalry regiment,' agreed Mr Beaumaris, rising, as Mr Scunthorpe came back to the table. 'Meanwhile, do not draw the bustle with too much of a vengeance during this visit of yours to London!' He nodded to Mr Scunthorpe, and walked away, leaving that gentleman to explain to Bertram with the utmost earnestness just how greatly he had been honoured.

But Mr Beaumaris, quelling the ecstatic advances of his canine admirer, an hour or two later, said: 'If you had any real regard for me, Ulysses, you would be greeting me with condolences rather than with these uncalled-for raptures.'

Ulysses, considerably plumper, and with his flying ear more rebellious than ever, and his tail even more tightly curled over his back, stretched worshipfully before the god of his idolatry, and uttered an encouraging bark. After that he bustled to the door of the library, and plainly invited Mr Beaumaris to enter, and partake of refreshment there. Brough, tenderly relieving his master of his long cloak, and his hat and gloves, remarked that it was wonderful how knowing the little dog was.

'It is wonderful what encouragement he has

received from my staff to continue to burden me with his unwanted presence in my house!' retorted Mr Beaumaris acidly.

Brough, who had dealt with Mr Beaumaris for many years, permitted himself to give what in a lesser personage would have been a grin, and to say: 'Well, sir, if I had *known* you wanted him chased off, I'm sure I'd have done my best! Not but what he's so devoted to you that I doubt if he'd have gone, setting aside that it would go to my heart to chase off a dog that handles Alphonse like this one does.'

'If that misbegotten animal has been upsetting Alphonse, I'll wring his neck!' promised Mr Beaumaris.

'Oh, no, sir, nothing of that sort! When you're out, and Ulysses comes downstairs (as come he does), he behaves to Alphonse as though he hadn't had a bite to eat in a month, nor wouldn't think of touching so much as a scrap of meat he found on the kitchen floor. Well, as I said to Mrs Preston, if ever a dog could speak, that one does, telling Alphonse as plain as a Christian that he's the only friend he's got in the world. Quite won Alphonse over, he has. In fact, when two nice loin chops was found to be missing, Alphonse would have it the undercook was accusing the dog of having stolen them only to cover up his own carelessness, and Ulysses sitting there looking as if he didn't know what a chop tasted like. He buried the bones under the rug in your study, sir, but I have removed them.'

'You are not only an ill favoured specimen,' Mr Beaumaris informed Ulysses severely, 'but you have all the faults of the under-bred: toadeating, duplicity, and impudence!'

Ulysses sat down to relieve the irritation of a healing wound by a hearty scratch. He was rebuked, and since he had heard that note in Mr Beaumaris's voice before — as when he had expressed a vociferous desire to share his bedchamber with him — he stopped scratching, and flattened his ears placatingly.

Mr Beaumaris poured himself out a glass of wine, and sat down with it in his favourite chair. Ulysses sat before him, and sighed deeply. 'Yes, I daresay,' said Mr Beaumaris, 'but I have something better to do than to spend my time spreading ointment on your sores. You should remember, moreover, that you cannot be permitted to meet your benefactress again until you are entirely healed.' Ulysses yawned at him, and lay down with his head on his paws, as one who found the conversation tedious. Mr Beaumaris stirred him with one foot. 'I wonder if you are right?' he mused. 'A month ago I should have been sure of it. Yet I let her saddle me with a foundling-brat, and a mongrel-cur — you will forgive my plain speaking, Ulysses! — and I am now reasonably certain that neither of you is destined to be the most tiresome of my responsibilities. Do you suppose that that wretched youth is masquerading under a false name for reasons of his own, or in support of her pretensions? Do not look at me like that! You may consider that experience should have taught me wisdom, but I do not believe that it was all a clever plot to inveigle me into declaring myself. I am not even sure that she regards me with more than tolerance. In fact, Ulysses, I am not very sure of anything — and I think I will pay my grandmother a long overdue visit.'

In pursuance of this resolve, Mr Beaumaris sent for his curricle next morning. Ulysses, who had shared his breakfast, bundled ahead of him down the steps of his house, leaped into the curricle, and disposed himself on the passenger's seat with all the air of a dog born into the purple.

'No!' said Mr Beaumaris forcibly. Ulysses descended miserably from the curricle, and prostrated himself on the flag-way. 'Let me tell you, my friend,' said Mr Beaumaris, 'that I have a certain reputation to maintain, which your disreputable appearance would seriously jeopardize! Do not be alarmed! — I am not, alas, going out of your life for ever!' He climbed into the curricle, and said: 'You may stop grinning, Clayton, and let 'em go!'

'Yes, sir!' said his groom, obeying both these behests, and swinging himself expertly up on to the curricle as it passed him. After a minute or two, having twice glanced over his shoulder, he ventured to inform Mr Beaumaris that the little dog was following him.

Mr Beaumaris uttered an oath, and reined in his reluctant pair. The faithful hound, plodding valiantly along, with heaving ribs, and several inches of tongue hanging from his parted jaws, came up with the curricle, and once more abased himself in the road. 'Damn you' said Mr. Beaumaris. 'I suppose you are capable of following me all the way to Wimbledon! It now remains to be seen whether my credit is good enough to enable me to carry you off. Get up!'

Ulysses was very much out of breath, but at these words he mustered up enough strength to scramble into the curricle once more. He wagged a grateful tail, climbed on to the seat beside Mr Beaumaris, and sat there panting blissfully. Mr Beaumaris read him a short lecture on the evils of blackmail, which sorely tried the self-control of his groom, discouraged him peremptorily from hurling a challenge at a mere pedestrian dog in the gutter, and proceeded on his way to Wimbledon.

The Dowager Duchess of Wigan, who was the terror of four sons, three surviving daughters, numerous grandchildren, her man of business, her lawyer, her physician, and a host of dependants, greeted her favourite grandson characteristically. He found her imbibing nourishment in the form of slices of toast dipped in tea, and bullying the unmarried daughter who lived with her. She had been a great belle in her day, and the ravages of her former beauty were still discernible in the delicate bones of her face. She had a way of looking at her visitors with an eagle-like stare, had never been known to waste politeness on anyone, and was scathingly contemptuous of everything modern. Her children were inordinately proud of her, and lived in dread of her periodical commands to them to present themselves at her house. Upon her butler's ushering Mr Beaumaris into her morning-room, she directed one of her piercing looks at him, and said: 'Oh! So it's you, is it? Why haven't you been to see me since I don't know when?'

Mr Beaumaris, bowing deeply over her hand, replied imperturbably: 'On the occasion of my last visit, ma'am, you told me you did not wish to see me again until I had mended my ways.'

'Well, have you?' said the Duchess, conveying another slip of soaked toast to her mouth.

'Certainly, ma'am: I am in a fair way to becoming a philanthropist,' he replied, turning to greet his aunt.

'I don't want any more of *them* about me,' said her grace. 'It turns my stomach enough already to have to sit here watching Caroline at her everlasting knitting for the poor. In *my* day, we gave 'em vails, and there was an end to it. Not that I believe you. Here, take this pap away, Caroline, and ring the bell! Maudling one's inside with tea never did any good to anyone yet, and never will. I'll tell Hadleigh to fetch up a bottle of Madeira — the lot your grandfather laid down, not that rubbish Wigan sent me t'other day!'

Lady Caroline removed the tray, but asked her parent in a shrinking tone if she thought that Dr Sudbury would approve.

'Sudbury's an old woman, and you're a fool, Caroline!' replied the Duchess. 'You go away, and leave me to talk to Robert! I never could abide a pack of females hangin' round me!' She added, as Lady Caroline gathered up her knitting: 'Tell Hadleigh the *good* Madeira! He knows. Well, sir, what have you to say for yourself now you *have* had the impudence to show your face here again?'

Mr Beaumaris, closing the door behind his aunt, came back into the room, and said with deceptive meekness that he was happy to find his grandmother in such excellent health and spirits.

'Graceless jackanapes!' retorted the Duchess with relish. She ran her eye over his handsome person. 'You look very well — at least, you would if you didn't make such a figure of yourself in that rig! When I was a girl, no gentleman would have dreamed of paying a social call without powder, let me tell you! Enough to make your grandfather turn in his grave to see what you've all come to, with your skimpy coats, and your starched collars, and not a bit of lace to your neckcloth, or your wristbands! If you can sit down in those skin-tight breeches, or pantaloons, or whatever you call 'em, do so!'

'Oh, yes, I can sit down!' said Mr Beaumaris, disposing himself in a chair opposite to hers. 'My pantaloons, like Aunt Caroline's gifts to the poor, are knitted, and so adapt themselves reasonably well to my wishes.'

'Ha! Then I'll tell Caroline to knit you a pair for Christmas. That'll send her into hysterics, for a bigger prude I never met!'

'Very likely, ma'am, but as I am sure that my aunt would obey you, however much her modesty was offended, I must ask you to refrain. The embroidered slippers which reached me last Christmas tried me high enough. I wonder what she thought I should do with them?'

The Duchess gave a cackle of laughter. 'Lord

bless you, she don't *think!* You shouldn't send her handsome gifts.'

'I send you very handsome gifts,' murmured Mr Beaumaris, 'but you never reciprocate!'

'No, and I never shall. You've got more than's good for you already. What have you brought me this time?'

'Nothing at all — unless you have a fancy for a mongrel-dog?'

'I can't abide dogs, or cats either. Fifty thousand a year if you've a penny, and you don't bring me as much as a posy! Out with it, Robert! what did you come for?'

'To ask you whether you think I should make a tolerable husband, ma'am.'

'What?' exclaimed her grace, sitting bolt upright in her chair, and grasping the arms with her frail, jewelled hands. 'You're never going to offer for the Dewsbury girl?'

'Good God, no!'

'Oh, so that's yet another idiot who's wearing the willow for you, is it?' said her grace, who had her own ways of discovering what was going on in the world from which she had retired. 'Who is it now? One of these days you'll go a step too far, mark my words!'

'I think I have,' said Mr Beaumaris.

She stared at him, but before she could speak her butler had entered the room, staggering under a specimen of the ducal plate which her grace had categorically refused to relinquish to the present Duke, on the twofold score that it was her personal property, and that he shouldn't have married anyone who gave his mother such a belly-ache as that die-away ninny he had set in her place. This impressive tray Hadleigh set down on the table, casting, as he did so, a very expressive look at Mr Beaumaris. Mr Beaumaris nodded his understanding, and rose, and went to pour out the wine. He handed his grandmother a modest half-glass, to which she instantly took exception, demanding to know whether he had the impertinence to suppose that she could not carry her wine.

'I daresay you can drink me under the table,' replied Mr Beaumaris, 'but you know very well it's extremely bad for your health, and also that you cannot bully me into pandering to your outrageous commands.' He then lifted her disengaged hand to his lips, and said gently: 'You are a rude and an overbearing old woman, ma'am, but I hope you may live to be a hundred, for I like you so much better than any other of my relatives!'

'I daresay that's not saying much,' she remarked, rather pleased by this audacious speech. 'Sit down again, and don't try to hoax me with any of your faradiddles! I can see you're going to make a fool of yourself, so you needn't wrap it up in clean linen! You haven't come here to tell me you're going to marry that brass-faced lightskirt you had in keeping when I last saw you?'

'I have not!' said Mr Beaumaris.

'Just as well, for laced mutton being brought into the family is what I won't put up with! Not that I think you're fool enough for that.'

'Where *do* you learn your abominable

expressions, ma'am?' demanded Mr Beaumaris.

'*I* don't belong to your mealy-mouthed generation, thank God! Who is she?'

'If I did not know from bitter experience, ma'am, that nothing occurs in London but what you are instantly aware of it, I should say that you had never heard of her. She is — or at any rate, she says she is — the latest heiress.'

'Oh! Do you mean the chit that that silly Bridlington woman, has staying with her? I'm told she's a beauty.'

'She *is* beautiful,' acknowledged Mr Beaumaris. 'But that's not it.'

'Well, what is it?'

He reflected. 'She is the most enchanting little wretch I ever encountered,' he said. 'When she is trying to convince me that she is up to every move in the social game, she contrives to appear much like any other female, but when, as happens all too often for my comfort, her compassion is stirred, she is ready to go to any lengths to succour the object of her pity. If I marry her, she will undoubtedly expect me to launch a campaign for the alleviation of the lot of climbing-boys, and will very likely turn my house into an asylum for stray curs.'

'Oh, she will, will she?' said her grace, staring at him with knit brows. 'Why?'

'Well, she has already foisted a specimen of each on to me,' he explained. 'No, perhaps I wrong her. Ulysses she certainly foisted on to me, but the unspeakable Jemmy I actually offered to take under my protection.'

The Duchess brought her hand down on the

arm of her chair. 'Stop trying to gammon me!' she commanded. 'Who is Ulysses, and who is Jemmy?'

'I have already offered to make you a present of Ulysses,' Mr Beaumaris reminded her. 'Jemmy is a small climbing-boy whose manifest wrongs Miss Tallant is determined to set right. I wish you might have heard her telling Bridlington that he cared for nothing but his own comfort, like all the rest of us; and asking poor Charles Fleetwood to imagine what his state might now be had he been reared by a drunken foster-mother, and sold into slavery to a sweep. Alas that I was not privileged to witness her encounter with the sweep! I understand that she drove him from the house with threats of prosecution. I am not at all surprised that he cowered before her: I have seen her disperse a group of louts.'

'She sounds to me an odd sort of a gal,' remarked her grace. 'Is she a lady?'

'Unquestionably.'

'Who's her father?'

'That, ma'am, is a mystery I have hopes that you may be able to unravel.'

'I?' she exclaimed. 'I don't know what you think I can tell you!'

'I have reason to believe that her home is within easy reach of Harrowgate, ma'am, and I recall that you visited that watering-place not so very long ago. You may have seen her at an Assembly — I suppose they do have Assemblies at Harrowgate? — or have heard her family spoken of.'

'Well, I didn't!' replied her grace bitterly. 'What's more I don't want to hear anything more about Harrowgate! A nasty, cold, shabby-genteel place, with the filthiest waters I ever tasted in my life! They did me no good at all, as anyone but a fool like that snivelling leech of mine would have known from the outset! Assemblies, indeed! It's no pleasure to me to watch a parcel of country-dowds dancing this shameless waltz of yours! Dancing! *I* could give you another name for it!'

'I have no doubt that you could, ma'am, but I must beg you to spare my blushes! Moreover, for one who is for ever railing against the squeamishness of the modern miss, your attitude towards the waltz seems a trifle inconsistent.'

'I don't know anything about consistency,' retorted her grace, with perfect truth, 'but I do know indecency when I see it!'

'We are wandering from the point,' said Mr Beaumaris firmly.

'Well, I never met any Tallants in Harrowgate, or anywhere else. When I wasn't trying to swallow something that no one is ever going to make me believe wasn't drained off from the kennels, I was sitting watching your aunt knot a fringe in the most uncomfortable hole of a lodging I've been in yet! Why, I had to take all my own bed-linen with me!'

'You always do, ma'am,' said Mr Beaumaris, who had several times been privileged to see the start of one of the Duchess's impressive journeys. 'Also your own plate, your favourite chair, your steward, your — '

'I don't want any of your impudence, Robert!' interrupted her grace. 'I don't always *have* to take 'em!' She gave her shawl a twitch. 'It's nothing to me whom you marry,' she said. 'But why you must needs dangle after a wealthy woman beats me!'

'Oh, I don't think she has any fortune at all!' replied Mr Beaumaris coolly. 'She only said she had to put me in my place.'

He came under her eagle-stare again. 'Put you in your place? Are you going to tell me, sir, that she ain't tumbling over herself to catch you?'

'Far from it. She holds me at arm's length. I cannot even be sure that she has even the smallest *tendre* for me.'

'Been seen in your company often enough, hasn't she?' said her grace sharply.

'Yes, she says it does her a great deal of good socially to be seen with me,' said Mr Beaumaris pensively.

'Either she's a devilish deep 'un,' said her grace, a gleam in her eye, 'or she's a good gal! Lord, I didn't think there was one of these niminy-piminy modern gals alive that had enough spirit not to toadeat you! Should I like her?'

'Yes, I think you would, but to tell you the truth, ma'am, I don't care a button whether you like her or not.'

Surprisingly, she took no exception to this, but nodded, and said: 'You'd better marry her. Not if she ain't of gentle blood, though. You ain't a Caldicot of Wigan, but you come of good stock. I wouldn't have let your mother marry into your

253

family if it hadn't been one of the best — not for five times the settlements your father made on her!' She added reminiscently: 'A fine gal, Maria: I liked her better than any other of my brats.'

'So did I,' agreed Mr Beaumaris, rising from his chair. 'Shall I propose to Arabella, risking a rebuff, or shall I address myself to the task of convincing her that I am not the incorrigible flirt she has plainly been taught to think me?'

'It's no use asking me,' said her grace unhelpfully. 'It wouldn't do you any harm to get a good set-down, but I don't mind your bringing the gal to see me one day.' She held out her hand to him, but when he had punctiliously kissed it, and would have released it, her talon-like fingers closed on his, and she said: 'Out with it, sir! What's vexing you, eh?'

He smiled at her. 'Not precisely that, ma'am — but I have the stupidest wish that she would tell me the truth!'

'Pooh, why should she?'

'I can think of only one reason, ma'am. That is what vexes me!' said Mr Beaumaris.

12

On his way home from Wimbledon, Mr Beaumaris drove up Bond Street, and was so fortunate as to see Arabella, accompanied by a prim-looking maidservant, come out of Hookham's Library. He pulled up immediately, and she smiled, and walked up to the curricle, exclaiming: 'Oh, how much better he looks! I told you he would! Well, you dear little dog, do you remember me, I wonder?'

Ulysses wagged his tail in a perfunctory manner, suffered her to stretch up a hand to caress him, but yawned.

'For heaven's sake, Ulysses, try to acquire a little polish!' Mr Beaumaris admonished him.

Arabella laughed. 'Is that what you call him? Why?'

'Well, he seemed, on the evidence, to have led a roving life, and judging by the example we saw it must have been adventurous,' explained Mr Beaumaris.

'Very true!' She watched Ulysses look up adoringly into his face, and said: 'I knew he would grow to be attached to you: only see how he looks at you!'

'His affection, Miss Tallant, threatens to become a serious embarrassment.'

'Nonsense! I am sure you must be fond of him, or you would not take him out with you!'

'If that is what you think, ma'am, you can have

no idea of the depths to which he can sink to achieve his own ends. Blackmail is an open book to him. He is well aware that I dare not deny him, lest I should lose what little reputation I may have in your eyes.'

'How absurd you are! I knew, as soon as I saw how well you handled him, that you know just how to use a dog. I am so glad you have kept him with you.'

She gave Ulysses a last pat, and stepped back on to the flag-way. Mr Beaumaris said: 'Will you not give me the pleasure of driving you to your door?'

'No, indeed, it is only a step!'

'No matter: send your maid home! Ulysses adds his entreaties to mine.'

As Ulysses chose this moment to scratch one ear, this made her laugh.

'Mere bashfulness,' explained Mr Beaumaris, stretching down his hand. 'Come!'

'Very well — since Ulysses wishes it so much!' she said, taking his hand, and climbing into the curricle. 'Mr Beaumaris will see me home, Maria.'

He spread a light rug across her knees, and said over his shoulder: 'I have recalled, Clayton, that I need something from the chemist's. Go and buy me a — a gum-plaster! You may walk home.'

'Very good, sir,' said the groom, at his most wooden, and sprang down into the road.

'A *gum-plaster*?' echoed Arabella, turning wide eyes of astonishment upon Mr Beaumaris. 'What in the world can you want with such a thing, sir?'

'Rheumatism,' said Mr Beaumaris defiantly, setting his horses in motion.

'*You?* Oh, no, you must be quizzing me!'

'Not at all. I was merely seeking an excuse to be rid of Clayton. I hope Ulysses will prove himself an adequate chaperon. I have something to say to you, Miss Tallant, for which I do not desire an audience.'

She had been stroking the dog, but her hands were stilled at this, and the colour receded from her cheeks. Rather breathlessly, she asked: 'What is it?'

'Will you do me the honour of becoming my wife?'

She was stunned, and for a moment could not utter a word. When she was able to control her voice a little, she said, 'I think you *must* be quizzing me.'

'You must know that I am not.'

She trembled. 'Yes, yes, let us say that that was all it was, if you please! I am very much obliged to you, but I cannot marry you!'

'May I know why you cannot, Miss Tallant?'

She was afraid that she was about to burst into tears, and answered in a shaken tone: 'There are many reasons. Pray believe it is impossible!'

'Are you quite sure that these reasons are insuperable?' he asked.

'Quite, quite sure! Oh, please do not urge me further! I had never dreamed — it never entered my head — I would not for the world have given you cause to suppose — Oh, *please* say no more, sir!'

He bowed, and was silent. She sat staring

down at her clasped hands in great agitation of spirit, her mind in a turmoil, tossed between surprise at such a declaration, coming from one whom she had believed to have been merely amusing himself, and the shock of realizing, for the first time, that there was no one she would rather marry than Mr Beaumaris.

After a slight pause, he said in his usual calm way: 'I believe there is always a little awkwardness attached to such situations as this in which we now find ourselves. We must strive not to allow it to overcome us. Is Lady Bridlington's ball to rank amongst the season's greatest squeezes?'

She was grateful to him for easing the tension, and all the discomfort of the moment, and tried to reply naturally. 'Yes, indeed, it is! I am sure quite three hundred cards of invitation have been sent out. Shall — shall you find time to look in, I wonder?'

'Yes, and shall hope that even though you will not *marry* me you may be persuaded to *dance* with me.'

She replied she scarcely knew what: it was largely inaudible. He shot a quick look at her averted profile, hesitated, and then said nothing. They had reached Park Street by this time, and in another moment he had handed her down from the curricle.

'Do not come with me to the door! I know you do not like to leave your horses!' she said, in a hurried tone. 'Good-bye! I shall see you at the ball.'

He waited until he had seen her admitted into

the house, and then got into the curricle again, and drove off. Ulysses nudged his nose under his arm. 'Thank you,' he said dryly. 'Do you think I am unreasonable to wish that she would trust me enough to tell me the truth?'

Ulysses sighed heavily; he was rather sleepy after his day in the country.

'I suppose I shall end by telling her that I have known it all along. And yet — Yes, Ulysses, I am quite unreasonable. Did it seem to you that she was not as indifferent to me as she would have had me believe?'

Understanding that something was expected of him, his admirer uttered a sound between a yelp and a bark, and furiously wagged his tail.

'You feel that I should persevere?' said Mr Beaumaris. 'I was, in fact, too precipitate. You may be right. But if she had cared at all, would she not have told me the truth?'

Ulysses sneezed.

'At all events,' remarked Mr Beaumaris, 'she was undoubtedly pleased with me for bringing you out with me.'

Whether it was due to this circumstance, or to Ulysses' unshakeable conviction that he was born to be a carriage-dog, Mr Beaumaris continued to take him about. Those of his intimates who saw Ulysses, once they had recovered from the initial shock, were of the opinion that the Nonpareil was practising some mysterious jest on society, and only one earnest imitator went so far as to adopt an animal of mixed parentage to ride in his own carriage. He thought that if the Nonpareil was setting a new fashion it would become so much the rage that it might be difficult hereafter to acquire a suitable mongrel. But Mr Warkworth, a more profound thinker, censured this act as being rash and unconsidered. 'Remember when the Nonpareil wore a dandelion in his buttonhole three days running?' he said darkly. 'Remember the kick-up there was, with every sap-head in town running round to all the flower-women for dandelions, which they hadn't got, of course. Stands to reason you couldn't buy dandelions! Why, poor Geoffrey drove all the way to Esher looking for one, and Altringham went to the trouble of rooting up half-a-dozen out of Richmond Park, and having a set-to with the keeper over it, and then planting 'em in his window-boxes. Good idea, if they *had* become the mode: clever fellow, Altringham! — but of course the Nonpareil was only hoaxing us! Once he had the whole lot of us decked out with them, he never wore one again, and a precious set of gudgeons we looked! Playing the same trick again, if you ask me!'

Only in one quarter did unhappy results arise from the elevation of Ulysses. The Honourable Frederick Byng, who had for years been known by the sobriquet of Poodle Byng from his habit of driving everywhere with a very highly-bred and exquisitely shaved poodle sitting up beside him, encountered Mr Beaumaris in Piccadilly one afternoon, and no sooner clapped eyes on his disreputable companion than he pulled up his horses all standing, and spluttered out: 'What the devil — ?'

Mr Beaumaris reined in his own pair, and

looked enquiringly over his shoulder. Mr Byng, his florid countenance suffused by an angry flush, was engaged in backing his curricle, jabbing at his horses' mouths in a way that showed how greatly moved he was. Once alongside the other curricle, he glared at Mr Beaumaris, and demanded an explanation.

'Explanation of what?' said Mr Beaumaris. 'If you don't take care, you'll go off in an apoplexy one of these days, Poodle! What's the matter?'

Mr Byng pointed a trembling finger at Ulysses. 'What's the meaning of *that*?' he asked belligerently. 'If you think I'll swallow any such damned insult —!'

He was interrupted. The two dogs, who had been eyeing one another measuringly from their respective vehicles, suddenly succumbed to a mutual hatred, uttered two simultaneous snarls, and leaped for one another's throats. Since the curricles were too far apart to allow them to come to grips, they were obliged to vent their feelings in a series of hysterical objurgations, threats, and abuse, which drowned the rest of Mr Byng's furious speech.

Mr Beaumaris, holding Ulysses by the scruff of his neck, laughed so much that he could hardly speak: a circumstance which did nothing to mollify the outraged Mr Byng. He began to say that he should know how to answer an attempt to make him ridiculous, but was obliged to break off in order to command his dog to be quiet.

'No, no, Poodle, don't call me out!' said Mr Beaumaris, his shoulders still shaking. 'Really, I

261

had no such intention! Besides, we should only make fools of ourselves, going out to Paddington in the cold dawn to exchange shots over a pair of dogs!'

Mr Byng hesitated. There was much in what Mr Beaumaris said; moreover Mr Beaumaris was acknowledged to be one of the finest shots in England, and to call him out for a mere trifle would be an act of sheer foolhardiness. He said suspiciously: 'If you're not doing it to make a laughing-stock of me, why *are* you doing it?'

'Hush, Poodle, hush! You are treading on delicate ground!' said Mr Beaumaris. 'I cannot bandy a lady's name about in the open street!'

'What lady? I don't believe a word of it! Why can't you make that damned mongrel be quiet?'

In lamentable contrast to his well-trained adversary, who was now seated virtuously beside his master again, and affecting a maddening deafness, Ulysses, convinced that he had cowed the contemptible dandy, was hurling extremely ignoble taunts at him. Mr Beaumaris cuffed him, but although he cowered under the avenging hand he was quite unrepentant, and resumed his threats with unabated fervour.

'It is all jealousy, Poodle!' Mr Beaumaris said soothingly. 'The hatred of the vulgar for the aristocrat! I think we had better part, don't you?'

Mr Byng gave an angry snort, and drove off. Mr Beaumaris released Ulysses, who shook himself, sighed his satisfaction, and looked up for approbation. 'Yes, you will, I perceive, ruin me yet,' said Mr Beaumaris severely. 'If I am any judge of the matter, you picked your language up in the back-slums, and have probably been the associate of dustmen, coal-heavers, bruisers, and other such low persons! You are quite unfit for polite circles.'

Ulysses lolled his tongue out, and grinned cheerfully.

'At the same time,' said Mr Beaumaris, relenting, 'I daresay you would have made mincemeat of the creature, and I must own that I am not entirely out of sympathy with you. But poor Poodle will certainly cut me for a week at least.'

However, at the end of five days Mr Byng unbent, adopting a tolerant attitude towards Ulysses. It had been borne in upon him that to drive past the Nonpareil's curricle, staring rigidly ahead, was provocative of just the amusement amongst his acquaintances which he particularly wished to discourage.

Mr Beaumaris and Miss Tallant met again in the dazzling splendour of the Circular Room at Carlton House, on the night of the Regent's Dress-party. Arabella was so much impressed by the elegance of the sky-blue draperies, and the almost intolerable glare of a huge cut-glass chandelier, reflected, with its myriads of candles, in four large pier-glasses, that she momentarily forgot her last meeting with Mr Beaumaris, and greeted him by saying impulsively: 'How do you do? I have never seen anything like it in my life! Each room is more magnificent than the last!'

He smiled. 'Ah, but have you yet penetrated to the Conservatory, Miss Tallant? Our Royal host's *chef d'auvre*, believe me! Let me take you there!'

By this time she had recollected under what circumstances they had parted, so short a time previously, and her colour had risen. Many tears had been shed over the unhappy circumstance which had made it impossible for her to accept Mr Beaumaris's suit, and it had required all the excitement of a party at Carlton House to make her forget for one evening that she was the most miserable girl alive. She hesitated now, but Lady Bridlington was nodding and beaming, so she placed her hand on Mr Beaumaris's arm, and went with him through a bewildering number of apartments, all full of people, up the grand stairway, and through several saloons and antechambers. In the intervals of bowing to acquaintances, and occasionally exchanging a word of greeting, Mr Beaumaris entertained her with an account of Ulysses' quarrel with Mr Byng's poodle, and this made her laugh so much that a good deal of her constraint vanished. The Conservatory made her open her eyes very wide indeed, as well it might. Mr Beaumaris watched her, a look of amusement in his face, while she gazed silently round the extraordinary structure. Finally, she drew a breath, and uttered one of her unexpectedly candid remarks. 'Well, I don't know why he should call it a Conservatory, for it is a great deal more like a cathedral, and a very bad one too!' she said.

He was delighted. 'I thought you would be pleased with it,' he said, with deceptive gravity.

'I am not at all pleased with it,' replied Arabella severely. 'Why is there a veil over that statue?'

Mr Beaumaris levelled his glass at Venus Asleep, under a shroud of light gauze. 'I can't imagine,' he confessed. 'No doubt one of Prinny's flashes of taste. Would you like to ask him? Shall I take you to find him?'

Arabella declined the offer hastily. The Regent, an excellent host, had already managed to spend a minute or two in chat with nearly every one of his guests, and although Arabella was storing up the gracious words he had uttered to her, and meant to send home to the Vicarage an exact account of his amiability, she found conversation with such an exalted personage rather overpowering. So Mr Beaumaris took her back to Lady Bridlington, and after staying beside her for a few minutes was buttonholed by a gentleman in very tight satin knee-breeches, who lisped that the Duchess of Edgeware commanded his instant attendance. He bowed, therefore, to Arabella, and moved away, and although she several times afterwards caught a glimpse of him, he was always engaged with friends, and did not again approach her. The rooms began to seem hot, and overcrowded; the company the most boring set of people imaginable; and the vivacious, restless, and scintillating Lady Jersey, who flirted with Mr Beaumaris for quite twenty minutes, an odious creature.

Lady Bridlington's ball was the next social event of importance. This promised to be an event of more than ordinary brilliance, and although the late Lord Bridlington, to gratify an ambitious bride, had added a ballroom and a conservatory to the back of the house, it seemed

265

unlikely that all the guests who had accepted her ladyship's invitation could be accommodated without a degree of overcrowding so uncomfortable as to mark the evening as an outstanding success. An excellent band had been engaged for the dancing. Pandean pipes were to play during supper, extra servants were hired, police-officers and link-boys warned to make Park Street their special objective, and refreshments to supplement the efforts of Lady Bridlington's distracted cook ordered from Gunter's. For days before the event, housemaids were busy moving furniture, polishing the crystal chandeliers, washing the hundreds of spare glasses unearthed from a storeroom in the basement, counting and recounting plates and cutlery, and generally creating an atmosphere of bustle and unrest in the house. Lord Bridlington, who combined an inclination for ceremonious hospitality with a naturally frugal mind, was torn between complacency at having drawn to his house all the most fashionable persons who adorned the *ton*, and a growing conviction that the cost of the party would be enormous. The bill for wax candles alone threatened to rise to astronomical heights, and not his most optimistic calculations of the number of glasses of champagne likely to be drunk reduced the magnums that must be ordered to a total he could contemplate with anything but gloom. But his self-esteem was too great to allow of his contemplating for more than a very few minutes the expedient of ekeing out the precious liquor by making it into an iced cup. Cups there must certainly be, as well as

266

lemonade, orgeat, and such milder beverages as would please the ladies, but unless the party were to fall under the stigma of having been but a shabby affair after all the best champagne must flow throughout the evening in unlimited quantities. His mind not being of an order to question his own consequence, his gratification on the whole outweighed his misgivings, and if a suspicion did enter his head that he had Arabella to thank for the flattering number of acceptances which poured into the house, he was easily able to banish it. His mother, rather shrewder than he, gave honour where it was due, and, in a fit of reckless extravagance, was moved to order a new gown for Arabella from her own expensive dressmaker. But she was not, after all, so sadly out of pocket over the transaction, since a very few words whispered into the ear of Mme Dumaine were enough to convince that astute woman of business that the réclame of designing a toilette for the great Miss Tallant would fully justify her in making a substantial reduction in the price of a gown of figured lace over a white satin robe, with short, full, plaited sleeves, fastened down the front with pearl buttons to match the edging of pearls to the overdress. Arabella, ruefully surveying the depredations caused by a succession of parties to her glove-drawer, was obliged to purchase a new pair of long white gloves, as well as new satin sandals, and a length of silver net to drape round her shoulders in the style known as à l'Ariane. There was not very much left, by this time, of the Squire's handsome present to her; and when she considered how impossible her own folly had made it for her to requite her family's generosity in the only way open to a personable young female, she was overcome by feelings of guilt and remorse, and could not refrain from shedding tears. Nor could she refrain from indulging her fancy with the contemplation of the happiness which might even now have been hers, had she not allowed her temper to lead her so grossly to deceive Mr Beaumaris. This was a thought more bitter than all the rest, and it was only by the resolute exercise of her commonsense that she was able to regain some degree of calm. It was not to be supposed that the haughty Mr Beaumaris, related as he was to so many noble houses, so distinguished in his bearing, so much courted, and so much pursued, would ever have looked twice at a girl from a country Vicarage, with neither fortune nor connection to recommend her to his notice.

It was therefore with mixed feelings that Arabella awaited the arrival of the first guests on the appointed night. Lady Bridlington, thinking that she looked a little hagged (as well she might, after a week of such nerve-racking preparation) had tried to persuade her to allow Miss Crowle to rub a little — a *very* little! — rouge into her cheeks, but after one look at the result of this delicate operation Arabella had washed it away, declaring that never would she employ such aids to beauty as must, could he but see them, destroy for ever Papa's affection for his eldest daughter. Lady Bridlington pointed out, very reasonably, that there could be no fear of Papa's seeing them, but as Arabella remained adamant, and showed alarming signs of being about to burst into tears, she pressed her no more, consoling herself with the reflection that even without her usual blooming colour her god-daughter could not fail to appear lovely in the exquisite gown of Mme Dumaine's making.

One cause at least for satisfaction was granted to Arabella: although some guests might arrive early, and leave betimes to attend another function; others walk in past two o'clock, having relegated Lady Bridlington's ball to the third place on their list of the evening's engagements, so that the ball was rendered chaotic by the constant comings and goings, and Park Street echoed hideously for hours to the shouts of My lord's carriage! or My lady's chair! and heated police-officers quarrelled with vociferous link-boys, and chairmen exchanged insults with coachmen, Bertram arrived punctually at ten o'clock, and nobly remained throughout the proceedings.

He had recklessly ordered an evening dress from the obliging Mr Swindon, rightly deeming the simple garments he had brought with him from Heythram quite inadequate to the occasion. Mr Swindon had done well by him, and when Arabella saw him mount the stairway between the banks of flowers which she had helped all day to revive by frequent sprinklings of water, her heart swelled with pride in his appearance. His dark blue coat set admirably across his shoulders; his satin knee-breeches showed scarcely a crease; and nothing could have been more chaste than his stockings or his waistcoat. With his dark, curly locks rigorously brushed into the fashionable Brutus, his handsome, aquiline countenance interestingly pale from the nervousness natural to a young gentlemen attending his first *ton* party, he looked almost as distinguished as the Nonpareil himself. Arabella, fleetingly clasping his hand, bestowed on him so speaking a look of admiration that he was betrayed into a grin so boyish and attractive as to cause another early arrival to demand of her companion, who was that handsome boy?

Emboldened by the intensive coaching of a noted French dancing-master, whom he had found the time to visit, he claimed his sister's hand for the first waltz, and, being a graceful youth, taught by the athletic sports at Harrow to move with precision and a complete control over his limbs, acquitted himself so well that Arabella was moved to exclaim: 'Oh, Bertram, how elegantly you dance! Do, pray, let us make up a set for the quadrille, and dance together in it!'

This, however, he did not feel himself capable of doing. It was true that he had acquired the rudiments of the more simple steps, but he doubted his ability to go through the *grande ronde* or the *pas de zéphyr* without muffing these figures. Gazing up into his face, it occurred to Arabella that he too was looking a trifle hagged. She anxiously asked him if he were quite well, and he assured her that he had never been better in his life, very creditably refraining from confiding to her that his adventurous career had made so deep a hole in his purse that the question of how he was to meet his liabilities had

270

been causing him some sleepless nights. Since she had not seen him since a furtive assignation in the Mall one morning, under the vague chaperonage of the nursemaids who aired their charges there, and bought glasses of milk for them, fresh from the cows that lent so rural an air to the scene, she could not but feel uneasy about him. The faint rakishness that now hung about him did nothing to allay her fears, and she rather unjustly blamed Mr Scunthorpe for setting his feet upon a path Papa would certainly not have wished him to tread: She had formed no very favourable opinion of Mr Scunthorpe, and, with the praiseworthy notion of introducing Bertram into better company, made him known to one of the most disinterested of her admirers, young Lord Wivenhoe, heir to an affluent Earldom, and known to the greater part of London as Chuffy Wivenhoe, an affectionate sobriquet earned for him by his round, good-humoured countenance. This lively young nobleman, although he had not so far offered for her hand, formed one of Arabella's court, and was one of her favourites, being blessed with ingenuous manners, and an overflowing friendliness. She introduced Bertram to him with the best of intentions, but had she known that the engaging Chuffy had been reared by a misguided parent according to the principles laid down by the late Mr Fox's father, she might have refrained from so doing. In spite of every evidence to disprove them, the Earl of Chalgrove held Lord Holland's maxims in high esteem, and blandly encouraged his heir to indulge in every

271

extravagance that captured his erratic fancy, discharging his gaming-debts as cheerfully as he discharged the bills that poured in from his tailor, his coachbuilder, his hatter, and a host of other tradesmen who enjoyed his patronage.

The two young gentlemen took an instant liking to one another. Lord Wivenhoe was some years Bertram's senior, but his mind was as youthful as his countenance, whereas Bertram's aquiline features, and superiority of intellectual attainment, added several years to his true age. They found themselves with much in common, and before they had enjoyed one another's society for more than a very few minutes had arranged to go together to a forthcoming race-meeting.

Meanwhile, Miss Tallant's pleasure in dancing with her young friend from Yorkshire had not passed unnoticed. Gloom was struck into several hearts that had cherished hopes of winning the heiress, for not the most sanguine amongst her suitors could persuade himself that she had ever smiled up into his face with such unshadowed affection as she bestowed upon Bertram, or had talked so much or so confidentially to him. It struck that acute observer, Mr Warkworth, that there was an elusive resemblance between the pair. He mentioned the matter to Lord Fleet-wood, who had been so fortunate as to secure the promise of Arabella's hand for the quadrille, and was being incorrigibly blind to the claims of the less well-favoured damsels who had not been solicited to waltz, and were consequently chatting animatedly together in gilt chairs placed round the walls of the ballroom.

Lord Fleetwood stared hard at the Tallants for a minute or two, but could perceive no likeness, which, indeed, existed more in an occasional expression than in their lineaments. 'No, dash it!' he said. 'The little Tallant ain't got a beak of a nose!'

Mr Warkworth acknowledged it, and excused his lapse by explaining that it was only a sudden notion he had taken into his head.

Mr Beaumaris did not arrive until after midnight, and consequently failed to secure a waltz with Arabella. He seemed to be in one of his more inaccessible moods, and, having exerted himself to say a few civil things to his hostess, to dance once with a lady to whom she presented him, and once with his cousin, Lady Wainfleet, occupied himself in strolling through the various saloons, talking languidly to acquaintances, and surveying the company through his quizzing-glass with a faintly bored air. After about half-an-hour, when two sets were forming for a country-dance, he went in search of Arabella, who had disappeared from the ballroom in the direction of the conservatory, at the end of the last dance, accompanied by Mr Epworth, who protested that there had never been such a jam in the history of London balls, and offered to procure her a cooling glass of lemonade. Whether he redeemed this promise or not, Mr Beaumaris never knew, but when he walked into the conservatory a few minutes later, it was to find Arabella shrinking back in a chair in a state of the greatest discomfort, and trying to disengage her hands from the fervent clasp of Mr Epworth, romantically on his knees before her. Everyone else having left the conservatory to take their places in the new sets, the enterprising Mr Epworth, fortified by liberal doses of Lord Bridlington's champagne, had seized the opportunity once more to press his suit upon the heiress. Mr Beaumaris entered in time to hear her utter in a tone of distress: 'Oh, pray do not! Mr Epworth, I implore you, get up! I am very much obliged to you, but I shall never, never change my mind! It is ungentlemanly of you to tease me like this!'

'Do try not to be such a dead bore, Epworth!' said Mr Beaumaris, with all his usual sangfroid. 'I came to ask you if you would stand up with me for the next dance, Miss Tallant.'

She was blushing furiously, and returned rather an incoherent answer. Mr Epworth, considerably mortified at having been found in such a posture by one whose contempt he dreaded, got to his feet, muttered something about taking his leave, and left the conservatory. Mr Beaumaris, taking her fan from Arabella's hand, unfurled it, and began gently to wave it beside her heated countenance. 'How many times has he proposed to you?' he enquired conversably. 'How very ridiculous he looked, to be sure!'

She was obliged to laugh, but said warmly: 'He is the most odious little man, and seems to think he has only to persevere to make me receive his advances with complaisance!'

'You must make allowances for him,' said Mr

Beaumaris. 'If he did not believe you to be a wealthy woman he would cease to trouble you.'

Her bosom swelled; she said in a low, shaking voice: 'Had it not been for *you* sir, he would never have known it!'

He was silent, as much from disappointment as from the rueful knowledge that although Fleetwood's had been the tongue which had spread the rumour, it had been his own idly malicious words which had convinced Fleetwood of the truth of Arabella's claim.

After a moment, she said in a subdued tone: 'Shall we take our places in the set?'

'No, the numbers must by now be made up,' he replied, continuing to fan her.

'Oh! Well — well, perhaps we should go back into the ballroom, at all events!'

'Don't be alarmed!' said Mr Beaumaris, with a touch of asperity. 'I have not the smallest intention of embarrassing you by kneeling at your feet!'

Her colour rushed up again; she turned away her head in confusion, her lip slightly trembling. Mr Beaumaris shut the fan, and gave it back to her. He said gently: 'I am not, I hope, such a coxcomb as to distress you by repeated solicitations, Miss Tallant, but you may believe that I am still of the same mind as I was when I made you an offer. If your sentiments should undergo a change, one word — one look! — would be sufficient to apprise me of it.' She lifted her hand in a gesture imploring his silence. 'Very well,' he said. 'I shall say no more on that head. But if you should stand in need of a friend at any time, let me assure you that you may depend upon me.'

These words, delivered, as they were, in a more earnest tone than she had yet heard him use, almost made her heart stand still. She was tempted to take the risk of confessing the truth; hesitated, as the dread of seeing his expression change from admiration to disgust took possession of her; turned her eyes towards him; and then hurriedly rose to her feet, as another couple entered the conservatory. The moment was lost; she had time not only to recollect what might be the consequences if Mr Beaumaris treated her second confidence with no more respect than he had treated her first; but also to recall every warning she had received of the danger of trusting him too far. Her heart told her that she might do so, but her scared brain recoiled from the taking of any step that might lead to exposure, and to disgrace.

She went back into the ballroom with him; he relinquished her to Sir Geoffrey Morecambe, who came up to claim her; and within a very few minutes had taken leave of his hostess, and left the party.

13

Bertram's acquaintance with Lord Wivenhoe prospered rapidly. After a day spent together at the races, each was so well pleased with the other that further assignations were made. Lord Wivenhoe did not trouble to enquire into his new friend's age, and Bertram naturally did not confess that he was only just eighteen years old. Wivenhoe drove him to Epsom in his curricle, with a pair of dashing bays harnessed in the bar, and finding that Bertram was knowledgeable on the subject of horseflesh, good-naturedly offered to hand over the ribbons to him. So well did Bertram handle the pair, and at such a spanking pace did he drive them, showing excellent judgment in the feathering of his corners, and catching the thong of his whip just as the Squire had taught him, that he needed no other passport to Wivenhoe's favour. Any man who could control the kind of prime cattle his lordship liked must be a capital fellow. When he could do so without abating his cheerful conversation, he was clearly a right 'un, at home to a peg, and worthy of the highest regard. After some very interesting exchanges of reminiscences about incurable millers, roarers, lungers, half-bred blood-cattle, gingers, and slugs, which led inevitably to still more interesting stories of the chase, during the course of which both gentlemen found themselves perfectly in accord in their contempt of such ignoble persons as roadsters and skirters, and their conviction that the soundest of all maxims was, Get over the ground if it breaks your neck, formality was at an end between them, and his lordship was not only begging Bertram to call him Chuffy, as everyone else did, but promising to show him some of the rarer sights in town.

Bertram's fortunes, ever since he had come to London, had fluctuated in a bewildering manner. His first lucky evening with what he had swiftly learnt to refer to as St Hugh's Bones had started him off on a career that seriously alarmed his staider friend, Mr Scunthorpe. He had been encouraged by his luck to order a great many things from the various shops and warehouses where Mr Scunthorpe was known, and although a hat from Baxter's, a pair of boots from Hoby's, a seal from Rundell and Bridge, and a number of trifling purchases, such as a walking cane, a pair of gloves, some neckcloths, and some pomade for his hair were none of them really expensive, he had discovered, with a slight shock, that when added together they reached rather an alarming total. There was also his bill at the inn to be taken into account, but since this had not so far been presented he was able to relegate it to the very back of his mind.

The success of that first evening's play had not been repeated: in fact, upon the occasion of his second visit to the discreet house in Pall Mall he had been a substantial loser, and had been obliged to acknowledge that there might have been some truth in Mr Scunthorpe's dark warning. He was quite shrewd enough to realize that he had been a pigeon amongst hawks, but he was inclined to think that the experience would prove of immense value to him, since he was not one to be twice caught with the same lure. Playing billiards with Mr Scunthorpe at the Royal Saloon, he was approached by an affable Irishman, who applauded his play, offered to set him a main or two, or to accompany him to a snug little ken where a penchant for faro, or rouge-et-noir could be enjoyed. It was quite unnecessary for Mr Scunthorpe to whisper in his ear that this was a nibble from an ivory-turner: Bertram had no intention of going with the plausible Irishman, had scented a decoy the moment he saw him, and was very well-pleased with himself for being no longer a flat, but, on the contrary, a damned knowing one. A pleasantly convivial evening at Mr Scunthorpe's lodging, with several rubbers of whist to follow an excellent dinner, convinced him that he had a natural aptitude for cards, a belief that was by no means shaken by the vicissitudes of fortune which followed this initiation. It would be foolish, of course, to frequent gaming-halls, but once a man had made friends in town there were plenty of unexceptionable places where he could enjoy every form of gaming, from whist to roulette. On the whole, he rather thought he was lucky at the tables. He was quite sure that he was lucky on the Turf, for he had several very good days. It began to be a regular habit with him to look in at Tattersall's, to watch how the sporting men bet their money there, and sometimes to copy them, in his modest way, or at others to back his own choice. When he became intimate with Chuffy Wivenhoe, he accompanied him often, either to advise him on the purchase of a prad, to watch some ruined man's breakdowns being sold, or to lay out his blunt on a forthcoming race. Once he had fallen into the way of going with Wivenhoe it was impossible to resist spending a guinea for the privilege of being made free of the subscription-room; and once the very safe man whom his lordship patronized saw the company he kept it was no longer necessary for him to do more than record his bets, just as the Bloods did, and wait for settling-day either to receive his gains, or to pay his losses. It was all so pleasant, and every day was so full of excitement, that it went to his head, and if he was sometimes seized by panic, and felt himself to be careering along at a pace he could no longer control, such frightening moments could not endure when Chuffy was summoning him to come and try the paces of a capital goer, or Jack Carnaby carrying him off to the theatre, or the Fives-court, or the Daffy Club. None of his new friends seemed to allow pecuniary considerations to trouble them, and since they all appeared to be constantly on the brink of ruin, and yet contrived, by some fortunate bet, or throw of the dice, to come about again, he began to fall insensibly into the same way of life, and to think that it was rustic to treat a temporary insolvency as more than a matter for jest. It did not occur to him that the tradesmen who apparently gave Wivenhoe and

Scunthorpe unlimited credit would not extend the same consideration to a young man whose circumstances were unknown to them. The first hint he received of the different light in which he was regarded came in the form of a horrifying bill from Mr Swindon. He could not believe at first that he could possibly have spent so much money on two suits of clothes and an overcoat, but there did not seem to be any disputing Mr Swindon's figures. He asked Mr Scunthorpe, in an airy way, what he did if he could not meet his tailor's account. Mr Scunthorpe replied simply that he instantly ordered a new rig-out, but however much Bertram had been swept off his feet he retained enough native shrewdness to know that this expedient would not answer in his case. He tried to get rid of a very unpleasant feeling at the pit of his stomach by telling himself that no tailor expected to be paid immediately, but Mr. Swindon did not seem to be conversant with this rule. After a week he presented his bill a second time, accompanied by a courteous letter indicating that he would be much obliged by an early settlement of his account. And then, as though they had been in collusion with Mr Swindon, other tradesmen began to send in their bills, so that in less than no time one of the drawers in the dressing-table in Bertram's bedroom was stuffed with them. He managed to pay some of them, which made him feel much easier, but just as he was convincing himself that with the aid of a judicious bet, or a short run of luck, he would be able to clear himself from debt altogether, a polite but implacable gentleman

281

called to see him, waited a good hour for him to come in from a ride in the Park, and then presented him with a bill which he said he knew had been overlooked. Bertram managed to get rid of him, but only by giving him some money on account, which he could ill-spare, and after an argument which he suspected was being listened to by the waiter hovering round the coffee-room door. This fear was shortly confirmed by the landlord's sending up his account with the Red Lion next morning. Matters were becoming desperate, and only one way of averting disaster suggested itself to Bertram. It was all very well for Mr Scunthorpe to advise against racing and gaming: what Mr Scunthorpe did not understand was that merely to abstain from these pastimes would in no way solve the difficulty. If Mr Scunthorpe found himself at Point Non Plus he had trustees who, however much they might rate him, would certainly come to his rescue. It was quite unthinkable that Bertram should appeal to his father for assistance: he would rather, he thought, cut his throat, for not only did the very thought of laying such a collection of bills before the Vicar appal him, but he knew very well that the settlement of them must seriously embarrass his father. Nor would it any longer be of any use to sell his watch, or that seal he had bought, or the fob that hung beside it from his waistband: in some inexplicable way his expenses seemed to have been growing ever larger since he had begun to frequent the company of men of fashion. A vague, and rather dubious notion of visiting a moneylender was vetoed by Mr Scunthorpe, who told him that since the penalties attached to the lending of money at interest to minors were severe, not even Jew King could be induced to advance the smallest sum to a distressed client under age. He added that he had once tried that himself, but that the cents-per-cent were all as sharp as needles, and seemed to smell out a fellow's age the moment they clapped eyes on him. He was concerned, though not surprised, to learn of Bertram's having got into Queer Street, and had the quarter not been so far advanced that he himself was at a standstill, he would undoubtedly have offered his friend instant relief, for he was one, his intimates asserted, who dropped his blunt like a generous fellow. Unfortunately he had no blunt to drop, and knew from past experience that an application to his trustees would result in nothing but unfeeling advice to him to rusticate at his house in Berkshire, where his Mama would welcome him with open arms. To do him justice, Bertram would have been exceedingly reluctant to have accepted pecuniary assistance from any of his friends, since he saw no prospect, once he had returned to Yorkshire, of being able to reimburse them. There was only one way of getting clear, and that was the way of the Turf and the Table. He knew it to be hazardous, but as he could not see that it was possible for him to be in a worse case than he was already, it was worth the risk. Once he had paid his debts he rather thought that he should bring his visit to London to an end, for although he had enjoyed certain aspects of it enormously, he by no means enjoyed insolvency, and was beginning to realize that to stand continually on the edge of a financial precipice would very soon reduce him to a nervous wreck. An interview with a creditor who was not polite at all, but, on the contrary, extremely threatening, had shaken him badly: unless he made a speedy recovery it could only be a matter of days before the tipstaffs would be on his heels, even as Mr Scunthorpe had prophesied.

It was at this stage in his career that two circumstances occurred which seemed to hold out hopes of delivery. A fortunate evening playing faro for modest stakes encouraged him to think that his luck had turned again; and Chuffy Wivenhoe, earwigged by a jockey at Tattersall's, passed on to him the name of the *certain bet* thus disclosed. It really seemed as though Providence was at last aiding Bertram. It would be madness not to bet a substantial amount on the horse, for if it won he would have solved all his difficulties at one blow, and would have enough money left over to pay for his fare back to Yorkshire on the stage-coach. When Wivenhoe laid his own bet, he followed suit, and tried not to think of the predicament he would be in on settling-day if that infallible jockey had for once in his life been mistaken in his judgment.

'I'll tell you what, Bertram,' said Wivenhoe, as they strolled out of the subscription-room together, 'if you should care for it, I'll take you along with me to the Nonesuch Club tonight: all

284

the go, y'know, and devilish exclusive, but they'll let you in if you come with me.'

'What is it?' Bertram asked.

'Oh, faro and hazard, for the most part! It was started by some of the great guns only this year, because Watier's is becoming damned flat: they say it won't last much longer — never been the same since Brummell had to run for it! The Nonesuch is devilish good sport, I can tell you. There ain't many rules, for one thing, and though most of the men bet pretty heavily, the patrons fixed the minimum stake at twenty guineas, and there's only one faro-table. What's more, it ain't a shabby business enterprise, like half the gaming-clubs, and if you want to play hazard you appoint the croupier from amongst your set, and someone will always volunteer to call the odds. None of these paid croupiers and groom-porters, which make the Great Go more like a hotel than a social club. The whole idea is to make it a friendly affair, keep out the scaff and raff, and do away with all the rules and regulations which get to be such a dead bore! For instance, there's no damned syndicate running the faro-bank: they take it in turns, the well-breeched swells, like Beaumaris, and Long Wellesley Pole, and Golden Ball, and Petersham, and the rest of that set. Oh, it's the Pink of the Mode, I can tell you — top-of-the-trees!'

'I'd like to go with you,' Bertram said, 'only — Well, the fact is I'm none too plump in the pocket just now! Had a shocking run of luck!'

'Oh, no need to fret over that!' said his insouciant friend. 'I keep telling you it ain't like

Watier's! No one cares whether you bet twenty guineas or a hundred! You come: a man's luck is bound to change if he sticks to it — one of the things my governor told me, and *he* should know!'

Bertram was undecided, but since he was already engaged to dine at Long's Hotel with Lord Wivenhoe there was no need for him to return a definite answer to the invitation until he had thought it over rather more carefully. His lordship said that he should depend upon him, and there the matter for the moment rested.

It was not to be supposed that Bertram's protracted sojourn in London was causing his sister no anxiety. Arabella was very anxious indeed, for although she was not taken into his confidence she could not doubt, from his appearance, that he was spending money far more lavishly than the winning of a hundred pounds in a lottery justified him in doing. She seldom set eyes on him, and when they did meet she could not think that he was looking well. Late nights, unaccustomed potations, and worry, were taking their toll. But when she told him that he was looking fagged to death, and implored him to return to Yorkshire, he was able to retort with a good deal of truth that she was not particularly blooming herself. It was true. Her bright colour had faded a little, and her eyes had begun to seem a trifle large for her face, etched in, as they were, with shadows. Lord Bridlington, observing this, ascribed it to the absurd exigencies of a London season, and moralized on the folly of females with social ambitions. His mother, who had not failed to take note of the fact that her charge was no longer driving in the Park so frequently with Mr Beaumaris, and had developed a habit of evading his visits to the house, drew more correct conclusions, but failed signally to induce Arabella to confide in her. Whatever Frederick chose to say, Lady Bridlington was by this time convinced that the Nonpareil was very much in earnest, and she could not imagine what could be holding Arabella back from encouraging his advances. Divining that her reasons would be quite inexplicable to the good lady, Arabella preferred to keep her own counsel.

It had not escaped the notice of the Nonpareil that his tiresome love was not enjoying her customary good-looks and spirits, nor was it unknown to him that she had lately refused three advantageous offers of marriage, since the rejected suitors made no secret of the fact that their hopes were quite cut-up. She had excused herself from dancing with him at Almack's, but three times during the course of the evening he had been aware that her eyes were following him.

Mr Beaumaris, rhythmically drawing Ulysses' flying ear through his hand — a process which reduced Ulysses to a state of blissful idiocy — said meditatively: 'It is a melancholy reflection, is it not, that at my age I can be such a fool?'

Ulysses, his eyes half-closed, his senses swooning in ecstasy, gave a sigh which his god might, if he chose, interpret as one of sympathy.

'What if she proves to be the daughter of a

tradesman?' said Mr Beaumaris. 'I do owe something to my name, you know. It might even be worse, and surely I am too old to be losing my head for a pretty face!'

Since his hand was still, Ulysses nudged him. Mr Beaumaris resumed his steady pulling of that shameful ear, but said: 'You are quite right: it is not her pretty face. Do you believe her to be entirely indifferent to me? Is she really afraid to confess the truth to me? She must not be — no, Ulysses, she must not be! Let us look on the darker side! Is she ambitious to acquire a title? If that is so, why, then, has she sent poor Charles to the rightabout? You believe her to be aiming higher? But she cannot suppose that Witney will come up to scratch! Nor do I think that your suspicions are correct, Ulysses.'

Ulysses, catching the note of severity in his voice, cocked an anxious eye at him. Mr Beaumaris took his muzzle in his hand, and gently shook it. 'What do you advise me to do?' he asked. 'It appears to me that I have reached Point Non Plus. Should I — ' He broke off, and rose suddenly to his feet, and took a turn about the room. 'What a saphead I am!' he said. 'Of course! Ulysses, your master is a fool!' Ulysses jumped up to place his forepaws against those elegant pantaloons, and uttered a protesting bark. All this walking about the room, when Mr Beaumaris might have been better employed, was not at all to his taste. 'Down!' commanded Mr Beaumaris. 'How many more times am I to request you not to sully the purity of my garments by scrabbling at them with your ignoble, and probably dirty, paws? Ulysses, I shall be leaving you for a space!'

Ulysses might find this a little beyond him, but he fully understood that his hour of bliss was at an end, and so lay down in an attitude of resignation. Mr Beaumaris's subsequent actions filled him with vague disquiet, for although he was unacquainted with the significance of portmanteaux, some instinct warned him that they boded no good to little dogs. But these inchoate fears were as nothing when compared to the astonishment, chagrin, and dismay suffered by that peerless gentleman's gentleman, Mr Painswick, when he apprehended that his employer proposed to leave town without the support and expert ministration of a valet whom every Tulip of Fashion had at one time or another attempted to suborn from his service. He had accepted with equanimity the information that his master was going out of town for perhaps as much as a week, and was already laying out, in his mind, the raiment suitable for a sojourn at Wigan Park, or Woburn Abbey, or Belvoir, or perhaps Cheveley, when the full horror of the event burst upon him. 'Put up enough shirts and neckcloths to last me for seven days,' said Mr Beaumaris. 'I'll travel in riding-dress, but you may as well pack the clothes I have on, in case I should need them. I shan't take you with me.'

It took a full minute for the sense of this pronouncement to penetrate to the mind of his valet. He was shocked, and could only gaze at Mr Beaumaris in stupefaction.

'Tell 'em to have my travelling-chaise, and the bays, at the door by six o'clock,' said Mr Beaumaris. 'Clayton can accompany me for the first couple of stages, and bring the horses home.'

Mr Painswick found his voice. 'Did I understand you to say, sir, that you would not be requiring Me?' he asked.

'You did,' responded Mr Beaumaris.

'May I enquire, sir, who then is to wait upon you?' demanded Mr Painswick, in a voice of ominous quiet.

'I am going to wait upon myself,' replied Mr Beaumaris.

Mr Painswick accorded this attempt at humour the perfunctory smile it deserved. 'Indeed, sir? And who, if you please, will press your coat for you?'

'I suppose they are accustomed to pressing coats at the posting-houses,' said Mr Beaumaris indifferently.

'If you can call it pressing,' said Mr Painswick darkly. 'Whether you will be pleased with the result, sir, is, if I may be permitted to say so, Another Matter.'

Mr Beaumaris then said something so shocking that it gave his henchman, as he afterwards reported to Brough, a Very Nasty Spasm. 'I daresay I shan't,' he said, 'but it won't signify.'

Mr Painswick looked searchingly at him. He did not bear the appearance of one bordering on delirium, but there could be little doubt that his case was serious. Mr Painswick spoke in the tone of one soothing a refractory patient. 'I think, sir, it will be best for me to accompany you.'

'I have already told you that I don't need you. You may have a holiday.'

'I should not, sir, have the Heart to enjoy it,' returned Mr Painswick, who invariably spent his holidays in indulging nightmareish visions of his understudy's sending Mr Beaumaris forth with his clothes improperly brushed, his boots dulled by neglect, or, worst of all, a speck of mud on the skirts of his driving-coat. 'If I may say so without offence, sir, you cannot Go Alone!'

'And if *I* may say so without offence, Painswick,' retorted Mr Beaumaris, 'you are being foolish beyond permission! I will readily own that you keep my clothes in excellent order — I should not continue to bear with you, if you did not — and that the secret of imparting a gloss to my Hessians, which you so jealously guard, makes you not wholly undeserving of the extortionate wage I pay you; but if you imagine that I am unable to dress myself creditably without your assistance, your powers of self-deception must be greater than even I was aware of! Upon occasion — and merely to reward you! — I have permitted you to shave me; I allow you to help me into my coats, and to hand me my neckcloth. But at no time, Painswick, have I allowed you to dictate to me what I should wear, to brush my hair, or to utter a word — a sound! — while I am engaged in arranging that neckcloth! I shall do very well without you. But you must put up enough neckcloths to allow for some failures.'

Mr Painswick swallowed these insults, but tried one last, desperate throw. 'Your Boots, sir! You will never use a *iack*!'

'Certainly not,' said Mr Beaumaris. 'Some menial shall pull them off for me.'

Mr Painswick gave a groan. 'With greasy hands, sir! And only I know what it means to get a thumb-mark off your Hessians!'

'He shall handle them through gloves,' promised Mr Beaumaris. 'You need not lay out my knee-breeches: I am going to the Nonesuch Club tonight.' He added, possibly to atone for his harshness: 'Don't wait up for me, but call me at five o'clock tomorrow morning!'

Mr Painswick responded in a voice trembling with suppressed passion: 'If, sir, you choose to dispense with my services upon your journey, I am sure it is not for me to utter a word of criticism, nor would I so far demean myself as to remonstrate with you, whatever my feelings may be. But retire from my post before I have put you to bed, sir, and removed your raiment for proper attention, nothing will prevail upon me to do!'

'As you please,' said Mr. Beaumaris, unmoved. 'Far be it from me to interfere in your determination to become a martyr in my cause!'

Mr Painswick could only throw him a look of searing reproach, being, as he afterwards confided to Brough, unable to trust himself to say more. It had been Touch and Go with him, he said, whether he remained another day in the service of one so lost to the sense of what was due to himself and his valet. Brough, who was perfectly well-aware that wild horses would not

292

have parted his colleague from Mr Beaumaris, sympathized in suitable terms, and produced a bottle of Mr Beaumaris's second-best port. The healing properties of port, when mixed with a judicious quantity of gin, soon exercised a beneficial effect upon Mr Painswick's wounded feelings, and remarking that there was nothing like a glass of flesh-and-blood for setting a man up, he settled down to discuss with his crony and rival all the possible reasons that might be supposed to underlie Mr Beaumaris's rash and unbecoming conduct.

Mr Beaumaris, meanwhile, after dining at Brooks's, strolled across St James's Street towards Ryder Street, where the Nonesuch Club was established. Thus it was that when, rather later in the evening, Bertram Tallant entered the faro-room under the protective chaperonage of Lord Wivenhoe, Mr Beaumaris was afforded an excellent opportunity of estimating in just what manner Miss Tallant's enterprising young relative had been spending his time in London.

Two circumstances had decided Bertram in favour of visiting the Nonesuch Club. The first was the news that that sure winner, Fear-not-Victorious, had been unplaced in his race; the second the discovery of a twenty-pound bill amongst the tangle of accounts in the dressing-table. Bertram had sat staring at it quite numbly for some minutes, not even wondering how he had come to mislay it. He had suffered a terrible shock, for he had argued himself into believing that Fear-not-Victorious was bound to win, and had not seriously considered how he was to meet his creditor at Tattersall's on Monday if the animal were unplaced. The utter impossibility of meeting him at all burst upon him with shattering effect, so that he felt sick with apprehension, and could see nothing but a hideous vision of the Fleet Prison, where he would no doubt languish for the rest of his days, since it did not appear to him that his father could be expected to do more for so depraved a son than to expunge his name from the family tree, and forbid all mention of him at the Vicarage.

Rendered reckless by this last and most crushing blow, he rang the bell for the waiter, and demanded a bottle of brandy. It was then borne in upon him that orders had been issued in the tap not to supply him with any liquor for which he did not put down his blunt. Flushing darkly, he drove his hand into his breeches' pocket, and dragged out his last remaining handful of coins. Throwing one of these on the table, he said: 'Fetch it, damn you! — and you may keep the change!'

This gesture a little relieved his feelings, and the first glass of brandy, tossed at one gulp down his throat, had a still more heartening effect upon him. He looked again at the twenty-pound bill, still clasped between his fingers. He remembered that Chuffy had named twenty pounds as the minimum stake permitted to punters at the Nonesuch. Such a coincidence was surely too marked to be ignored. The second glass of brandy convinced him that here in his hand lay his last chance of saving himself from irretrievable ruin and disgrace.

Not being accustomed to drinking neat brandy, he was obliged before setting out for Long's Hotel to swallow a damper in the form of a glass of porter. This had a sobering effect, and the walk through the streets to Long's put him in tolerable shape to do justice to *maintenon* cutlets, and the hotel's famed Queensberry hock. He had made up his mind to be guided by Fate. He would lay down his twenty guineas upon a card chosen at random from the livret: if it turned up, he would take it for a sign that his luck had changed at last, and play on until he had covered all his debts; if it lost, he would be very little worse off than he was already, and could, at the worst, cut his throat, he supposed.

When he and Lord Wivenhoe entered the faro-room at the Nonesuch, Mr Beaumaris, holding the bank, had just completed a deal, and had tossed the pack on to the floor. He raised his eyes, as a waiter laid a fresh pack before him, and looked straight across to the door. The lure of hazard had drawn all but one other of the club's doyens from the room, and that one, Lord Petersham, was lost in one of his fits of deep abstraction.

Damn Petersham! thought Mr Beaumaris, on the horns of a dilemma. Why must he choose this of all moments to dream of tea?

That amiable but vague peer, perceiving Lord Wivenhoe, smiled upon him with the doubtful air of one who seemed to recollect seeing his face before. If he took notice of a youthful stranger within the sacred precincts of the club, he gave no sign of it. Mr. Warkworth stared very hard at Bertram, and then glanced towards the head of the table. Lord Fleetwood, filling his glass, frowned, and also looked to the Nonpareil.

Mr Beaumaris gave an order to the waiter to bring him another bottle of burgundy. One blighting word from him, and the stranger would have nothing to do but bow himself out with what dignity he could muster. There was the rub: the boy would be unbearably humiliated, and one could not trust that young fool, Wivenhoe, to smooth over the rebuff. He would be far more likely to kick up a dust over the exclusion of one of his friends, placing the unhappy Bertram in a still more intolerable position.

Lord Wivenhoe, finding places for himself and Bertram at the table, was casually making Bertram known to his neighbours. One of these was Fleetwood, who favoured Bertram with a curt nod, and again looked under his brows at the Nonpareil; the other, like most of the men in the room, was content to accept any friend of Chuffy's without question. One of the older men said something under his breath about babes and sucklings, but not loudly enough to be overheard.

Mr Beaumaris glanced round the table. 'Stakes, gentlemen,' he said calmly.

Bertram, who had changed his bill for one modest rouleau, thrust it in a quick movement towards the queen in the livrat. Other men were placing their bets; someone said something which made his neighbour laugh; Lord Petersham sighed deeply, and deliberately pushed forward several large rouleaus, and ranged them about his chosen cards; then he drew a delicately enamelled snuff-box from his pocket, and helped himself to a pinch of his latest blend. A pulse was beating so hard in Bertram's throat that it almost hurt him; he swallowed, and fixed his eyes on Mr Beaumaris's hand, poised above the pack before him.

The boy has been having some deep doings, thought Mr Beaumaris. Shouldn't wonder if he's rolled-up! What the devil possessed Chuffy Wivenhoe to bring him here?

The bets were all placed; Mr Beaumaris turned up the first card, and placed it to the right of the pack.

'Scorched again!' remarked Fleetwood, one of whose bets stood by the card's counterpart.

Mr Beaumaris turned up the Carte Anglaise, and laid it down to the left of the pack. The Queen of Diamonds danced before Bertram's eyes. For a dizzy moment he could only stare at the card; then he looked up, and met Mr Beaumaris's cool gaze, and smiled waveringly. That smile told Mr Beaumaris quite as much as he had need to know, and did nothing to increase his enjoyment of the evening ahead of him. He picked up the rake beside him, and pushed two twenty-guinea rouleaus across the table. Lord Wivenhoe called for wine for himself and his friend, and settled down to plunge with his ususal recklessness.

For half-an-hour the luck ran decidedly in Bertram's favour, and Mr Beaumaris was encouraged to hope that he would rise from the table a winner. He was drinking fairly steadily, a flush of excitement in his cheeks, his eyes, glittering a little in the candlelight, fixed on the cards. Lord Wivenhoe sat cheerfully losing beside him. He was soon punting on tick, scrawling his vowels, and tossing them over to the bank. Other men, Bertram noticed, did the same. There was quite a pile of paper before Mr Beaumaris.

The luck veered. Three times did Bertram bet heavily on the bank's card. He was left with only two rouleaus, and staked them both, sure that the bank could not win his money four times in succession. It could. To his own annoyance, Mr Beaumaris turned up the identical card.

From then on, he accepted, with an unmoved countenance, vowel upon vowel from Bertram. It was quite impossible to tell the boy either that he would not take his vouchers, or that he would be well-advised to go home. It was even doubtful whether Bertram would have listened to him. He was in the grip of a gamester's madness, betting recklessly, persuaded by one lucky chance that the luck smiled upon him again, convinced when he lost that ill-fortune could not last. That he had the least idea of the sum he already owed the bank, Mr Beaumaris cynically doubted.

The evening broke up rather earlier than usual, Mr Beaumaris having warned the company that he did not sit after two o'clock, and Lord Petersham sighing that he did not think he should take the bank over tonight. Wivenhoe, undaunted by his losses, said cheerfully: 'In the basket again! What do I owe, Beaumaris?'

Mr Beaumaris silently handed his vowels to him. While his lordship did rapid sums in mental addition, Bertram, the flush dying out of his cheeks, sat staring at the paper still lying in front of Mr Beaumaris. He said jerkily: 'And I?' and stretched out his hand.

'Dipped, badly dipped!' said Wivenhoe, shaking his head. 'I'll send you a draught on my bank, Beaumaris. The devil was in it tonight!'

Other men were totting up their losses; there was a noise of lighthearted conversation dinning in Bertram's ears; he found that his vowels totalled six hundred pounds, a sum that seemed vast to him, almost incredible. He pulled himself together, pride coming to his rescue, and rose. He looked very white now, and ridiculously boyish, but he held his head well up, and spoke to Mr Beaumaris perfectly calmly. 'I may have to keep you waiting for a few days, sir,' he said. 'I — I have no banking accommodation in London, and must send to Yorkshire for funds!'

What do I do now? wondered Mr Beaumaris. Tell the boy the only use I have for his vowels is as shaving-papers? No: he would enact me a Cheltenham tragedy. Besides, the fright may do him a world of good. He said: 'There is no hurry, Mr Anstey. I am going out of town tomorrow for a week, or five days. Come and see me at my house — let us say, next Thursday. Anyone will tell you my direction. Where are you putting up?'

Bertram replied mechanically: 'At the Red Lion, in the City, sir.'

'Robert!' called Fleetwood, from the other side of the room, where he was engaged in a lively argument with Mr Warkworth. 'Robert, come and bear me out! *Robert!*'

'Yes, in a moment!' Mr Beaumaris returned. He detained Bertram a moment longer. 'Don't fail!' he said. 'I shall expect to see you on Thursday.'

He judged it to be impossible to say more, for there were people all round them, and it was plain that the boy's pride would not brook a suggestion that his gaming-debts should be consigned to the flames.

But he was still frowning when he reached his house, some time later. Ulysses, gambolling and squirming before him, found that his welcome was not receiving acknowledgment, and barked at him. Mr Beaumaris bent, and patted him absentmindedly. 'Hush! I am not in the mood for these transports!' he said. 'I was right when I told you that you were not destined to be the worst of my responsibilities, was I not? I think I ought to have set the boy's mind at ease: one never knows, with boys of that age — and I didn't like the look in his face. All to pieces, I have little doubt. At the same time, I'll be damned if I'll go out again at this hour of night. A night's reflection won't hurt him.'

He picked up the branch of candles that stood upon the hall-table, and carried it into his study, and to his desk by the window. Seeing him sit down, and open the ink-standish, Ulysses indicated his sentiments by yawning loudly. 'Don't let me keep you up!' said Mr Beaumaris, dipping a pen in the standish, and drawing a sheet of paper towards himself.

Ulysses cast himself on the floor with a flop, gave one or two whines, bethought him of a task left undone, and began zealously to clean his forepaws.

Mr Beaumaris wrote a few rapid lines, dusted his sheet, shook off the sand, and was just about to fold the missive, when he paused. Ulysses looked up hopefully. 'Yes, in a minute,' said Mr Beaumaris. 'If he has quite outrun the constable — ' He laid down the paper, drew out a fat pocket-book from his inner pocket, and extracted from it a bill for a hundred pounds. This he folded up in his letter, sealed the whole with a wafer, and directed it. Then he rose, and to Ulysses' relief indicated that he was now ready to go to bed. Ulysses, who slept every night on the mat outside his door, and regularly, as a matter of form, challenged Painswick's right to enter that sacred apartment each morning, scampered ahead of him up the stairs. Mr Beaumaris found his valet awaiting him, his expression a nice mixture of wounded sensibility, devotion to duty, and long-suffering. He gave the sealed letter into his hand. 'See that that is delivered to a Mr Anstey, at the Red Lion, somewhere in the City, tomorrow morning,' he said curtly. 'In person!' he added.

14

Not for three days did any news of the disaster which had overtaken Bertram reach his sister. She had written to beg him to meet her by the Bath Gate in the Green Park, and had sent the letter by the Penny Post. When he neither appeared at the rendezvous, nor replied to her letter, she began to be seriously alarmed, and was trying to think of a way of visiting the Red Lion without her godmother's knowledge when Mr Scunthorpe sent up his card, at three o'clock one afternoon. She desired the butler to show him into the drawing-room, and went down immediately from her bedchamber to receive him.

It did not at once strike her that he was looking preter-naturally solemn; she was too eager to learn tidings of Bertram, and went impetuously towards him with her hand held out, exclaiming: 'I am so very glad you have called to see me, sir! I have been so much worried about my brother! Have you news of him? Oh, do not tell me he is ill?'

Mr Scunthorpe bowed, cleared his throat, and grasped her hand spasmodically. In a somewhat throaty voice he replied: 'No, ma'am. Oh, no! Not *ill*, precisely!'

Her eyes eagerly scanned his face. She now perceived that his countenance wore an expression of deep melancholy, and felt immediately sick with apprehension. She managed to say: 'Not — not — *dead?*'

'Well, no, he ain't dead,' replied Mr Scunthorpe, but hardly in reassuring tones. 'I suppose you might say it ain't as bad as that. Though, mind you, I wouldn't say he won't be dead, if we don't take care, because when a fellow takes to — But never mind that!'

'Never mind it?' cried Arabella, pale with alarm.

'Oh, what can be the matter? Pray, pray tell me instantly!'

Mr Scunthorpe looked at her uneasily. 'Better have some smelling-salts,' he suggested. 'No wish to upset a lady. Nasty shock. Daresay you'd like a glass of hartshorn and water. Ring for a servant!'

'No, no, I need nothing! Pray do not! Only put me out of this agony of suspense!' Arabella implored him, clinging with both hands to the back of a chair.

Mr Scunthorpe cleared his throat again. 'Thought it best to come to you,' he said. 'Sister. Happy to be of service myself, but at a standstill. Temporary, of course, but there it is. Must tow poor Bertram out of the River Tick!'

'River?' gasped Arabella.

Mr Scunthorpe perceived that he had been misunderstood. He made haste to rectify this. 'No, no, not drowned!' he assured her. 'Swallowed a spider!'

'Bertram has swallowed a spider?' Arabella repeated, in a dazed voice.

Mr Scunthorpe nodded. 'That's it,' he said.

'Blown up at Point Non Plus. Poor fellow knocked into horse-nails!'

Arabella's head was by this time in such a whirl that she was uncertain whether her unfortunate brother had fallen into the river, or had been injured in some explosion, or was, more mildly, suffering from an internal disorder. Her pulse was tumultuous; the most agitating reflections made it impossible for her to speak above a whisper. She managed to utter: 'Is he dreadfully hurt? Have they taken him to a hospital?'

'Not a case for a hospital, ma'am,' said Mr Scunthorpe. 'More likely to be screwed up.'

This pronouncement, conjuring up the most horrid vision of a coffin, almost deprived Arabella of her senses. Her eyes started at Mr Scunthorpe in a look of painful enquiry. 'Screwed up?' she repeated faintly.

'The Fleet,' corroborated Mr Scunthorpe, sadly shaking his head. 'Told him how it would be. Wouldn't listen. Mind, if the thing had come off right, he could have paid down his dust, and no harm done. Trouble was, it didn't. Very rarely does, if you ask me.'

The gist of this speech, gradually penetrating to Arabella's understanding, brought some of the colour back to her face. She sank into a chair, her legs trembling violently, and said. 'Do you mean he is in *debt*?'

Mr Scunthorpe looked at her in mild surprise. 'Told you so, ma'am!' he pointed out.

'Good God, how could I possibly guess — ? Oh, I have been so afraid that something of the

304

sort must happen! Thank you for coming to me, sir! You did very right!'

Mr Scunthorpe blushed. 'Always happy to be of service!'

'I must go to him!' Arabella said. 'Will you be so kind as to escort me? I do not care to take my maid on such an errand, and I think perhaps I should not go alone.'

'No, wouldn't do at all,' Mr Scunthorpe agreed. But better not go, ma'am! Not the thing for you. Delicate female — shabby neighbourhood! Take a message.'

'Nonsense! Do you think I have never been to the City? Only wait until I have fetched a bonnet, and a shawl! We may take a hackney, and be there before Lady Bridlington comes downstairs.'

'Yes, but — Fact is, ma'am, he ain't at the Red Lion!' said Mr Scunthorpe, much disturbed.

She had sprung up from her chair, but at this she paused. 'Not? But how is this? Why has he left the inn?'

'Couldn't pay his shot,' explained Mr Scunthorpe apologetically. 'Left his watch. Silly thing to do. Might have come in useful.'

'Oh!' she cried out, horror in her voice. 'Is it as bad as *that*?'

'Worse!' said Mr Scunthorpe gloomily. 'Got queered sporting his blunt on the table. Only hadn't enough blunt. Took to signing vowels, and ran aground.'

'*Gaming*!' Arabella breathed, in a shocked voice.

'Faro,' said Mr Scunthorpe. 'Mind, no question of any Greeking transactions! No fuzzing, or handling the concavesuit! Not but what it makes it worse, because a fellow has to be dashed particular in all matters of play and pay, if he goes to the Nonesuch. All the go, I assure you: Corinthian club — best of good *ton*! They play devilish high there — above my touch!'

'Then it was not you who took him to such a place!'

'Couldn't have been,' said Mr Scunthorpe simply. 'Not a member. Chuffy Wivenhoe.'

'Lord Wivenhoe! Oh, what a fool I have been!' cried Arabella. 'It was I who made him known to Lord Wivenhoe!'

'Pity,' said Mr Scunthorpe, shaking his head.

'But how wicked of him to have led Bertram to such a place! Oh, how could he have done so? I had no suspicion — I thought him so agreeable, and gentlemanlike — !'

'Polite to a point,' agreed Mr Scunthorpe. 'Very good sort of a man: very well-liked. Daresay he did it for the best.'

'How could he think so?' Arabella said hotly.

'Very exclusive club,' he pointed out.

She said impatiently, 'It is of no use for us to argue on that head. Where is Bertram?'

'Don't think you'd know the place, ma'am. It's — it's near Westminster!'

'Very well, let us go there at once!'

In considerable agitation, Mr Scunthorpe said: 'No, dash it! Can't take a lady to Willow Walk! You don't quite understand, ma'am! Poor Bertram — couldn't pay his shot — not a meg on him — duns in his pocket — tipstaffs after him — had to give 'em all the bag! Can't quite make out exactly how it was, but think he must have gone back to the Red Lion when he left the Nonesuch, because he has his portmanteau with him. Seems to have bolted for it to Tothill Fields. Very low back-slum, ma'am. Silly fellow ought to have come and knocked me up — happy to have given him my sofa!'

'Good God, why did he not?'

He coughed in an embarrassed way. 'Might have been a little bit on the go,' he said diffidently. 'Scared of being pounded by the tipstaffs, too. Come to think of it, might easily be if he stayed with me. Dashed tradesmen know he's a friend of mine! At all events, he ain't with me — didn't send me word where he was till this morning — feeling too blue-devilled, I daresay. Don't blame him: would myself!'

'Oh, poor Bertram, poor Bertram!' she cried, wringing her hands. 'I do not care where he is, see him I must, if I have to go to this Willow Walk alone!'

'Good God, ma'am, mustn't do that!' he exclaimed, appalled. 'Very rough set of coves in Willow Walk! Besides —' He paused, looking acutely uncomfortable. 'Not quite himself!'

'Oh, he must be ill with worry, and despair! Nothing would keep me from him at such a time! I will fetch my bonnet, and we may be off directly!'

'Ma'am, he won't like it!' Mr Scunthorpe said desperately. 'Very likely be ready to murder me only for telling you! You *can't* see him!'

'Why can I not?'

'He's been in the sun a trifle! You see — very

understandable thing to do! — shot the cat!'

'*Shot the cat?*'

'Can't blame him!' Mr Scunthorpe pleaded. 'Wouldn't have told you, if you hadn't been so set on seeing him! Felt desperate — shot the cat — felt better — kept on swallowing balls of fire — result, looking as queer as Dick's hatband, when I saw him!'

'Do you mean that he has been drinking?' demanded Arabella. 'What, in heaven's name, is a ball of fire?'

'Brandy,' said Mr Scunthorpe. 'Devilish bad brandy too. Told him to make Blue Ruin the preferred suit. Safer.'

'Every word you say makes me the more determined to go to him!' declared Arabella.

'Assure you much better to send him some blunt, ma'am!'

'I will take him all I have, but oh, it is so little! I cannot think yet what is to be done!'

Mr Scunthorpe pointed significantly to the ceiling. 'You don't think the old lady — ?' he suggested delicately.

She shook her head. 'Oh, no, no! Impossible!'

Mr Scunthorpe looked a little thoughtful. 'In that case, ma'am, better take you to him. Talking very wildly this morning. No saying what he might do.'

She almost ran to the door. 'We have not a moment to waste, then!'

'No, no!' he assured her. 'No need to be on the fret! Won't cut his throat today! Told the girl to hide his razor.'

'What girl?'

He became very much confused, blushed, and uttered: 'Girl he sent to my lodging with a message. Been looking after him.'

'Oh, God bless her!' Arabella cried fervently. 'What is her name? How much I must owe her!'

As the lady in question had introduced herself to Mr Scunthorpe as Leaky Peg, he was obliged to take refuge in prevarication, and to hope devoutly that they would not encounter her in Willow Walk. He said that he had not caught her name. Arabella seemed a little disappointed, but since this was no time for wasting over trifles she said no more, but ran out of the room to fetch her bonnet and shawl.

It was impossible for her to leave the house without the butler's being aware of it, but although he looked surprised, he made no comment, and in a few minutes' time she and Mr Scunthorpe were seated in a ramshackle hackney coach, which seemed as though, many years before, it had formed part of a nobleman's equipage, but which had fallen into sad decay. The coverings to the seats and the squabs were tattered and dirty, and the vehicle smelled strongly of beer and old leather. These evils Arabella scarcely noticed, in such a turmoil was her mind. It was a struggle to support her spirits at all; she felt ready to sink; and was unable, while in such a state of agitation, to form any plan for Bertram's relief. The only solution which had so far presented itself to her mind was an instinctive impulse, no sooner thought of than recoiled from, to send off an express to Heythram. Mr Scunthorpe's suggestion of applying to Lady Bridlington she well knew to be useless, nor would her pride tolerate the putting of herself under such added obligation to her godmother. Wild notions of selling Mama's diamonds, and the pearl necklet that had belonged to Grandmama Tallant, could not, she knew, be entertained, for these trinkets were not hers to dispose of at will.

Beside her, Mr Scunthorpe, feeling vaguely that her spirits required support, tried to entertain her by pointing out, conscientiously, the various places of interest the hackney drove past. She scarcely heeded him, but when they reached Westminster, began to look about her a little, insensibly cheered by the respectability of the neighbourhood. But the hackney lumbered on, and in a surprisingly short space of time it was hard to realize that she must be within a stone's throw of the Abbey, so squalid were her surroundings. An unlucky attempt made by Mr Scunthorpe to divert her, by pointing out an ugly brick structure which he said was the Tothill Fields Bridewell, made her shudder so alarmingly that he hastily informed her that it was so crammed to overflowing with felons that there was no room for another soul behind its walls. A row of squat almshouses was the next object of interest to be seen. This was followed by a charity school, but the district seemed to Arabella to be largely composed of wretched hovels, ancient mansions, fallen into depressing decay, and a superfluity of taverns. Frowsy looking women stood in the doorways of some of the hovels; half-naked urchins turned cartwheels on the dirty cobbles, in the hope of gaining largesse from persons well-breeched enough to travel in hackney coaches; at one corner, a fat woman, seated behind an iron cauldron appeared to be dispensing tea to a curiously ill-assorted crowd of persons, ranging from bricklayers to bedizened young women; various street-cries echoed in the narrow streets, from offers of coal to entreaties for old iron; and the male population seemed to consist entirely of scavengers, sweeps, and unidentifiable persons with blue jowls, and mufflers round their necks in place of collars.

After passing the entrances to several noisome alleys, the hackney turned into Willow Walk, and proceeded down it for some way before drawing up outside a dingy house, whose windows showed, besides fluttering oddments of washing hung out to dry, several broken panes of glass. In the open doorway, an old woman sat in a rocking-chair, puffing at a clay pipe, and engaged in conversation with a younger female, who held a squalling infant on one arm, which she from time to time shook, or refreshed from a black bottle, from which she herself took frequent pulls. Arabella had no positive knowledge of what was in that black bottle, but that it must contain strong liquor she felt convinced. The thought of Bertram was momentarily banished from her head; as Mr Scunthorpe handed her down from the hackney, and punctiliously brushed off the straws that clung to the flounce of her simple cambric dress, she opened her reticule, hunted in it for a shilling, and

311

astonished the mother of the infant by pressing it into her hand, and saying earnestly: 'Pray buy the baby some milk! Oh, pray do not give it that horrid stuff!'

Both women stared at her with fallen jaws. The old Irishwoman, the first to regain command over her faculties, burst into a cackle of mirth, and informed her that she was talking to no less a personage than Quartern Sue. This conveyed little to Arabella, but while she was still puzzling over the appellation, Quartern Sue, recovering from her stupefaction, had launched forth into a catalogue of her embarrassments, and was holding her hand cupped suggestively. Mr Scunthorpe, beads of sweat standing upon his brow, took it upon himself to hustle his charge into the house, whispering to her that she must not get into talk with such ill-famed women. Quartern Sue, never one to let slip an opportunity, followed them, her beggar's whine rising to a crescendo, but was repulsed at the foot of a rickety, uncarpeted stairway by a strapping young woman, with a tousle of greasy yellow hair, a countenance which not all the ravages of gin had entirely deprived of comeliness, and a tawdry dress, stained in various places, and with the bodice cut so low as to reveal glimpses of a dirty shift. This lady, having driven Quartern Sue forth by a series of remarks, not one of which was intelligible to Arabella, turned and confronted the genteel visitors with a belligerent look on her face, and her arms set widely akimbo. She demanded of Mr Scunthorpe, with whom she appeared to be

312

acquainted, what he meant by bringing a flash mort to the ken. Mr Scunthorpe uttered the one word, Sister! in strangled accents, upon which the blonde beauty turned a pair of fierce, bloodshot eyes upon Arabella, and ejaculated: 'Ho! Sister, is it?'

'Girl who brought me the message!' explained Mr Scunthorpe in a blushful aside to Arabella.

The blonde beauty needed no other passport to Arabella's favour. If she was conscious — as she could hardly have failed to have been — of the strong aroma of daffy which hung about the person of Leaky Peg, she gave no sign of it, but started forward, with her hands held out, and impulsive words on her lips. 'Oh, are you the girl who has been kind to my brother? You must let me thank you! I can never, never repay you! Mr Scunthorpe here has been telling me that it was you who took care of him when he — when he came to this place!'

Leaky Peg stared very hard at her for a moment, and then said pugnaciously: 'I found the covey on the mop, blue as megrim, see? And him no more than a mouth! Half flash and half foolish, that's him. Strike me, I don't know what I see in the hick!'

'Miss Tallant, better come upstairs!' said the anguished Mr Scunthorpe, to whom Leaky Peg's vocabulary was rather more intelligible than to Arabella.

'You dub your mummer, you death's head on a mop-stick!' Leaky Peg advised him. 'Leave me and the swell mort be!' She turned back to Arabella, and said roughly: 'Lurched, ain't he?

313

He tells me there's a fastener out after him. He hadn't so much as a meg in his truss when I come up with him in the boozing-ken. I took him along with me — strike me if I know why!' She jerked her thumb towards the stairs. 'You want to take him away: this ain't his lay, nor it ain't mine neither! Spouting a kid's mish all to buy him mutton and smash, which he don't eat! Me! You take him off; you're welcome!'

Gathering from these words that Leaky Peg had been keeping Bertram supplied with food, Arabella, tears standing in her eyes, seized one of her hands, and pressed it fervently between both her own, saying: 'How good you are! Indeed, I thank you! He is only a boy, you know, and what must have become of him without you I dare not think!'

'Well, it's little enough I got from it!' remarked Leaky Peg caustically. 'You and him with your breakteeth words! You get up them dancers, you and that moulder alongside you that looks like a toothdrawer! First door on the right: stale-drunk, he is, but he ain't backt yet!'

With these heartening words she turned on her heel, and strode out of the house, driving before her Quartern Sue, who had had the temerity to venture on to the threshold again. Mr Scunthorpe made haste to usher Arabella up the stairs, saying reproachfully: 'Shouldn't talk to her, ma'am! Not at all the thing! Assure you!'

'The thing!' she exclaimed scornfully. 'She has a kind heart, sir!'

Abashed, Mr Scunthorpe begged pardon, and tapped at a door at the head of the stairs.

Bertram's voice sounded from within the room, and without waiting for her escort to usher her in Arabella lifted the latch and quickly entered.

The apartment, which looked out on to a filthy yard, where lean cats prowled amongst garbage-heaps, was small, rather dark, and furnished with a sagging bed pushed up against one wall, a deal table, two wooden chairs, and a strip of threadbare carpet. The remains of a loaf of bread, a heel of cheese, together with a glass, a jug, and an empty bottle stood on the table; and on the mantelshelf, presumably placed there by Leaky Peg, was a cracked mug containing a wilting bunch of flowers. Bertram, who was stretched on the bed, raised himself on his elbow as the door opened, an apprehensive look in his face. He was fully dressed, but was wearing a handkerchief knotted round his neck, and looked both ill and unkempt. When he saw Arabella, he uttered something like a sob, and struggled up, and to his feet. 'Bella!'

She was in his arms on the word, unable to prevent herself from bursting into tears, but passionately clasping him to her. His breath reeked of spirits, but although this shocked her, she did not recoil from him, but hugged him more tightly still.

'You should not have come!' he said unsteadily. 'Felix, how *could* you have brought her here?'

'Warned her she wouldn't like it,' Mr Scunthorpe excused himself. 'Very set on seeing you!'

Bertram gave a groan. 'I did not mean you to know!'

She disengaged herself, wiped her tears away, and sat down on one of the chairs. 'Bertram, you know that is nonsense!' she said. 'Whom should you turn to if not to me? I am so sorry! What you must have suffered in this dreadful house!'

'Pretty, ain't it?' he said jeeringly. 'I don't know how I came here: Leaky Peg brought me. You may as well know, Bella, I was so foxed I don't remember anything that happened after I bolted from the Red Lion!'

'No, I quite see,' she said. 'But, Bertram, pray do not go on drinking! It is all so bad, and that makes it worse! You look sadly out of sorts, and no wonder! Have you a sore throat, dearest?'

He flushed, his hand going instinctively to the handkerchief round his neck. 'This! Oh, no! Gammoning the draper, my dear!' He saw her look of bewilderment, and added, with a short laugh: 'You would be surprised at the cant I have learnt from my hosts here! I've become a spouter — at least Peg manages the business for me! Pawned, Bella, pawned! Shan't have a rag to my back soon — not that that will signify!'

Mr Scunthorpe, seated on the edge of the bed, exchanged a meaning look with Arabella. She said briskly: 'It would signify very much! We must think what is to be done. Only tell me what you owe!'

He was reluctant to divulge the sum, but she insisted, and after a little while he blurted out: 'It comes to more than seven hundred pounds! There is no possibility of my being able to get clear!'

She was aghast, for she had not supposed that he could owe nearly so much. The sum seemed vast beyond belief, so that she could not be surprised when Bertram, casting himself into the other chair, began to talk in a wild way of putting a period to his existence. She let him run on, guessing that his despair needed the relief of just such mad outpourings, and having no very real fear that he would put his violent threats into execution. While he talked she cudgelled her brains for a solution to his difficulties, only lending half an ear to him, but patting his hand soothingly from time to time. Mr Scunthorpe intervened at last, saying with great common-sense: 'Don't think you ought to jump into the river, dear old boy. Sister wouldn't like it. Bound to leak out. Your governor might not like it either: never can tell!'

'No, indeed!' Arabella said. 'You must not talk of it any more, Bertram. You know how wicked it would be!'

'Well, I suppose I shan't kill myself,' Bertram said, a shade sulkily. 'Only, I can tell you this: I'll never face my father with *this!*'

'No, no!' she agreed. 'Seven hundred pounds! Bertram, how has it been possible?'

'I lost six hundred at faro,' he said, dropping his head in his hands. 'The rest — Well, there was the tailor, and the horse I hired, and what I owe at Tatt's, and my shot at the inn — oh, a dozen things! Bella, what am I to do?'

He sounded much more like the younger brother she knew when he spoke like that, a scared look in his face, and in his voice an unreasoning dependence on her ability to help him out of a scrape.

'Bills don't signify,' pronounced Mr Scunthorpe. 'Leave town: won't be followed. Not been living under your own name. Gaming debts another matter. Got to raise the wind for that. Debt of honour.'

'I know it, curse you!'

'But all debts are debts of honour!' Arabella said. 'Indeed, you should pay your bills first of all!'

A glance passed between the two gentlemen, indicative of their mutual agreement not to waste breath in arguing with a female on a subject she would clearly never understand. Bertram passed his hand over his brow, heaving a short sigh, and saying: 'There's only one thing to be done. I have thought it all over, Bella, and I mean to enlist, under a false name. If they won't have me as a trooper, I'll join a line regiment. I should have done it yesterday, when I first thought of it, only that there's something I must do first. Affair of honour. I shall write to my father, of course, and I daresay he will utterly cast me off, but that can't be helped!'

'How can you think so?' Arabella cried hotly. 'Grieved he must be — oh, I dare not even think of it! — but you must know that never, never would he do such an unchristian thing as to cast you off! Oh, do not write to him yet! Only give me time to think what I can do! If Papa knew that you owed all that money, I am very sure he would pay every penny of it, though it ruined him!'

'How can you suppose I would be such a gudgeon as to tell him *that?* No! I shall tell him that my whole mind is set on the army, and I had as lief start in the ranks as not!'

This speech struck far more dismay into Arabella's heart than his previous talk of committing suicide, for to take the King's shilling seemed to her a likely thing for him to do. She uttered, hardly above a whisper: 'No, no!'

'It must be, Bella,' he said. 'I'm sure the army is all I'm fit for, and I cannot show my face again with a load of debt hanging over me. Particularly a debt of honour! O God, I think I must have been mad!' His voice broke, and he could not speak for a moment. In the end he contrived to summon up the travesty of a smile, and to say: 'Pretty pair, ain't we? Not that *you* did anything as wrong as I have.'

'Oh, I have behaved so dreadfully!' she exclaimed. 'It is even my fault that you are reduced to these straits! Had I never presented you to Lord Wivenhoe — '

'That's fudge!' he said quickly. 'I had been to gaming-houses before I met him. He was not to know I wasn't as well-blunted as that set of his! I ought not to have gone with him to the Nonesuch. Only I had lost money on a race, and I thought — I hoped — Oh, talking pays no toll! But to say it was your fault is all gammon!'

'Bertram, who won your money at the Nonesuch?' she asked.

'The bank. It was faro.'

'Yes, but someone holds the bank!'

'The Nonpareil.'

She stared at him. 'Mr Beaumaris?' she gasped. He nodded. 'Oh, no, do not say so! How

319

could he have let you —No, no, Bertram!'

She sounded so much distressed that he was puzzled. 'Why the devil shouldn't he?'

'You are only a boy! He must have known! And to accept notes of hand from you! Surely he might have refused to do so much at least!'

'You don't understand!' he said impatiently. 'I went there with Chuffy, so why should he refuse to let me play?'

Mr Scunthorpe nodded. 'Very awkward situation, ma'am. Devilish insulting to refuse a man's vowels.'

She could not appreciate the niceties of the code evidently shared by both gentlemen, but she could accept that they must obtain in male circles. 'I must think it wrong of him,' she said. 'But never mind! The thing is that he is — that I am particularly acquainted with him! Don't be in despair, Bertram! I am persuaded that if I were to go to him, explain that you are not of age, and not a rich man's son, he will forgive the debt!'

She broke off, for there was no mistaking the expressions of shocked disapprobation in both Bertram's and Mr Scunthorpe's faces.

'Good God, Bella, what will you say next!'

'But, Bertram, indeed he is not proud and disagreeable, as so many people think him! I — I have found him particularly kind, and obliging!'

'Bella, this is a *debt of honour!* If it takes me my life long to do it, I must pay it, and so I shall tell him!'

Mr Scunthorpe nodded judicial approval of this decision.

'Spend your life paying six hundred pounds to

a man who is so wealthy that I daresay he regards it no more than you would a shilling?' cried Arabella. 'Why, it is absurd!'

Bertram looked despairingly at his friend. Mr Scunthorpe said painstakingly: 'Nothing to do with it, ma'am. Debt of honour is a debt of honour. No getting away from that.'

'I cannot agree! I own, I do not like to do it, but I *could* do it, and I know he would never refuse me!'

Bertram grasped her wrist. 'Listen, Bella! I daresay you don't understand — in fact, I can see that you don't! — but if you dared to do such a thing I swear you'd never see my face again! Besides, even if he did tear up my vowels I should still think myself under an obligation to redeem them! Next you will be suggesting that you should ask him to pay those damned tradesmen's bills for me!'

She coloured guiltily, for some such idea had just crossed her mind. Suddenly, Mr Scunthorpe, whose face a moment before had assumed a cataleptic expression, uttered three pregnant words. 'Got a notion!'

The Tallants looked anxiously at him, Bertram with hope, his sister more than a little doubtfully.

'Know what they say?' Mr Scunthorpe demanded. 'Bank always wins!'

'I know that,' said Bertram bitterly. 'If that's all you have to say — '

'Wait!' said Mr Scunthorpe. 'Start one.' He saw blank bewilderment in the two faces confronting him, and added, with a touch of impatience: 'Faro!'

'Start a faro-bank?' said Bertram incredulously. 'You must be mad! Why, even if it were not the craziest thing I ever heard of, you can't run a faro-bank without capital!'

'Thought of that,' said Mr Scunthorpe, not without pride. 'Go to my trustees. Go at once. Not a moment to be lost.'

'Good God, you don't suppose they would let you touch your capital for such a cause as that?'

'Don't see why not!' argued Mr Scunthorpe. 'Always trying to add to it. Preaching at me for ever about improving the estate! Very good way of doing it: wonder they haven't thought of it for themselves. Better go and see my uncle at once.'

'Felix, you're a gudgeon!' said Bertram irritably. 'No trustee would let you do such a thing! And even if they would, good God, we neither of us want to spend our lives running a faro-bank!'

'Shouldn't have to,' said Mr Scunthorpe, sticking obstinately by his guns. 'Only want to clear you of debt! One good night's run would do it. Close the bank then.'

He was so much enamoured of this scheme that it was some time before he could be dissuaded from trying to promote it. Arabella, paying very little heed to the argument, sat wrapped in her own thoughts. That these were by no means pleasant would have been apparent, even to Mr Scunthorpe, had he been less engrossed in the championing of his own plans, for not only did her hands clench and unclench in her lap, but her face, always very expressive, betrayed her. But by the time Bertram had

322

convinced Mr Scunthorpe that a faro bank would not answer, she was sufficiently mistress of herself again to excite no suspicion in either gentleman's breast.

She turned her eyes towards Bertram, who had sunk back, after his animated argument, into a state of hopeless gloom. 'I shall think of something,' she said. 'I *know* I shall contrive to help you! Only please, please do not enlist, Bertram! Not yet! Only if I should fail!'

'What do you mean to do?' he demanded. 'I shan't enlist until I have seen Mr Beaumaris, and — and explained to him how it is! That I *must* do. I — I told him I had no funds in London, and should be obliged to send into Yorkshire for them, so he asked me to call at his house on Thursday. It is of no use to look at me like that, Bella! I couldn't tell him I was done-up, and had no means of paying him, with them all there, listening to what we were saying! I would have died rather! Bella, have you any money? Could you spare me enough to get my shirt back? I can't go to see the Nonpareil like this!'

She thrust her purse into his hand. 'Yes, yes, of course! If only I had not bought those gloves, and the shoes, and the new scarf! There are only ten guineas left, but it will be enough to make you more comfortable until I have thought how to help you, won't it? Do, do remove from this dreadful house! I saw quite a number of inns on our way, and one or two of them looked to be respectable!'

It was plain that Bertram would be only too ready to change his quarters, and after a brief dispute, in which he was very glad to be worsted, he took the purse, gave her a hug, and said that she was the best sister in the world. He asked wistfully whether she thought Lady Bridlington might be induced to advance him seven hundred pounds, on a promise of repayment over a protracted period, but although she replied cheerfully that she had no doubt that she could arrange something of the sort, he could not deceive himself into thinking it possible, and sighed. Mr Scunthorpe, prefixing his remark with one of his deprecating coughs, suggested that as the hackney had been told to wait for them, he and Miss Tallant ought, perhaps, to be taking their leave. Arabella was much inclined to go at once in search of a suitable hostelry for Bertram, but was earnestly dissuaded, Mr Scunthorpe promising to attend to this matter himself, and also to redeem Bertram's raiment from the pawnbroker's shop. The brother and sister then parted, clinging to one another in such a moving way that Mr Scunthorpe was much affected by the sight, and had to blow his nose with great violence.

Arabella's first action on reaching Park Street again was to run up to her bedchamber, and without pausing to remove her bonnet to sit down at the little table in the window, and prepare to write a letter. But in spite of the urgency of the matter she had no sooner written her opening words than all inspiration appeared to desert her, and she sat staring out of the window, while the ink dried on her pen. At last she drew a breath, dipped the pen in the standish again, and resolutely wrote two lines. Then she stopped, read them over, tore up the paper, and drew a fresh sheet towards her.

It was some time before she had achieved a result that satisfied her, but it was done at last, and the letter sealed up with a wafer. She then rang the bell-pull, and upon a housemaid's coming in answer to the summons desired the girl to send Becky to her, if she could be spared from her duties. When Becky presently appeared, shyly smiling and twisting her hands together in her apron, Arabella held out the letter, and said: 'If you please, Becky, do you think you could contrive to slip out, and — and carry that to Mr Beaumaris's house? You might say that I have asked you to go on an errand for me, but — but I shall be very much obliged to you if you will not disclose to anyone what it is!'

'Oh, miss!' breathed the handmaid, scenting a romance. 'As though I would say a word to a living soul!'

'Thank you! If — if Mr Beaumaris should be at home, I should be glad if you would wait for an answer to the letter!'

Becky nodded her profound understanding of this, assured Arabella that she might trust her through fire and water, and departed.

Nothing could have been more conspiratorial than her manner of entering Arabella's room half-an-hour later, but she brought bad news: Mr Beaumaris had gone into the country three days ago, and had said that he might be away from London for a week.

15

Mr Beaumaris returned to his London house in time to partake of a late breakfast on Tuesday morning, having been absent for six days. It had been considered probable by his dependants that he would be away for a full week, but as he rarely gave any positive information on his movements, counted no cost, and had accustomed his highly-paid servants to live in a constant state of expectation of being obliged, at a moment's notice, to provide suitable entertainment for himself, or for a score of guests, his premature arrival caused no one any dismay. It caused one member of his household a degree of joy bordering on delirium. A ragged little mongrel, whose jauntily curled tail had been clipped unhappily between his legs for six interminable days, and who had spent the major part of this time curled into a ball on the rug outside his master's door, refusing all sustenance, including plates of choice viands prepared by the hands of the great M. Alphonse himself, came tumbling down the stairs, uttering canine shrieks, and summoned up enough strength to career madly round in circles before collapsing in an exhausted, panting heap at Mr Beaumaris's feet. It spoke volumes for the light in which Mr Beaumaris's whims were regarded by his retainers that the condition to which his disreputable protégé had wilfully reduced himself brought every member of the household who might have been

326

considered in some way responsible into the hall to exonerate himself from all blame. Even M. Alphonse mounted the stairs from his basement kingdom to describe to Mr Beaumaris in detail the chicken-broth, the ragout of rabbit, the shin of beef, and the marrow-bone with which he had tried to tempt Ulysses' vanished appetite. Brough broke in on his Gallic monologue to assure Mr Beaumaris that he for one had left nothing undone to restore Ulysses' interest in life, even going to the lengths of importing a stray cat into the house, in the hope that this outrage would galvanize one notoriously unsympathetic towards all felines to activity. Painswick, with a smug air that rendered him instantly odious to his colleagues, drew attention to the fact that it had been his superior understanding of Ulysses' processes of thought which Mr Beaumaris had to thank for his finding himself still in possession of his low-born companion: he had conceived the happy notion of giving Ulysses one of Mr Beaumaris's gloves to guard.

Mr Beaumaris, who had picked Ulysses up, paid no heed to all these attempts at self-justification, but addressed himself to his adorer. 'What a fool you are!' he observed. 'No, I have the greatest dislike of having my face licked, and must request you to refrain. Quiet, Ulysses! quiet! I am grateful to you for your solicitude, but you must perceive that I am in the enjoyment of my customary good health. I would I could say the same of you. You have once more reduced yourself to skin and bone, my friend, a process which I shall take leave to inform you I consider as unjust as it is ridiculous. Anyone setting eyes on you would suppose that I grudged you even the scraps from my table!' He added, without the slightest change of voice, and without raising his eyes from the creature in. his arms: 'You would also appear to have bereft my household of its senses, so that the greater part of it, instead of providing me with the breakfast I stand in need of, is engaged in excusing itself from any suspicion of blame and — I may add — doing itself no good thereby.'

Ulysses, to whom the mere sound of Mr Beaumaris's voice was ecstasy, looked adoringly up into his face, and contrived to lick the hand that was caressing him. On his servants, Mr Beaumaris's voice operated in quite another fashion: they dispersed rapidly, Painswick to lay out a complete change of raiment; Brough to set the table in the breakfast-parlour; Alphonse to carve at lightning speed several slices of a fine York ham, and to cast eggs and herbs into a pan; and various underlings to grind coffee-beans, cut bread, and set kettles on to boil. Mr Beaumaris tucked Ulysses under one arm, picked up the pile of letters from the table in the hall, and strolled with them into his library. To the zealous young footman who hastened to fling open the door for him, he said: 'Food for this abominable animal!' — a command which, relayed swiftly to the kitchen, caused M. Alphonse to command his chief assistant instantly to abandon his allotted task, and to prepare a dish calculated to revive the flagging appetite of a Cambacérès.

Mr Beaumaris, tossing a pile of invitations and

bills aside, came upon a billet which had not been delivered through the medium of the Penny Post, and which was superscribed, *Urgent*. The writing, certainly feminine, was unknown to him. 'Now, what have we here, Ulysses?' he said, breaking the wafer.

They had not very much. '*Dear Mr Beaumaris*,' ran the missive, '*I should be very much obliged to you if you would do me the honour of calling in Park Street as soon as may be convenient to you, and requesting the butler to inform me of the event. I remain, Ever yours most sincerely, Arabella Tallant*.'

This model of the epistolary art, which had caused Miss Tallant so much heart-searching, and so many ruined sheets of hot-pressed notepaper, did not fail of its effect. Mr Beaumaris cast aside the rest of his correspondence, set Ulysses down on the floor, and bent his powerful mind to the correct interpretation of these few, heavily underlined, words. He was still engaged on this task when Brough entered the room to announce that his breakfast awaited him. He carried the letter into the parlour, and propped it against the coffee-pot, feeling that he had not yet got to the bottom of it. At his feet, Ulysses, repairing with enthusiasm the ravages of his protracted fast, was rapidly consuming a meal which might have been judged excessive for the satisfaction of the appetite of a boa-constrictor.

'This,' said Mr Beaumaris, 'was delivered here three days ago, Ulysses!'

Ulysses, whose keen olfactory sense had

discovered the chicken giblets cunningly hidden in the middle of his plate, could spare no more than a perfunctory wag of the tail for this speech; and to Mr Beaumaris's subsequent demand to know what could be in the wind he returned no answer at all. Mr Beaumaris pushed away the remains of his breakfast, a gesture which was shortly to operate alarmingly on the sensibilities of the artist belowstairs, and waved aside his valet, who had just entered the room. 'My town dress!' he said.

'I have it ready, sir,' responded Painswick, with dignity. 'There was just one matter which I should perhaps mention.'

'Not now,' said Mr Beaumaris, his eyes still bent upon Miss Tallant's tantalizing communication.

Painswick bowed, and withdrew. The matter was not, in his fastidious estimation, of sufficient importance to justify him in intruding upon his employer's evident preoccupation; nor did he broach it when Mr Beaumaris presently came upstairs to change his riding-dress for the blue coat, yellow pantaloons, chaste waistcoat, and gleaming Hessians with which he was wont to gratify the eyes of beholders in the Metropolis. This further abstention was due, however, more to the sense of irretrievable loss which had invaded his soul on the discovery that a shirt was missing from Mr Beaumaris's execrably packed portmanteau than from a respect for his master's abstraction. He confined his conversation to bitter animadversions on the morals of inn-servants, and the depths of depravity to which some unknown boots had sunk in treating Mr Beaumaris's second-best pair of Hessians with a blacking fit only to be used on the footwear of country squires. He could hardly flatter himself that Mr Beaumaris, swiftly and skilfully arranging the folds of his neckcloth in the mirror, or delicately paring his well-cared-for finger-nails, paid the least heed to his discourse, but it served in some measure to relieve his lacerated feelings.

Leaving his valet to repair the damage to his wardrobe, and his faithful admirer to sleep off the effects of a Gargantuan meal, Mr Beaumaris left the house, and walked to Park Street. Here he was met by the intelligence that my lord, my lady, and Miss Tallant had gone out in the barouche to the British Museum, where Lord Elgin's much disputed marbles were now being exhibited, in a wooden shed built for their accommodation. Mr Beaumaris thanked the butler for this information, called up a passing hackney, and directed the jarvey to drive him to Great Russell Street.

He found Miss Tallant, her disinterested gaze fixed upon a sculptured slab from the Temple of Nike Apteros, enduring a lecture from Lord Bridlington, quite in his element. It was Lady Bridlington who first perceived his tall, graceful figure advancing across the saloon, for since she had naturally seen the collection of antiquities when it was on view at Lord Elgin's residence in Park Lane, and again when it was removed to Burlington House, she felt herself to be under no obligation to look at it a third time, and was more profitably engaged in keeping a weather eye cocked for any of her acquaintances who might have elected to visit the British Museum that morning. Upon perceiving Mr Beaumaris, she exclaimed in accents of delight: 'Mr Beaumaris! What a lucky chance, to be sure! How do you do? How came you not to be at the Kirkmichael's Venetian Breakfast yesterday? Such a charming party! I am persuaded you must have enjoyed it! Six hundred guests — only fancy!'

'Amongst so many, ma'am, I am flattered to know that you remarked my absence,' responded Mr Beaumaris, shaking hands. 'I have been out of town for some days, and only returned this morning. Miss Tallant! 'Servant, Bridlington!'

Arabella, who had started violently upon hearing his name uttered, and quickly turned her head, took his hand in a clasp which seemed to him slightly convulsive, and raised a pair of strained, enquiring eyes to his face. He smiled reassuringly down into them, and bent a courteous ear to Lady Bridlington, who was making haste to assure him that she had come to the Museum merely to show the Grecian treasures to Arabella, who had not been privileged to see them on their *first* showing. Lord Bridlington, not averse from any aggrandizement to his audience, began in his consequential way to expound his views on the probable artistic value of the fragments, a recreation which would no doubt have occupied him for a considerable period of time had Mr Beaumaris not cut him short by saying, in his most languid way: 'The pronouncements of

West, and of Sir Thomas Lawrence, must, I imagine, have established the aesthetic worth of these antiquities. As to the *propriety* of their acquisition, we may, each one of us, hold to our own opinion.'

'Mr Beaumaris, do you care to visit Somerset House with us?' interrupted Lady Bridlington. 'I do not know how it comes about that we were not there upon Opening Day, but such a rush of engagements have we been swept up in that I am sure it is a wonder we have time to turn round! Arabella, my love, I daresay you are quite tired of staring at all these sadly damaged bits of frieze, or whatever it may be called — not but what I declare I could feast my eyes on it for ever! — and will be glad to look at pictures for a change!'

Arabella assented to it, throwing so beseeching a look at Mr Beaumaris that he was induced to accept a seat in the barouche.

During the drive to the Strand, Lady Bridlington was too much occupied in catching the eyes of chance acquaintances, and drawing their attention to the distinguished occupant of one of the back seats by bowing and waving to them, to have much time for conversation. Arabella sat with her eyes downcast, and her hand fidgeting with the ribands tied round the handle of her sunshade; and Mr Beaumaris was content to watch her, taking due note of her pallor, and the dark shadows beneath her eyes. It was left to Lord Bridlington to entertain the company, which he did very willingly, prosing uninterruptedly until the carriage turned into the courtyard of Somerset House.

Once inside the building, Lady Bridlington, whose ambitions had for some time been centred on promoting a match between Arabella and the Nonpareil, seized the first opportunity that offered of drawing Frederick away from the interesting pair. She stated her fervent desire to see the latest example of Sir Thomas Lawrence's art, and dragged him away from a minute inspection of the President's latest enormous canvas to search for this fashionable masterpiece.

'In what way can I serve you, Miss Tallant?' said Mr Beaumaris quietly.

'You — you had my letter?' faltered Arabella, glancing fleetingly up into his face.

'This morning. I went instantly to Park Street, and, apprehending that the matter was of some urgency, followed you to Bloomsbury.'

'How kind — how *very* kind you are!' uttered Arabella, in accents which could scarcely have been more mournful had she discovered him to have been a monster of cruelty.

'What is it, Miss Tallant?'

Bearing all the appearance of one rapt in admiration of the canvas before her, she said: 'I daresay you may have forgot all about it, sir, but — but you told me once — that is, you were so obliging as to say — that if my sentiments underwent a change — '

Mr Beaumaris mercifully intervened to put an end to her embarrassment. 'I have certainly not forgotten it,' he said. 'I perceive Lady Charnwood to be approaching, so let us move on! Am I to understand, ma'am, that your sentiments

334

have undergone a change?'

Miss Tallant, obediently walking on to stare at one of the new Associates' *Probationary Pictures* (described in her catalogue as 'An Old Man soliciting a Mother for Her Daughter who was shewn Unwilling to consent to so disproportionate a match') said baldly: 'Yes.'

'My surroundings,' said Mr Beaumaris, 'make it impossible for me to do more than assure you that you have made me the happiest man in England, ma'am.'

'Thank you,' said Arabella, in a stifled tone. 'I shall try to be a — to be a conformable wife, sir!'

Mr Beaumaris's lips twitched, but he replied with perfect gravity: 'For my part, I shall try to be an unexceptionable husband, ma'am!'

'Oh, yes, I am *sure* you will be!' said Arabella naively. 'If only — '

'If only — ?' prompted Mr Beaumaris, as she broke off.

'Nothing!' she said hastily. 'Oh, dear, there is Mr Epworth!'

'A common bow in passing will be enough to damp his pretensions,' said Mr Beaumaris. 'If that does not suffice, I will look at him through my glass.'

This made her give an involuntary gurgle of laughter, but an instant later she was serious again, and evidently struggling to find the words with which to express herself.

'What very awkward places we do choose in which to propose to one another!' remarked Mr Beaumaris, guiding her gently towards a red-plush couch. 'Let us hope that if we sit down, and appear to be engrossed in conversation no one will have the bad manners to interrupt us!'

'I do not know what you must think of me!' said Arabella.

'I expect I had better not tell you until we find ourselves in a more retired situation,' he replied. 'You always blush so delightfully when I pay you compliments that it might attract attention to ourselves.'

She hesitated, and then turned resolutely towards him, tightly gripping her sunshade, and saying: 'Mr Beaumaris, you do *indeed* wish to marry me?'

'Miss Tallant, I do *indeed* wish to marry you!' he asserted.

'And — and you are so wealthy that my — my fortune can mean nothing to you?'

'Nothing at all, Miss Tallant.'

She drew an audible breath. 'Then — will you marry me at once?' she asked.

Now, what the devil's the meaning of this? thought Mr Beaumaris, startled. Can that damned young cub have been getting up to more mischief since I left town?

'At once?' he repeated, voice and countenance quite impassive.

'Yes!' said Arabella desperately. 'You must know that I have the greatest dislike of — of all *formality*, and — and the nonsense that always accompanies the announcement of an engagement! I — I should wish to be married very quietly — in fact, in the strictest secrecy — and before anyone has guessed — that I have

336

accepted your very obliging offer!'

The wretched youth must have been deeper under the hatches than I guessed, thought Mr Beaumaris, and still she dare not tell me the truth! Does she really mean to carry out this outrageous suggestion, or does she only think that she means it? A virtuous man would undoubtedly, at this juncture, disclose that there is not the smallest need for these measures. What very unamusing lives virtuous men must lead!

'You may think it odd of me, but I have always thought it would be so very romantic to elope!' pronounced Papa's daughter defiantly.

Mr Beaumaris, whose besetting sin was thought by many to be his exquisite enjoyment of the ridiculous, turned a deaf ear to the promptings of his better self, and replied instantly. 'How right you are! I wonder I should not have thought of an elopement myself! The announcement of the engagement of two such notable figures as ourselves must provoke a degree of comment and congratulation which would not be at all to our taste!'

'Exactly so!' nodded Arabella, relieved to find that he saw the matter in so reasonable a light.

'Consider, too, the chagrin of such as Horace Epworth!' said Mr Beaumaris, growing momently more enamoured of the scheme. 'You would be driven to distraction by their ravings!'

'Well, I do think I might be,' said Arabella.

'There is not a doubt of it. Moreover, the formality of making application to your father for permission to address you is quite antiquated, and we shall do well to dispense with it. If some

337

little feeling still exists in the minds of old-fashioned persons against marrying minors out of hand, it need not concern us, after all.'

'N-no,' agreed Arabella, rather doubtfully. 'Do you think people will — will be very much shocked, sir?'

'No,' said Mr Beaumaris, with perfect truth. 'No one will be in the least shocked. When would you like to elope?'

'Would tomorrow be too soon?' asked Arabella anxiously.

Mr Beaumaris might wish that his love would give him her confidence, but it would have been idle to have denied that he was hugely enjoying himself. Life with Arabella would contain few dull moments; and although her estimate of his morals was unflattering enough to have discomposed any man of sensibility it left his withers unwrung, since he was well-aware that her assumption of his readiness to behave in so improper a fashion sprang from an innocence which he found enchanting. He replied with great promptness: 'Not a moment too soon! But for the recollection that there are one or two preparations which perhaps I should make I should have suggested that we should leave this building together at once.'

'No, that would be impossible,' said Arabella seriously. 'In fact — I do not know very much about such things, but I cannot but feel that it will be excessively difficult for me to escape from Park Street without anyone's knowing! For I must carry a valise with me, at least, besides my dressing-case, and how may it be contrived?

338

Unless I crept out at dead of night, of course, but it would have to be very late indeed, for the porter always waits up for Lord Bridlington to come in. And I might fall asleep,' she added candidly.

'I have a constitutional dislike of eloping at dead of night,' said Mr Beaumaris firmly. 'Such exploits entail the use of rope-ladders, I am credibly informed, and the thought of being surprised perhaps by the Watch in the very act of throwing this up to your window I find singularly unnerving.'

'Nothing,' said Arabella, 'would prevail upon me to climb down a rope-ladder! Besides, my bedroom is at the back of the house.'

'Perhaps,' said Mr Beaumaris, 'you had better leave me to make the necessary arrangements.'

'Oh, yes!' responded Arabella gratefully. 'I am sure you will know just how it should be contrived!'

This reflection upon his past career Mr Beaumaris bore with an unmoved countenance. 'Just so, Miss Tallant,' he said gravely. 'Now, it occurs to me that, tomorrow being Wednesday, there will be a gala night at Vauxhall Gardens.'

'Yes, Lady Bridlington thought at one time of taking me to it,' agreed Arabella. 'But then, you know, she recalled that it is the night of the party at Uxbridge House.'

'A very dull affair, I have no doubt. I shall invite Lady Bridlington — and Bridlington, I suppose — to do me the honour of joining *my* party at Vauxhall. You will naturally be included in this invitation, and at a convenient moment during the course of the evening, we shall slip away together to the street entrance, where my chaise will be awaiting us.'

Arabella considered this proposition, and discovered two objections to it. 'Yes, but how very odd it would seem to Lady Bridlington if you were to go away in the middle of your own party!'

The reflection that Lady Bridlington might well deem this eccentricity the least odd feature of the affair Mr Beaumaris kept to himself. He said: 'Very true. A note shall be delivered to her after our departure.'

'Well, I suppose that would be better than nothing,' Arabella conceded. 'Oh, will she ever forgive me for treating her so?' This involuntary exclamation seemed to escape her without her knowledge. She raised the second of her objections. 'And in any event it will not answer, because I cannot take a valise to Vauxhall!'

'That you will also leave to me,' said Mr Beaumaris.

'But you cannot call in Park Street to fetch it!' she pointed out.

'Certainly not.'

'And I will *not* elope without a change of clothes, or my hairbrushes, or my tooth-powder!' declared Arabella.

'Most improper,' agreed Mr Beaumaris. 'All these things shall be forthcoming.'

'You cannot buy such things for me!' gasped Arabella, shocked.

'I assure you I should enjoy doing it.'

She stared at him, and then exclaimed

340

wretchedly: 'How dreadful it all is! I never, never thought I should come to this! I daresay it seems the merest commonplace to you, but to me — But I see that it is of no use to cavil!'

The tell-tale muscle at the corner of Mr Beaumaris's mouth quivered, and was sternly repressed. 'Well, perhaps not precisely commonplace,' he said. 'It so happens that I have not previously eloped with anyone. However, to a man of ordinary ingenuity the affair should not prove impossible to achieve creditably, I trust. I perceive Mrs Penkridge, who is hoping to catch either your eye or mine. We shall permit her to do so, and while she asks you to say if you do not think Nollekens's bust over there most like, I shall go in search of Lady Bridlington, and engage her to bring you to Vauxhall tomorrow evening.'

'Oh, pray do not! I dislike Mrs Penkridge excessively!' she whispered.

'Yes, an odious woman, but impossible to avoid,' he returned.

Seeing him rise to his feet, Mrs Penkridge bore down upon him, her acidulated smile on her lips. Mr Beaumaris greeted her with his smooth civility, stayed for perhaps a minute, and then, to Arabella's indignation, made his bow, and went off in the direction of the next room.

Either Lady Bridlington proved hard to find, or he must have fallen a victim to her garrulity, Arabella thought, for it seemed a very long time before she set eyes on him again. When he did reappear, Lady Bridlington was walking beside him, wreathed in smiles. Arabella made her

341

excuses to Mrs Penkridge, and went across to her godmother, who greeted her with the cheerful intelligence that Mr Beaumaris had formed the most delightful scheme for an evening at Vauxhall. 'I did not scruple to accept, my love, for I knew you would like it of all things!' she said.

'Yes,' said Arabella, feeling that she was now committed to an irrevocable and reprehensible course which she would no doubt regret her life long. 'I mean, oh, yes! how very agreeable!'

16

Upon leaving Somerset House, Mr Beaumaris got into a hackney, and drove to the Red Lion inn. What he learned at that hostelry threw abundant light on to Arabella's conduct. Since he had his own reasons for believing Arabella's heart to have been won long since, he was not in the least wounded by the discovery that she proposed to marry him as a means of rescuing her brother from debt, but, on the contrary, considerably amused. Having paid Bertram's bill at the inn, and received his watch back from the landlord, he returned to his own house in yet another hackney.

The same delight in the ridiculous which had made him wear a dandelion in his button-hole for three consecutive days for no better purpose than to enjoy the discomfiture of his misguided friends and copyists made him deeply appreciative of the situation in which he now found himself; and he beguiled the tedium of the drive to Mount Street in wondering when it would cross his absurd love's mind that the disclosure, following hard upon the wedding-ceremony, that she required a large sum of money from him without a moment's loss of time, might be productive of a little awkwardness. He could not resist picturing the scene, and was still laughing softly when he reached his house, a circumstance which considerably surprised his butler.

'Send round to the stables for my tilbury, will you, Brough?' he said. 'And desire Painswick — oh, you're there, are you?' he added, as his valet descended the stairs. 'I want to hear no more about missing shirts, on which excessively boring subject I can see from your expression you are prepared to discourse at length, but you may tell me this! Where is the letter I gave into your hands to be delivered at the Red Lion, to a Mr Anstey, and why did you not tell me that it had not been so delivered?'

'You may perhaps recall, sir,' said Painswick reproachfully, 'that I mentioned to you while you sat at breakfast that there was a matter which I deemed it my duty to bring to your notice. Upon which, sir, you said, Not now.'

'Did I? I had no idea you could be so easily silenced. Where is the letter?'

'I placed it, sir, at the bottom of the pile that was awaiting you on the table here,' replied Painswick, tacitly disclaiming further responsibility.

'In that case it is in the library. Thank you: that is all.'

Ulysses, who had been lying stretched out in the library, enjoying the sleep of the replete, awoke at Mr Beaumaris's entrance, yawned, got up, shook himself, sneezed several times, stretched, and indicated by his cocked ears and wagging tail that he was now ready for any adventure.

'I am glad to see you restored to your usual self,' said Mr Beaumaris, running through the mass of his neglected correspondence, and picking up his own letter to Bertram. 'You know, you should not have dissuaded me from going out again that evening! Just look what has come of it! And yet I don't know. I would not have missed this morning's interview for a thousand pounds! I suppose you think that I am behaving very badly? I am, of course, but do me the justice to own that she deserves it for being such an adorable little fool!'

Ulysses wagged his tail. He was not only willing to do Mr Beaumaris justice, but presently indicated his readiness to accompany him on whatever expedition he had in mind.

'It would be useless to suggest, I suppose, that you are occupying Clayton's seat?' said Mr Beaumaris, mounting into his tilbury.

Clayton, grinning, expressed himself as being agreeable to taking the little dog on his knees, but Mr Beaumaris shook his head.

'No, no, I fear he would not like it. I shan't need you,' he said, and drove off, remarking to his alert companion: 'We are now faced with the wearing task of tracking down that foolish young man's inarticulate friend, Felix Scunthorpe. I wonder whether, in the general medley, there is any bloodhound strain in you?'

He drew blank at Mr Scunthorpe's lodging, but on being informed that Mr Scunthorpe had mentioned that he was going to Boodle's, drove at once to St James's Street, and was so fortunate as to catch sight of his quarry, walking up the flag-way. He reined in, and called imperatively: 'Scunthorpe!'

Mr Scunthorpe had naturally perceived who

was driving a spanking chestnut between the shafts of the tilbury, but as he had no expectation of being recognized by the Nonpareil this summons surprised him very much. He was even a little doubtful, and said cautiously: 'Me, sir?'

'Yes, you. Where is young Tallant?' He saw an expression of great wariness descend upon Mr Scunthorpe's face, and added impatiently: 'Come, don't be more of a fool than you can help! You don't suppose I am going to hand him over to the tipstaffs, do you?'

'Well, he's at the Cock,' disclosed Mr Scunthorpe reluctantly. 'That is to say,' he corrected himself, suddenly recalling his friend's incognito, 'he is, if you mean Mr Anstey.'

'Have you any brothers?' demanded Mr Beaumaris.

'No,' said Mr Scunthorpe, blinking at him. 'Only child.'

'You relieve my mind. Offer my congratulations to your parents!'

Mr Scunthorpe thought this over, with knit brow, but could make nothing of it. He put Mr Beaumaris right on one point. 'Only one parent,' he said. 'Father died three months after I was born.'

'Very understandable,' said Mr Beaumaris. 'I am astonished that he lingered on for so long. Where is this Cock you speak of?'

'Thing is — not sure I ought to tell you!' said Mr Scunthorpe.

'Take my word for it, you will be doing your misguided friend an extremely ill-turn if you don't tell me!'

'Well, it's at the corner of Duck Lane, Tothill Fields,' confided Mr Scunthorpe, capitulating.

'Good God!' said Mr Beaumaris, and drove off.

The Cock inn, however, though a small, squat building, proved to be more respectable than its situation had led Mr Beaumaris to suppose. Duck Lane might abound in filth of every description, left to rot in the road, but the Cock seemed to be moderately clean, and well-kept. It even boasted an ostler, who emerged from the stable to gape at the tilbury. When he understood that the swell handling the ribbons had not merely stopped to enquire the way, but really did desire him to take charge of his horse and carriage, a vision of enormous largesse danced before his eyes, and he hastened to assure this noble client that he was ready to bestow his undivided attention on the equipage.

Mr Beaumaris then descended from the tilbury, and walked into the tap of the inn, where his appearance caused a waterman, a jarvey off duty, two bricklayer's labourers, a scavenger, and the landlord to break off their conversation in mid-sentence to stare at him.

'Good-morning!' said Mr Beaumaris. 'You have a Mr Anstey putting up here, I think?'

The landlord, recovering from his surprise, came forward, bowing several times. 'Yes, your honour! Oh, yes, indeed, your honour! — Chase that cur out of here, Joe! — If your honour will —'

'Do nothing of the sort, Joe!' interrupted Mr Beaumaris.

'Is he *yours*, sir?' gasped the landlord.

'Certainly he is mine. A rare specimen: his family tree would surprise you! Is Mr Anstey in?'

'He'll be up in his room, sir. Keeps hisself *to* hisself, in a manner of speaking. If your honour would care to step into the parlour, I'll run up and fetch him down before the cat can lick her ear.'

'No, take me up to him,' said Mr Beaumaris. 'Ulysses, do stop hunting for rats! We have no time to waste on sport this morning! Come to heel!'

Ulysses, who had found a promising hole in one corner of the tap, and was snuffing at it in a manner calculated to keep its occupant cowering inside it for the next twenty-four hours at least, regretfully obeyed this command, and followed Mr Beaumaris up a steep, narrow stairway. The landlord scratched on one of the three doors at the top of this stair, a voice bade him come in, and Mr Beaumaris, nodding dismissal to his guide, walked in, shut the door behind him, and said cheerfully: 'How do you do? I hope you don't object to my dog?'

Bertram, who had been sitting at a small table, trying for the hundredth time to hit upon some method of solving his difficulties, jerked up his head, and sprang to his feet, as white as his shirt. '*Sir!*' he uttered, grasping the back of his chair with one shaking hand.

Ulysses, misliking his tone, growled at him, but was called to order. 'How many more times am I to speak to you about your total lack of polish, Ulysses?' said Mr Beaumaris severely.

'Never try to pick a quarrel with a man under his own roof! Lie down at once!' He drew off his gloves, and tossed them on to the bed. 'What a very tiresome young man you are!' he told Bertram amiably.

Bertram, his face now as red as a beetroot, said in a choked voice: 'I was coming to your house on Thursday, as you bade me!'

'I'm sure you were. But if you hadn't been so foolish as to leave the Red Lion so — er — hurriedly, there would not have been the slightest need for this rustication of yours. *You* would not have worried yourself half-way to Bedlam, and *I* should not have been obliged to bring Ulysses to a locality you can see he does not care for.'

Bertram glanced in a bewildered way towards Ulysses, who was sitting suggestively by the door, and said: 'You don't understand, sir. I — I was rolled-up! It was that, or — or prison, I suppose!'

'Yes, I rather thought you were,' agreed Mr Beaumaris. 'I sent a hundred pound banknote to you the next morning, together with my assurance that I had no intention of claiming from you the vast sums you lost to me. Of course, I should have done very much better to have told you so at the time — and better still to have ordered you out of the Nonesuch at the outset! But you will agree that the situation was a trifle awkward.'

'Mr Beaumaris,' said Bertram, with considerable difficulty, 'I'c-can't redeem my vowels now, but I pledge you my word that I *will* redeem

349

them! I was coming to see you on Thursday, to tell you the whole, and — and to beg your indulgence!'

'Very proper,' approved Mr Beaumaris. 'But it is not my practice to win large sums of money from schoolboys, and you cannot expect me to change my habits only to accommodate your conscience, you know. Shall we sit down, or don't you trust the chairs here?'

'Oh, I beg pardon!' Bertram stammered, flushing vividly. 'Of course! I don't know what I was thinking about! Pray, will you take this chair, sir? But it will not do! I must and I will — Oh, can I offer you any refreshment? They haven't anything much here, except beer and porter, and gin, but if you would care for some gin — '

'Certainly not, and if that is how you have been spending your time since last I saw you I am not surprised that you are looking burned to the socket.'

'I haven't been — at least, I did at first, only it was brandy — but not — not lately,' Bertram muttered, very shamefaced.

'If you drank the brandy sold in this district, you must have a constitution of iron to be still alive,' remarked Mr Beaumaris. 'What's the sum total of your debts? Or don't you know?'

'Yes, but — *You* are not going to pay my debts, sir!' A dreadful thought occurred to him; he stared very hard at his visitor, and demanded: 'Who told you where I was?'

'Your amiable but cork-brained friend, of course.'

'*Scunthorpe?*' Bertram said incredulously. 'It was not — it was not someone else?'

'No, it was not someone else. I have not so far discussed the matter with your sister, if that is what you mean.'

'How do you know she is my sister?' Bertram said, staring at him harder than ever. 'Do you say that Scunthorpe told you that too?'

'No, I guessed it from the start. Have you kept your bills? Let me have them!'

'Nothing would induce me to!' cried Bertram hotly. 'I mean, I am very much obliged to you, sir, and it's curst good of you, but you must see that I couldn't accept such generosity! Why, we are almost strangers! I cannot conceive why you should think of doing such a thing for me!'

'Ah, but we are not destined to remain strangers!' explained Mr Beaumaris. 'I am going to marry your sister.'

'Going to marry *Bella*?' Bertram said.

'Certainly. You perceive that that puts the whole matter on quite a different footing. You can hardly expect me either to win money from my wife's brother at faro, or to bear the odium of having a relative in the Fleet. You really must consider *my* position a little, my dear boy.'

Bertram's lip quivered. 'I see what it is! She *did* go to you, and *that* is why — But if you think, sir, that I have sunk so low I would let Bella sacrifice herself only to save me from disgrace —'

Ulysses, taking instant exception to the raised voice, sprang to Mr Beaumaris's side, and barked a challenge at Bertram. Mr Beaumaris dropped a hand on his head. 'Yes, very rude, Ulysses,' he agreed. 'But never mind! Bear in

351

mind that it is not everyone who holds me in such high esteem as you do!'

Much confused, Bertram stammered: 'I didn't mean — I beg your pardon! I only meant —She never said a word of this to me!'

'Didn't she? How secretive females are, to be sure! Perhaps she felt that her parents should be the first persons to learn the news.'

'Well, I suppose she *might*,' Bertram said doubtfully. 'But considering she said she couldn't marry anyone, because she made 'em all think she was an heiress — '

'She didn't make me think anything of the sort,' said Mr Beaumaris.

'Oh, I *see*!' said Bertram, his brow clearing. 'Well, I must say, sir, I'm dashed glad, because I had a notion she liked you more than all the rest! I — I wish you very happy! And, of course, I do see that it makes a difference to my debt to *you*, only I don't think I should let you pay the other debts, because it is not in the least your affair, and — '

'Now, don't let us go into all that again!' begged Mr Beaumaris. 'Just tell me what you propose to do if I don't pay your debts!'

'I thought of enlisting in a cavalry regiment, if they would take me,' confessed Bertram. 'Under an assumed name, of course!'

'I should think that a cavalry regiment would suit you very well,' said Mr Beaumaris. 'But it will be very much more comfortable for you, and for all of us, if you join it under your own name, and as a cornet. What do you want? a Hussar regiment?'

These incredible words made Bertram turn first red, and then white, swallow convulsively, and finally blurt out; 'You *c-couldn't* mean that! After *this*! I — Oh, sir, *do* you mean it?'

'Yes, of course, but give me your bills!'

'I don't deserve anyone should do anything for me!' Bertram said, overcome.

'The bills!'

Bertram, already floating in some beatific dream, started, and said: 'The bills? Oh! Oh, yes, I have them all here — only you will be very much shocked to see how much I have spent, and —'

'Nothing ever shocks me,' replied Mr Beaumaris, holding out a hand. He stuffed the sheaf of crumpled papers into the pocket of his driving-coat, and said: 'I will settle all these so that none of your creditors will know that it was not you who paid them. Do you owe anything in this neighbourhood beyond your shot here?'

Bertram shook his head. 'No, for Bella gave me all the money she had, when she came to see me. I am afraid you would not have liked her doing so, sir, and nor did I, but Felix brought her, like the saphead he is! It — it was a horrid place, and I think I ought to tell you that it was all my fault that she ever went to such a back-slum!'

'You fill me with dismay,' said Mr Beaumaris. 'I do trust she did not set eyes on any destitute person whom she may feel it to be her duty to befriend?'

'Well, I don't *think* she did,' Bertram replied. 'Felix did say that she told a woman they all call

353

Quartern Sue not to give her baby gin to drink, and gave her a shilling to buy it some milk. And I am excessively sorry, sir, and I would not have had it happen for the world, but Felix says that they walked smash into Leaky Peg, who — who took me to the place when I was so castaway I didn't know even where I was, or how I came there. She — she *was* very good to me, in her way, you know, and Bella got it into her head she owed her a debt of gratitude for looking after me! But that's all right, because I gave Peg five pounds out of the money Bella left for me!'

'Heaven help me!' said Mr Beaumaris. 'She will undoubtedly expect me to house this doxy! *Leaky Peg*, did you say? Good God!'

'No, no,'sir, of course she won't!' exclaimed Bertram. 'Why *should* she?'

'Because that is her invariable practice,' said Mr Beaumaris bitterly. 'You don't suppose, do you, that I voluntarily adopted that animal over there?'

'You don't mean Bella gave him to you? Well, that's a great deal too bad of her! I must say, I thought it was a queer sort of a dog for *you* to have, sir!'

'The whole of London thinks it is a queer sort of a dog for me to have. Even the landlord of this tavern tried to chase him from the taproom!' He drew out his pocket-book, and extracted from it several banknotes, and pushed them across the table. 'There you are: pay your shot here, redeem whatever lies in pawn, and book yourself the box-seat on the first stage to Harrowgate. I believe the northern-bound coaches leave at

354

some godless hour of the morning, so you had better spend tonight at whatever inn they set out from. A few days in the fresh air will, I trust, repair the ravages of all the brandy you imbibed, and make it possible for you to meet your father without arousing suspicion.'

Bertram tried to speak, failed, tried once more, and managed to say in a very gruff voice: 'I c-can't thank you as I should, and of course I know it is for Bella's sake! But I *can* do one thing, and I will! I shall confess the whole to my father, sir, and — and if he says I may not join a Hussar regiment, after behaving so badly, well — well it will serve me right!'

'Yes,' said Mr Beaumaris, 'that is very noble of you, of course, but I have always found it to be an excellent plan, before one indulges in an orgy of expiation, to consider whether the recipient of the sort of confession you have in mind may not be made to suffer a great deal of quite unnecessary pain.'

Bertram was silent for a moment, as this sank into his brain. 'You don't think I should tell my father, sir?'

'I not only don't think you should: I utterly forbid you to mention the matter to him.'

'I don't quite like to deceive him,' Bertram said shyly. 'You see —'

'I am sure you don't, so if your mind is set on doing penance, that will serve your turn excellently. You have been staying in Berkshire with Scunthorpe. Just bear that in mind, and forget that you have ever been within ten miles of London!' He rose, and held out his hand. 'Now I

355

must go. Don't harrow yourself with thinking that you have broken all the ten commandments! You have only done what four out of five young fools do, if set loose upon the town. Incidentally, you have acquired a deal of valuable experience, and when next you come to London you will do much better.'

'I shall never be able to show my face in London again, sir,' said Bertram wistfully. 'But thank you!'

'Nonsense! A few years' service, and you will become a dashing Captain, I daresay, with a fine pair of military whiskers. No one will recognize you. By the way, don't call to take leave of your sister: she is very much occupied today. I will tell her that you are safely despatched to Yorkshire. Ulysses, stop scratching! Do try to be a little more worthy of me! Yes, we are now going, but it is quite unnecessary, and, indeed, extremely uncivil, to caper about in that joyful fashion!' He picked up his gloves, shook hands, and walked to the door, but bethought him of something, and put a hand into his inner pocket. 'Association with that hound — the boon companion of every prig in town, I have not a shadow of doubt — is fast undermining my morals. Your watch, Bertram!'

17

Mr Beaumaris's subsequent proceedings, during the short space of time that elapsed before his elopement, were many and varied, but although they included precise instructions to his coachman and his postilion, and a drive out of London, there was one curious omission: he took no steps to procure a special licence, so that it was to be inferred that he contemplated a flight to the Border, and a ceremony performed across the anvil at Gretna Green: a departure from the canons of good taste which would have staggered any of his associates who had had the least suspicion of his clandestine intentions. But as no one who met him detected anything out of the ordinary in his demeanour no one except his prospective bride speculated at all on the course of action he meant to pursue.

Arabella, naturally enough, employed every moment that was unoccupied by social engagements in a great deal of speculation, but as she was wholly ignorant of the rules governing hasty marriages the need of a special licence did not occur to her. She certainly supposed that she would be driven to Gretna Green, and, having once accepted this hateful necessity, resolutely turned her thoughts away from it. Romantic though such an adventure might be, no young lady, reared, as she had been, in the strictest propriety, could embark on it without feeling herself to have sunk to irreclaimable depths of depravity. How she was ever to explain such conduct to the satisfaction of Papa was an unanswerable question. Only the thought of Bertram's predicament in any way sustained her. She snatched ten minutes between seeing a balloon-ascent and dressing for a more than ordinarily splendid ball, in scribbling a letter to Bertram, assuring him that he need only wait patiently at the Cock for a few more days before he should infallibly be rescued from all his embarrassments.

Of Mr Beaumaris she saw nothing until she met him at Vauxhall Gardens. He was not present at the ball on the night previous to their assignation, a circumstance of which she hardly knew whether to be glad or sorry.

Perhaps it was fortunate that Lady Bridlington's plans for their amusement left her with so little time for reflection. The indulgence of a quiet hour or two in her own bedchamber was not granted her. Try as she would she was unable to stay awake after that splendid ball, and only awoke next morning when Maria drew back her window-blinds. The day was full to overflowing with engagements: she was dressing for Mr Beaumaris's Vauxhall Gardens party, before, as it seemed to her, she well realized what she was about.

It so happened that through the press of invitations which had showered down upon the house in Park Street Arabella had never before visited the famous gardens. They took sculls across the river, to enter by the water-gate, and at any other time she must have been transported by the sight which met her eyes. The gardens, which were laid out in groves and colonnades, were lit (as Lord Bridlington instructively informed her) by no fewer than thirty-seven thousand lamps, some of them suspended in graceful festoons between the pillars of the colonnades. The orchestra, detected across the principal grove, was established in a giant kiosk, glittering all over with coloured lights; there was a spacious Pavilion, lined with mirrors, which formed the principal supper-room for those who did not care to go to the expense of hiring one of the boxes which opened on to the various colonnades; a Rotunda, where excellent concerts were held throughout the season; several magnificent fountains; and innumerable walks where lovers could lose themselves at will.

Mr Beaumaris met his guests at the water-entrance, and conducted them to the Rotunda, where, since it was past eight o'clock, the concert was already in progress. Arabella could scarcely meet his eyes, but forced herself to look up once, very fleetingly, into his face. He smiled at her, but no private speech passed between them.

After the first act of the concert, at about ten o'clock, a bell rang, and those who had no ear for music poured into the Rotunda to witness the marvels of the Grand Cascade. Even though feelings of guilt were in danger of overcoming her, Arabella could not help uttering an exclamation of delight when a dark curtain arose

359

to reveal a rural scene, done in miniature, but amazingly life-like, of a cascade, a watermill, a bridge, and a succession of coaches, wagons, and other vehicles passing with every appearance of verisimilitude across the stage. Even the sound of the wheels, and the rush of the waters was ingeniously counterfeited, so that she thought it no matter for wonder that people should visit Vauxhall three and four times only to see this marvel.

When the curtain descended again, Mr Beaumaris suggested that his guests might like to partake of supper instead of waiting to hear the second part of the concert. This being agreed to, they edged their way out of the row where they were sitting and strolled down one of the colonnades to the supper-box which had been hired for their accommodation. This was in an excellent position, not too close to the orchestra in the kiosk to make conversation a labour, and commanding a splendid view of the principal grove. No one, of course, could visit Vauxhall without eating the wafer-thin slices of ham for which the suppers were famous, or tasting the rack-punch; but in addition to these delicacies Mr Beaumaris had ordered a meal so excellently chosen as to tempt the most fugitive appetite. Even Arabella, whose appetite had deserted her several days before, could enjoy the chicken, cooked before her eyes in a chafing-dish; and was persuaded to toy with a trifle. Mr Beaumaris prepared a peach for her with his own hands, and since an imminent elopement was no excuse, she believed, for a present lapse of good manners, she ate this too, smiling shyly and gratefully at him. She found little to say beyond the merest commonplace throughout supper, but this silence passed unnoticed in the spate of Lord Bridlington's discourse. He kindly explained to the ladies the mechanism which produced the wonders of the Grand Cascade; sketched the history of the Gardens; extensively examined their claim to be considered a development of the old Spring Gardens; and disposed of the tradition which linked the district with the name of Guy Fawkes. He was only interrupted when it became necessary to exchange greetings with some acquaintance who happened to walk past the box; and since his mother murmured encouraging remarks every now and then, and Mr Beaumaris, with great self-control, forbore to utter one of his blighting snubs, he enjoyed himself very much, and was sorry when his host suggested that Miss Tallant would like to see the Fireworks.

He was allowed to take Arabella on his arm on their way to the part of the grounds whence these could best be seen, while Mr Beaumaris followed beside Lady Bridlington, but just as he had secured two excellent places he found himself, quite how he did not know, supplanted, and was obliged to attend to his Mama, who did not like her situation, and insisted on his finding her a place where her view of the set-pieces would not be obscured by the head-dress of a lady who favoured immensely tall ostrich plumes.

Arabella momentarily forgot her troubles in enchantment, and clapped her hands when the rockets soared skywards, and burst into stars. Mr Beaumaris, inured to fireworks, derived even more entertainment through watching her round-eyed delight; but after the first of the set-pieces had burnt itself out, he consulted his watch, and said gently: 'Shall we go, Miss Tallant?'

These words brought her to earth with a shock. An impulse to tell him that she had changed her mind had to be sternly repressed, and all the miseries poor Bertram must be enduring recalled. She clutched her taffeta cloak round her, and said nervously: 'Oh, yes! Is it already time? Yes, let us go at once!'

There was not the least difficulty in detaching themselves unnoticed from a crowd of persons all intent upon the evolutions of a giant Catherine-wheel; Arabella laid a cold hand on Mr Beaumaris's arm, and went with him down an alley, past the Fountain of Neptune, most tastefully illuminated, along one of the colonnades, and so to the land-entrance. Several carriages were awaiting their owners here, and amongst them Mr Beaumaris's travelling chaise, with a pair of horses harnessed to it, and his head-coachman, and one postilion in attendance. Neither of these individuals betrayed the smallest surprise at seeing a lady on his master's arm, and although Arabella was too much embarrassed to raise her eyes she was aware that they were conducting themselves as though this elopement were an everyday occurrence in their lives. They sprang to well-trained activity as soon as they saw their master; the cloths were swept from the back of Mr Beaumaris's highly-bred horses; the steps of the chaise were let down, the doors opened, and Mr Beaumaris handed his bride tenderly up into the luxurious vehicle. So little time had she been kept waiting in the road that she did not even look to see whether any baggage was strapped to the back of the chaise. Mr Beaumaris paused only to exchange a word with the coachman, and then sprang up, and took his place beside Arabella on the comfortably cushioned seat; the doors were shut on them; the postilion swung himself into the saddle, and the equipage moved forward.

Mr Beaumaris spread a soft rug over Arabella's legs, and said: 'I have a warmer cloak here: may I put it round your shoulders?'

'Oh, no, thank you! I am quite warm!' Arabella said nervously.

He took her hand, and kissed it. After a moment she drew it away, and sought desperately for something to say to relieve the tension of the moment.

'How very well-sprung your chaise is, sir!' she achieved.

'I am glad you are pleased with it,' he responded, in the same polite tone which she had used. 'I remembered, of course, that we are alike in detesting hired vehicles.'

'Are — are we?' she said doubtfully. 'I mean, of course —'

'We exchanged opinions, the first time we met, on the only tolerable way of travel,' Mr Beaumaris reminded her.

This recollection not unnaturally deprived her

of speech. Mr Beaumaris, most obligingly, forbore to press her for an answer, but talked agreeably about the concert they had heard that night. Arabella, who had experienced a few moments' panic on finding herself shut up with her bridegroom in a chaise, travelling to an unknown but probably remote destination, was overwhelmingly grateful to him for behaving precisely as though he were escorting her home from some place of entertainment. She had been much afraid that he would perhaps have tried to make love to her. She had not much experience in such matters, but it had occurred to her that a gentleman starting on an elopement might expect some demonstration of affection from his beloved. A week earlier, safe in the darkness of her bedchamber, her cheek on a damp pillow, Arabella had owned to herself that life could hold no greater happiness for her than for Mr Beaumaris to take her in his arms; now, miserably conscious of her duplicity, she could imagine nothing more unnerving. But Mr Beaumaris, surely the calmest of runaway-bridegrooms, showed no desire to succumb to his ardour. Finding that he was being answered in monosyllables, he presently gave up trying to engage Arabella in genteel conversation, and leaned back in his corner of the chaise, his head a little turned against the squabs behind it towards her, so that he could watch her face in the dim moonlight that penetrated into the vehicle. Arabella was scarcely aware that he had stopped talking to her. She was lost in her own thoughts, seated bolt upright, and clinging with one hand to the strap that hung from the wall of the chaise beside her. She could see the postilion bobbing up and down before her, and, when the cobbles were left behind, was vaguely conscious of having left the streets and to be driving through the countryside. In what direction they were travelling, or where she would find herself at the first halt, she had no idea, nor were these the questions that troubled her mind. The impropriety of her conduct she had from the start known to be unforgiveable; what now filled her with repugnance was the sudden realization that in marrying Mr Beaumaris while he still laboured under a misapprehension she was treating him so shabbily that it was doubtful if he would ever pardon her, much less continue to regard her with even a shred of affection. At this melancholy reflection a small sob escaped her, which had the effect of making Mr Beaumaris say: 'What is it, my love?'

'Nothing! Nothing!' whispered Arabella, much agitated.

To her relief, he appeared to accept this, for he said no more. She decided, in a wave of remorse, that he was the greatest gentleman of her acquaintance, with the best manners, the most delicate forbearance, and quite the kindest disposition. It was at this point that the moment for which Mr Beaumaris had been waiting arrived. All at once Arabella wondered how soon after the wedding-ceremony she could break the news to him that she required him not only to forgive her brother's debt to him, but also to bestow a hundred pounds on him for the settlement of all his other liabilities; and what words she could find with which most unexceptionably to express this urgent necessity. There were no such words, as a very little cudgelling of her brain sufficed to convince her. She could not imagine how she could ever have been foolish enough to have supposed that the thing could be done, or that such a confession could be made without afterwards rendering it impossible for her to convince him that she did indeed love him.

These, and still more disagreeable thoughts, were jostling one another in Arabella's frightened mind when the pace at which they were travelling seemed suddenly to slacken. The chaise swung round at so sharp an angle that only her clutch on the strap saved Arabella from being thrown on to Mr Beaumaris's shoulder. It proceeded for a very little way, and then drew up. Arabella turned towards the dupe beside her, and said breathlessly: 'I cannot! I cannot! Mr Beaumaris, I am *very* sorry, but it was all a mistake! Please take me back to London at once! Oh, please take me back!'

Mr Beaumaris received this daunting request with a remarkable degree of composure, merely replying, as the door of the chaise was opened: 'Shall we discuss this matter in a more private spot? Let me assist you to alight, my love!'

'Please take me back! I — I don't want to elope, after all!' said Arabella, in an urgent whisper.

'Then we won't elope,' returned Mr Beaumaris reassuringly. 'I must own that I think it quite unnecessary for us to do so. Come!'

Arabella hesitated, but since he seemed determined that she should descend from the chaise, and perhaps wanted to rest his horses, she allowed him to hand her down. They seemed to be standing before a large building, but it showed none of the welcoming lights to be expected of a posting-inn, nor had the chaise driven into a courtyard. At the top of a flight of broad, shallow stone steps a large door opened, and a beam of light from the interior of the building showed Arabella neat flower-beds flanking the entrance. Before she had recovered from the surprise of finding herself at what was plainly a private residence, Mr Beaumaris had led her up the steps, and into a lofty hall, furnished in a massive style, and lit by candles in wall-chandeliers. An elderly butler bowed them in, and said 'Good-evening sir.' One powdered and liveried footman divested Mr Beaumaris of his cloak, another relieved him of his hat and gloves.

Arabella stood turned to stone as all the implications of her surroundings burst upon her. Mr Beaumaris's soothing assurance to her that they would not elope now became invested with the most sinister significance, and it was a pathetically white and frightened face which she turned towards him. He smiled at her, but before either of them had time to speak, the butler had informed Mr Beaumaris that he would find the Yellow Saloon in readiness; and a most respectable-looking housekeeper, with neat white hair under a starched cap, had appeared upon the scene, and was dropping a curtsy to Arabella.

'Good-evening, miss! Good-evening, Mr Robert! Please to take Miss into the saloon, while I see that the maids unpack her trunk! You will find a nice fire, for I am sure Miss must be chilled after the drive, so late as it is. Let me take your cloak, miss! I shall bring you up a glass of hot milk directly: I am sure you will be glad of it.'

The promise of a glass of hot milk, which hardly seemed to be in keeping with the hideous vision of seduction and rape which had leapt to her mind, a little reassured Arabella. One of the footmen had thrown open a door at the back of the hall; Mr Beaumaris possessed himself of a trembling, icy little hand, and said: 'I want to make you known to Mrs Watchet, my love, who is a very old friend of mine. Indeed, one of my earliest allies!'

'Now, Master Robert! I'm sure I am very happy to see you here, miss — and mind, now, don't let Master Robert keep you out of your bed till all hours!'

The fear that Master Robert had quite different intentions receded still farther. Arabella summoned up a smile, said something in a shy little voice, and allowed herself to be led into a saloon, fitted up in the first style of elegance, and offering her all the comfort of a small fire, burning in a brightly polished grate.

The door was softly closed behind them; Mr Beaumaris drew a chair invitingly forward, and said: 'Come and sit down, Miss Tallant! You know, I cannot but be glad that you have decided after all not to elope with me. To tell you the truth, there is one circumstance at least that makes me reluctant to proceed with you to Scotland — a journey that would occupy six or seven days, I daresay, before we found ourselves back in London.'

'Oh!' said Arabella, sitting down primly on the edge of the chair, and regarding him out of scared, doubtful eyes.

'Yes,' said Mr Beaumaris. 'Ulysses!'

Her eyes widened. 'Ulysses?' she repeated blankly.

'The animal you were so obliging as to bestow upon me,' he explained. 'Most unfortunately, he has developed so marked a predilection for my society that he frets himself to skin and bone if I am absent from him for more than a night. I did not quite like to bring him with me upon our elopement, for I can discover no precedent for taking a dog with one upon such an occasion, and one scarcely cares to violate the conventions at such a moment.'

The door opened just then to admit Mrs Watchet, who came in, carrying a glass of steaming milk on a silver tray. This, with a plate of macaroons, she set down on a small table at Arabella's elbow, telling her that when she had drunk it, and said goodnight to Master Robert, she should be escorted upstairs to her bed-chamber. With a slightly severe injunction to Mr Beaumaris not to keep Miss talking to him too long, she then curtsied herself out of the room.

'Sir!' said Arabella desperately, as soon as they were alone again: 'What is this house to which you have brought me?'

'I have brought you to my grandmother's house, at Wimbledon,' he replied. 'She is a very old lady, and keeps early hours, so you must forgive her for not being downstairs to receive you. You will meet her tomorrow morning. My aunt, who lives with her, would undoubtedly have sat up to receive you had she not gone a few days ago to stay with one of her sisters for a short time.'

'Your grandmother's house?' exclaimed Arabella, almost starting from her chair. 'Good God, why have you brought me to such a place, Mr Beaumaris?'

'Well, you know,' he explained, 'I could not but feel that it was possible you might think better of that notion of eloping. Of course, if, after a night's repose, you still believe we should go to Gretna Green, I assure you I shall escort you there, whatever Ulysses' claims upon me may be. For myself, the more I consider the matter, the more I am convinced that we should do better to steel ourselves to meet the felicitations of our friends, and announce our betrothal in the columns of the society journals in the accepted manner.'

'Mr Beaumaris,' interrupted Arabella, pale but resolute, 'I cannot marry you!' She added, on another of her small sobs: 'I don't know why you should ever have wanted to marry me, but —'

'I have lost my entire fortune on 'Change, and must instantly repair it,' he interrupted promptly.

Arabella rose jerkily, and confronted him. 'I have not a penny in the world!' she announced.

'In that case,' responded Mr Beaumaris, maintaining his calm, 'you really have no choice in the matter: you must obviously marry me. Since we are being frank with one another, I will confess that my fortune is still intact.'

'I deceived you! I am not an heiress!' Arabella said, feeling that he could not have understood her words.

'You never deceived me for a moment,' said Mr Beaumaris, smiling at her in a way which made her tremble still more violently.

'I *lied* to you!' cried Arabella, determined to bring him to a sense of her iniquities.

'Most understandable,' agreed Mr Beaumaris. 'But I am really quite uninterested in heiresses.'

'Mr Beaumaris,' said Arabella earnestly, 'the whole of London believes me to be a wealthy woman!'

'Yes, and since the whole of London must certainly continue in that belief, you have, as I have already pointed out to you, no choice but to marry me,' he said. '*My* fortune, happily, is so large that *your* lack of fortune need never be suspected.'

'Oh, why didn't you tell me you knew the truth?' she cried, wringing her hands.

He possessed himself of them, and held them lightly. 'My dearest goose, why didn't you trust me, when I assured you that you might?' he countered. 'I have cherished throughout the belief that you would confide in me, and you see I was quite right. So certain was I that you would not, when the time actually came, run off with me in this absurd fashion, that I visited my

371

grandmother yesterday, and told her the whole story. She was very much diverted, and commanded me to bring you to stay for a few days with her. I hope you will not object to this: she frightens half the world, but you will have me to support you through the ordeal.'

Arabella pulled her hands resolutely away, and turned from him to hide her quivering lips, and suffused eyes. 'It is worse than you know!' she said, in a stilled tone. 'When you know all the truth, you will not wish to marry me! I have been worse than untruthful: I have been shameless! I can never marry you, Mr Beaumaris!'

'This is most disturbing,' he said. 'Not only have I sent the notice of our betrothal to the *Gazette*, and the *Morning Post*, but I have obtained your father's consent to our marriage.'

At this, she spun round to face him again, a look of utter astonishment in her face. '*My father's consent?*' she repeated incredulously.

'It is usual, you know,' explained Mr Beaumaris apologetically.

'But you do not know my father!'

'On the contrary. I made his acquaintance last week, and spent two most agreeable nights at Heythram,' he said.

'But — Did Lady Bridlington tell you?'

'No, not Lady Bridlington. Your brother let slip the name of his home once, and I have an excellent memory. I am sorry, by the way, that Bertram should have been having such an uncomfortable time during my absence from town. That was quite my fault: I should have sought him out, and settled his difficulties before

I left for Yorkshire. I did write to him, but he had unfortunately departed from the Red Lion before the delivery of my letter. However, you won't find that the experience has harmed him, so I must hope to be forgiven.'

Her cheeks were now very much flushed. 'You know it all then! Oh, what must you think of me? I asked you to marry me because — because I wanted you to give me seven hundred pounds to save poor Bertram from a debtor's prison!'

'I know you did,' said Mr Beaumaris cordially. 'I don't know how I contrived to keep my countenance. When did it occur to you, my ridiculous little love, that to demand a large sum of money from your bridegroom as soon as the ring was on your finger might be a trifle awkward?'

'Just now — in your chaise!' she confessed, covering her face with her hands. 'I couldn't do it! I have behaved very, very badly, but when I realized what I was about — oh, indeed, I knew I could never do it!'

'We have both behaved very badly,' he agreed. 'I encouraged Fleetwood to spread the news that you were a great heiress: I even allowed him to suppose that I knew all about your family. I thought it would be amusing to see whether I could make you the rage of London — and I blush to confess it, my darling: it *was* amusing! Nor do I really regret it in the least, for if I had not set out on this most reprehensible course we might never have come much in one another's way again, after our first meeting, and I might never have discovered that I had found the very girl I had been looking for for so long.'

'No, no, how can you say so?' she exclaimed, large tears standing on the ends of her lashes. 'I came to London in the hope of — of contracting an eligible marriage, and I asked you to marry me because you are so very rich! You *could* not wish to marry such an odious creature!'

'No, perhaps I couldn't,' he replied. 'But although you may have forgotten that when I first addressed myself to you, you declined my offer, I have not. If wealth was all your object, I can't conceive what should have induced you to do so! It seemed to me that you were not entirely indifferent to me. All things considered, I decided that my proper course was to present myself to your parents without further loss of time. And I am very glad I did so, for not only did I spend a very pleasant time at the Vicarage, but I also enjoyed a long talk with your mother — By the way, do you know how much you resemble her? More, I think, than any of your brothers and sisters, though they are all remarkably handsome. But, as I say, I enjoyed a long talk with her, and was encouraged to hope, from what she told me, that I had not been mistaken in thinking you were not indifferent to me.'

'I never wrote a word to Mama, or even to Sophy, about — about — not being indifferent to you!' Arabella said involuntarily.

'Well, I do not know how that may be,' said Mr Beaumaris, 'but Mama and Sophy were not at all surprised to receive a visit from me. Perhaps you may have mentioned me rather frequently in your letters, or perhaps Lady Bridlington gave Mama a hint that I was the most determined of your suitors.'

The mention of her godmother made Arabella start, and exclaim: 'Lady Bridlington! Good God, I left a letter for her on the table in the hall, telling her of the dreadful thing I had done, and begging her to forgive me!'

'Don't disturb yourself, my love: Lady Bridlington knows very well where you are. Indeed, I found her most helpful, particularly when it came to packing what you would need for a brief sojourn at my grandmother's house. She promised that her own maid should attend to the matter while we were listening to that tedious concert. I daresay she has long since told that son of hers that he may look for the notice of our engagement in tomorrow's *Gazette*, together with the intelligence that we have both of us gone out of town to stay with the Dowager Duchess of Wigan. By the time we reappear in London, we must hope that our various acquaintances will have grown so accustomed to the news that we shall not be quite overwhelmed by their astonishment, their chagrin, or their felicitations. But I am strongly of the opinion that you should permit me to escort you home to Heythram as soon as possible: *you* will naturally wish your father to marry us, and *I* am extremely impatient to carry off my wife without any loss of time. My darling, what in the world have I said to make you cry?'

'Oh, nothing, nothing!' sobbed Arabella. 'Only that I don't deserve to be so happy, and I n-never was indifferent to you, though I t-tried very hard to be, when I thought you were only trifling with m-me!'

Mr Beaumaris then took her firmly into his arms, and kissed her; after which she derived much comfort from clutching the lapel of his elegant coat, and weeping into his shoulder. None of the very gratifying things which Mr Beaumaris murmured into the curls that were tickling his chin had any other effect on her than to make her sob more bitterly than ever, so he presently told her that even his love for her could not prevail upon him to allow her to ruin his favourite coat. This changed her tears to laughter, and after he had dried her face, and kissed her again, she became tolerably composed, and was able to sit down on the sofa beside him, and to accept from him the glass of tepid milk which he told her she must drink if she did not wish to incur Mrs Watchet's displeasure. She smiled mistily, and sipped the milk, saying after a moment: 'And Papa gave his consent! Oh, what will he say when he knows the whole? What did you tell him?'

'I told him the truth,' replied Mr Beaumaris.

Arabella nearly dropped the glass. 'All the truth?' she faltered, dismay in her face.

'All of it — oh, not the truth about Bertram! His name did not enter into our conversation, and I strictly charged him, when I sent him off to Yorkshire, not to divulge one word of his adventures. Much as I like and esteem your father, I cannot feel that any good purpose would be served by distressing him with *that* story. I told him the truth about you and me.'

'Was he — dreadfully displeased with me?' asked Arabella, in a small, apprehensive voice.

'He was, I fear, a little grieved,' owned Mr Beaumaris. 'But when he understood that you would never have announced yourself to have been an heiress had you not overheard me talking like a coxcomb to Charles Fleetwood, he was soon brought to perceive that I was even more to blame for the deception than you.'

'*Was* he?' said Arabella doubtfully.

'Drink your milk, my love! Certainly he was. Between us, your Mama and I were able to show him that without my prompting Charles would never have spread the rumour abroad, and that once the rumour had been so spread it was impossible for you to deny it, since naturally no one ever asked you if it were true. I daresay he may give you a little scold, but I am quite sure you are already forgiven.'

'Did he forgive you too?' asked Arabella, awed.

'*I* had all the merit of making the confession,' Mr Beaumaris pointed out virtuously. 'He forgave me freely. I cannot imagine why you should look so much surprised: I found him in every way delightful, and have seldom enjoyed an evening more than the one I spent conversing with him in his study, after your Mama and Sophy had gone to bed. Indeed, we sat talking until the candles guttered in their sockets.'

Arabella's awed expression became even more marked. 'Dear sir, what — what did you talk *about?*' she enquired, quite unable to visualize Papa and the Nonpareil hobnobbing together.

'We discussed certain aspects of Wolf's *Prolegomena ad Homerum*, a copy of which work I chanced to see upon his bookshelf,' replied Mr Beaumaris calmly. 'I myself picked up a copy when I was in Vienna last year, and was much interested in Wolf's theory that more than one hand was employed in the writing of the *Iliad* and the *Odyssey*.'

'Is — is *that* what the book is about?' asked Arabella.

He smiled, but replied gravely: 'Yes, that is what it is about — though your father, a far more profound scholar than I am, found the opening chapter, which treats of the proper methods to be used in the recension of ancient manuscripts, of even more interest. He took me a little out of my depth there, but I hope I may have profited by his very just observations.'

'Did you *enjoy* that?' demanded Arabella, much impressed.

'Very much. In spite of my frippery ways, you know, I do occasionally enjoy rational conversation, just as I can spend a very agreeable evening playing at lottery-tickets with Mama, and Sophy, and the children.'

'You did not do *that*!' she cried. 'Oh, you are quizzing me! You must have been shockingly bored!'

'Nothing of the sort! The man who could be bored in the midst of such a lively family as yours must be an insufferable fellow, above being pleased by anything. By the by, if that uncle of yours does not come up to scratch, we must do something towards helping Harry to achieve his burning ambition to become a second Nelson. Not the eccentric uncle who died, and left you his entire fortune, but the one who still lives.'

'Oh, pray don't speak of that dreadful fortune ever again!' begged Arabella, hanging down her head.

'But I must speak of it!' objected Mr Beaumaris. 'Since I presume that we shall frequently be inviting the various members of your family to stay with us, and can hardly pass them all off as heirs and heiresses, *some* explanation of your superior circumstances must be forthcoming! Your Mama — an admirable woman! — and I decided that the eccentric uncle would serve our turn very well. We were further agreed, quite tacitly, you know, that it will be unnecessary, and, indeed, quite undesirable, to mention the matter to Papa.'

'Oh, no it would never do to tell him that!' she said quickly. 'He would not like it at all, and when he is grieved with any of us —Oh, if only he does not discover the scrape Bertram fell into, and if only Bertram didn't fail to pass that examination at Oxford, which I am much afraid he may have, because it did not sound to me as though — '

'It is not of the slightest consequence,' he interrupted. 'Bertram — though Papa does not yet know it — is not going to Oxford: he is going to join a good cavalry regiment, where he will feel very much more at home, and, I daresay, become a great credit to us all.'

At this, Arabella caught his hand in her free one, and kissed it, exclaiming, with a sob in her voice: 'How good you are! How much, much *too* good you are, my *dear* Mr Beaumaris!'

'Never,' said Mr Beaumaris, snatching his hand away, and taking Arabella into his arms so ungently that the rest of the milk in the glass was spilt over her gown, 'Never, Arabella, dare to do such a thing again! And don't talk such fustian to me, or persist in calling me Mr Beaumaris!'

'Oh, I must!' protested Arabella, into his shoulder. 'I can't call you — I can't call you — Robert!'

'You have called me Robert very prettily, and you will find, if you persevere, that it will rise quite easily to your lips in a very short space of time.'

'Well, if it will please you, I will *try* to say it,' said Arabella. She sat up s uddenly, as a thought occurred to her, and said in her impulsive way: 'Oh, Mr Beau — I mean, dear Robert! — there was an unfortunate female, called Leaky Peg, in that horrid house where I went to see poor Bertram, and she was so very kind to him! Do you think —?'

'No, Arabella,' said Mr Beaumaris firmly. 'I do not!'

She was disappointed, but docile. 'No?' she said.

'No,' said Mr Beaumaris, drawing her back into his arms.

'I thought we might have taken her away from that dreadful place,' suggested Arabella, smoothing his coat-lapel with a coaxing hand.

'I am quite sure you did, my love, but while I am prepared to receive into my household climbing-boys and stray curs, I must draw the line at a lady rejoicing in the name of Leaky Peg.'

'You don't think she might learn to become a housemaid, or something of that sort? You know — '

'I only know two things,' interrupted Mr Beaumaris. 'The first is that she is not going to make the attempt in any house of mine; and the second, and by far the more important, is that I adore you, Arabella!'

Arabella was so much pleased by this disclosure that she lost interest in Leaky Peg, and confined herself to the far more agreeable task of convincing Mr Beaumaris that his very obliging sentiments were entirely reciprocated.

We do hope that you have enjoyed reading
this large print book.

Did you know that all of our titles
are available for purchase?

We publish a wide range of high quality
large print books including:
Romances, Mysteries, Classics
General Fiction
Non Fiction and Westerns

Special interest titles available in
large print are:
The Little Oxford Dictionary
Music Book
Song Book
Hymn Book
Service Book

Also available from us courtesy of
Oxford University Press:
Young Readers' Dictionary
(large print edition)
Young Readers' Thesaurus
(large print edition)

For further information or a free
brochure, please contact us at:
Ulverscroft Large Print Books Ltd.,
The Green, Bradgate Road, Anstey,
Leicester, LE7 7FU, England.
Tel: (00 44) 0116 236 4325
Fax: (00 44) 0116 234 0205

SPRIG MUSLIN

Georgette Heyer

Sir Gareth Ludlow has decided he'll never fall in love again — but Fate has other ideas ... A chance encounter with Amanda, a young and devastatingly pretty runaway, inspires him to set her on a path towards a good life, despite the fact that she is determined to keep her identity a secret. But Sir Gareth has been neck-deep in a life of debauchery and hedonism ever since his fiancee's death, and Amanda's startlingly lively imagination proves to be more than he bargained for. As they match each other lie for outrageous lie, will the truth eventually prevail?

COTILLION

Georgette Heyer

The three great-nephews of cantankerous
Mr Penicuik know better than to ignore his
summons, especially when it concerns the
bestowal of his fortune. The wily old gentleman has hatched an outrageous plan for his
stepdaughter's future and his own amusement: his fortune will be lovely Catherine
Charing's dowry if she marries one of his
great-nephews. To the spirited Kitty, the
conditions of her guardian's will before she
can inherit a tuppence are intolerable. But
while the beaux are scrambling for her hand,
Kitty counters with her own inventive, if
daring, scheme: a sham engagement that
should help keep wedlock at bay . . .

'The gothic landscape of the Cemetery of Forgotten Books – the winding streets of Barcelona's old quarter – haunt a novel about books and writing and secrets. **Wonderful**'   Kate Mosse

'Bold, serious and shocking. His treatment of Spain's tortured history in the 20th century is as significant as his literary skill. These are things that belong not just to one city, but to the world'   *The Times*

'The prose is intelligent but unpretentious, and the author is clear in his intentions to provide a rollicking, fun read . . . the novel's themes address the power of narrative, and many sharp lines pertain to storytelling . . . hugely enjoyable'   *Daily Telegraph*

'If the previous book celebrated the ecstasies of reading then this one – no less in love with literature, and no less crammed with archetypal plots – explores the agonies of writing. **Zafón thrillingly tiptoes along the fine line between paranormal events and psychological delusion** . . . One virtuoso hyper-Gothic scene snaps at the heels of another'   *Independent*

'*The Angel's Game* draws with relish on all the conventions beloved of Wilkie Collins, Dickens and even the penny dreadfuls . . . then weaves them into something entirely original and surprisingly moving that hold the reader's expectations until the final twist'   *Observer*

'**A delicious blend of literary thriller and romance**. Zafón is a master of the atmospheric . . . its faith in the power of fiction is **endearing, and addictive**'   *Financial Times*

'Starts off as an intelligent literary thriller, but morphs into action-packed adventure with a hefty body count'   *Daily Express*

'The Cemetery of Forgotten Books – "a colossal labyrinth of bridges, passages and shelves" – is **a wonderful creation**'   *Sunday Telegraph*

'Carlos Ruiz Zafón has followed up his masterly debut, *The Shadow of the Wind*, with a work of no less brilliance . . . it **has wit, style, great sex and a hugely entertaining plot**'   *Mail on Sunday*

'His narrative style embraces relentless pace and fantastical and magical diversions . . . [Zafón] takes us into sinful corners, indulging fantasies that are erotic, magical or violent'   *Guardian*

The Prisoner of Heaven

'Zafón combines sincere engagement with genre tradition with clever touches of the literary post-modern ... **This is explicitly, and joyously, a book about books, about what can be learned from them and what is lost when they are lost'**   *Guardian*

'Zafón's characters and dialogue are **as lively and full-blooded as ever'**
                                                                                                        Observer

'The story has heart, menace, torture, kindness, cruelty, sacrifice, and a deep devotion to what makes humans tick'   *New York Journal of Books*

'This **wonderfully atmospheric**, historical mystery is an adventure story of the highest class – **fast paced and stylishly written'**   *Good Book Guide*

The Labyrinth of the Spirits

'Zafón is a master storyteller, combining the postmodern and the traditional in an enchanting hymn to literature ... **Magnificent**: a dizzying tale of drama, intrigue and passion'   *Mail on Sunday*

'**A colossal, genre-crossing achievement** ... it is to be hoped that Zafón's next books deal as seriously and enjoyably with the present and future of Barcelona'   *Guardian*

'Moving and engaging. This is a novel to lose oneself in, and it promotes the sort of reading experience we remember from childhood – of complete absorption into a fantasy world'   *Irish Times*

'**Sprawling, seductive and hugely atmospheric'**   *Sunday Express*

'Rich, ambitious storytelling'   *Sunday Times*

'Neither too geeky nor too highbrow, Zafón's genre-mashing novels provide a high-definition, alternative account of Spain's turbulent 20th-century history, with added Hollywood blockbuster thrills. I was hooked' *Daily Mail*

'This is a suspenseful story of loss, betrayal and redemption'   *Independent*

The City of Mist

'As well as allusions to the Forgotten Books novels themselves, there's everywhere evidence of the **storytelling skill and intoxicating tropes** – Faustian pacts, fateful meetings, labyrinthine architecture and nested stories – that made Zafón such a phenomenon' *Daily Mail*

'The Dickens of Barcelona . . . A **flamboyant farewell** from a grand contemporary writer' *Sydney Morning Herald*

'Ruiz Zafón's many fans are sure to find his collection of short stories both familiarly **satisfying and poignant** . . . Readers will once again luxuriate in his florid descriptions of his hometown of Barcelona that bring to life that magical and mysterious city . . . [they] will encounter new characters but also find familiar names, offering fresh perspectives on fictional lives we already know so well' *Washington Post*

'A posthumous parting gift from Ruiz Zafón to his millions of fans . . . with much-loved places and characters making fleeting reappearances, it's a fitting coda to his life and world' *Observer*

'**Mysterious, imbued with a sense of menace, and told with the warmth, wit, and humor of Zafón's inimitable voice** . . . the stories contained within this posthumous collection summon up the mesmerizing magic of their brilliant creator and invite us to come dream along with him' *Book Riot*

The Shadow of the Wind

'*Shadow* is the real deal, a novel full of cheesy splendour and creaking trapdoors, a novel where even the subplots have subplots . . . **one gorgeous read**' Stephen King

'*The Shadow of the Wind* is **a triumph** of the storyteller's art. I couldn't put it down. Enchanting, hilarious and heartbreaking, **this book will change your life. An instant classic**' *Daily Telegraph*

'Carlos Ruiz Zafón's complex thriller, *The Shadow of the Wind*, has proved **a runaway, word-of-mouth success** across Europe. In Zafón's native Barcelona, you are the odd one out if you haven't read it' *The Times*

'**Irresistib** . . . . a and you'll glimpse t . . . . *Guardian*

4000000165566 3

'Tremendously enjoyable . . . the book's 400 pages whip past with incredible speed'   *Sunday Telegraph*

'This is highly-sophisticated, fun reading that keeps you gripped and tests the brain cells all at the same time. **What more could you ask for?**'
                                                                              Scotsman

'**One of those rare novels that combine brilliant plotting with sublime writing** . . . word of mouth alone is sure to make it a bestseller'
                                                        James Daunt, *Sunday Times*

'Everything about *The Shadow of the Wind* is smooth. The language purrs along, while the plot twists and unravels with a languid grace . . . Zafón's novel is **atmospheric, beguiling and thoroughly readable**'   *Observer*

'Set in the author's native Barcelona in the years after the Spanish Civil War, this gripping novel **has the feel of a gothic ghost story**, complete with crumbling, ivy-covered mansions, gargoyles and dank prison cells . . .'
                                                                              Daily Mail

'A **stunning** thriller about the discovery of a forgotten book, which leads to a hunt for an elusive author. I loved it so much that I bought six copies for my friends'   *Sunday Express*

'*The Shadow of the Wind* is a novel that is prompting superlatives and winning fans. It is likely to become one of those word-of-mouth recommendations that grows into a worldwide hit'   *Independent*

'**I couldn't put it down but I didn't want to rush it** as every sentence is beautifully crafted and every character unique'   *Evening Standard*

'The translation by Lucia Graves is excellent, mixing formality with poetry, so the rambling prose occasionally sparkles with lovely phrases . . . The twists of the story, which folds in on itself again and again like complicated origami, eventually reveal a simple shape. Love and deception are at the heart of the literary mystery – aren't they always?'   *Scotland on Sunday*

'Anyone who enjoys novels that are scary, erotic, touching, tragic and thrilling should **rush right out to the nearest bookstore and pick up *The Shadow of the Wind***'   *Washington Post*

THE
CITY of MIST

Also by Carlos Ruiz Zafón

THE
CITY of MIST
CARLOS RUIZ ZAFÓN

Translated from Spanish by Lucia Graves
With two stories translated by Carlos Ruiz Zafón
And one story written in English by Carlos Ruiz Zafón

W&N
WEIDENFELD & NICOLSON

First published in Great Britain in 2021 by Weidenfeld & Nicolson,
This paperback edition first published in Great Britain in 2022
by Weidenfeld & Nicolson,
an imprint of The Orion Publishing Group Ltd
Carmelite House, 50 Victoria Embankment
London EC4Y 0DZ

An Hachette UK Company

1 3 5 7 9 10 8 6 4 2

Support for the translation of this book was provided by Acción Cultural Española,
AC/E.

AC/E
ACCIÓN CULTURAL
ESPAÑOLA

A CIP catalogue record for this book is
available from the British Library.

ISBN (Mass Market Paperback) 978 1 4746 2313 1
ISBN (eBook) 978 1 4746 2314 8
ISBN (Audio) 978 1 4746 2315 5

Typeset by Input Data Services Ltd, Somerset
Printed in Great Britain by Clays Ltd, Elcograf S.p.A.

www.weidenfeldandnicolson.co.uk
www.orionbooks.co.uk

Soon afterwards, like figures made of mist, father and son disappear into the crowd of the Ramblas, their steps lost forever in the shadow of the wind.

The Shadow of the Wind

CONTENTS

FOREWORD

This collection of ten tales invites the reader for a final visit to the labyrinth of Carlos Ruiz Zafón. What a dream is to reality, this labyrinth is to Barcelona and its turbulent, melancholic deep-rooted history. Readers familiar with Zafón's bestselling Cemetery of Forgotten Books quartet will relish the encounters with the familiar faces, names and bloodlines that pepper these tales. For readers new to Zafón, *The City of Mist* is an elegant side-door into one of our century's notable literary microcosms. The book showcases the breadth and depth of the author's imagination, and to lure the unwary newcomer, an excerpt from *The Shadow of the Wind* is included here. My advice? Get hooked. The quartet of novels is wonderful.

Nothing comes from nowhere, and Zafón's labyrinth is derived from promiscuous reading. Unencumbered by notions of high and low culture, the author absorbed – and was informed by – Gothic romance, hard-boiled crime, comics, fable and legend, war reportage, graphic novels, Hollywood, metafictional *divertimenti*, as well as the Spanish and world literature one would expect. Yet if Zafón was magpie-minded, he was wholly his own magpie, and each page of *The City of Mist* authenticates its provenance. Certainly, if you write in Spanish about labyrinths and mystical bibliophilia the spectre of Borges never fails to appear: but Zafón, unlike the librarian of Buenos Aires, is a dextrous juggler of genre, crafts memorable dialogue and is deeply curious about the human heart. As the following pages testify.

While *The City of Mist* is replete with Zafónesque tropes and belongs to the same creative mural as his quartet, it also exhibits the author's range and versatility. Be warned, dear Reader. You will suffer the ache of long-ago lost love. Scurry through 1940s Barcelona with a war orphan. Eavesdrop on a Faustian pact. Shadow a world-weary assassin who knows a peaceful retirement is not an option. Converse with prostitutes, pimps and prisoners. Get to know a Grand Inquisitor dreaming of sainthood better than you might wish. Travel with both Miguel de Cervantes and Cervantes' fictional Cervantes. Kiss a stranger as the world ends. Cross the Atlantic on a steamship with Antoni Gaudí. So many and such varied leaps in perspective, within the ten stories and between them . . . all without a single plot creak, or a feeling of being wrenched – for this reader, at least. Trying to predict where Zafón's labyrinth will take you, or who we'll meet there, is a fool's errand. Give in to its twists and turns. The impossibility of guessing 'What happens next?' is one of the principal joys of this author.

An accomplished prose style that harmonises with the story is a holy ghost that elevates the good to the excellent. Thanks to translator Lucia Graves, it is evident to the Anglophone reader that Zafón is a most accomplished stylist. My own Spanish translator once told me about the difficulties of rendering the noun 'understatement' in his native tongue. For me, Zafón is a great stylistic 'understater'. This quality serves simultaneously to anchor and to heighten his fantastical passages; and to burnish the moments of poetry embedded in the unfussy prose. A character's pupils 'narrow like the eyes of a wolf at the sight of fresh blood'. Buildings are 'gutted by bombs and poverty'. Speaking of bombs, bombers appear like 'a swarm of black angels [that] spread over the red sky of Barcelona'. Zafón has a keen eye for well-crafted phrases and dictums. 'The long night of history had only just begun.' 'Death, which always follows gold, is moving to Madrid.' 'One man's hell is another's paradise lost.' These are arresting enough to interrupt the flow of reading, but only momentarily. I soon dive back in for more, with an enhanced understanding of the fictional world; and, perhaps, of my world, as well.

A work of fiction is the totality of countless decisions made by the writer. What and who is the story about? When and where is it set? What language should it be told in? What motivates the characters? What are their journeys, trials and endings? How any given writer answers these questions not only constructs the narrative, decision by decision: it also puts the writer on display like some MRI scan of the soul. 'Fiction is the lie that tells the truth,' says Neil Gaiman – truths about the world, the heart and everything in between, certainly, but also truths about the writer. I was never lucky enough to meet Carlos Ruiz Zafón in person, so I know him only via his work and interviews on the internet. But the stories of *The City of Mist* speak of a human who knew that injustice and cruelty are a pandemic; but also, that the imagination is a vaccine, a refuge and a cradle of resistance. That any individual can be flawed, selfish and cruel; and, equally, capable of grace that startles even themselves. That reading is an act of seance and survival. That life is both very long and all too brief. Mr Zafón left this world too early, but he bequeathed his past, present and future readers one imperishable labyrinth.

Step this way. Mind the gap.

David Mitchell
September 2021

BLANCA AND THE
DEPARTURE

(FROM THE IMAGINED MEMOIRS
OF ONE DAVID MARTÍN)

Translated by Lucia Graves

I

I've always envied the ease with which some people are able to forget – people for whom the past is only a set of last season's clothes or a pair of old shoes that can simply be condemned to the back of a cupboard to ensure they're unable to retrace lost footsteps. I had the misfortune of remembering everything, and that everything in turn, remembered me. I recall my early childhood days of cold and loneliness, of dead moments spent gazing at greyness; and the dark mirror that haunted my father's eyes. Yet I can barely bring back the memory of a single friend. I can conjure up the faces of children in the Ribera neighbourhood with whom I sometimes played or quarrelled in the street, but none I would wish to rescue from that land of indifference. None except Blanca's.

Blanca was about two years older than me. I met her one day in April outside my front door. She was walking hand in hand with a maid who had come to collect some books from a small antiquarian bookshop, opposite the building site for the concert hall. By a quirk of fate the bookshop didn't open until twelve o'clock that day and the maid had arrived at eleven thirty, leaving a half-hour gap during which, unbeknown to me, my fate was about to be sealed. Had it been up to me, I would never have dared exchange a single word with her. Her clothes, her smell and her elegant bearing spoke of a wealthy girl cosseted by silks and velvet; she clearly didn't belong to my world, and even less did I belong to hers. We were separated by only a few metres of street and miles of invisible laws. I merely gazed at her, the way one admires objects that have been consigned to a glass cabinet or to the display window of one of those shops that may look open, but you know you'll never enter. I've often thought that, were it not for my father's firm strictures regarding my personal cleanliness, Blanca would never have noticed me. My father was of the opinion that he'd seen enough filth during the war to fill nine lives and although we were as poor as church mice, he had taught me, from a very early age, to become used to the freezing water that ran – when it felt like it – from the tap above the sink, and to those soap bars that smelled of bleach and scraped everything off you, even your regrets. That is how, when I'd just turned eight, yours truly, David Martín, a clean nonentity and a future candidate for third-rate author, managed to gather enough composure not to look away when that well-to-do doll set her eyes on me and smiled timidly. My father had always told me that in life one should pay people back in kind. He was referring to slaps in the face and other such offences, but I decided to follow his teachings and return that smile – and while I was at it, throw in a small nod. She was the one who walked over, slowly and, looking me up and down, held out her hand, a gesture nobody had ever made to me, and said:

'My name is Blanca.'

Blanca held out her hand the way young ladies do in drawing-room comedy, palm down and with the detachment of a Parisian damsel. I didn't realise that what was expected of me was to lean forward and brush her hand with my lips, and after a while Blanca removed her hand and raised an eyebrow.

'I'm David.'

'Are you always so bad-mannered?'

I was working on a rhetorical way out that would compensate for my uncouth plebeian background, rescuing my image with a display of ingenuity and wit, when the maid walked over, a look of alarm on her face, and stared at me the way one stares at a rabid dog let loose on the street. She was a young, severe-looking woman with deep, dark eyes that held no sympathy for me. Grabbing Blanca by the arm, she pulled her out of reach.

'Who are you speaking to, Miss Blanca? You know your father doesn't like you to talk to strangers.'

'He's not a stranger, Antonia. This is my friend David. My father knows him.'

I froze while the maid studied me out of the corner of her eye.

'David what?'

'David Martín, madam. At your service.'

'Nobody is at Antonia's service, David. She's the one who serves us. Isn't that right, Antonia?'

It was just an instant, an expression nobody would have noticed but me – for I was watching her closely. Antonia darted a brief, dark glance at Blanca, a look that was poisoned with hatred and turned my blood to ice, before she concealed it with a smile of resignation and a shake of the head, playing down the matter.

'Kids,' she muttered under her breath as she turned to walk back to the bookshop, which was now opening its doors.

Blanca then made as if to sit down on the front doorstep. Even a yokel like me knew that the dress she wore could not come into contact with the base materials covered in soot with which my home was built. I took off my patched-up jacket and spread it over the step like a doormat. Blanca sat on my best garment, gazing at the street and the people walking by. From the bookshop door, Antonia didn't take her eyes off us, and I pretended not to notice.

'Do you live here?' Blanca asked.

I nodded, pointing at the adjacent building.

'Do you?'

Blanca looked at me as if that were the stupidest question she'd heard in her short life.

'Of course not.'

'Don't you like the neighbourhood?'

'It smells bad, it's dark and cold and the people are ugly and noisy.'

It had never occurred to me to size up the world I knew in such a way, but I found no solid arguments with which to contradict her.

'So why do you come here?'

'My father has a house near the Borne Market. Antonia brings me here to visit him almost every day.'

'And where do you live?'

'In Sarriá, with my mother.'

Even a poor wretch like me had heard of Sarriá, but I'd never actually been there. I imagined it as a sort of citadel made up of large mansions and lime-tree avenues, luxurious carriages and leafy gardens, a world inhabited by people like that girl, only taller. Hers was a perfumed, luminous world, no doubt, a world of fresh breezes and good-looking, quiet citizens.

'So how come your father lives here and not with you and your mother?'

Blanca shrugged and looked away. The subject seemed to make her uncomfortable so I decided not to insist.

'It's just for a while,' she added. 'He'll come back home soon.'

'Of course,' I said, without quite knowing what we were talking about, but adopting that commiserating tone of those already born defeated, experts at recommending resignation.

'The Ribera isn't that bad, you'll see. You'll get used to it.'

'I don't want to get used to it. I don't like this neighbourhood, nor the house my father has bought. I don't have any friends here.'

I gulped.

'I can be your friend, if you like.'

'And who are you?'

'David Martín.'

'You've already said that.'

'I suppose I'm also someone who doesn't have any friends.'

Blanca turned her head to look at me with a mixture of curiosity and hesitation.

'I don't like playing hide-and-seek, or ball games,' she warned me.

'Neither do I.'

Blanca smiled and held out her hand again. This time I did my utmost to brush it with my lips.

'Do you like stories?' she asked.

'That's what I like best in the whole world.'

'I know a few stories that very few people have heard,' she said. 'My father writes them for me.'

'I also write stories. Well, I invent them and learn them by heart.'

Blanca frowned.

'Let's see. Tell me one.'

'Now?'

She nodded, defiantly.

'I hope it's not about little princesses,' she threatened. 'I hate little princesses.'

'Well, it does have one princess . . . but she's a very bad one.'

Blanca's face lit up.

'How bad?'

2

That morning Blanca became my first reader, my first audience. I told her, as best I could, my story about princesses and sorcerers, maledictions and poisoned kisses in a universe of spells and living palaces that slithered along a misty wilderness like infernal beasts. When the narrative came to an end and the heroine had sunk into the frozen waters of a black lake holding a cursed rose in her hands, Blanca set the course of my life forever: moved with emotion, she shed a tear and, casting aside any high-flown airs, murmured that she thought my story was beautiful. I would have given my life for that moment never to disappear. Antonia's shadow stretching over our feet brought me back to the humdrum reality.

'We're going now, Miss Blanca. Your father doesn't like us to be late for lunch.'

The maid snatched her away and led her down the street, but I held Blanca's gaze until her figure vanished and I saw her waving at me. I picked up my jacket and put it on again, feeling Blanca's warmth and aroma over me. Then I smiled to myself and, although it was just for a few seconds, I became aware that for the first time in my life I was happy, and that after tasting that poison my existence would never be the same again.

That night, while we were having our dinner of soup and bread, my father looked at me severely.

'You seem different,' he said. 'Has something happened?'

'No, Father.'

I went to bed early, fleeing from his irritable mood. I lay down on my bed in the dark, thinking about Blanca, about the stories I wanted to invent for her, and I realised that I didn't know where she lived or when, if ever, I was going to see her again.

I spent several days searching for Blanca. After lunch, as soon as my father fell asleep or closed his bedroom door, succumbing to his personal oblivion, I would go out and head for the lower part of the neighbourhood, where I'd walk through the dark, narrow side streets surrounding Paseo del Borne in the hope of finding Blanca or her sinister maid. I managed to memorise every hidden corner and every shadow of that labyrinth of streets whose walls seemed to lean against one another and blend into a network of tunnels. The ancient lanes of the medieval guilds formed a web of corridors that commenced at the basilica of Santa María del Mar and then intertwined to form a knot of incomprehensible passages, arches and curves where the sun barely penetrated more than a few minutes a day. Gargoyles and relief sculptures marked the crossings where old, ruined palaces met buildings that grew, one on top of the other, like rocks forming a cliff edge of windows and towers. In the evening I would return home exhausted just as my father was waking up.

On the sixth day, when I was beginning to think that I'd dreamed that encounter, I walked up Calle de los Mirallers towards the side entry of Santa María del Mar. A thick mist had dropped over the city and was creeping through the streets like a silvery veil. The church door was open and there I saw two figures, both dressed in white – a woman and a girl – silhouetted against the arched entrance. A second later the mist had wrapped them in an embrace. I ran to the door and stepped inside the basilica. The draught dragged the mist into the building and a ghostly mantle of vapour, glowing in the candlelight, floated over the pews in the nave. I spied Antonia, the maid, kneeling by one of the confessionals, her expression contrite and pleading. I was sure that harpy's confession had the colouring and consistency of tar. Blanca was sitting in one of the pews, waiting, her legs dangling, staring absently at the altar. I walked over to the end of the pew and she turned her head. When she saw me her face lit up and she smiled, making me instantly forget the endless days of misery I'd spent trying to find her. I sat down next to her.

'What are you doing here?' she asked.

'I was coming to mass,' I improvised.

'It's not the time for mass,' she laughed.

I didn't want to lie to her, so I just lowered my eyes. There was no need to say anything.

'I've also missed you,' she said. 'I thought you might have forgotten me.'

I shook my head. The hazy atmosphere and the muffled whispers emboldened me and I blurted out a declaration I'd devised for one of my tales about magic and heroism.

'I would never be able to forget you,' I said.

Those were words that would have sounded empty and ridiculous, except when spoken by an eight-year-old boy who probably didn't know what he was saying, but felt it. Blanca looked into my eyes with a strange sadness that did not belong to a child's gaze, and she pressed my hand firmly.

'Promise you'll never forget me.'

Antonia, the maid, now apparently free of sin and ready to re-offend, was observing us with hostility from the end of the pew.

'Miss Blanca?'

Blanca kept her eyes fixed on mine.

'Promise.'

'I promise.'

Once again the maid took away my only friend. I saw them walk down the nave and disappear through the back door that led to Paseo del Borne. But this time a touch of malice suffused my melancholy. Something told me that the maid was a woman with a fragile conscience who regularly visited the confessional to purge her faults. The church bells struck four o'clock and the germ of a plan began to form in my mind.

From that day on, every afternoon at a quarter to four I would go to Santa María del Mar and sit in one of the pews near the confessionals. I only had to wait two days before they reappeared. I waited for the maid to kneel down in front of the confessional and then stepped over to where Blanca was standing.

'Every other day at four,' she whispered.

Without wasting a second I grabbed her hand and took her on a tour of the basilica. I'd prepared a story for her that took place precisely there, among the columns and chapels of the church, with a final duel between an evil spirit made of ashes and blood, and a heroic knight, fought in the crypt beneath the altar. It would become the first episode of a series of finely detailed adventures, terrors and romances that I invented for Blanca, titled *The Cathedral Ghosts* and which, with my immense vanity as a novice author, seemed to me near perfection. I finished recounting the first episode just in time for us to get back to the confessional and meet up with the maid, who didn't see me this time because I hid behind a pillar. For a couple of weeks Blanca and I met there every other day. We shared our kids' stories and dreams, while the maid tortured the parish priest with exhaustive accounts of her sins.

At the end of the second week the confessor, a priest who looked liked a retired boxer, noticed my presence and quickly put two and two together. I was about to slip away when he beckoned me to approach the confessional. His pugilistic appearance convinced me and I hastened to obey. I knelt down, trembling in the knowledge that my ruse had been discovered.

'Hail Mary, full of grace,' I murmured through the latticed opening.

'Do I look like a nun to you, you little rascal?'

'I'm sorry, Father. I wasn't sure what I was meant to say.'

'Don't they teach you this at school?'

'The teacher is an atheist and says you priests are an instrument of the capitalist system.'

'And what's he an instrument of?'

'He didn't say. I think he considers himself a free agent.'

The priest laughed.

'Where did you learn to speak like that? In school?'

'Reading.'

'Reading what?'

'Whatever I can.'

'And do you read the word of the Lord?'

'Does the Lord write?'

'Keep acting like a smart aleck and you'll end up burning in hell.'

I gulped.

'Do I have to tell you my sins now?' I whispered anxiously.

'There's no need. They're stamped on your forehead. What's this business that's going on with the maid and the girl almost every day?'

'What business?'

'Let me remind you that this is a confessional and if you lie to a priest Our Lord may well strike you down with a deadly bolt on your way out,' the confessor threatened.

'Are you sure?'

'If I were you I wouldn't risk it. Come on, spit it out.'

'Where do I begin?'

'Skip the playing with yourself and the swear words and tell me what it is you do every day in my parish at four o'clock in the afternoon.'

The kneeling, the darkness and the smell of wax have something about them that invite one to unburden one's conscience. I even confessed my first sneeze. The priest listened in silence, clearing his throat every time I stopped. At the end of my confession, when I supposed he was going to send me straight to hell, I heard him chuckling.

'Aren't you going to give me a penance?'

'What's your name, kid?'

'David Martín, sir.'

'It's "father", not "sir". One would say "sir" to your father, and "Lord" to the Most High. But I'm not your father, I'm *a* father, in this case, Father Sebastián.'

'Forgive me, Father Sebastián.'

'Just "father" will be fine. And the one who forgives is the Lord. I only do the administering. Now: back to business. For today I'll let you go with only a warning and a couple of Hail Marys. And as I believe that the Lord, in his infinite wisdom, has chosen this most unusual path to persuade you to come to church, I'll offer you a deal. Every other day, half an hour before you meet up with your little damsel, you come and help me clean the sacristy. In exchange I'll keep the maid here for at least half an hour to give you more time.'

'You'll do this for me, Father?'

'*Ego te absolvo in nomine Patris et Filii et Spiritus Sancti.* And now clear off.'

3

Father Sebastián proved to be a man of his word. I would arrive half an hour early and help him in the sacristy, for the poor fellow was almost lame and could barely manage on his own. He liked to listen to my stories, which according to him were little blasphemies of a venial nature, but which amused him, especially the ones about ghosts and curses. He seemed to me as solitary a person as I was, and when I admitted that Blanca was my only friend, he agreed to help me. I lived for those meetings.

Blanca always arrived looking pallid and cheerful, dressed in ivory-coloured clothes. She always wore new shoes and necklaces with silver medals. She listened to the tales I invented for her and told me about her world and the large dark house, close by, where her father had gone to live, a frightening place she loathed. Sometimes she talked about her mother, Alicia, with whom she lived in the old family house in Sarriá. Other times, speaking almost in tears, she mentioned her father, whom she adored but who, she said, was ill and now barely left the house.

'My father is a writer,' she explained. 'Like you. But he doesn't write stories for me any more, the way he used to. Now he only writes stuff for a man who sometimes comes to the house at night to visit him. I've never seen him, but once I spent the night there and I heard them talking until very late, locked up in my father's study. That man isn't good. He scares me.'

14

Every afternoon, when we parted, I walked back home day-dreaming about the moment when I would rescue her from that existence marked by absences, from that night visitor who scared her, from that pampered life that stole the light from her with every passing day. Every afternoon I told myself that I wasn't going to forget her and that, so long as I remembered her, I'd be able to save her.

One November day – it had dawned blue with frosty windows – I went out to meet her as usual, but Blanca didn't come to our rendezvous. For two weeks I waited in vain for my friend to appear in the basilica. I looked everywhere for her, and when my father caught me weeping at night I lied to him and told him I had toothache, although no tooth could hurt as much as that absence. Father Sebastián, who began to worry every time he saw me waiting there like a lost soul, sat down next to me one day and tried to comfort me.

'Perhaps you should forget your friend, David.'

'I can't. I promised I would never forget her.'

A month had gone by since her disappearance when I noticed I was beginning to forget her. I'd stopped going to the church every other day, I'd stopped inventing stories for her and holding her image in the dark every night as I fell asleep. I had begun to forget the sound of her voice, her smell and the light of her face. When I realised that I was losing her, I wanted to go and see Father Sebastián to beg his forgiveness, to beg him to pull away the pain that was devouring me, the pain that was telling me to my face that I'd broken my promise and had been incapable of remembering the only friend I'd ever had.

The last time I saw Blanca was at the beginning of that December. I'd gone down to the street and was standing by the front door staring at the rain when I caught sight of her. She was walking alone in the rain, her white patent shoes and her ivory-coloured dress stained with muddy water. I ran towards her and saw that she was weeping. I asked her what had happened and she hugged me. Blanca told me that her father was very ill and that she'd run away from home. I told her not to be afraid, we would run away together. If necessary I'd steal the money to buy two train tickets and we'd leave the city forever. Blanca smiled and embraced me. We stood like that, hugging silently beneath the scaffolding of the concert hall, until a large black carriage appeared through the mist of the downpour and stopped in front of us. A dark figure stepped out of the carriage. It was Antonia, the maid. She pulled Blanca from my arms and shoved her inside the carriage. Blanca screamed and when I tried to grab her arm the maid turned and slapped me as hard as she could. I fell backwards on the cobblestones, dazed by the blow. When I got up again the carriage was moving into the distance.

I ran after the carriage in the rain until I reached the roadworks for the construction of Vía Layetana. The new avenue was a long valley of waterlogged ditches that was destroying the jungle of side streets and houses in the Ribera quarter as it advanced with hammer blows of dynamite and demolition cranes. I saw the carriage dodging potholes and puddles, getting further and further away from me. In an attempt not to lose sight of it I climbed onto a ridge of cobblestones and earth that ran alongside a ditch flooded by the rain. Suddenly I felt the earth give way beneath my feet and I slipped. I tumbled into the ditch, falling face down into the well of water that had collected below. When I managed to stand up and get my head out of the liquid that covered me up to my waist, I realised that the water was poisoned and alive with black spiders that floated and walked over the surface. The insects hurled themselves over me and covered my hands and my arms. I screamed, waving my arms about and climbing up the mud walls of the trench, panic-stricken. By the time I got out of the flooded ditch it was too late. The carriage was disappearing into the upper reaches of the city, its outline enveloped in the blanket of rain. Soaked to my bones I dragged myself back home where my father was still asleep and locked up in his room. I took my clothes off and got into bed trembling with anger and cold. I noticed that my arms were covered in tiny red, bleeding dots. Bites. The spiders in the ditch hadn't wasted their time. I could feel the poison burning in my blood and then I lost consciousness, falling into a crater of darkness somewhere between awareness and sleep.

I dreamed that I was walking through the deserted streets of the neighbourhood looking for Blanca in the storm. Black rain pounded the facades and through flashes of lightning I could make out distant figures. A large black carriage crept along in the fog. Blanca travelled inside the carriage, shouting and banging the windows with her fists. I followed her shouts as far as a narrow, murky street where I saw the carriage come to a halt opposite a tall, dark house – a house that seemed to twist upwards, forming a tower that pierced the sky. Blanca was stepping out of the carriage and looking at me, stretching her pleading hands towards me. I wanted to run to her but my steps would only advance a few metres. It was then that the large, dark silhouette appeared, standing at the door of the house – a huge angel with a face of marble that looked at me and smiled like a wolf, spreading its black wings over Blanca and wrapping her in an embrace. I screamed, but utter silence had descended over the city. During an endless moment the rain was left suspended in mid-air, a million glass tears floating in the void, and I saw the angel kiss her on the forehead, its lips leaving a mark on her skin like that of a red-hot iron. When the rain brushed the ground they had both disappeared forever.

NAMELESS

Translated by Lucia Graves

Years later, I was told that she was last seen walking up that sombre avenue leading to the gates of the Pueblo Nuevo Cemetery. Evening was falling and an icy wind was dragging a cupola of red clouds over the city. She walked alone, shivering with cold and leaving a wake of uncertain footsteps on the mantle of snow that had started to fall in mid-afternoon. When she reached the entrance to the graveyard she paused for a moment to catch her breath. A forest of angels and crosses peered over the walls. The stench of dead flowers, lime and sulphur licked her face, inviting her in. She was about to start walking again when a stabbing pain throbbed through her entrails like a red-hot iron. She put her hands on her belly and took a deep breath, trying to stop the nausea. For an endless moment all she could feel was agony and the fear of being unable to take another step, of collapsing by the entrance to the cemetery and being discovered there at dawn, clinging to its spiked gates like a figure of bile and frost, with the child she was carrying trapped hopelessly in an icy sarcophagus.

It would have been so easy to give in, there and then, stretched out on the snow, and close her eyes forever. But she could feel the breath of life beating inside her, a breath that did not want to be extinguished, that kept her upright, and she knew she would not succumb to the suffering or the cold. She gathered all the strength she didn't possess and got back on her feet. Ribbons of pain knotted themselves in her belly but she ignored them and hastened on. She didn't stop until she'd left the labyrinth of tombs and mouldy statues behind her. Only then, when she raised her head to look, did a ray of hope flash through her: for silhouetted against the murky twilight stood the large wrought-iron door that led to the Old Book Factory.

Further on, the Pueblo Nuevo neighbourhood spread towards a horizon of ashes and shadows. The city of factories outlined the dark reflection of a Barcelona bewitched by hundreds of chimneys that exhaled their black breath over the scarlet of the sky. As the young woman entered the maze of narrow streets entangled among cavernous stores and warehouses, her eyes recognised some of the large structures that shored up the neighbourhood, from the factory of Can Saladrigas to the great water tower. The Old Book Factory stood out among them all. Turrets and hanging bridges emerged from its extravagant profile, suggesting the work of a diabolical architect who had discovered how to flout the laws of perspective. Domes, minarets and chimney stacks seemed to charge through a chaos of vaults and naves supported by dozens of flying buttresses and columns. Sculptures and reliefs snaked along its walls, and rotundas, speckled with windows, sent out shafts of ghostly light.

The girl observed the row of gargoyles along its cornices – they oozed streaks of vapour, spreading a bitter perfume of ink and paper. Feeling another wave of pain coming she hurried to the large front door and pulled the bell rope. The muffled echo of a chime could be heard behind the large wrought-iron door. The girl looked behind her and noticed that in just a few seconds the snow had covered the trail of her footsteps. A cold, biting wind cornered her against the iron door. She pulled the bell rope again, harder and repeatedly, but no answer came. All around her, the faint light seemed to be vanishing with every passing second and shadows began to spread quickly at her feet. Well aware that she was running out of time, she stepped back a little and scanned the large windows of the main facade. A motionless figure was silhouetted against one of the windows with smoked-glass panes, like a spider in the centre of its web. The girl couldn't see its face; all she could make out was a female body, but she knew she was being observed. She waved her arms and called out for help. The figure remained immobile until suddenly the light went out. The window was now in complete darkness, but the girl noticed that the two eyes that had been piercing hers were still there, in the shadow, unmoving, shining in the twilight. For the first time fear made her forget the cold and the pain. She pulled the bell rope a third time and when she realised that ringing the bell would get no response she started shouting and banging the door with her fists. She struck the door until her hands bled and she begged for help until her voice broke and her legs could no longer hold her up. Then she collapsed into an icy puddle, closed her eyes and listened to the throbbing of life in her womb. Soon the snow began to cover her face and her body.

Evening was already spreading like a pool of ink when the door opened, casting a fan of light over the girl. Two figures carrying gas lamps knelt down beside her. One of the men, heavily built and pock-marked, pushed the hair away from her forehead. She opened her eyes and smiled at him. The two men exchanged glances and the second man, who was younger and small, pointed at something shining on the girl's hand. A ring. He was about to snatch it from her but his companion stopped him.

They helped her up. The older and stronger of the two took her in his arms and told the other one to run and get help. The younger man agreed reluctantly and disappeared into the dusk. The girl kept her eyes fixed on those of the heavily built man who was carrying her in his arms, murmuring words that wouldn't form on her cracked lips. *Thank you, thank you.*

The man, who had a slight limp, took her to what looked like a coach house next to the factory entrance. Once they were inside, the girl heard other voices and felt various arms holding her and laying her on a wooden table opposite a fire. Slowly, the heat from the flames melted the frozen beads of ice on her hair and face. Two women, both as young as her and wearing maids' uniforms, wrapped her in a blanket and began to rub her arms and legs. Two hands that smelled of spices brought a glass of hot wine to her lips. The liquid spread through her like a balm.

As she lay on the table, the girl glanced round the room and realised she was in a kitchen. One of the maids placed a few tea towels under her head and the girl tilted her forehead backwards. From this position she could see the room upside down – the pots, frying pans and utensils hanging against gravity. That is how she saw her come in. The pale, serene face of the lady in white was slowly approaching from the door as if she were walking on the ceiling. The maids stood aside as she went by and the heavily built man looked down fearfully and quickly moved out of the way. The girl heard footsteps and voices leaving the room and sensed she was now alone with the lady in white. She saw her bend over her and felt her warm, sweet breath.

'Don't be afraid,' whispered the lady.

The lady was studying her quietly with her grey eyes; the back of her hand, the softest skin the girl had ever known, brushed her cheek. It occurred to the girl that the lady had the presence and the manners of a broken angel, fallen from heaven amid forgotten cobwebs. She searched her eyes for protection. The lady smiled at her and stroked her face with infinite tenderness. They remained like that for almost half an hour, almost in silence, until she heard loud voices in the courtyard and the maids returned, together with the younger man and a gentleman wearing a thick coat and carrying a large black doctor's bag. The doctor stood by her side and proceeded to take her pulse. His eyes observed her nervously. He prodded her belly and sighed. The girl struggled to understand the orders the doctor was giving the maids and the male servants who had gathered round the fire. Only then did she find the strength to recover her voice and ask whether her child would be born in good health. The doctor who, judging from his expression, thought neither of them would live, merely exchanged a look with the lady in white.

'David,' murmured the girl. 'He'll be called David.'

The lady nodded and kissed the girl on her forehead.

'Now you must be strong,' whispered the lady, holding her hand firmly.

Years later I learned that that girl, who was barely seventeen, lay completely silent, without uttering even a whimper, her eyes open and tears falling down her cheeks while the doctor opened her belly with a scalpel and brought a child into the world, a boy who would only be able to remember her through the words of strangers. Time and time again I've wondered whether she ever saw the lady in white as she turned her back on her to take the baby and hold it close, cuddling it against her white silk chest while she, the girl, stretched her arms out and begged to be allowed to see her child. I've often wondered whether that girl was able to hear the sound of her son crying as he was taken away in the arms of another woman and she was left alone in that room where she lay in a pool of her own blood until they returned to wrap her body, still trembling, in a shroud. I've wondered whether she felt how one of the maids struggled with the ring on her left hand, tearing her skin to steal it from her while they dragged her body back into the night, and the two men who had rescued her now loaded it into a cart. I've asked myself so many times whether she was still breathing when the horses stopped and the two individuals took the shroud and flung it into the gully that dragged the sewage from a hundred factories towards the tundra of cardboard-and-reed shacks that covered the Bogatell beach.

I've wanted to believe that at that last moment, when the putrid waters spat her into the sea and the shroud that wrapped her unfolded in the current to deliver her body into the darkness of the deep, she knew that the boy she had given birth to would live and would always remember her.

I never knew her name.

That girl was my mother.

A YOUNG LADY FROM
BARCELONA

Translated by Lucia Graves

Laia was five years old the first time her father sold her. It was an innocent, kind-hearted arrangement, with no malice other than that inspired by hunger and pressing debts. Eduardo Sentís, a hapless, penniless portrait photographer, had just inherited the studio of the man who had been his mentor and boss for over twenty years. He had started work there as an unpaid trainee, had then become an assistant and finally, after obtaining the required qualifications, though not the salary, had moved on to become photographer and junior manager. The studio's premises occupied a spacious ground floor on Calle Consejo de Ciento and consisted of four sets, two developing rooms and a storage room bursting with out-of-date equipment in a dilapidated state. Aside from the studio, Eduardo had also inherited the numerous unpaid bills left by his boss, who had been more of a man of lenses and plates than one of clarity in his accounts. At the time of his boss's demise, Eduardo Sentís had not received his wages for over six months. In the words of the executor, the post-mortem takeover of the business and the miserable inheritance that came with it were supposed to be a just reward for his loyal and austere dedication. But as soon as light and accountants fell on the company's business books, Eduardo Sentís realised that what his boss had left him in return for having offered him his youth and his efforts was no inheritance but a simple curse. He had to fire all the employees and confront the survival of the studio, and his own survival, alone. Until then, a large part of the business generated by the studio focused on family celebrations of various kinds, from weddings and christenings to funerals and Holy Communions. Work related to funeral parlours and burials were a speciality of the house, and over time Eduardo Sentís had found it easier to light and photograph the deceased than the living. The dead never looked out of focus in long exposures because they didn't move or have to hold their breath.

It was his reputation as a photographer of bereavement that secured him a job which, at first sight, seemed straightforward and uncomplicated. Margarita Pons, the five-year-old daughter of a wealthy married couple with a mansion on Avenida del Tibidabo and an industrial estate on the banks of the River Ter, had died from some strange fever on New Year's day of 1901. Her mother, Doña Eulalia, had suffered a nervous breakdown which the family doctors had hastened to mitigate with generous doses of laudanum. Don Federico Pons, paterfamilias and a gentleman with no room or time for sentimentalities, who had seen more than one of his children die, did not shed a tear or utter a groan. He already had a healthy and talented first-born heir. The loss of a daughter, for all its sadness, also meant an obvious saving in family expenditure, both long- and medium-term. What Don Federico wanted was to hold the funeral service without delay, followed by the burial in the family vault in Montjuïc Cemetery, so that he could resume his daily work routine as soon as possible. But Doña Eulalia, a fragile creature who was prone to the influence of the sinister ladies of The Light, a spiritualist society on Calle Elisabets, was in no fit state to turn the page as resolutely as her husband. In order to silence her sighs, Don Federico allowed her to have a series of photographs taken of the deceased princess before the undertakers proceeded with the body's eternal consignment to an ivory coffin adorned with pieces of blue glass.

Eduardo Sentís, photographer of the dead, was summoned to the Pons family mansion on Avenida del Tibidabo. The property lay hidden inside a dense grove accessed through a wrought-iron gate on the corner of the avenue and Calle José Garí. It was a grey, grim day, a sliver of that harsh, misty winter that had brought such bad luck on poor Sentís. As he didn't have anyone with whom to leave his daughter Laia, he took her with him. Holding the girl with one hand and his lens-and-bellows case in the other, Sentís took the blue tram and turned up at the mansion, determined to start the year with some hard cash income. He was welcomed by a servant who led him through the garden to the house, where he was shown to a small waiting room. Laia was fascinated by everything she saw, because she'd never seen a place like that. It looked like something straight out of a fairy tale, but one of those about an evil stepmother and mirrors that were poisoned by bad memories. Glass chandeliers hung from the ceiling, statues and paintings lined the walls and thick Persian carpets covered the floors. As he gazed at all that weighty fortune, Sentís was tempted to put up his price. He was received by Don Federico, who barely looked at him and addressed him in the tone he reserved for servants and factory workers. He was given an hour to take a set of photographs of the deceased child. When he saw Laia, Don Federico frowned disapprovingly. It was a widely accepted dogma among the males of his family that the utility of the female gender was confined to the bedroom, the table or the kitchen, and that brat had neither the age nor the pedigree to be considered for any of the three. Sentís excused the child's presence claiming that the urgency of the job had not given him enough time to find someone to take care of her. Don Federico sighed unsympathetically and told the photographer to follow him up the stairs.

The little princess had been placed in a room on the first floor. She lay on a wide bed covered in white lilies, her hands crossed over her chest and clutching a crucifix. A tiara of flowers adorned her forehead and she wore a diaphanous silk dress. Two silent male servants guarded the door. A shaft of ashen light from the window fell on the child's face. Her skin, almost transparent, had taken on the colour and appearance of marble, with blue and black veins running through it. Her eyes had sunk into their sockets and her lips were purple. The room stank of dead flowers.

Sentís told Laia to wait in the corridor and began setting up his tripod and camera in front of the bed. He thought he'd create six plates in all. Two close-ups with one of the long lenses, two mid-range shots from the waist up and a couple of general, full-body shots. All from the same angle, because he suspected that a profile or a three-quarter shot would draw attention to the web of veins and dark capillaries under the girl's skin and produce pictures that might look more sinister than the situation required. A slight overexposure would whiten the skin and soften the image, giving a warmer, more diffuse aura to the body and a greater depth of field and detail to the surrounding area. While he prepared the lenses he noticed something moving at the far end of the room. What he had thought was yet another statue when he came in turned out to be a woman in black with her face covered by a veil. It was Doña Eulalia, the princess's mother, who was sobbing quietly as she crept around the room like a lost soul. She approached the dead girl and stroked her cheek.

'My angel speaks to me,' she told Sentís. 'Can't you hear her?' Sentís nodded and continued with his preparations. The sooner he got out of there, the better. When he was ready to start taking the first images, the photographer asked the mother to move out of the camera's field of vision for a few moments. She kissed the corpse on the forehead and stood behind the camera.

Sentís was concentrating so hard on his task he hadn't noticed that Laia had stepped into the room and was standing next to him, petrified, staring at the dead girl laid out on the bed. Before he was able to react, Señora Pons walked over to Laia and knelt down in front of her. 'Hello, sweetheart,' she said. 'Are you my angel?' The lady of the house took Sentís's daughter in her arms and pressed her against her chest. Sentís felt his blood freeze. The mother of the deceased child was singing a lullaby to Laia as she rocked her in her arms, telling her that she was her angel and they would never again be parted. At that moment Don Federico appeared. He pulled the girl from his wife's arms and led Doña Eulalia out of the room, while she begged to be left with her angel, her arms extended towards Laia. As soon as they were left alone, the photographer exposed the plates as fast as he could and put away his equipment. On his way out, Don Federico was waiting for him in the entrance hall, holding the payment for his services in an envelope. Sentís noticed that the envelope contained twice the amount they had agreed upon. Don Federico was looking at him with a mixture of hope and disdain. He made him an offer then and there: in exchange for a generous sum of money the photographer would bring his daughter to the mansion the following day and leave her there until the evening. Stupefied, Sentís looked at his daughter and then at Pons. The industrialist doubled the amount he'd offered. Sentís silently shook his head. 'Think about it,' was all Pons said when he bid him goodbye.

The photographer spent a sleepless night. Laia found him crying in the pale light of the studio and held his hand. She told him to take her to that house: she would be the angel and would play with the lady. By mid-morning they were both standing outside the mansion's gates. Sentís was handed the money by a servant and told to return at seven o'clock in the evening. He saw Laia disappear inside the large house and he dragged himself down the avenue until he found a café at the top of Calle Balmes where they served him a glass of brandy, and then another, and a further one, and as many as were necessary until it was time for him to go and pick up his daughter.

Laia spent that day playing with Doña Eulalia and the dolls that had belonged to the deceased. Doña Eulalia dressed her in the dead girl's clothes, kissed her and held her in her arms, telling her stories and talking to her about the girl's brothers, about her aunt, about a cat they'd once had but had run away. They played hide-and-seek and went up to the attic. They ran around the garden and had a snack by the fountain, throwing breadcrumbs to the coloured fish that darted through the water of the pond. At sunset, Doña Eulalia lay down on her bed with Laia by her side and drank her glass of water with laudanum. And so, embracing in the dark, the two fell asleep until one of the male servants woke Laia up and took her to the front door where her father was waiting, his eyes reddened with shame. When he saw her he fell on his knees and hugged her. The servant handed him an envelope with the money and instructed him to bring his daughter back the following day at the same time.

Every day of that week Laia went to the mansion to become the little angel, to play with her toys and wear her clothes, to answer to her name and disappear into the shadow of the dead girl who haunted every corner of that dark, sad house. By the sixth day, Laia's memories were those of little Margarita, and her past existence had evaporated. She had become that longed-for presence and had learned to embody it with more intensity than the deceased herself. She had learned to interpret looks and longings, to hear the trembling of hearts broken with loss and find the gestures and the touch that consoled the inconsolable. Without realising, she'd learned to become another person, to be nothing and nobody, to live in the skin of others. She never asked her father not to take her to that place, nor did she tell him what happened during the long hours she spent inside. The photographer, intoxicated with money and relief, salved his conscience by telling himself that this was an act of charity and Christian piety. 'If you don't want to, you don't have to go to that house any more, do you hear me?' her father would say every night when they came back from the mansion. 'But we're doing a good deed.'

The little angel disappeared on the seventh day. They said that Doña Eulalia had woken up at dawn and when she didn't find the girl next to her she had begun searching frantically for her all over the house, thinking they were still playing hide-and-seek. The laudanum and the darkness led her to the garden where she thought she heard a voice and then thought she could see a little angel – its face lined with blue veins, its lips black with poison – looking at her from the depths of the pond, calling her, inviting her to submerge herself and accept the frozen, silent embrace of the shadow that was pulling at her and whispering: 'Mother, now we'll always be together, just as you wanted.'

For years the photographer and his daughter travelled to every city and town in the country with their circus act of deceptions and pleasures. By the time she was seventeen Laia had learned to embody lives and faces aided by a few sheets of paper, an old photograph, a forgotten story or a handful of memories that refused to die. Sometimes her art served to bring back the longing of a first secret and forbidden love, and her trembling body would awaken beneath the hands of older lovers, individuals who had been able to buy everything in life except what they most desired and had allowed to slip away.

Businessmen endowed with too much money and too little life would imagine themselves, perhaps for only a few minutes, in bed with women whom the girl had conjured up from a secret longing, from the pages of a diary or a family portrait – and whose memory would stay with them the rest of their lives. Sometimes the miracle of her artistry achieved such perfection that the client forgot it was all a fantasy with which to cloud his senses and poison them with pleasure for a few moments. The client then believed the young girl was who she was pretending to be, that the object of his desire had come alive, and he did not want to let it go. He was prepared to lose his fortune or the empty, barren life he'd lugged behind him until then in order to live the rest of his dream in the arms of that girl who could become what one most desired.

When this happened – and it had been happening more and more frequently because Laia had learned to read the souls and the desires of men with such precision that even her father sometimes felt the game had gone too far – they would both run away like fugitives at dawn and hide in another city, in other streets, for weeks on end. Then Laia would spend the day hidden in the suite of a luxury hotel, sleeping most of the day, buried in a lethargy of silence and sadness, while her father did the rounds of the city's casinos and lost, in just a few days, the fortune they had accrued. Her father's promises of abandoning that life would be broken again: he would hug her and whisper that there would only be one more time, one more client, and then they would retire to a house by a lake where Laia would never again have to give life to the secret desires of some wealthy gentleman sick with loneliness. Laia knew that her father lied without realising he was lying, as all great liars do who first lie to themselves and are then unable to see the truth even if it's stabbing them in their hearts. She knew he was lying and she forgave him because she loved him and because, deep down, she wanted the game to continue, she wanted to find another character whose life she could awaken and with whom she could fill, for a few hours at least, that huge void that was growing inside her and was eating her alive at night as she waited, between silk sheets, in the suite of some grand hotel, for her father to return, inebriated with liquor and failure.

Once a month Laia received the visit of an older man wearing a dejected expression, whom her father liked to call Doctor Sentís. The doctor, a fragile person who tried to hide a look of despair and defeat behind his glasses, had seen better days. When he was young, in more affluent times, Doctor Sentís had owned a prestigious surgery on Calle Ausias March, visited by damsels of a marriageable age and dames who were more prone to reminisce. In that surgery, legs open and spread out in the blue-ceilinged room, the cream of Barcelona's bourgeoisie had no secrets or modesty before the kind doctor. His hands had delivered hundreds of children from wealthy homes and his care and advice had saved the lives and often the reputation of patients who had been deliberately kept ignorant about an important part of their bodies, the part that most burned and throbbed, so that it held more secrets for them than the mystery of the Holy Trinity.

Doctor Sentís had the quiet manners and the friendly and reassuring disposition of someone who sees no shame or embarrassment in the facts of life. Calm and affable, he knew how to gain the trust and appreciation of women and young girls, once terrorised by nuns and friars who only touched their private parts in the dark and at the devil's bidding. He would explain, with no awkwardness or fuss of any sort, how their bodies worked, and taught them not to feel bashful about what, according to him, was only the work of God. Naturally, a talented, successful man who was also decent and honest could not last long in good society, and sooner rather than later, his moment came. The fall of the righteous is always brought about by people who are most indebted to them. One doesn't betray those who want to ruin us but those who offer us a hand, even if only because we don't wish to acknowledge the debt of gratitude we owe them.

In the case of Doctor Sentís, betrayal had been in the offing for some time. For years the kind doctor had attended a lady of noble pedigree who journeyed through a marriage – lacking in contact and even words – to a man she barely knew and with whom she had shared a bed twice in twenty years. Out of habit, the lady had learned to live with cobwebs round her heart, but she refused to smother the fire between her legs, and in a city where so many gentlemen liked to treat their own wives as saints and virgins, and those of others as sluts and whores, it was easy enough for her to find lovers and fleeting devotees with whom to kill the tedium and remind herself that she was still alive, even if only from the neck down. Adventures and misadventures in others' beds carried their risks and the lady kept no secrets from the good doctor, who made sure that her pale, longing thighs did not fall prey to diseases and disreputable ailments. The doctor's potions, ointments and wise advice had kept the lady in a state of immaculate ardour for years.

As life would have it – and it usually does, given a chance – the doctor's good turns were repaid with bile and spite. Any city's polite society is a world as small as its reserves of honesty, and it was a foregone conclusion that the accursed day would come when one of those half-hour lovers, out of meanness or spite, or better still, out of self-interest, would reveal the secret and passionate life of a sad and lonely woman to the sharp eyes of her companions in jealousy. The story of the whore in silk stockings, a nickname with which some gossip-monger with literary pretensions christened her, spread like wildfire among the chattering members of a community that thrived on slander and suspicions.

Distinguished gentlemen guffawed as they described, in spiteful detail, the charms of the lady-turned-whore in silk stockings, and their no less distinguished and disdained wives spoke under their breath about how that fallen hooker, who had once been considered their friend, had performed unmentionable acts and corrupted the souls and the nether regions of their husbands and sons on all fours and with her mouth full, performing linguistic acrobatics they hadn't learned in their eleven years at the School of the Sacred Heart. The story, which was on everyone's lips and had grown increasingly outlandish, did not take long to reach the august husband of the so-called whore in silk stockings. Later, people said that nobody was to blame, that it was the lady's own decision to leave the family home, abandon her clothes and jewels and move into a cold apartment on Calle Mallorca, a place with no light and no furniture. And there, one January day, she lay down on the bed facing an open window and drank half a glassful of laudanum, until her heart stopped and her eyes, open to the icy wind of winter, shattered in the frost.

They found her naked, in the company of only a long letter – the ink not yet dry – in which she confessed her story, blaming everything on Doctor Sentís, who had confused her with his potions and his crafty words into adopting a life of abandon and lust from which only prayer and the encounter with the Lord at the doors of Purgatory could save her.

The letter, in facsimile copies or in spoken accounts, circulated widely among respectable people and in a matter of weeks the appointment book in Doctor Sentís's surgery was empty, and his quiet, calm expression had turned into that of a pariah who is barely offered a word or a look. After months of utter destitution, the doctor tried to find work in the city's hospitals. But none of them would accept him because the husband of the deceased, who had gone from being a whore in silk stockings to a saintly martyr dressed in white, was a man of great influence and had ordered and threatened that anyone who offered Doctor Sentís an opening would join him in the land of the forgotten.

With the help of time and invisibility, the kind doctor descended from the cotton-wool clouds of wealthy Barcelona and went on to live in the endless basement of its streets, where hundreds of whores with no silk stockings and other deprived souls welcomed his services and his honesty, if not with money, which they barely had, then with respect and gratitude. The kind doctor, who had been obliged to sell off his surgery on Calle Ausias March and his villa in the San Gervasio neighbourhood to survive during those difficult years, bought a modest flat on Calle Condal, where he would die many years later, happy and tired, with no regrets.

It was during those first years, when Doctor Sentís did the rounds of brothels and rooms for hire in the Raval quarter, armed with medication and common sense, that he came across the photographer, who tried to lend him his daughter's talents, free of charge. The photographer had heard how the doctor had lost his fourteen-year-old daughter, whose name was Laia, and how his wife had abandoned him shortly afterwards, unable to bear the loss they shared. Those who knew the doctor said he was haunted by the tragic death of his daughter, for he'd been unable to save her despite all his efforts. The photographer, whom the doctor had cured of an ear infection that had almost cost him his hearing and his sanity, wanted to pay him back in kind, and was convinced that, if his daughter could study photographs and tokens the doctor kept of his own dead daughter, she would be able to bring her back to life and return to him what he had most loved in the world, even if only for a few minutes. Doctor Sentís declined the offer, but struck up a friendship with the photographer and ended up becoming his daughter's doctor, visiting her once a month and keeping her safe from diseases and ailments common to her profession.

Laia adored the doctor and longed for his visits. He was the only man she knew who didn't look at her with desire, or project barren fantasies onto her. She could talk to him about things she would never have mentioned to her father and speak to him in confidence about her fears and anxieties. The doctor, who never judged his patients or the occupations life had chosen for them, couldn't hide his distaste for the way the photographer was selling the best years of his daughter's life. Sometimes he would talk to Laia about the daughter he had lost, and without anyone having to tell her, she knew she was the only person in whom the doctor confided his secrets and memories. Privately, she wished she could take the place of the other Laia, become the daughter of that sad, benevolent man, and abandon the photographer – whom greed and lies had turned into a stranger walking in her father's clothes. Death would grant her what life had denied her.

*

Not long after her seventeenth birthday, Laia knew she was pregnant. The father could have been any of the customers who, at a rate of three a week, supported the photographer's gambling debts. At first Laia hid her pregnancy from her father and made up a thousand excuses to avoid Doctor Sentís's visits during the first few months. Corsets and the art of making others only see in her what they wished to see did the rest. By the fourth month, one of her customers, a doctor who had been Doctor Sentís's rival and had now inherited a large part of his patients, became aware of her situation during a game in which Laia, wearing restraining cuffs on hands and feet, was made to undergo a cruel medical examination by the doctor, a man who was aroused by his patients' cries of pain. He left her bleeding, naked and handcuffed on the bed, where her father found her hours later.

When he discovered the truth, the photographer panicked and rushed his daughter to see a woman who practised forbidden arts in a basement on Calle Aviñón, where he asked her to get rid of the noble bastard Laia carried inside her. Surrounded by candles and buckets of smelly water, lying on a dirty, blood-stained, makeshift bed, Laia told the old witch that she was afraid and didn't want to hurt the innocent child she carried in her womb. At a nod from the photographer, the witch gave her a thick, greenish liquid to drink, which clouded her understanding and removed her willpower. She felt her father holding her wrists and the witch opening her thighs. She felt something cold and metallic making its way inside her like a tongue of ice. In her delirium, she thought she could hear the cries of a baby twisting inside her, begging her to let it live. It was then that the explosion of pain – like a thousand blades gnawing her insides, like fire blazing within – overpowered her and made her lose consciousness. The last thing she remembered was sinking into a well of steaming black blood and something, or someone, pulling her legs.

She woke up on the same dirty old bed, under the indifferent gaze of the witch. She felt weak. A dull, burning pain ravaged her lower abdomen and thighs, as if her entire body were a raw scar. Her feverish eyes met the witch's. She asked after her father. The witch shook her head in silence. Laia lost consciousness again and the next time she opened her eyes she knew dawn was breaking because of the light filtering through a tiny window that looked out at street level. The witch was standing with her back to her, preparing some concoction that smelled of honey and alcohol. Laia asked after her father. The woman handed her a hot cup and told her to drink. It would make her feel better, she said. She drank, and the warm, gelatinous balm slightly eased the gnawing agony inside her.

'Where's my father?'

'Was that your father?' asked the witch with a bitter smile.

The photographer had abandoned her, thinking she was dead. Her heart had stopped beating for two minutes, the witch explained. When he saw her lying there, dead, her father had made a run for it.

'I also thought you were dead. But a couple of minutes later you opened your eyes and started breathing again. Count yourself lucky, kid. Someone up there must love you a lot, because you've been reborn.'

When Laia had gathered enough strength to stand up and walk over to the Hotel Colón, in whose rooms they'd lived for the past three weeks, the receptionist informed her that the photographer had left the day before without leaving an address. He had taken all her clothes. The only thing he'd left behind was Laia's photograph album.

'Didn't he leave a note for me?'

'No, miss.'

Laia spent a week searching for him all over the city. Nobody had seen him recently in the casinos and cafés where he was a regular customer, but they all reminded her to tell him, if she saw him, to come and settle his outstanding debts and bills. By the second week she knew she'd never see him again. With no home and no friends, Laia went to see Doctor Sentís, who realised, the moment he saw her, that there was something wrong, and insisted on examining her. When the kind doctor discovered the damage the old witch had caused to Laia's insides, he wept inconsolably. That day he recovered a daughter and, for the first time, Laia found a father.

They lived together in the doctor's modest flat on Calle Condal. The doctor's income was minimal but enough to enrol Laia in a school for young ladies and keep up the fantasy that all would be fine for the coming year. His advanced age and the occasional carelessness in the doses of ether he secretly took to ease the pain of his existence had affected him. His hands had begun to shake and he was losing his eyesight. The man was fading and Laia left her school to look after him.

As he lost his sight, the kind doctor also began to lose awareness of reality and to believe that she was his real daughter who had come back from the dead to take care of him. Sometimes, when she held him in her arms and let him cry, Laia also believed it. When his small savings had run out, Laia was forced to unearth her arts and go back to the fray.

Now that she was free of her father's constraints, Laia discovered that her powers had increased. In just a few months the best establishments in town were fighting for her services. She limited herself to one client a month, at the highest price. For weeks she would study the case and create the persona in the fantasy she was going to embody for a few hours. She never saw the same client twice. She never revealed her real identity.

Word got round the neighbourhood that the old man was living with a stunningly beautiful young woman, and after years of abandonment his resentful wife resurfaced out of the shadows. She returned home to ruin the old age of a man who could no longer see or remember, and whose only reality was the company of a young girl whom he believed to be his dead daughter, a girl who read him books and held him in her arms, calling him, and considering him to be, her father. With the help of judges and policemen, Señora Sentís managed to throw Laia out of the house and, almost, out of the doctor's life. Laia found shelter in an institution run by an old bedroom professional, Simone de Sagnier, and spent a few years trying to forget who she was, trying to forget that her only way of feeling alive was by giving life to others. When his wife allowed her, Laia would go to the doctor's flat on Calle Condal to fetch him and take him out for a stroll. They went to places and gardens he remembered having enjoyed with his daughter and there Laia, the Laia he remembered, read books to him or brought back memories which she had not lived but had made her own. Almost three years went by like this, with old Doctor Sentís fading away week after week, until that rainy day when I followed her to the doctor's home and Laia was given the news that her father, the only father she had ever known, had died that night with her name on his lips.

ROSE OF FIRE

Translated by Lucia Graves

And so, when 23 April came round, the prisoners in the block turned to David Martín, who lay in the shadows of his cell with his eyes closed, and begged him to tell them a story with which to alleviate their tedium. 'I'll tell you a story,' he replied. 'A story about books, dragons and roses, as befits the date,[1] but above all, a story about shadows and ashes, as befits the times . . .'

(from the lost fragments of *The Prisoner of Heaven*)

---

[1] 23 April, St George's Day (World Book Day), is celebrated in Catalonia with gifts of roses and books.

I

The chronicles tell us that when the maker of labyrinths reached Barcelona on board a vessel hailing from the East, he already carried with him the germ of a curse that was to stain the city's skies with fire and blood. It was the year of Our Lord 1454. A plague had decimated the population during the winter and the city lay under a blanket of ochre-coloured smoke that rose from bonfires ablaze with hundreds of corpses and shrouds. From afar one could see the noxious pall spiralling upwards. It crept through towers and palaces and soared like an omen of death, warning travellers to continue on their way and not approach the city walls. The Holy Office had ordered the city to be sealed off and had carried out an investigation. After days of brutal interrogation it was established without a shadow of a doubt that the plague had originated in a well close to the Jewish quarter, also known as the Call de Sanaüja, where Semitic moneylenders had conjured up a demonic plot to poison its waters. The usurers' substantial goods were seized and what was left of their bodies was cast into a pit in the marshes. Now, all that anyone could do was hope that the prayers of honest citizens might bring God's blessing back to Barcelona. Every day fewer people died and more people believed that the worst was over. However, as fate would have it, the former turned out to be the fortunate ones and the latter would soon envy them for having already left that vale of misery. By the time a timid voice dared to suggest that a terrible punishment might fall upon them from Heaven to purge the vile act committed against the Jewish traders *in nomine Dei*, it was too late. Nothing fell from Heaven except ash and dust. Evil, for once, arrived by sea.

2

The ship was sighted at dawn. Some fishermen, mending their nets by the sea wall, saw it emerging out of the mist, carried in by the swell. When the prow ran aground on the shore and the hull listed to port, the fishermen clambered aboard. A powerful stench rose from the bowels of the ship: the hold was flooded and a dozen sarcophagi floated among the debris. Edmond de Luna, maker of labyrinths and sole survivor of the voyage, was found tied to the helm and burnt by the sun. At first they thought he was dead, but when they took a closer look they noticed that his wrists were still bleeding where they were tied and a cold breath issued from his lips. He carried a leather-bound notebook under his belt but none of the fishermen was able to lay his hands on it because by then a group of soldiers had turned up in the port and their captain, following instructions from the Bishop's Palace – which had been alerted to the ship's arrival – ordered the dying man to be taken to the neighbouring Hospital de Santa Marta. The captain then posted his men around the shipwreck to guard it until representatives of the Holy Office were able to inspect the vessel and make a proper Christian appraisal of the events. Edmond de Luna's notebook was handed over to the Grand Inquisitor Jorge de León, a brilliant and ambitious defender of the Church who trusted that his efforts to cleanse the world of sin would soon earn him the titles of Blessed, Saint and Beacon of the Christian Faith. After a brief inspection, Jorge de León concluded that the notebook had been written in a language unbeknown to Christianity and he ordered his men to go and find a printer named Raimundo de Sempere. Sempere had a modest workshop next to the gate of Santa Ana and, because he had travelled during his youth, knew more languages than it was prudent for a good Christian to know. Under threat of torture, Sempere the printer was made to swear he would keep the secret of what was revealed to him. Only then was he allowed to inspect the notebook, in a heavily guarded room above the library of the archdeacon's house, next to the cathedral. Jorge de León watched over him avidly.

'I think the text is written in Persian, your Holiness,' murmured a terrified Sempere.

'I'm not a saint yet,' clarified the Inquisitor. 'All in good time. Continue . . .'

And so it was that the printer spent the entire night reading and translating for the Grand Inquisitor the secret diary of Edmond de Luna, adventurer and bearer of the curse that was to bring the beast to Barcelona.

3

Thirty years earlier, Edmond de Luna had set sail from Barcelona, bound for the East, in search of wonders and adventures. His sea voyage had taken him to forbidden islands that did not appear on navigation charts, to lie with princesses and creatures of an unmentionable nature, to learn secrets of civilisations buried by time and to initiate himself in the science and art of building labyrinths, a talent that would make him famous and provide him with employment and fortune at the service of sultans and emperors. As the years went by, the accumulation of pleasure and wealth no longer meant anything to him. He had satisfied greed and ambition beyond the dreams of any mortal, and upon reaching maturity, aware that he was fast approaching the twilight of his life, he told himself that he would never again offer his services to anyone unless it were in exchange for the greatest of rewards: forbidden knowledge. For years he refused invitations to build the most prodigious and intricate labyrinths because nothing offered in payment seemed desirable to him. He thought there could be no treasure in the world that had not already been presented to him, when news came that the Emperor of the city of Constantinople required his services, for which he was prepared to reward him with a thousand-year-old secret to which no living soul had been privy for centuries. Bored, and tempted by a last opportunity to revive the flame of his soul, Edmond de Luna visited Emperor Constantine in his palace. Constantine was utterly convinced that sooner or later the siege of the Ottoman sultans would bring his empire to an end and all the knowledge that the city of Constantinople had built up over the centuries would be banished from the face of the earth. He therefore wanted Edmond to plan the greatest labyrinth ever created, a secret library, a city of books hidden beneath the catacombs of the cathedral of Hagia Sophia, where forbidden works and the prodigies of centuries of thoughts could be preserved for ever. In exchange, Emperor Constantine offered Edmond no treasure, but only a flask: a small cut-glass phial containing a scarlet liquid that shone in the dark. Constantine smiled strangely as he showed Edmond the bottle.

'I've waited many years to find a man worthy of this gift,' the Emperor explained. 'In the wrong hands, this could be an instrument for evil.'

Fascinated and intrigued, Edmond examined the bottle.

'It's a drop of blood from the last dragon,' murmured the Emperor. 'The secret of immortality.'

4

For months on end Edmond de Luna worked on the project for the great labyrinth of the books, making and remaking the plans, never satisfied with them. By then he had realised that he no longer cared about the payment, for his immortality would be secured by that prodigious library and not by some legendary magic elixir. The Emperor, patient but concerned, kept reminding him that the final siege of the Ottomans was drawing nigh and there was no time to waste. When, at long last, Edmond de Luna solved the mighty conundrum, it was too late: the troops of Mehmed II the Conqueror had besieged Constantinople. The end of the city and of the empire was imminent. The Emperor marvelled when he received the plans, but realised that he would never be able to build the labyrinth under the city that bore his name. So he asked Edmond to try to escape the siege together with so many other artists and thinkers who were about to set off for Italy.

'Dear friend,' he said, 'I know you will find the perfect place to build the labyrinth.'

In gratitude, the Emperor handed him the phial with the blood of the last dragon, but a shadow of concern clouded his face as he did so.

'When I offered you this gift, I was appealing to your avid mind, to tempt you, dear friend. I now want you also to accept this humble amulet, which one day will appeal to the wisdom of your soul if the price of ambition is too high . . .'

The Emperor removed a medal that hung round his neck and handed it to him. The pendant contained neither gold nor jewels, just a small stone that looked like a simple grain of sand.

'The man who gave it to me told me it was a tear shed by Christ.' Edmond frowned. 'I know you're not a man of faith, Edmond, but faith is found when one isn't looking for it and the day will come when your heart, and not your mind, will long for the purification of the soul.'

Edmond did not wish to contradict the Emperor so he hung the insignificant medal round his neck. With no more baggage than the plan for his labyrinth and the scarlet flask, he departed that very night. Constantinople and the empire would fall shortly afterwards, following a bloody siege, while Edmond traversed the Mediterranean in search of the city he had left in his youth.

He sailed with a group of mercenaries who had offered him passage, taking him to be a rich merchant whose pouch they could empty once they attained the high seas. When they discovered that he carried no riches upon him they decided to throw him overboard, but Edmond persuaded them to let him stay by narrating some of his adventures in the manner of Scheherazade. The trick consisted in always leaving them craving for another morsel, as a wise dweller of Damascus had once taught him. 'They will despise you for it, but they will want you even more.'

In his spare time he began to record his experiences in a notebook and in order to keep it from the prying eyes of those pirates, he wrote in Persian, an extraordinary tongue he had learned during the years he had spent in ancient Babylon. Halfway through the journey they came across a ship that was sailing adrift with no voyagers or crew. It carried large amphorae of wine which they took aboard and with which the pirates got drunk every night while listening to the stories recounted by Edmond – who was not allowed to taste a single drop of it. After a few days the crew began to fall ill and soon one after the other the mercenaries died, poisoned by the stolen wine.

Edmond, the only survivor, placed them one by one in sarcophagi the pirates carried in the ship's hold – the bounty from one of their pillages. Only when he was the last man left alive on the ship and feared he might die adrift on the high seas in the most terrible solitude did he dare open the scarlet bottle and sniff its contents for a second. An instant sufficed for him to glimpse the chasm that threatened to take possession of him. He felt the vapour creeping up from the phial over his skin and for a moment saw his hands being covered in scales and his nails turning into claws, sharper and deadlier than the most fearsome sword. He then clutched the humble grain of sand hanging round his neck and prayed for his salvation to a Christ in whom he did not believe. The dark abyss of the soul faded away and Edmond breathed anew, seeing his hands becoming normal human hands again. He closed the bottle and cursed himself for being so naïve, realising then that the Emperor had not lied to him. He also knew that this was no payment or blessing of any sort. It was the key to hell.

5

When Sempere had finished translating the notebook, the first light of dawn peered through the clouds. Shortly afterwards the Inquisitor, without uttering a word, left the room and two sentries came in to fetch Sempere and lead him to a cell from which he felt sure he would never emerge alive.

While Sempere was being flung into the dungeon, the Grand Inquisitor's men were sent to the ship's hulk where, hidden in a metal coffer, they were to find the scarlet phial. Jorge de León was waiting for them in the cathedral. They had not managed to find the medal with the supposed tear of Christ to which Edmond's text referred, but the Inquisitor was unconcerned because he felt that his soul did not need any cleansing. With his eyes poisoned by greed, the Inquisitor grabbed the scarlet bottle, raised it above the altar to bless it and, thanking God and hell for that gift, downed the contents in a single gulp. A few seconds went by and nothing happened. Then the Inquisitor began to laugh. The soldiers looked at one another, disconcerted, wondering whether Jorge de León had lost his mind. For most of them this was the last thought of their lives. They saw the Inquisitor fall to his knees as a gust of icy wind swept through the cathedral, dragging with it the wooden benches, knocking down statues and lighted candles.

Then they heard his skin and his limbs cracking, and amid agonising howls Jorge de León's voice was lost in the roar of the beast emerging from his flesh, rapidly growing into a bloody tangle of scales, claws and wings. A tail punctuated by sharp edges, like the blades of an axe, fanned out like a gigantic snake and when the beast turned and showed them its face lined with fangs, its eyes alight with fire, the soldiers had no courage left to turn and run. The flames caught them as they stood there, rooted to the ground. It tore the flesh off their bones like a hurricane tearing leaves off a tree. The beast then spread its wings and the Inquisitor, saint and dragon all in one, took flight, passing through the cathedral's large rose window in a storm of glass and fire, then rising over the roofs of Barcelona.

6

For seven days and seven nights the beast sowed panic, knocking down churches and palaces, setting fire to hundreds of buildings and dismembering with its claws the trembling figures it found begging for mercy under the roofs it ripped off. Every day the scarlet dragon grew, devouring all it found in its path. Torn bodies rained down from the sky and flames from the beast's breath flowed down the streets like a torrent of blood.

On the seventh day, when everyone thought the beast was about to raze the city and kill all its inhabitants, a lone figure came out to meet it. Barely recovered, Edmond de Luna limped up the staircase leading to the very top of the cathedral. There he waited for the dragon to catch sight of him. The beast emerged from black clouds of smoke and embers, flying low, close to the roofs of Barcelona. It had grown so much that it was now larger than the church from which it had sprung.

Edmond de Luna could see himself reflected in those eyes that resembled huge pools of blood. Flying like a cannonball over the city, tearing off terrace roofs and towers, the beast opened its jaws to snap him up. Edmond de Luna then pulled out that miserable grain of sand hanging round his neck and pressed it in his fist. He recalled the words of Constantine and told himself that faith had at last found him and that his death was a very small price to pay to purify the black soul of the beast, which was none other than the soul of all men. Raising the fist that held the tear of Christ, Edmond closed his eyes and offered himself up. In a flash, the jaws swallowed him and the dragon rose high above the clouds.

Those who remember that day say that the heavens split in two and a great brightness lit up the firmament. The beast was enveloped in the flames that poured out through its teeth and as it flapped its wings it formed a huge rose of fire that covered the entire city. Silence ensued and when they opened their eyes again, the sky was shrouded as in the darkest of nights and a gentle rain of bright ash flakes was falling from on high, covering the streets, the burned ruins and the entire city of tombs, churches and palaces with a white mantle that melted when one touched it and smelled of fire and damnation.

7

That night Raimundo de Sempere managed to escape from his cell and return to his home to discover that his family and his book-printing workshop had survived the catastrophe. At dawn, the printer approached the Sea Wall. Debris from the shipwreck that had brought Edmond de Luna to Barcelona swayed on the water. The sea had begun to break up the hull and Sempere was able to enter it, as one would enter a house with a wall removed. Walking through the bowels of the ship in the ghostly light of dawn, the printer at last found what he was looking for. Salt residue had partly erased the outlines, but the plans for the great labyrinth of books were still intact, just as Edmond de Luna had conceived it. Sempere sat on the sand and unfolded the plans. His mind could not encompass the complexity and the arithmetic holding that marvel together, but he told himself that there would be other illustrious minds capable of understanding its secrets. Until then, until the time when other men wiser than him found the means of saving the labyrinth and remembering the price exacted by the beast, he would keep the plans in the family chest where some day, he had no doubt, they would find the maker of labyrinths worthy of such a challenge.

THE PRINCE OF
PARNASSUS

Translated by Lucia Graves

A bloodstained sun was sinking below the line of the horizon when Antoni de Sempere, the gentleman whom everyone called *the maker of books*, climbed up to the very top of the walls that sealed the city and sighted the cortege approaching in the distance. It was the year of Our Lord 1616 and a mist that smelled of gunpowder snaked over the rooftops of a Barcelona made of stone and dust. The maker of books turned to look at the city and his gaze became lost in the mirage of towers, palaces and narrow streets throbbing in the miasma of a perpetual darkness that was barely broken by torches and by carriages crawling along close to the walls.

'One day the walls will fall and Barcelona will spread beneath the sky like a teardrop of ink over holy water.'

The maker of books smiled as he remembered those words, spoken by his good friend when he left the city six years earlier.

'I'm taking with me its memory, for I am bound by the beauty of its streets and indebted to its dark soul, to which I vow I will return to offer my own soul and seek the embrace of its sweetest oblivion.'

The echo of hoofs approaching the city walls rescued him from his daydreaming. The maker of books turned to the east and caught sight of the cortege, already on the road leading to the large gate of San Antonio. The black hearse, escorted by two horsemen, was adorned with carved reliefs and figures winding round a glass frame that was veiled with velvet curtains. Four steeds, decorated with plumes and other funeral finery, pulled the hearse, and the turning wheels raised a cloud of dust in the amber of sunset. The coachman, his face covered, could be seen on the driver's seat and behind him, crowning the hearse like a figurehead, rose the silhouette of a silver angel.

The maker of books lowered his eyes and sighed dolefully. All of a sudden, he knew he was not alone and did not even have to turn his head to verify the presence of the gentleman standing next to him. He could feel that gust of cold air and that perfume of dry flowers that always accompanied him.

'They say a good friend is one who knows how to remember as well as how to forget,' said the gentleman. 'I see you have not forgotten the meeting, Sempere.'

'Nor have you forgotten the debt, *Signore*.'

The gentleman came closer until his pale face was but a handspan away from the maker of books and Sempere was able to catch his own reflection in the dark mirror of those pupils that changed colour and narrowed like the eyes of a wolf at the sight of fresh blood. The gentleman had not aged a single day and wore the same formal attire. Sempere felt a shiver and a deep desire to run away, but all he did was nod politely.

'How did you find me?' he asked.

'The smell of ink gives you away, Sempere. Have you printed anything good recently? Anything you could recommend?'

The maker of books noticed the volume in the gentleman's hands.

'Mine is a modest press that cannot attract authors worthy of your taste. Besides, it would appear that the *signore* already has something to read for the evening.'

The gentleman exhibited his smile, revealing a string of sharp white teeth. The maker of books fixed his attention on the cortege, which was now reaching the city walls. He felt the gentleman's hand rest on his shoulder and clenched his teeth to stop himself from trembling.

'Don't be afraid, Sempere, my friend. The death rattles of Avellaneda[2] and that pack of envious scoundrels published by your friend Sebastián de Cormellas are as likely to reach posterity as the soul of my dear Antoni de Sempere is to enter the humble domain over which I preside. You have nothing to fear from me.'

'You said something similar to Don Miguel forty-six years ago.'

'Forty-seven. And I wasn't lying.'

The maker of books exchanged a brief glance with the gentleman and for a wistful moment thought he perceived the same huge sadness in his face as was engulfing his own heart.

'I thought this was a day of triumph for you, *Signore* Corelli,' he remarked.

'Beauty and knowledge are the only lights that shine on this miserable hovel that I am condemned to inhabit, Sempere. His loss is the greatest of my sufferings.'

Down below, the funeral cortege was passing through the gate of San Antonio. The gentleman made a sign to the printer, inviting him to lead the way.

'Come with me, Sempere. Let's welcome our good friend Don Miguel to the Barcelona he loved so much.'

And with those words, old Sempere abandoned himself to reminiscence, recalling that distant day when, not far from this very place, he'd met a young man named Miguel de Cervantes

---

2   Alonso Fernández de Avellaneda is the pseudonym used by the man who wrote his own Part II to Cervantes's *Don Quixote*.

Saavedra, whose destiny and whose memory were to become linked to his own fate and to his own name in the night of time . . .

BARCELONA, 1569

Those were legendary times when history's only tool was the memory of what had never happened, and the only dreams life could attain were brief and fleeting. In those days, aspiring poets carried swords on their belts and rode their horses without thought or destination, dreaming of verses tinged with venom. Barcelona was then a fortified town cradled by an amphitheatre of mountains replete with bandits, a city hiding behind a wine-coloured sea riddled with light and pirates. Outside its gates thieves and villains were hanged to drive away unlawful greed, and inside its walls, filled to bursting point, traders, wise men, courtiers and *hidalgos* of every condition and vassalage fought at the behest of a labyrinth of conspiracies, monies and alchemies whose fame reached the horizons and yearnings of the known and the imagined world. It was said that kings and saints had shed their blood there, that words and knowledge found shelter in that town, and that any adventurer with a coin in his hands and a lie on his lips could taste glory, sleep with death and wake up the following dawn among tall towers and cathedrals feeling blessed and able to achieve fame and fortune.

At such a place, which never existed and whose name he was condemned to remember all the days of his life, there arrived one midsummer's night a young *hidalgo* of the pen-and-sword variety, riding an emaciated nag that could barely stand on its four legs after having galloped for several days. On its back it carried the then destitute Miguel de Cervantes Saavedra, who hailed from no place and from everywhere, and a young woman whose face, one might say, looked as if it had been stolen from the canvas of one of the great masters. And it would be rightly said, for it was later known that the young girl's name was Francesca di Parma, born and raised in the Eternal City barely nineteen springtides past.

As fate would have it, the scrawny nag, foaming at the mouth after having concluded its heroic trot, collapsed in exhaustion a few steps away from the gates of Barcelona and the two lovers – for that was their secret condition – ambled along the sands of the beach beneath a sky bleeding with stars until they came to the boundary marked by the walls and then, seeing the breath of a thousand bonfires rising skywards and tinting the night the colour of liquid copper, decided to look for lodging and shelter in that place that resembled a dark palace built on Vulcan's forge itself.

Don Miguel de Cervantes's arrival in Barcelona with his beloved Francesca was later recounted in similar but less florid words to the noted maker of books, Don Antoni de Sempere – whose workshop and home stood next to the gate of Santa Ana – by a limping young man of humble appearance, imposing nose and sharp wit named Sancho Fermín de la Torre who, aware of the needs of the new arrivals, kindly offered to be their guide in exchange for a few coins. That is how the couple found accommodation and sustenance in a sombre house twisted upon itself like a gnarled tree trunk. And that is how, thanks to Sancho's skills and the workings of chance, the maker of books became acquainted with the young Cervantes, with whom he would share a deep friendship to the end of his days.

Little do the experts know about the circumstances preceding Don Miguel de Cervantes's arrival in the city of Barcelona. Initiates in such matters report severe hardships and much suffering before that moment in the author's life and warn that many more, from battles to unfair sentences and prison, or to the virtual loss of a hand in combat lay ahead of him before he was able to enjoy a short time of peace in his waning years. Whatever the ins and outs of fate that had brought him there, from what the cheerful Sancho was able to gather, a great wrong and an even greater threat were hot on his heels.

Sancho, partial to tales of glowing romances and to religious plays of robust moral instruction, managed to deduce that the stimulus at the heart of such a hefty plot had to be the presence of that young woman of supernatural beauty and charms whose name was Francesca. Her skin was like a breath of light, her voice a sigh that set hearts racing, her eyes and lips a promise of pleasures whose description escaped the rhyming talents of poor Sancho, for the magic suggested by the shapes beneath those clothes of silk and lace was enough to alter his pulse and his reason. And so Sancho concluded that the young poet, having tasted that heavenly poison, was in all likelihood beyond salvation, for there could be no honest man on this earth who would not have sold his soul, his horse and even his mind for a moment of bliss in the arms of that siren.

'Cervantes, my friend,' Sancho asserted, 'it is not for a sad peasant like me to tell Your Excellency that a countenance and frame so magnificent will cloud the mind of any man in breathing condition, but my nose, which after my gut is my shrewdest organ, leads me to think that wherever it was that Your Honour removed that marvellous example of womanhood from, you will not be forgiven for it, and there is not enough room on earth in which to hide a Venus of such delicious substance.'

Needless to say, in pursuit of the drama and the scene-setting, the words and musicality of good Sancho's drivel have been rearranged and improved by the pen of this your humble and reliable narrator, but the essence and wisdom of his judgement remain untouched and unadulterated.

'Oh, my friend, were I to tell you . . .' sighed a mortified Cervantes.

And tell him he did, for the wine of storytelling ran through his veins and, as the heavens would have it, it was his practice to firstly tell himself the things of the world in order to understand them and then tell them to others, draped in the music and light of literature, because he sensed that if life was not a dream it was at least a pantomime where the cruel absurdity of the narrative always ran behind the scenery, and there was no greater or more effective vengeance twixt heaven and earth than to sculpt beauty and wit by dint of words if one was to find sense in the nonsense of things.

The account of how he had arrived in Barcelona, fleeing from monumental dangers, and which was the origin and nature of that prodigious creature named Francesca di Parma, was expounded by Don Miguel de Cervantes seven nights later. At Cervantes's request, Sancho had put him in touch with Antoni de Sempere, for it appears that the young poet had written a play, some sort of romance about mysterious enchantments, spells and wild passions, which he wished to see committed to paper.

'It is of extreme importance that I see my work printed before the next moon, Sancho. My life and that of Francesca depend on it.'

'How can someone's life depend on a bunch of verses and the conjunction of the moon, Master?'

'Believe me, Sancho. I know what I'm saying.'

Sancho, who secretly did not believe in any poetry or astronomy other than those promised by a fine meal and a generous tumble in the hay with some plump and cheerful lass, trusted in his patron's words and performed the necessary tasks to bring about the meeting. Leaving the beautiful Francesca in her room, fast asleep in the arms of the nymphs, the two men departed at nightfall. They had arranged to meet Sempere at an inn that lay in the shadow of the fishermen's great cathedral – known as the basilica of Santa María del Mar – and there, sitting in a corner by candlelight, all three partook of a good wine and a loaf of bread with rashers of salted pork. The clientele was made up of fishermen, pirates, murderers and sundry visionaries. Laughter, quarrels and thick clouds of smoke floated in the golden darkness of the tavern.

'Tell Don Antoni about your comedy,' Sancho encouraged the author.

'Actually, it's a tragedy,' Cervantes clarified.

'And pray, what is the difference, if the master will forgive my utter ignorance of fine lyric genres?'

'Comedy shows us that one must not take life too seriously, and tragedy teaches us what happens when we pay no attention to what comedy teaches us,' Cervantes explained.

Sancho nodded without batting an eyelid and rounded off the job with a fierce bite at his bacon.

'Isn't poetry grand?' he mumbled.

Sempere, somewhat bereft of orders in those days, listened with interest to the young poet. Cervantes carried a bundle of papers in a folder, which he showed the maker of books. The latter examined them carefully, stopping here and there to cast his eye over certain turns of phrase in the text.

'There's work here for quite a few days . . .'

Cervantes pulled a bag from his belt and dropped it on the table. A handful of coins peeped out of it. As soon as the filthy lucre shone in the candlelight, Sancho hid it with an anguished expression.

'For God's sake, Master, don't show such fine fodder around here – these places are stuffed with villains and cut-throats who would slice your gullet and ours too with just one whiff of the aroma given off from these doubloons.'

'Sancho is right, my friend,' Sempere confirmed, eyeing the crowd.

Cervantes hid the monies and sighed.

Sempere poured him another glass of wine and began examining the poet's pages in more detail. The work, described by the author as a tragedy in three acts and an epistle, was titled *A Poet in Hell* and narrated the hardships of a young Florentine artist who, accompanied by Dante's ghost, penetrates the depths of the underworld in order to rescue the soul of his beloved, the daughter of a cruel and corrupt family of nobles who had sold her to the Prince of Darkness in exchange for fame, fortune and glory in the finite, earthly world. The last scene took place inside the Duomo, where the hero had to prise the lifeless body of his chosen damsel from the claws of an angel of light and fire.

Sancho thought it sounded like some sinister puppet tale, but didn't say anything because he sensed that regarding such matters bookworms had a thin skin and didn't take any criticism easily.

'Tell me how you came to compose this work, my friend,' Sempere inquired.

Cervantes, who had already knocked back three or four glasses of wine, nodded. It was evident that he wanted to unburden himself of the secret that was weighing him down.

'Rest assured that Sancho and I will keep your secret, my friend, whatever it may be.'

Sancho raised his goblet of wine to that noble sentiment.

Cervantes hesitated. 'My story is the story of a curse,' he began.

'Like that of all apprentice poets,' said Sempere. 'Pray continue.'

'It's the story of a man in love.'

'Agreed. But fear not, such tales are highly favoured by the public,' Sempere reassured him.

Sancho nodded repeatedly.

'Love is the only creature that doesn't learn from its mistakes,' he agreed. 'And wait until you see the lass in question, Sempere,' he added, suppressing a belch. 'She's of the kind that truly lifts one's spirit.'

Cervantes stared at him censoriously.

'Please forgive me, sir,' Sancho ventured. 'It's this wicked wine that's taking hold of me. The virtue and purity of the lady plainly speak for themselves, and may the very heavens fall on my empty head if at any moment I entertained a single impure thought in this regard.'

The three men looked briefly up at the tavern's ceiling, and seeing that the Creator was not on duty and no mishap had taken place, they smiled, raised their glasses and toasted the happy occasion of their encounter. And that is how the wine, which makes men become sincere when they least need to, and gives them courage when they should hold back, persuaded Cervantes to tell the story within the story, that which fools and murderers call the truth.

A POET IN HELL

According to the proverb, a man must walk while he still has legs, speak while he still has a voice and dream while he still preserves his innocence, because sooner or later he will be unable to stand up, his breath will falter and the only dream he will long for is the eternal night of oblivion. With these words as his saddlebags, an arrest warrant out for him – because of a duel that had taken place in murky circumstances – and the fire of youth in his veins, Miguel de Cervantes departed from the town of Madrid in the year of Our Lord 1569, heading for the legendary cities of Italy in search of wonders, beauty and science which, according to those who knew them, they possessed in far greater measure and grace than any other place to be found on the maps of the kingdom. Many were the adventures and misfortunes that befell him in those lands, but the greatest of them all was his happening upon that creature of extraordinary radiance whose name was Francesca, from whose lips he tasted heaven and hell, and in whose desire he was to seal his destiny forever.

Barely nineteen, Francesca had already lost all hope in life. She was the last daughter of a despicable and destitute family who scraped together a living in an old house that leaned over the waters of the River Tiber in the ancient city of Rome. Her brothers – deceitful, malicious good-for-nothings – lazed about and committed thefts and petty crimes with which they barely managed to put a crust of bread in their mouths. Her prematurely aged parents, who insisted they had conceived her in the autumn of their unhappy lives, were just a couple of miserly swindlers who had found little Francesca crying in the still warm arms of her real mother, a nameless young girl who had died giving birth to her under the arches of the old bridge of Castel Sant'Angelo.

As they debated whether to fling the baby into the river and just take the copper medal her mother wore round her neck, the two villains noticed the child's astonishing perfection and decided to keep her, for surely such a gift would fetch a good price among the most refined and wealthy families, those providing an entry to the doors of the court. As the days, weeks and months went by, their greed intensified, for day by day the little girl showed herself to be a creature of such beauty and charm that in the minds of her captors her price and value could only rise. When she was ten, a Florentine poet who was passing through Rome noticed her one day as she went down to the river for water – not far from where she had been born and had lost her mother. Faced with the magic in her eyes, the poet dedicated a few lines to her and gave her what would be her name, Francesca, for her adoptive family had not even bothered to give her one. And so Francesca grew, until she blossomed into a woman of exquisite fragrance whose very presence stopped conversations and brought time to a halt. Only the immeasurable sadness of her eyes tarnished the picture of a beauty beyond words.

Very soon, artists from all corners of Rome began to offer enticing sums to her scheming parents to be allowed to use her as a model for their works. When they saw her they were convinced that if anyone with talent and skill were able to capture only a tenth of her enchantment on canvas or marble, he would pass into history as the greatest artist of all time. The demand for her services did not cease, and the one-time beggars now basked in the splendour of new wealth, riding about in garish carriages fit for a cardinal, dressed in coloured silks and smearing their private parts with scent to disguise the shame that covered their hearts.

When Francesca came of age, her parents, fearing they might lose the treasure that had built their fortune, decided to offer her hand in marriage. Contrary to the usual practice of providing a dowry, as was expected of the bride's family in those days, their audacity led them to request a substantial payment in exchange for granting the damsel's hand and body to the highest bidder. An unprecedented auction took place which was won by one of the most celebrated and renowned artists in the city, Don Anselmo Giordano. Giordano was by then a mature man in his declining years, with body and soul damaged by decades of excess, and a heart poisoned by greed and envy because, despite all the tributes, wealth and praise his work had garnered, his secret dream had been to surpass Leonardo in both name and reputation.

The great Leonardo had been dead for five decades, but Anselmo Giordano had never been able to forget, or forgive, the day when, still only an adolescent, he had gone to the master's workshop to offer his services as an apprentice. Leonardo examined some of the sketches he had brought with him and said a few kind words about them. Young Anselmo's father was a well-known banker to whom Leonardo owed a favour or two, and the boy was convinced that his place in the workshop of the greatest artist of the day was guaranteed. Much to his surprise, Leonardo, not without sadness, added that although he appreciated a certain talent in his lines, it was not enough to make him any different from a thousand and one aspirants like him who would never even reach mediocrity. He told him that he did have some ambition, but not enough to distinguish him from so many other apprentices who would never be capable of sacrificing what was needed to deserve the light of true inspiration. And finally, he told him that perhaps he could acquire some skill, but never enough to make it worth his while to devote his life to a profession where only geniuses managed to get by.

'Young Anselmo,' said Leonardo, 'don't let my words distress you. Consider them a blessing, for your kind father will make you a wealthy man for life, one who will not have to fight with brush and chisel for a living. You will be a fortunate man, you will be a man loved and respected by your fellow citizens, but what you will never be, even if you possessed all the gold in the world, is a genius. Few fates can be as cruel or as bitter as that of a mediocre artist who spends his life envying and cursing his rivals. Don't waste your life on an inauspicious destiny. Let art and beauty be created by others who have no choice. And in time, learn to forgive my honesty which will hurt today but tomorrow, if you accept it with good grace, will save you from your own hell.'

With these words, Master Leonardo dismissed young Anselmo, who was to wander for hours through the streets of Rome weeping tears of anger. When he returned to his father's house he announced that he did not wish to study with Leonardo, whom he considered a fraud, a producer of vulgar pieces for ignorant masses who were incapable of appreciating true art.

'I will be a pure artist, only for a select few who will be able to understand the depth of my commitment.'

His father, who was a patient man and, like all bankers, had more understanding of human nature than the wisest of cardinals, embraced him and told him to fear not, as he would never want for anything – not sustenance, or admirers, or praise for his work. Before dying, the banker made sure that it would be so.

Anselmo Giordano never forgave Leonardo, because a man can forgive everything except being told the truth. Fifty years later, his hatred and his wish to see the false master discredited were greater than ever.

When Anselmo Giordano heard the fabulous tale of young Francesca told by poets and artists, he sent his servants with a bagful of gold coins to the family's home and requested their presence. The young woman's parents, dressed like circus monkeys on a visit to the court of Mantua, turned up at Giordano's residence escorting the lass, who was clad in humble rags. When the artist's eyes rested upon Francesca his heart seemed to stop for a moment. Everything he had heard about her was true, nay, more than true. Nowhere in the world did such beauty exist – nor had it ever existed – and he knew, as only an artist can know, that her charm did not stem, as everyone believed, from that skin, or that shapely body, but from the luminosity emanating from within her, from her sad, forlorn eyes, from her lips silenced by fate.

So strong was the impression Francesca di Parma made on Master Giordano that he was convinced he must not let her escape, that he could not allow her to sit for any other painter and that such a marvel of nature must belong to him and to him alone. It was the only way he would be able to create a body of work that would earn him the people's favour over that of the contemptible and odious Leonardo. It was the only way his fame and reputation would surpass those of the deceased Leonardo, whose name he would no longer need to scorn in public, because once he had reached the pinnacle he would be the one who could permit himself to ignore him and claim that his work had only ever existed to excite the coarse and the ignorant. Then and there, Giordano made an offer that exceeded the most lavish dreams of the vile couple who called themselves Francesca's parents. The wedding was to take place a week later in the chapel of Giordano's palace. Francesca did not utter a single word during the transaction.

Seven days later, young Cervantes was ambling through town in search of inspiration, when the retinue accompanying a large golden carriage cleared the way through the crowd. The procession halted for an instant as it crossed Via del Corso, and it was then that he saw her. Francesca di Parma, wearing the most delicate silks woven by Florentine craftsmen, gazed at him in silence from the carriage window. So profound was the sadness he read in her eyes, and such was the power of that stolen spirit as it was being led to prison, that Cervantes was seized by the cold certainty that for the first time in his life he had seen the path of his true destiny in the face of an unknown woman.

As he watched the procession disappear into the distance, Cervantes asked who that creature could be, and the people walking by told him the story of Francesca di Parma. Listening to them, he recalled having heard rumours and gossip about her, but he had dismissed these, attributing them to the wild fabrications of local bards. And yet, the fable was true. Sublime beauty had become embodied in a simple, humble woman and, as could be expected, people had done nothing but ensure her misfortune and humiliation. Young Cervantes wanted to follow the procession to Giordano's palace, but he couldn't find the strength. To him, the celebrations and merrymaking sounded like some ominous music, and all he could see was a tragedy: the destruction of purity and perfection by men's greed, wickedness and ignorance.

Pressing against the crowds who wished to follow the nuptial ceremonies outside the famous artist's palace, Cervantes walked back to his inn, filled with sadness almost as great as that which he had perceived in the eyes of the mysterious young woman. That very night, while Master Giordano removed the silks draped over Francesca di Parma's body and caressed every inch of her skin with lust and incredulity, the house of the young woman's family, built on a dangerous location above the Tiber and unable to take the weight of the treasures and glittering ornaments accumulated at her expense, collapsed into the freezing waters of the river, taking with it all the members of the clan, whom nobody would ever see again.

Not far from there, a wakeful Cervantes confronted ink and paper by the light of an oil lamp, preparing to write down everything he'd witnessed that day. With a faltering hand, and lost for words, he attempted to describe the impression made on him by that brief exchange of glances with the damsel Francesca on Via del Corso. All the art he thought he possessed withered on the tip of his pen and not a single word settled on the page. He told himself that if perchance his writing could ever capture a mere tenth of the magic radiating from that presence, his name and reputation would rise among those of the greatest poets in history and he would become a king among narrators, a prince of Parnassus whose light would illuminate the lost paradise of literature and, moreover, wipe from the earth the odious reputation of that perfidious playwright Lope de Vega, on whom both fortune and glory did not cease to smile, a man who had attained unprecedented triumphs since early youth, while he was barely able to complete a single line of poetry that would not embarrass the paper on which it was written. Moments later, understanding the darkness of his desire, he felt ashamed of his vanity and of the insane envy that was eating away at him, and he told himself that he was no better a man than old Giordano, who at that very moment must be licking the forbidden honey with his mendacious lips and exploring, with trembling hands reeking of infamy, the secrets he had stolen by dint of doubloons.

In his infinite cruelty, Cervantes presumed, God had abandoned Francesca di Parma's beauty to the hands of men to remind them of the ugliness of their souls, the meanness of their endeavours and the rancour of their desires.

Days passed, but the memory of that brief encounter would not die away. Cervantes sat at his desk trying to assemble the pieces of a drama that would satisfy the public and capture their imagination, like the ones Lope seemed to write effortlessly, but all his mind was able to evoke was the sense of loss Francesca di Parma's image had planted in his heart. As for the play he had decided to write, his pen filled page after page of a troubled romance in whose verses he tried to recreate the young woman's lost story. In his account, Francesca had no memory, she was a blank page; her character was a fate as yet untold that only he could make up, a promise of purity that would restore his determination to believe in something clean and innocent set in a world of lies and deceit, a world of trickery, meanness and blame. He spent sleepless nights hammering his imagination, pulling at the strings of his ingenuity to the point of exhaustion and despite all that, when he reread his folios at dawn he would toss them into the fire because he knew they did not deserve to share the light of day with the being who had inspired them, the woman who was slowly wasting away in the prison that Giordano, whom he had never seen but already loathed with every fibre of his being, had built for her inside the walls of his palace.

The days became weeks and the weeks turned into months, and soon half a year had passed since the wedding between Anselmo Giordano and Francesca di Parma, during which time nobody in the whole of Rome had set eyes on them again. People knew that the best merchants in town delivered provisions to the palace gates and these were received by Tomaso, the master's personal servant. They knew that once a week Antonio Mercanti's workshop provided the master with canvases and other materials for his work. But not a soul could say they'd seen the artist or his young wife in person. On the day that marked six months since the nuptials, Cervantes was visiting a famous impresario who managed some of the most important theatres in the city and was always on the lookout for new authors with talent, hunger and a willingness to work for a pittance. Thanks to the recommendation of various colleagues of his, Cervantes had been granted an audience with Don Leonello, an extravagant gentleman of pompous manners and noble attire who kept on his desk a collection of glass vials containing, or so they said, the intimate secretions of great courtesans whose virtue he had deflowered. Leonello, who wore a small brooch on his lapel in the shape of an angel, kept him standing while he skimmed over the pages of his play, feigning boredom and disdain.

'*A Poet in Hell*,' murmured the impresario. 'That's been done. This story has been told by others before you, and better too. What I'm looking for, let's say, is innovation. Audacity. Vision.'

Cervantes knew from experience that people who say they look for these noble virtues in art are the ones who are normally most incapable of recognising them, but he also knew that an empty stomach and a light pocket can remove all arguments and rhetoric from the best of us. If his instinct told him anything, it was that Leonello, who wore the appearance of an old fox, did at least feel perturbed by the nature of the material he had brought to him.

'I'm sorry to have wasted Your Lordship's time—'

'Not so fast,' Leonello cut in. 'I said this is nothing new, but not that it is, let's say, excremental. You do have some talent, but you lack professional skills. And what you don't have, let's say, is taste. Or a sense of opportunity.'

'I thank you for your generosity.'

'And I you for your sarcasm, Cervantes. You Spaniards suffer from too much pride and not enough perseverance. Don't give up so soon. Learn from your compatriot Lope de Vega. A true genius – *genio y figura* as you Spaniards say.'

'I'll bear that in mind. Does Your Excellency then see any possibility of accepting my work?'

Leonello burst out laughing.

'Do pigs fly? Nobody wants to see, let's say, bleak dramas telling them that the human heart is rotten, and that hell is oneself and one's neighbour, Cervantes. People go to the theatre to laugh, to cry and to be reminded of how good and noble one is. You've not yet lost your naivety and you think you have, let's say, the truth to tell. You'll be cured of it in a few years, or at least that's what I hope, because I wouldn't like to see you burned at the stake or rotting away in a prison cell.'

'So you don't think my play could interest anybody . . .'

'That's not what I said. Let's say that I know someone who perhaps might be interested.'

Cervantes felt his pulse race.

'Hunger is so predictable,' sighed Leonello.

'Hunger, unlike Spaniards, has no pride and is brimming with perseverance,' suggested Cervantes.

'You see? You do have some training. You know how to turn a sentence around and construct, let's say, a dramatic line as a reply. It's only a beginner's effort, but plenty of louts whose plays have been performed can't even write an exit stage left . . .'

'Can you help me, then, Don Leonello? I'll do whatever it takes and I learn quickly.'

'I've no doubt about that . . .'

Leonello observed him doubtfully.

'Anything, Your Excellency. I beg you . . .'

'There *is* something that might interest you. But it entails, let's say, some risks.'

'Risks don't scare me. No more than poverty, at least.'

'In that case . . . I know a certain gentleman with whom I have, let's say, an agreement. When a promising young man with some talent, like you, let's say, comes across my path, I send him off to see him and he, let's say, is grateful. In his own way.'

'I'm all ears.'

'That's what worries me . . . It so happens that the gentleman in question is, let's say, passing through the city.'

'Is the gentleman a theatre impresario like Your Excellency?'

'Let's say he's something like that. A publisher.'

'Even better . . .'

'If you say so. He has a presence in Paris, Rome and London and he's always on the lookout for a special type of talent. Like yours, let's say . . .'

'I'm enormously grateful for—'

'Don't thank me. Go and see him and tell him I sent you. But hurry up. I know he's only in town for a few days . . .'

Leonello wrote a name down on a sheet of paper and handed it to him.

Andreas Corelli
Stampa della Luce

'You'll find him in the Locanda Borghese, in the evening.'

'Do you think he'll be interested in my play?'

Leonello smiled mysteriously.

'Good luck, Cervantes.'

At nightfall Cervantes put on the only clean set of clothes he possessed and walked over to the Locanda Borghese, a villa surrounded by canals and gardens, not far from Anselmo Giordano's palace. At the foot of the stairway he was startled by a discreet servant who announced that he was expected and that Andreas Corelli would receive him shortly in one of the halls. Cervantes imagined that perhaps Leonello was kinder than he portrayed himself to be and had sent a note recommending him to his publisher friend. The servant led Cervantes to a large oval library. The room lay in the shadows and was heated by a fire that cast an intense amber glow dancing over endless walls of books. Two large armchairs faced one another by the fireplace. After a moment's hesitation, Cervantes sat in one of them and was soon enveloped by the warm aura and the hypnotic dance of the flames. It took him a couple of minutes to realise that he was not alone. A tall, angular figure occupied the opposite armchair. He was dressed in black and wore a silver angel that was identical to the one he'd seen on Leonello's lapel that afternoon. What he first noticed about him were his hands, the largest he had ever seen, pale and displaying long, sharp fingers. Then he noticed his eyes: two mirrors reflecting the flames and Cervantes's own face, eyes that never blinked and seemed to alter the shape of their pupils without moving a single muscle.

'My good friend Leonello tells me you're a man of great talent, but little fortune.'

Cervantes swallowed hard.

'Don't allow my appearance to trouble you, Señor Cervantes. Appearances do not always deceive, but frequently confound.'

Cervantes nodded but said nothing. Corelli smiled, tight-lipped.

'You've brought a play to show me. Am I wrong?'

Cervantes handed him the manuscript and noticed how Corelli smiled when he saw the title.

'It's a first draft,' ventured Cervantes.

'Not any longer,' said Corelli as he leafed through it.

Cervantes watched the publisher read calmly, occasionally smiling or raising his eyebrows in surprise. A wine glass and a bottle of some fine-looking liquid seemed to have materialised on the table between the two armchairs.

'Help yourself, Cervantes. Man cannot scrape a living on writing alone.'

Cervantes poured a glass of wine and raised it to his lips. A sweet, intoxicating aroma flooded his palate. He downed the wine in three gulps and felt an irrepressible desire to help himself to some more.

'Don't be shy, my friend. A glass with no wine is an insult to life.'

Soon Cervantes had lost count of the number of glasses he'd savoured. A gratifying and comforting drowsiness had taken hold of him and through half-closed eyelids he could see that Corelli was still reading the manuscript. He heard bells striking midnight in the distance. Shortly afterwards, the curtain of a deep sleep fell and Cervantes abandoned himself to the silence.

When he opened his eyes again, Corelli's silhouette was outlined against the fire. The publisher was facing the flames, standing with his back to Cervantes and holding the manuscript in his hand. Cervantes felt a hint of nausea, the sweet aftertaste of the wine in his throat, and wondered how much time had gone by.

'One day you'll write a masterpiece, Cervantes,' said Corelli, 'But this isn't it.'

Without further ado, the publisher threw the manuscript into the fire. Cervantes leaped towards the flames but the roar of the fire stopped him. He watched helplessly as the fruit of his labours burned, as the lines of ink turned into blue flames and trails of white smoke scurried over the pages like snakes of gunpowder. Devastated, he fell on his knees and when he turned to face Corelli he saw the publisher looking at him with pity.

'Sometimes a writer must burn a thousand pages before writing a single one that deserves bearing his signature. You've barely begun. Your work awaits you on the threshold of your maturity.'

'You had no right to do that . . .'

Corelli smiled and stretched out a hand to help him up from the floor. Cervantes hesitated, but finally accepted.

'I want you to write something for me, my friend. Without haste. Even if it takes you years, and believe me, it will. It will take longer than you imagine. Something in accord with your ambition and your desires.'

'What do you know about my desires?'

'Like most aspiring poets, Cervantes, you're like an open book. For that reason, because your *Poet in Hell* seems to me simply a child's game, a bout of measles you must go through, I choose to make you a firm offer. An offer for you to write a work that will meet your high standards, and mine.'

'You've burned everything I was able to write in months of work.'

'And I've done you a favour. Now tell me, from your heart, if you really think I'm wrong.'

It took him a while, but Cervantes agreed.

'And tell me whether I'm mistaken when I say that in your heart you cherish the hope of creating a work that will eclipse that of your rivals, that will sully the name of that Señor Lope and his prolific ingenuity . . .'

Cervantes wanted to protest, but the words wouldn't reach his lips. Corelli smiled again.

'You don't need to feel ashamed about that. Or to think that such a desire turns you into someone like Giordano . . .'

Cervantes looked up disconcertedly.

'Of course I know the story of Giordano and his muse,' replied Corelli, anticipating his question. 'I know it because I've known the old master for many years, before you were even born.'

'Anselmo Giordano is a vile person.'

Corelli laughed.

'No, he's not. He's just a man.'

'A man who deserves to pay for his crimes.'

'Is that what you think? Don't tell me you're also going to fight a duel with him.'

Cervantes paled. How could the publisher know he'd left Madrid months ago fleeing from an arrest warrant issued as a consequence of a duel?

Corelli gave him a wicked smile and pointed an accusing finger at him.

'And what crimes are those you're attributing to poor Giordano, aside from his tendency to paint bucolic scenes of goats, Virgin Marys and little shepherds to suit the tastes of traders and bishops, and madonnas with ample busts to cheer up parishioners during prayer?'

'He kidnapped that poor girl and keeps her imprisoned in his palace to satisfy his greed and his baseness. To hide his lack of talent. To erase his shame.'

'How quickly men judge their fellow humans for actions that they themselves would commit if the opportunity arose . . .'

'I would never do what he has done.'

'Are you sure?'

'Completely.'

'Would you dare to be put to the test?'

'I don't understand . . .'

'Tell me, Señor Cervantes. What do you know about Frances-ca di Parma? And don't give me that tale about the dishonoured maiden and her cruel childhood. You've already shown me that you've mastered the rudiments of theatre . . .'

'All I know is . . . that she doesn't deserve to live in a prison.'

'Is that because of her beauty? Do you think that ennobles her?'

'Because of her purity. Because of her goodness. Her inno-cence.'

Corelli licked his lips.

'You're still in time to abandon literature and embrace the sac-rament of priesthood, my friend Cervantes. Better pay, better lodg-ings, and, it goes without saying, hot and plentiful meals. One needs a great deal of faith to be a poet. More than you claim.'

'You make fun of everything.'

'Only of you, Cervantes.'

Cervantes stood up and made as if to go to the door.

'Then I'll leave Your Grace alone to laugh to your heart's con-tent.'

Cervantes was about to reach the door when it slammed shut in his face with such force that it knocked him over. He was trying to get back on his feet when he discovered that Corelli was leaning over him, a six-foot, bony figure, looking as if he were about to fling himself upon him and tear him apart.

'Get up,' he ordered.

Cervantes obeyed. The publisher's eyes seemed to have changed. Two huge black pupils spread across them. Cervantes had never been so frightened. He took a step back and bumped into the wall of books.

'I'm going to give you one opportunity, Cervantes. An opportunity to become yourself, to stop wandering along paths that would lead you to live lives that are not your own. And as with every opportunity, the final choice will be yours. Do you accept my offer?'

Cervantes shrugged.

'This is my offer. You will write a masterpiece, but in order to do so you will have to lose what you love most. Your work will be praised, envied and imitated till the end of time, but a void will open in your heart, a void a thousand times greater than the glory and the vanity of your inventiveness, because only then will you understand the true nature of your feelings and only then will you know whether or not you are, as you now believe you are, a better man than Giordano and all those who, like him, have already fallen on their knees at the sight of their own reflection when they have accepted this challenge ... Do you accept it?'

Cervantes sought to avert Corelli's eyes.

'I can't hear you.'

'I accept it,' he heard himself say.

Corelli stretched out his hand and Cervantes shook it. The publisher's fingers closed over his like a spider and he felt the cold breath of Corelli on his face. It smelled of dug-up earth and dead flowers.

'Every Sunday, at midnight, Tomaso, Giordano's servant, opens the door to an alleyway that lies hidden among trees on the eastern side of the palace. He sets off to fetch a bottle of tonic which Avianno, the healer, prepares for him with spices and rosewater, and with which Tomaso hopes he will recover the spirit of youth. This is the only night in the week when the master's servants and guards are not at work, and the next shift doesn't commence until dawn. During the half-hour the servant is away, the door is open and nobody guards the palace . . .'

'And what do you expect of me?' stammered Cervantes.

'The question is what you expect of yourself, dear sir. Is this the life you wish to live? Is this the man you wish to be?'

The flames in the fireplace flickered and went out, the shadows moved along the library walls like stains of spilt ink, enveloping Corelli. When Cervantes was about to reply, he was already alone.

That Sunday at midnight, Cervantes waited, hidden among the trees that flanked Giordano's palace. The bells had just finished striking twelve when a small side door opened and the hunched figure of the artist's old servant set off down the alley. Cervantes waited for his shadow to disappear in the night and crept towards the door. He grasped the handle and pushed. Just as Corelli had predicted, the door opened. Cervantes took one last look outside and, trusting he had not been seen, entered. As soon as the door closed behind him he realised he was surrounded by utter darkness and he cursed his lack of common sense for not having brought a candle or a lamp to guide him. He felt the walls, which were damp and slippery like the guts of a beast, and groped his way forward until he bumped into the first step of what seemed to be a spiral staircase. Slowly he ascended and soon a pale glimmer of light outlined a stone arch leading to a wide corridor. The floor of the corridor was patterned with large black and white marble squares, resembling those of a chessboard. Like a pawn advancing furtively in a move, Cervantes made his way into the imposing palace. Even before he had reached the end of that gallery he began to notice frames and canvases abandoned by the walls, or thrown on the floor and forming what looked to him like debris from a shipwreck strewn all over the abode. He walked past the entrances to rooms and halls where unfinished portraits were piled up on shelves, tables and chairs. A marble staircase leading to the upper floors was covered with broken canvases, some of them proof of the fury with which their creator had destroyed them. When he reached the central atrium, Cervantes found himself standing beneath a great beam of ethereal lunar light that filtered down from the dome crowning the palace, where pigeons fluttered about, sending the echo of their wings through dilapidated corridors and rooms. He knelt down in front of one of the portraits and recognised the blurred face on the canvas – an unfinished likeness, like all the others, of Francesca di Parma.

Cervantes looked around him and saw hundreds more like that one, all of them discarded, all of them abandoned. Then he understood why nobody had seen Master Giordano again. In his determination to recover his lost inspiration and capture the luminosity of Francesca di Parma, the artist had been losing his mind with every brushstroke. His madness had left its trace on unfinished canvases that were scattered all over the palace like the skin of a snake.

'I've been expecting you for a long time,' said a voice behind his back.

Cervantes turned around. An old, emaciated man, with long tangled hair, filthy clothes and glazed, bloodshot eyes, was watching him with a smile from a corner of the large hall. He was sitting on the floor, alone, holding a glass and a bottle of wine. Master Giordano, one of the most famous artists of his time, transformed into a mad beggar in his own home.

'You've come to take her, haven't you?' he asked. Cervantes didn't know what to reply. The old painter poured himself another glass of wine and raised a toast. 'My father built this palace for me, did you know? He said it would protect me from the world. But who can protect us from ourselves?'

'Where is Francesca?' asked Cervantes.

The painter gave him a long look, savouring the wine with a mocking expression.

'Do you really think you'll triumph where so many have failed?'

'I'm not looking for any triumph, Master. I simply wish to free a girl who does not deserve to live in a place like this.'

'A noble sentiment indeed coming from a man who even lies to himself,' Giordano declared.

'I've not come here to argue with you, Master. If you don't tell me where she is, I'll find her myself.'

Giordano downed his wine and nodded.

'And I won't be the one to stop you, young man.'

Giordano looked up at the stairway that rose through the mist towards the dome. Cervantes scanned the dark and saw her. Francesca di Parma, an apparition of light amid shadows, was descending the stairs slowly, naked and barefoot. Cervantes rushed to remove his cloak and cover her, enfolding her in his arms. The immeasurable sorrow in her eyes rested upon him.

'The gentleman must leave this accursed place while there is still time,' she murmured.

'I will leave, but in your company.'

From his corner, Giordano applauded the scene.

'Magnificent scene. The lovers at midnight on the stairway to heaven.'

Francesca looked at the old painter, the man who had held her prisoner for half a year, with tenderness and without any hint of resentment. Giordano smiled sweetly, like a lovesick youth.

'Forgive me, my love, for not having been what you deserved.'

Cervantes tried to draw the young girl away, but she kept her eyes riveted on her captor, a man who seemed close to his dying breath. Giordano filled his glass with wine again and offered it to her.

'One last farewell sip, my love.'

Letting go of Cervantes's embrace, Francesca walked over to

Giordano and knelt down beside him. She stretched out a hand and stroked his wrinkled face. The artist closed his eyes and lost himself in her touch. Before she left, Francesca accepted the glass and drank the wine he was offering her. She drank slowly, with her eyes closed, clutching the glass with both hands. Then she let it fall and it shattered into a thousand pieces at her feet. Cervantes held her and she surrendered to him. Without even a parting glance at the painter, Cervantes hastened to the main door of the palace with the girl in his arms. When he stepped outside the guards and the servants were waiting for him. Not one of them tried to stop him. One of the armed guards was holding a black horse and presented it to Cervantes. He hesitated, but as soon as he accepted the mount, the line of guards opened up to let him through and gazed at him silently as he climbed onto the horse with Francesca in his arms. He was already trotting northwards when flames began to pour from the dome of Giordano's palace and Rome's sky became alive with scarlet and ashes. The couple rode by day, spending their nights in hostels and inns where the coins Cervantes had found in the horse's saddlebags allowed them to shelter from the cold and from suspicions.

Two whole days went by before Cervantes noticed the smell of almond essence on Francesca's lips and saw the dark circles that were beginning to show round her eyes. Every night, when the girl offered him her naked body with abandon, Cervantes knew she was wasting away in his hands, that the poisoned goblet with which Giordano had wanted to free her and free himself of the curse was now burning in her veins and consuming her. During their journey they stopped at the best inns, where doctors and wise men examined her but were unable to determine what her ailment was. Francesca faded during the day, when she was barely able to speak or keep her eyes open, and came alive at night, in the darkness of the bed, bewitching the poet's senses and guiding his hands. One evening, at the end of the second week of their travels, he found her walking in the rain by a lake, near the hostel where they had stopped for the night. The rain ran down her body and the girl stood, open-armed, her face raised to heaven, as if she was hoping that the pearly drops covering her skin could tear out her accursed soul.

'You must leave me here,' she said. 'Forget me and continue on your journey.'

But Cervantes, who saw how the young woman's light was becoming fainter day by day, promised himself that he would never say farewell to her, that while there was a single breath left in her body he would fight to keep her alive. To keep her his.

They crossed the Pyrenees into the Peninsula through a pass near the Mediterranean coast and were soon on their way to the city of Barcelona. By then Cervantes had already completed a hundred pages of a manuscript he wrote every night while he watched Francesca trapped in the nightmares of her sleep. He felt that his words, the images and the perfumes conjured up by his writing were now the only means of keeping her alive. Every night, when she fell into his arms and succumbed to sleep, Cervantes tried feverishly to rewrite her soul through a thousand and one fictions. When, a few days later, his mount dropped dead near the walls of Barcelona, the play he had written was already finished and Francesca seemed to have recovered her colour and the sparkle of her eyes. While he rode, he had been daydreaming that he would find shelter and hope in that city by the sea, that a friendly soul would lead him to someone who would print his manuscript, and that once people read his story and became immersed in the universe of images and poetry he had created, the Francesca he had fashioned with paper and ink and the one who lay dying in his arms every night would become as one and she would return to a world where malediction and hardship could be defeated by the power of words, a world in which God, wherever he was hiding, would allow him to live with her one more day.

(Extract from *The Secret Chronicles of the City of the Damned*, by Ignatius B. Samson. Published by Barrido y Escobillas, S.A., Barcelona 1924)

BARCELONA, 1569

They buried Francesca di Parma two days later beneath a flaming sky that glided over the calm sea and lit up the sails of the boats anchored at the port. The young girl had expired during the night in Cervantes's arms, in the room they occupied on the top floor of an old building on Calle Ancha. The printer Antoni de Sempere and Sancho were both with him when she opened her eyes for the last time and, smiling at Cervantes, murmured 'Free me.'

That afternoon Sempere had finished printing an edition of the second version of *A Poet in Hell*, a play in three acts by Don Miguel de Cervantes Saavedra, and had brought with him a copy to show the author, who was too downcast to even read his name on the cover. The printer, whose family owned a small plot of land near the old gate of Santa Madrona, next to Calle de Trenta Claus, offered to have the young woman buried in that humble graveyard, where, in the worst times of the Inquisition, the Sempere family had saved books from being burned by hiding them in coffins and interring them in what was a burial ground-cum-book sanctuary. Overcome with gratitude, Cervantes accepted.

The following day, after setting fire, for the second and last time, to his *Poet in Hell* on the sands of the strand – where one day Bachelor Sansón Carrasco was to defeat the ingenious knight Alonso Quijano – Cervantes abandoned the city and departed, this time holding the memory and the light of Francesca in his soul.

Four decades were to pass before Miguel de Cervantes returned once more to the city where he had buried his innocence. A sea of misfortunes, failures and sorrows had dogged the story of his days. The sweetness of recognition, even in its most wretched and miserly form, had not smiled upon him until his later years. And while his admired contemporary, the playwright and adventurer Lope de Vega, had reaped fame, fortune and glory since his youth, Cervantes was awarded no laurels until it was too late, because applause can only be valued when it comes at the right moment. When it is a faded, withered flower it is no more than an insult and an offence.

By the year 1610, Cervantes was at last able to consider himself a famous author, even if one of very modest fortune, because money, the filthy lucre, had avoided him all his life and did not seem ready to change its mind in the final stages of his existence. Leaving aside the ironies of fate, experts on Cervantes maintain that he was happy during those three short months he spent in Barcelona in the year 1610, even if there are others who doubt whether he ever set foot in the city. Others still would protest vehemently at the mere suggestion that any of the events referred to in this modest apocryphal romance could have happened at any moment or place save in the decadent imagination of some heartless scribe.

Yet if we are to believe the legend and accept the currency

of fantasy and dreams, we can be sure that in those days Cervantes dwelt in a small studio opposite the harbour wall, with large windows open to the Mediterranean light that were not distant from the room where Francesca di Parma had died in his arms, and that every day he sat there to write some of the works that were to bring him so much fame, especially beyond the frontiers of his native kingdom. The building where he lived belonged to his old friend Sancho, who was now a wealthy merchant and father of six, with an affable nature that even his dealings with the world's ignominy had not managed to eradicate.

'And what are you writing, Master?' Sancho would ask every day when he saw him step out into the street. 'My esteemed wife is still awaiting further feats of valour and lance from our beloved Knight of La Mancha . . .'

Cervantes would just smile and never replied to his question. Sometimes, when it was getting dark, he would walk over to the printing press still run by old Antoni de Sempere and his son on Calle de Santa Ana, next to the church. Cervantes liked to spend time among books and pages waiting to be assembled, chatting with his old friend the printer and avoiding all mention of the memory they both kept alive in their minds.

One night, when it was time to leave the workshop until the following day, Sempere sent his son home and closed the shop doors. The printer seemed uneasy and Cervantes knew something had been bothering his good friend for the past few days.

'The other day a gentleman came by asking after you,' Sempere began. 'White hair, very tall, and his eyes were . . .'

'Like the eyes of a wolf,' Cervantes completed.

Sempere nodded.

'Precisely. He told me he was an old friend of yours and would like to see you if you ever happened to be in town . . . I wouldn't be able to tell you why, but the moment he left, I was seized by a great anxiety and began to think he must be the person you told me and good old Sancho about one fateful night in a tavern next to the basilica of Santa María del Mar. Needless to say, he wore a small silver angel on his lapel.'

'I thought you'd forgotten that story, Sempere.'

'I don't forget what I print.'

'I hope you didn't think of keeping a copy?'

Sempere gave him a tepid smile. Cervantes sighed.

'What did Corelli offer for your copy?'

'Enough for me to retire and hand over my business to the sons of Sebastián de Cormellas – and thus perform a good deed.'

'And did you sell it to him?'

Sempere did not reply. Instead, he turned round, walked over to a corner of his workshop, knelt down and, lifting a couple of floorboards, recovered an object wrapped in pieces of cloth, which he left on the table in front of Cervantes.

The novelist stared at the package for a few seconds and, at a nod from Sempere, removed the cloths to reveal the only extant copy of *A Poet in Hell*.

'May I take it with me?'

'It's yours,' answered Sempere. 'By virtue of authorship, and by payment of its publication costs.'

Cervantes opened the book and scanned the first few lines.

'A poet is the only being whose eyesight improves with age,' he said.

'Are you going to meet him?'

Cervantes smiled.

'Do I have a choice?'

A couple of days later, Cervantes went out for his customary long walk in the city, despite Sancho's warning that, according to the fishermen, a storm was brewing over the sea. At noon it began to rain heavily and black clouds covered the sky, throbbing with flashes of lightning and loud thunderclaps that seemed to be hammering the walls and threatening to destroy the entire city. Cervantes stepped into the cathedral to shelter from the storm. The church was deserted and the novelist sat in one of the pews of a side chapel where hundreds of candles burned warmly in the gloom. He was not surprised when he saw Andreas Corelli sitting next to him, his eyes fixed on the Christ figure hanging above the altar.

'Your Grace doesn't look a day older,' said Cervantes.

'Nor has your wit lessened, dear friend.'

'But perhaps my memory has, because I think I've forgotten that you and I were ever friends . . .'

Corelli shrugged.

'There he is, crucified to purge the sins of men, with no resentment, and you can't even forgive this poor devil . . .' Cervantes looked at him severely. 'Don't tell me blasphemy offends you now,' added Corelli.

'Blasphemy only offends whoever utters it to mock others.'

'It's not my intention to mock you, dear Cervantes.'

'What is your intention then, *Signore* Corelli?'

'To beg forgiveness of you?'

A long silence ensued between the two.

'One does not beg forgiveness with words.'

'I know. And what I'm offering is not words.'

'I hope it won't bother you if my enthusiasm flags when I hear the term "offer" from your lips.'

'Why should it bother me?'

'Perhaps Your Excellency has gone mad from reading too many missals? Perhaps you have started to believe, *Signore*, that you're riding through this vale of darkness to right the wrongs that our Saviour left for us all when he abandoned ship.'

Corelli crossed himself and smiled, baring those sharp, wolfish teeth.

'Amen,' he pronounced.

Cervantes stood up, bowed and turned to leave.

'Your company is most agreeable, dear *arcangelo*, but in the present circumstances I prefer the company of thunder and lightning. I'm off to enjoy the storm in peace.'

Corelli sighed.

'First listen to my offer.'

Cervantes walked slowly towards the exit. The cathedral door was slowly closing in front of him.

'I've seen this trick before.'

Corelli was waiting for him deep in the shadows of the doorway. Only his eyes were visible, lit up by the reflection of the candles.

'You once lost what you loved most, or what you thought you loved most, in exchange for the possibility of creating a masterpiece.'

'I never had a choice. You lied.'

'The choice was always in your hands, dear friend. And you know that.'

'Open the door.'

'The door is open. You can leave whenever you wish to.'

Cervantes stretched a hand out to the door and pushed it. The wind and the rain spat on his face. He stopped for a second before going out and, in the dark, the voice of Corelli whispered in his ear.

'I've missed you, Cervantes. My offer is simple: pick up the pen you've abandoned and reopen the pages you should never have closed. Bring your immortal book back to life and finish off the adventures of Don Quixote and his faithful squire for the pleasure and comfort of this poor reader whom you've turned into an orphan of wit and invention.'

'The story is finished, the Knight is buried and my voice is exhausted.'

'Do it for me and I'll give you back the company of what you loved most.'

From the door of the cathedral, Cervantes gazed at the ghostly tempest riding over the city.

'Do you promise?'

'I swear. In the presence of my Father and Lord.'

'Where's the catch this time?'

'There are no catches this time. This time, in exchange for the beauty of your creation, I'll give you what you most long for.'

And without further ado, the old novelist set off beneath the storm on the road to his destiny.

BARCELONA, 1616

That last night beneath the stars of Barcelona, old Sempere and Andreas Corelli accompanied the funeral cortege through the narrow streets of the city towards the private graveyard of the Sempere family, where many years earlier three friends with an unmentionable secret had buried the mortal remains of Francesca di Parma. The hearse advanced silently, lit up by torches, and people stood to one side. It made its way through the maze of passages and squares leading to the small cemetery that was secured with a gate of pointed spears. The hearse stopped when it reached the entrance. The two horsemen escorting the funeral carriage dismounted and, with the help of the coachman, unloaded the coffin, which bore no inscription or sign of any sort. Sempere opened the cemetery gates and let them through. They carried the coffin to the open grave that waited under the moon and let it rest on the ground. At a sign from Corelli, the attendants moved back to the entrance of the graveyard, leaving Sempere alone with the publisher. There was a sound of footsteps by the gate and when Sempere turned round he recognised old Sancho, who had come to bid farewell to his friend. Corelli gave a nod and the men let him through. When the three were standing before the coffin, Sancho knelt down and kissed the lid.

'I'd like to say a few words,' he whispered.

'Do proceed,' Corelli encouraged him.

'May God hold a great man and the best of friends in his everlasting glory. And if, in view of the present company, the Good Lord should assign duties to orders of a questionable rank, let the honour and the respect of his friends escort him on this his last journey to paradise, and may his immortal soul not lose its bearings along roads of sulphur and flames through some trickery of the defeated angel, for if that be so, by Heaven, I will gird myself with armour and lance and go forth to rescue him no matter how many plots and deceits the guardian of the underworld, in his malice, may decide to set before me.'

Corelli was looking at him coldly. Although he was scared to death, Sancho held his gaze.

'Is that all?' asked Corelli.

Sancho nodded, clasping his hands to stop them from shaking. Sempere looked questioningly at Corelli. The publisher took a few steps towards the coffin and, to everyone's surprise and alarm, opened it.

Cervantes's corpse lay inside the coffin clad in a Franciscan habit. His face was uncovered, his eyes were open and he had one hand on his chest. Corelli lifted Cervantes's hand and placed the book he carried with him underneath it.

'My friend, I hereby give these pages back to you: the sublime third and final part of the greatest of fables that you were good enough to write for this humble reader who knows that men will never be worthy of such beauty. That is why we bury it with you, so that you can take it to meet the person who has been waiting for you all these years and to whom, knowingly or not, you have always wished to return. Thus your greatest wish has been granted, your destiny and final prize.'

After those words, Corelli sealed the coffin.

'Here lie Francesca di Parma, a pure soul, and Miguel de Cervantes, light among poets, pauper among men and Prince of Parnassus. They will rest in peace among books and words and their eternal repose will never be perturbed or known by other mortals. May this place become a secret, a mystery whose origin and end will remain unknown. And may the spirit of the greatest teller of tales ever to walk the earth inhabit it forever more.'

Years later, on his deathbed, old Sempere would explain how at that very instant he thought he saw Andreas Corelli shed a tear which, when it hit Cervantes's tomb, turned to stone. He knew then that on that rock he would embark upon building a sanctuary, a cemetery of ideas and inventions, of words and marvels, a sanctuary that would grow over the ashes of the Prince of Parnassus and would, one day, house the greatest of all libraries, the one in which every persecuted title, every book hated through men's ignorance and spite would seek shelter, and wait there until it once again found the reader that every book carries within it.

'Cervantes, my friend,' he said, as he took his leave. 'Welcome to the Cemetery of Forgotten Books.'

*

This story is a simple divertimento that plays with some of the less known and less documented elements of the great author's life, in particular his journey to Italy in his youth and his stay or stays in Barcelona, the only city he mentions repeatedly in his work.

Unlike his admired contemporary Lope de Vega, who enjoyed great success from the start, Cervantes's pen was a late one and one that received little reward and recognition. The last years of the life of Miguel de Cervantes Saavedra were the most fertile of his turbulent literary career. After the publication of the first part of Don Quixote in 1605, perhaps the most famous work in the history of literature and the precursor of the modern novel, a period of relative calm and recognition allowed him to publish in 1613 the Exemplary Novels *and the following year his* Journey to Parnassus.

In 1615 the second part of Don Quixote *appeared. Miguel de Cervantes would die the following year in Madrid and would be buried, or so it was believed for years, in the convent of the Barefoot Trinitarians.*

There is nothing to prove that Cervantes ever wrote a third part of his most brilliant creation.

As of today, it is still not known for certain where his remains are buried.

A CHRISTMAS TALE

Translated by Lucia Graves

There was a time when the streets of Barcelona were tinted with gaslight at night, and at dawn the city awoke surrounded by a forest of chimney stacks that poisoned the sky with crimson. In those days Barcelona resembled a precipitous pile of basilicas and palaces, all tangled into a labyrinth of narrow streets and tunnels and trapped beneath a permanent mist, from which an imposing tower protruded. The building was shaped like a cathedral tower, with a Gothic spire, gargoyles and rose windows, and on its top floor lived the richest man in town, a lawyer named Eveli Escrutx.

Every night his silhouette could be seen outlined behind the golden glow of the attic window, watching the city at his feet like a sombre sentry. Escrutx had already made a fortune in his early youth by defending the interests of kid-gloved murderers, financiers who had grown rich in Latin America and industrialists of the new generation of steam and textile mills. They said that the hundred most powerful families in Barcelona paid him an exorbitant annuity in exchange for his counsel, and that all manner of statesmen and petty generals with imperial pretensions would queue up to be received in his office at the top of the tower. They said he never slept, that he spent the nights gazing at Barcelona from his large window and that he hadn't left the tower since the death of his wife thirty-three years earlier. They said the loss had driven a knife through his soul, that he hated everything and everyone, and that the only thing that drove him was his desire to watch the world consume itself with its own greed and meanness.

Escrutx had no friends or confidants. He lived alone at the top of the tower save for the company of Candela, a blind servant who, it was rumoured, was a bit of a witch and wandered through the streets of the old town offering sweets to poor children who were never seen again. The lawyer's only known passion, apart from the maid with her secret arts, was chess. Every year, on Christmas Eve, Escrutx would invite a person from Barcelona to meet him in his attic. He would serve him a delicious meal, washed down with the most superb wines. Then, at the stroke of midnight, when the bells rang from the cathedral, Escrutx would pour out two glasses of absinthe and challenge his guest to a game of chess. The lawyer promised the contender that if he won, he would hand over to him his entire fortune and properties. But if he lost, the guest would have to sign a contract whereby the lawyer became the exclusive owner and executor of his immortal soul. Every Christmas Eve.

Candela would ride through the streets of Barcelona in the lawyer's black carriage in search of a player. Beggars or bankers, murderers or poets, it made no difference. The game went on until dawn on Christmas Day. When the blood-red sun rose over the snow-capped rooftops of the Gothic quarter, the opponent invariably realised that he had lost the challenge. He walked out into the cold streets, carrying with him only the clothes on his back, while the lawyer picked up an emerald-coloured glass bottle, wrote the name of the loser on it, and added it to a display cabinet that held dozens of identical bottles.

They say that on that particular Christmas, the last in his long life, Escrutx, the lawyer, sent his white-eyed and black-lipped Candela, once again, to scour the streets in search of a new victim. A snowstorm loomed over the city, its cornices and terraced roofs all nickel-plated with ice. Flocks of bats fluttered between the cathedral towers and a red-hot copper moon poured its light over the narrow streets. The black steeds pulling the carriage stopped suddenly at the entrance to Calle del Obispo, their frosty breath betraying their fear. The silhouette stepped out of the fog, holding a bunch of red roses and wearing a long bride's veil that merged into the whiteness of the snow. Candela felt intoxicated by the woman's perfume and invited her to step into the carriage. She tried to feel her face, but all she found was ice and lips that were moist with bile. She took her to the tower, which in those days stood over the ruins of an old graveyard next to Calle Aviñón.

They say that when Escrutx saw her, he was struck dumb and ordered Candela to leave the room. The guest for that last Christmas Eve removed her veil and the lawyer, a soul wearied with age and eyes blinded by bitterness, thought he recognised the face of his deceased wife. Her lips were red and she shone like porcelain, and when Escrutx asked her her name she only smiled. Soon the midnight bells rang and the chess game began. Later, they would say that the lawyer was already tired, that he allowed himself to be defeated and that it was Candela who, driven mad with jealousy, started the blaze that would consume the tower, provoking an early dawn over the dark-purple skies of Barcelona. A group of children who had gathered round a bonfire in Plaza de San Jaime swore that a few moments before the flames streamed out of the windows they saw the lawyer step onto the balustrade, which was crowned with angels of alabaster, and open the emerald-green bottles to the wind, releasing plumes of vapour that dispersed into tears over all the terraced roofs of Barcelona. Serpents of fire knotted round one another as they ascended to the very top of the tower and the lawyer's silhouette was seen for the last time clasping his bride of fire, leaping from the tower into the void, their bodies crumbling into ashes which the wind took with it before they struck the cobblestones. The tower fell at daybreak, like a skeleton of shadows folding upon itself.

The legend ends by stating that after the collapse of the tower, a conspiracy of silence and forgetfulness perpetually deleted the name of the lawyer Escrutx from the city's chronicles. Poets and people with a pure spirit swear that even today, if one looks up to the heavens on Christmas Eve, one can still make out the ghostly shape of the burning tower in the midnight sky and see Escrutx, blinded by tears and repentance, freeing the first of the emerald-green bottles in his collection, the one that bore his name. But others will affirm that on that accursed dawn there were many who turned up at the ruins of the tower to take away one of the smouldering fragments, and that the charred remains of Candela's carriage can still be heard among the shadows of the old town, always in the dark, in search of the next candidate.

ALICIA, AT DAWN

Translated by Lucia Graves

The house where I last saw her no longer exists. In its place stands one of those buildings that slips from one's view and stamps its shadow on the sky. And yet, even today, every time I pass by, I remember those accursed days of Christmas 1938 when Calle Muntaner's long slope was lined with trams and palatial mansions. I was barely thirteen at the time, earning a few céntimos a week as an errand boy for a pawnshop on Calle Elisabets. The owner, Don Odón Llofriu, one hundred and fifteen kilos of meanness and suspicion, presided over his bazaar of trinkets complaining even of the air breathed by that shit of an orphan – one of the thousands the war spat out – whom he never called by his name.

'For heaven's sake, kid, turn off that light bulb, these are no times for luxuries! Mop the floor by candlelight, it stimulates the retina.'

And so our days went by, amid turbulent news from the National Front, which was advancing towards Barcelona, rumours of shootings and murders in the streets of the red-light district, and sirens warning of air raids. It was on one of those days in December 1938, when snow and ash peppered the streets, that I saw her.

She was dressed in white and seemed to have materialised out of the mist that swept the streets. When she stepped into the shop she paused in the small rectangle of light sliced out from the darkness by the shop window. In her hands she held a black velvet folder which she proceeded to open on the counter without saying a word. A garland of pearls and sapphires shone in the gloom. Don Odón grabbed his magnifying glass and examined the piece. I followed the scene from the chink in the back-room door.

'The piece isn't bad, but these are no times for luxuries, miss. I'll give you fifty duros, and I'll still lose money, but it's Christmas Eve and one isn't made of stone.'

The girl folded the cloth again and headed for the door without batting an eyelid.

'Kid!' bellowed Don Odón. 'Follow her.'

'That necklace is worth at least a thousand duros,' I remarked.

'Two thousand,' Don Odón corrected. 'So we're not going to let her get away. Follow her to her home and make sure nobody clobbers her and cleans her out. She'll be back, like all of them.'

The girl's footprints were already vanishing under the white blanket when I went out into the street. I followed her through the labyrinth of alleyways and buildings gutted by bombs and poverty, until she emerged into Plaza del Peso de la Paja and I managed to catch sight of her getting into a tram that was just heading up Calle Muntaner. I ran after the tram and jumped onto the back step.

We travelled uphill, cutting black tracks in the canvas of snow spread by the blizzard, while evening began to fall and the sky turned the colour of blood. By the time we reached the crossing with Travesera de Gracia my bones were aching with cold. I was about to abandon my mission and make up some lie to satisfy Don Odón, when I saw her alight and walk towards the large entrance of the mansion. I jumped off the tram and ran to hide behind the corner of the property. The girl slipped through the garden gate. I peeped between the bars and saw her cross the line of trees surrounding the house. She stopped by the front steps and turned round. I wanted to run off, but the icy wind had already robbed me of any will. The girl studied me with a slight smile and stretched out a hand. I realised she'd mistaken me for a beggar.

'Come,' she said.

Night was falling when I followed her through the dark mansion. A faint halo blurred the outlines. Fallen books and frayed curtains punctuated a scene of broken furniture, slashed paintings and dark stains spattering the walls like bullet marks. We came to a large hall that housed a mausoleum of old photographs, all of them redolent of absence. The girl knelt down in a corner near a fireplace and lit a fire with sheets of newspaper and the remains of a chair. I moved a bit closer to the heat and accepted the mug of warm wine she was offering me. She knelt down beside me, her gaze lost in the flames. She told me her name was Alicia. Her skin was the skin of a seventeen-year-old, but she was betrayed by that serious, unfathomable look of those who have become ageless, and when I asked whether those photographs were of her family she didn't reply.

I wondered how long she'd been living there, alone, hiding in that mansion in her white dress that was coming apart at the seams, selling jewels off cheaply in order to survive. She'd left the black velvet folder on the mantelpiece. Every time she bent forward to poke the fire I couldn't help glancing at it and imagining the necklace inside. Hours later we heard the bells strike midnight as we lay cuddled up quietly in front of the fire, and I thought that was how my mother would have hugged me if I could remember her. When the flames began to die away I wanted to throw a book into the fire, but Alicia snatched it from me and started to read aloud from its pages until we fell asleep.

I left shortly before dawn, unlocking myself from her

embrace and running in the dark towards the gate with the necklace in my hands and my heart pounding with anger. I spent the first few hours of that Christmas Day with two thousand duros' worth of pearls and sapphires in my pocket, cursing those streets that were swamped with snow and fury, cursing those who had abandoned me among flames, until a weak sun plunged a spear of light through the clouds and I retraced my steps to the mansion, dragging that necklace that weighed like a tombstone and was stifling me, hoping only to find her still asleep, asleep forever, so I could leave the necklace back on the mantelpiece above the embers and then flee without ever having to remember her look and her warm voice, the only pure touch I had ever known.

The door was open and a pearly light dripped through the cracks in the ceiling. I found her lying on the floor, still holding the book in her hands, her lips poisoned with frost and her eyes open in her white, icy face. A red tear lingered on her cheek and the wind blowing through that large wide-open window was burying her under dusty snow. I left the necklace on her chest and fled back to the street, to mingle with the walls of the city and hide in its silences, avoiding my reflection in shop windows for fear of seeing a stranger.

Shortly afterwards the sirens sounded again, silencing the Christmas bells, and a swarm of black angels spread over the red sky of Barcelona, dropping columns of bombs that would never be seen as they hit the ground.

MEN IN GREY

Translated by Lucia Graves

He never told me his name and I'd never wanted to ask. He was waiting for me, as usual, on that old bench in the Retiro Park, wedged inside a long line of linden trees that were bare from the winter and the rain. Dark glasses obscured the depth of his eyes. He was smiling. I took a seat next to him at the other end of the bench. The messenger handed me the envelope and I put it away without opening it.

'Aren't you going to count it?'

I shook my head.

'You should. This time the fee has tripled. Plus expenses and travel.'

'Where to?'

'Barcelona.'

'I don't handle Barcelona. They know that. Give it to Sanabria.'

'We already did. There was a problem.'

I pulled out the envelope with the money and passed it back to him.

'I don't handle Barcelona. They know that very well.'

'Aren't you going to ask me who the customer is?'

His smile oozed venom.

'It's all in the envelope. The ticket for tonight's train is in your name at the Atocha left-luggage office. The minister has asked me to convey his most sincere personal gratitude. He never forgets a favour.'

The messenger with dark glasses stood up and, with a slight bow, prepared to set off in the rain. We'd been meeting for three years in that same corner of the park, always at dawn, and we'd never exchanged a single word beyond what was strictly necessary. I watched him slip on his black leather gloves. His hands opened like spiders. He noticed me watching him and paused.

'Is there a problem?'

'Simple curiosity. What do you tell your friends when they ask you what your job is?'

When he smiled, his cadaverous face seemed to fuse into the shroud of his raincoat.

'Cleaning. I tell them I work in cleaning services.'

I nodded.

'And you?' he asked. 'What do you tell them?'

'I don't have friends.'

Splinters of frozen mist slithered over the vaulted ceiling of Atocha Station when I proceeded along the deserted platform on that 9 January 1942 to catch the midnight express to Barcelona. The minister's gratitude had earned me a first-class ticket and the velvet sanctuary of a private compartment. Even in those dark days the last thing lost among professionals was courtesy. The train slid off, scraping trails of vapour in the shadows, and soon the city disappeared into a cloud of faint lights and barren land. Only then did I open the envelope and pull out the neatly folded sheets, typed at one and a half spaces in blue ink. I was surprised to discover that there was no photograph in the envelope and wondered whether the only picture of the customer had been handed to Sanabria. I only had to read a couple of lines of the report to realise that this time there would be no photograph.

I switched off the light in the compartment and abandoned myself to a sleepless night, until dawn stained the horizon with scarlet blood and the silhouette of Montjuïc stood out in the distance. Three years earlier I had promised myself that I would never return to Barcelona. I'd fled from my city with a poisoned soul. A forest of ghostly factories and a sulphurous haze enveloped us and, moments later, the city sucked us into a tunnel that smelled of soot and doom. I opened the briefcase and began to load my revolver magazine with the bullets Sanabria had taught me to use during the years when I was his apprentice in the streets of the red-light district. Nine-millimetre shells, with hollow points made to turn into red-hot metal jaws on impact and drill exit wounds the size of a fist. When I got off the train and faced the iron cathedral of the Estación de Francia, I was welcomed by an icy, damp wind. I'd forgotten that the city still reeked of gunpowder. I set off towards Vía Layetana under a curtain of powdery snow that floated in the watery shadows of dawn. The trams opened pathways through the layer of white, and people, grey and faceless, wandered under the breath of flickering lamps that cast a violet light on the streets. I crossed Plaza Palacio and entered the web of narrow side streets surrounding the basilica of Santa María del Mar. The ruins from the air raids remained largely intact. Guts of buildings disembowelled by bombs – deserted dining rooms, bedrooms and bathrooms – stood next to empty lots piled high with rubble that served as shelters for black marketeers selling coal and other ragged faces whose gaze remained fixed to the ground.

When I reached Calle Platería I stopped to stare at the skeleton of the building where I grew up. All that remained was part of the facade, damaged by fire, and the adjacent walls. One could still see the scars from the incendiary bombs that had drilled through the floors and spread a tornado of flames through the stairwell and the skylight. I walked over to the front door and remembered the name of the first girl I kissed there one summer's night in 1913. Her name was Merche and she lived on the third floor, in flat number one, with her blind mother who always disliked me. Merche never married. Later, I was told that in one of the explosions they'd seen her being tossed into the air from the balcony, naked and wrapped in flames, her body skewered onto a thousand hot glass splinters. The sound of a footstep behind me brought me back to the present. I turned to discover an ashen figure looking like a replica of the messenger with dark glasses. I could barely tell the difference between them any more. Their look and their breath always smelled of death.

'You, identity card,' he muttered triumphantly.

Here and there I noticed brief looks from passers-by and the hasty steps of emaciated figures. I examined the secret police agent. I reckoned he was just over forty, and weighed about seventy kilos. His shoulders were slightly bent and a few centimetres of his neck showed under the black scarf. A quick slash, with a short blade, could slice his throat and his jugular in less than a second: he would collapse to the ground, voiceless, shedding his life through his fingers over the canvas of dirty snow on which he stood. Men like that one had a family, and I had things to do. I offered him a tepid smile and the document stamped by the ministry. His arrogance vanished instantly and he gave it back to me with trembling hands.

'Please forgive me, sir. I didn't know . . .'

'Clear off.'

The agent nodded repeatedly and vanished behind the first corner he found. The bells of Santa María tolled behind me as I started walking again under the snow towards Calle Fernando to become another grey man merging with the flood of grey men that was beginning to clog up that winter morning. One of them, some twenty metres behind me, had been following me at a distance since the train station, probably convinced that I hadn't noticed his presence. I vanished into that comfortable, numb anonymity where murderers – professionals or mere amateurs – disguised themselves as accountants and trainees, and crossed the Ramblas towards Hotel Oriente. A doorman in uniform with a degree in reading people's eyes opened the door for me with a bow. The hotel retained its aura of a sunken ship. The receptionist recognised me instantly and brandished a hint of a smile. Through the half-open glass doors of the dining hall came the echo of an out-of-tune piano.

'Would the gentleman like room 406?'

'If it's available.'

I signed the hotel register while the receptionist signalled to a porter to take my briefcase and accompany me to the room.

'I know the way, thanks.'

A quick look from the receptionist and the porter beat a retreat.

'If there's anything we can do to make the gentleman's stay in Barcelona more pleasant, you only have to say.'

'Same as usual,' I replied.

'Yes, sir. Of course.'

I was on my way to the elevator when I stopped. The receptionist was still standing in his place, his smile frozen.

'Is Señor Sanabria staying in the hotel?'

He barely blinked, but it was enough for me.

'Señor Sanabria hasn't graced us with a visit for some time.'

Room 406 looked out over Paseo de la Rambla from a fourth floor with heavenly views over the spectre of a vanished city that was condemned to remember the pre-war years. My shadow waited for me below, crouching under the canopy of a newspaper stand. I closed the shutters, enough to fill the room with a pearly gloom, and lay down on my bed. The sounds of the city could be heard outside, creeping along the walls. I pulled the revolver out of the briefcase and, with my finger on the trigger, folded my hands over my chest and closed my eyes. I fell into a muddy, hostile sleep. Hours or minutes later I was awoken by moist lips brushing my eyelids. Candela's warm body was stretched out on the bed, her fingers, imperceptible, unfastening her clothes, and her white-sugar skin lit up by the glow from the street lamps.

'Such a long time,' she murmured, snatching the revolver from my hands and leaving it on the bedside table. 'If you like, I can stay all night.'

'I've got to work.'

'But you'll also have a bit of time for your Candela.'

Three years' absence had not erased the memory of Candela's body from my hands. These new times and the reopening of first-class hotels suited her well. Her breasts smelled of expensive perfume and I noticed a new firmness in her pale thighs, covered in those silk stockings she ordered from Paris. Patient and expert, Candela let me do as I wished until I'd quenched my thirst for her skin and moved to one side. I heard her walk over to the bathroom and run a tap. I got up and took the envelope with the money from the briefcase. I tripled her usual fee and left the folded notes on the chest of drawers. Then I lay on the bed and watched Candela as she walked over to the windows and opened the shutters. The snow falling behind the windowpanes left spots of shadow on her naked skin.

'What are you doing?'

'I like looking at you.'

'Aren't you going to ask me where he is?'

'Would you tell me if I did?'

She turned and sat down on the edge of the bed.

'I don't know where he is. I haven't seen him. It's the truth.'

I just nodded. Candela looked away and eyed the money on the chest of drawers.

'You're doing well,' she said.

'I can't complain.'

I began to get dressed.

'Do you have to go?'

I didn't reply.

'There's more than enough here for the whole night. If you like, I'll wait for you.'

'I'll be a long time, Candela.'

'I'm not in a hurry.'

I met Roberto Sanabria one night in 1917. It was a steamy August and the city was consumed with anger. Like almost every night, gunshots were heard in the neighbourhood before daybreak. I'd gone down to Paseo del Borne to fetch water from the fountain, and when I heard the shots I ran to hide in a doorway on Calle Montcada. Sanabria was lying in a black pool that spread at my feet like a slimy blanket, by the entrance to that narrow gap between old buildings that some people still call Calle de las Moscas, the street of flies. He held a smoking gun in his hands. I walked up to him and he smiled at me, with blood oozing from his lips.

'Don't worry, mate, I've got more lives than a cat.'

I helped him up and, supporting his considerable weight, brought him to a doorway in Calle de Baños Viejos, where we were attended by a large, morose woman with scabby skin. Sanabria had received two gunshots in the abdomen and had lost so much blood his skin was the colour of wax, but he didn't stop smiling at me while some quack who stank of muscatel cleaned his wounds with vinegar and surgical spirit.

'I owe you one, son,' he said before passing out.

Sanabria would survive that night and many other dark hours

of gunpowder and metal. Those were the days when Barcelona newspapers were steeped in reports warning that people were being killed in the streets. Unions for hired gunmen were doing well. Life was still as worthless as ever, but death had never been so cheap. It was Sanabria who, when I reached adulthood, taught me the trade.

'Unless you want to die a day labourer, like your father.'

To kill was a necessity, but to murder was an art, he maintained. His preferred tools were the revolver and the knife with a short curved blade that bullfighters used to finish a *faena* in the bullring with a quick dry stab. Sanabria taught me that one must only shoot a man in the face or in the chest, preferably at less than two metres' distance. He was a professional with principles. He didn't take on women or the elderly. Like so many others, he'd learned to kill in the Moroccan war. When he returned to Barcelona he started his career as a gunman in the ranks of the FAI,[3] but soon discovered that organised syndicates paid better and that their work was not polluted with high-sounding rhetoric. He liked music-hall shows and whores, interests which he instilled in me with paternal strictness and a scholarly touch.

'Nothing is truer in life than a good comedy or a good whore. Never treat them with disrespect or feel superior to them.'

It was Sanabria who introduced me to a seventeen-year-old Candela who carried the world on her skin and was destined to work in the best hotels, and to service council officials.

'Never fall in love with something that is priceless,' Sanabria advised me.

Once I asked him how many men he'd killed.

---

3   Iberian Anarchist Federation.

'Two hundred and six,' he replied. 'But better times are coming.'

My mentor was referring to the war that could already be sniffed in the air like the stench of a flooded sewer. Shortly before the summer of 1936, Sanabria told me that times were about to change and we'd soon have to leave Barcelona, because the city was reeling, with a stake plunged in its heart.

'Death, which always follows gold, is moving to Madrid,' he pronounced. 'And we're going with it. It's only a matter of time.'

The real bonanza began at the end of the war. The corridors of power twisted into new spider's webs and, just as my teacher had predicted, a million dead had only begun to quench the thirst for hatred that rotted the streets. Old contacts in the Barcelona organisation opened up big opportunities for us.

'No more killing poor devils in public urinals for a few pesetas,' Sanabria announced. 'We're now going to start working on quality clients.'

Almost two years of glory followed. Hard-working minds endowed with prodigious memories drew up endless lists of people who didn't deserve to live, miserable creatures whose breath contaminated the incorruptible spirit of the new era. Dozens of tremulous souls hid in dismal apartments fearing the light of day, without realising that they were living dead. Sanabria taught me how not to listen to their pleadings, their tears and moans, how to blow open their heads with a point-blank shot between the eyes before they could ask why. Death waited for them in the subway stations, in dark streets and in *pensiones* with no running water or light. Professors or poets, soldiers or intellectuals, they all recognised us the moment we exchanged glances. Some died without fear, calmly, eyes clear and fixed on their murderer. I don't remember their names, or what they did in life to earn death by my hands, but I remember their looks. Soon I lost count, or wished I could. Sanabria, who was beginning to feel the weight of years and the scars from staying in the business, handed me the best jobs.

'My bones are starting to complain. From now on I'll only deal with unimportant customers. One has to know when to stop.'

I used to meet the messenger with the dark glasses on the same bench of the Retiro Park once a week. There would always be an envelope and a new client. The money piled up in the account of a bank on Calle O'Donnell. The only thing Sanabria had not taught me was what to do with those stiff, scented, glossy notes straight out of the mint.

'Will they ever end?' I once asked the messenger.

It was the only time he removed his glasses. His eyes were as grey as his soul, dead and empty.

'There's always someone who doesn't adapt to progress.'

It was still snowing when I stepped out into the Ramblas. It was just an icy dust that didn't settle when it touched the ground and swirled about in the breeze, turning to specks of light in one's breath. I set off towards Calle Nueva, now reduced to a tunnel of darkness flanked by the forgotten carcasses of dilapidated dance halls and ghostly music-hall theatres that only a few years earlier had transformed the street into an avenue of light and noise until dawn. The pavements smelled of urine and coal. I walked down Calle Lancaster until I reached number thirteen. A couple of old street lamps hanging from the facade barely managed to scrape the darkness, but were sufficient to let one glimpse the poster nailed above the charred wooden door sealing the entrance.

THE SHADOW THEATRE
*Returns to Barcelona after a triumphant world tour to
present its new and magnificent puppet and automatons
show, with the exclusive and enigmatic first appearance
of the Paris music-hall star Madame Isabelle and her
exciting 'Dance of the Midnight Angel'.
Shows every night at midnight.*

I knocked twice with my fist, waited, then knocked again. About a minute went by before I heard footsteps on the other side of the large door. The oak panel opened a few centimetres to reveal the face of a woman with silvery hair and pupils so dilated they seemed to flood her eyes. A golden, liquid light poured from within.

'Welcome to the Shadow Theatre,' she announced.

'I'm looking for Señor Sanabria,' I said. 'I think he's expecting me.'

'Your friend isn't here, but if you wish to come in, the show is about to start.'

I followed the lady along a narrow corridor until we reached a staircase leading down to the basement. A dozen empty tables filled the auditorium. The walls were lined with black velvet and the footlights drilled needles of brightness through the vaporous atmosphere. Only a couple of customers languished on the edge of the darkness surrounding the auditorium. A drinks bar decorated with smoked mirrors and a pit for the pianist buried in a coppery light completed the scene. The closed scarlet curtain was embroidered with the figure of a harlequin puppet. I sat down at one of the tables in the auditorium facing the stage. Sanabria adored puppet shows. He used to say that puppets, more than anything else, reminded him of ordinary people.

'More than whores do.'

The barman served me what I supposed was a glass of brandy and walked away silently. I lit a cigarette and waited for the lights to dim. Once there was total darkness, the folds in the scarlet curtain slowly drew open. The figure of an exterminating angel, hanging from silver strings, descended onto the stage, flapping its black wings through puffs of blue vapour.

When, on the train to Barcelona, I'd opened the envelope containing the cash and the information, and had started to read the typed pages, I knew that this time there would be no photograph of the customer. There was no need. The night Sanabria and I had left Barcelona, my teacher, his hands stopping the bleeding that spurted over my chest, had fixed his eyes on mine and smiled.

'I owed you one, and I'm paying you back. We're quits now. One day somebody will come for me. One doesn't make it in this line of business without ending up sitting in the customer's chair. That's how it is. But when my time comes, and it's not that far off, I'd like it to be you.'

The ministerial report, as usual, spoke between the lines. Sanabria had returned to Barcelona three months earlier. His break with the network came from further back, when he'd refused to carry out a number of contracts, alleging that he was a man of principles in an age where principles no longer existed. The first mistake made by the ministry was to try to eliminate him. The second, a dreadful mistake, was to do it badly. From the first hit man they sent after him all that came back, by registered post, was his right hand. A man like Sanabria can be murdered, but he must never be insulted. A few days after his arrival in Barcelona, the operatives in the ministerial network began to be eliminated, one after the other. Sanabria worked by night and had perfected his skill with the short blade. Within two weeks he'd decimated the basic structure of the secret police in the city of Barcelona. By three weeks he'd begun to score in the most exclusive – and visible – sectors of the regime. Before panic spread, Madrid decided to send one of its best people to negotiate with Sanabria. The man from the ministry now rested beneath a marble stone in the morgue of the Raval quarter, with a wide smile knifed on his throat, identical to the smile that had ended the life of Lieutenant General Manuel Jiménez Salgado, shining star of the military government and a firm candidate for a brilliant career inside the ministries of the capital. That's when I was called. The report described the situation as a 'deep crisis'. Sanabria, in ministerial parlance, had decided to go freelance and had submerged himself in the Barcelona underworld in order to carry out a sort of personal vendetta against well-known members of the regime's military judiciary. The plot, said the report, must be 'rooted out, whatever the cost'.

'I was expecting you earlier,' murmured my mentor's voice in the dark. Even at his age the old murderer knew how to creep in the shadows with the same feline skill as in his youth.

'You look well,' I said.

Sanabria shrugged and pointed to the stage, where a lacquered wooden coffin was opening up to reveal the star of the automatons' show, Madame Isabelle and her 'Dance of the Midnight Angel'. The movements performed by Isabelle, a life-size puppet with human expressions, were hypnotic. Held up by filaments of light, she danced on the stage, catching the pianist's notes in flight.

'I come to see her every night,' murmured Sanabria.

'They're not going to let this continue, Roberto. If it's not me, it will be someone else.'

'I know. I'm glad it's you.'

We watched the automaton's dance for a few seconds, sheltering in the strange beauty of its movements.

'Who's pulling the strings?' I asked.

Sanabria just smiled back.

We left the Shadow Theatre shortly before daybreak, setting off down the Ramblas to the docks, a cemetery of masts in the mist. Sanabria wanted to see the sea for the last time, even if it was only that black, smelly water licking the steps of the quay. When a blade of amber cut across the skyline, Sanabria at last consented and we set off towards the room he rented in a third-rate brothel in Portal de Santa Madrona. Sanabria never felt safer than among his prostitutes. It was just a dark, damp cubicle, with no windows, that seemed to sway under the naked light bulb. A bare mattress was propped against the wall and a couple of bottles and dirty glasses completed the furniture.

'One day they'll come after you too,' said Sanabria.

We gazed at each other in silence and, having nothing left to say, I hugged him. He had the smell of a tired old man.

'Say goodbye to Candela for me.'

I closed the door of his room and walked off down that narrow corridor, with walls that sweated mould and ruin. A few seconds later the sound of the gunshot roared through the passageway. I heard the corpse slump onto the floor and flew down the stairs. One of the old whores watched me from a half-open door on the next landing, her eyes wet with tears.

I wandered aimlessly for a couple of hours through the accursed streets of the city before going back to the hotel. When I crossed the entrance hall the receptionist barely looked up from the hotel register. I took the elevator up to the top floor and walked all the way down the deserted corridor to my door at the end. I wondered whether Candela would believe me if I told her I'd let Sanabria go, that at that very moment our old friend was sailing on board a cruiser towards a safe destination. Perhaps, as always, a lie was what would most resemble the truth. I opened the door without turning on the light. Candela still lay asleep on the sheets, with the first breath of dawn clinging to her naked body. I sat on the edge of the bed and slid my fingertips down her back. She felt as cold as frost. Only then did I notice that what I'd taken for the shadow of her body was in fact blood spreading like an open flower over the bed. I turned round slowly and made out, obscured by the shadows, the barrel of the revolver pointing at me. The messenger's dark lenses shone on his face, beaded with sweat. He smiled.

'The minister gratefully thanks you for your invaluable collaboration.'

'But he doesn't trust my silence.'

'These are difficult times. The fatherland demands great sacrifices, my friend.'

I covered Candela's body with the sheet soaked in her blood.

'You never told me your name,' I said, turning my back to him.

'Jorge,' replied the messenger.

I spun round, the dagger's short blade just a flash of light between my fingers. The slash opened his abdomen at the pit of the stomach. The first shot from his gun went through my left hand. The second struck the top of one of the bedposts and pulverised it into a cascade of smouldering fragments. By then, the blade of the knife Sanabria admired so much had opened the messenger's throat, and the man lay on the floor choking on his own blood while his gloved hands tried desperately to keep his head joined to his trunk. I pulled out the revolver and stuck it in his mouth.

'I don't have friends.'

I took the train back to Madrid that very evening. My hand was still bleeding; the pain, like a red-hot splinter nailed into my memory. Otherwise, anyone could have taken me for another grey man amid the armies of grey men hanging from invisible strings that hovered over the scenery of those stolen times. Locked away in my compartment, gun in hand, gazing out of the window, I stared at that endless black night that opened up like a chasm over the bloodstained earth of the entire country. Sanabria's anger would be my anger, and Candela's skin would be my light. The wound that was drilling through my hand would never stop bleeding. When at dawn the infinite plain of Madrid came into view I smiled to myself. In just a few minutes my footsteps would become inscrutable, lost in the labyrinth of the city. As usual, my mentor had shown me the way, even in his absence. I knew that in all likelihood the papers would not mention me, that history books would try to bury my name amid political statements and fabrications. Little did it matter. Every day there would be more of us men in grey. Soon we'd be sitting next to you, in a café or on a bus, reading a newspaper or a magazine. The long night of history had only just begun.

KISS

Translated by Carlos Ruiz Zafón

I never told anybody, but getting that apartment was nothing short of a miracle. All I knew about Laura was that she worked part-time at the offices of the landlord on the first floor, and that she kissed like a tango. I met her on a July night when the skies blanketing Barcelona sizzled with steam and desperation. I had been sleeping on a bench in a nearby square when I was awakened by the brush of her lips.

Do you need a place to stay?

She led me to the lobby. The building was one of those vertical mausoleums that haunt the old town, a labyrinth of gargoyles and patched-up masonry, at the top of which you could still make out 1866 somewhere beneath the layer of soot.

I followed her upstairs, almost feeling my way in the darkness. The building creaked under my feet like an old ship. Laura never asked for any references, personal or financial. Good thing, because in prison you don't get either. The attic was the size of my former cell, a spare room perched over the endless roofworld of the old city.

I'll take it.

Truth be told, three years in the slammer had obliterated my sense of smell and the issue of voices leaking through the walls wasn't exactly a novelty for me. One man's hell is another's paradise lost.

Laura would come to me every night. Her cold skin and her misty breath were the only things that didn't burn during that scorching summer. At dawn she would silently vanish downstairs, leaving me to doze off during the day.

The neighbours had that meek kindness conferred by years of misery and oblivion. I counted six families, all with children and old-timers reeking of dead flowers and damp soil. My favourite was Don Florián, who lived below me and painted dolls and tin toys for a living. I spent weeks without venturing out of the building. Spiders were building arabesques in my doorway. But Doña Luisa, on the third floor, always brought me something to eat. Don Florián lent me old magazines and challenged me to endless domino matches. The kids in the building invited me to play hide-and-seek.

It was a good life. For the first time ever I felt welcomed. Even appreciated.

By midnight Laura would bring me her nineteen years wrapped in white silk and give herself to me as if it were the last time. I'd make love to her until the break of dawn, savouring in her body everything life had denied me. Afterwards, I'd dream in black and white, like dogs and cursed people. But even the lowest of the low sometimes get a taste of happiness in this world. That summer was mine.

When the demolition people came by in late August I mistook them for cops. The chief engineer told me he had nothing personal against squatters, but unfortunately they had to dynamite the place and raze it to the ground no matter what.

There must be a mistake.

Most chapters in my life begin with that line.

I ran downstairs to the landlord's office on the first floor looking for Laura. All I found was a coat hanger and two inches of dust. I went to Don Florián's. Fifty eyeless dolls rotting in the shadows. I went through the entire building looking for just one neighbour, one voice. Silent corridors lay covered in debris.

This property has been closed down since 1938, young man, the chief engineer informed me. *The bomb damaged the structure beyond repair.*

I believe we had some words. The wrong kind. My kind. I believe I pushed him. Down the stairs. Hard. This time the judge had a field day with me. My old cellmates, it turned out, were still waiting.

After all, you always come back.

Hernán, the library guy, found a ten-year-old newspaper article about the bombardment during the civil war. In the photograph the bodies are lined up in pine boxes, disfigured by shrapnel, but they were still recognisable to me. A shroud of blood spreads over the cobblestones. Laura is dressed in white, her hands crossed over her open chest.

*

It's been almost two years now, but in prison you live or die by memories. The guards think they're smart, but she knows how to sneak in past any walls.

At midnight I am awakened by the brush of her icy lips. She brings greetings from Don Florián and the others.

You'll love me always, won't you? she asks.

And I say yes.

GAUDÍ IN MANHATTAN

Translated by Carlos Ruiz Zafón

Many years later, as I watched the funeral procession for my master parade down Paseo de Gracia, I remembered the year I met Gaudí and my fate was sealed. I had arrived in Barcelona that autumn intent on gaining admission to the School of Architecture. My dreams of conquering the city depended on a grant that barely covered my tuition and the rent on a small room in a boarding house on Calle del Carmen. Unlike most of my fellow students, graced with patrician airs and fashionable attire, my wardrobe consisted solely of an old black suit I had inherited from my father that was several sizes too big and a few inches too short. In March 1908, Don Jaume Moscardó, the head of the department, summoned me to his office to pass judgement on my sterling academic performance and, I suspected, my lacklustre appearance.

'You look like a beggar, Miranda,' he pronounced. 'How do you expect to get work designing beautiful buildings when you look like a car crash? If you're running short of funds maybe I could offer you a hand. Word among the faculty is that you're quite a sharp young man. Tell me, what do you know about Gaudí?'

*

Gaudí. The mere mention of his name gave me the shivers. I had grown up dreaming of his impossible vaults, his neo-

Gothic reefs of stone and his futuristic primitivism. Gaudí was the principal reason I had wanted to become an architect. My main goal in life, other than not perishing from hunger during that first year of study, had been to try to absorb a tiny portion of the prodigious science with which that great man, my modern Prometheus, plotted the shape of his creations.

'I'm his greatest admirer,' I managed to answer.

Moscardó chuckled.

'I feared as much.'

I could detect in his voice the vaguely condescending tone that most people adopted when speaking about Gaudí in those days. Death bells were tolling everywhere for what some of us still called modernism, or art nouveau, and the majority simply deemed it an affront to good taste. The self-appointed new guard imposed a doctrine based on bare essentials, according to which the delirious baroque facades that in time would become the city's pride and joy were sentenced to public crucifixion. Over the years, Gaudí had earned a reputation as an extravagant, celibate and reclusive lunatic. He was generally regarded as a misguided visionary who was indifferent to fame and fortune, and whose sole obsession was the construction of his phantasmagoric cathedral, the Sagrada Familia. He had been living alone in the crypt of the unfinished church for years, sleeping on a camp bed in a corner of the sculpture workshop. He spent most of his time dressed in rags, drawing plans that defied the laws of geometry. He was utterly convinced that the only client he was answerable to was the Almighty.

'Gaudí is insane,' continued Moscardó. 'Now he's trying to put a madonna the size of the Colossus of Rhodes on top of Casa Milà in the heart of the city. He has balls, I'll give him that. But, crazy or not, there's never been and never will be an architect remotely like him.'

'That is my opinion precisely, sir,' I ventured.

'So then you'll have realised it's useless trying to become his successor?'

The august professor must have read the disappointment in my eyes.

'But perhaps you could become his assistant. One of the Llimona brothers working with him mentioned the other day that Gaudí is looking for somebody who speaks English. God knows why. If you ask me, what he really needs is someone who speaks Spanish because the stubborn son-of-a-bitch refuses to speak anything but Catalan, especially when ministers, princes and various court eunuchs from Madrid show their faces. I volunteered to find him a suitable candidate.'

A spy, more like, I thought, smiling meekly and pretending to be unaware of his real motives.

'I see,' I muttered.

'*Doo yoooo espik eengleesh*, Miranda?'

I guessed that the sounds emerging from Moscardó's mouth were supposedly the language of Shakespeare, although with his accent they could just as easily have been Aramaic or the symptom of some insidious throat infection. I swallowed hard and summoned the spirit of Machiavelli, patron saint of the expedient manoeuvre.

'*A leet-l*,' I replied in equally undecipherable gibberish.

Moscardó beamed, relieved.

'Well, *congratoolayshons*, and may the Lord have mercy on you.'

*

Later that afternoon, as the sun was beginning to sink, I set out for the building site of the Sagrada Familia. In those days, the confines of the city began to fade around Paseo de San

Juan, beyond which unfolded a mirage of fields, factories and isolated buildings that stood like lonely sentinels in the grid of a future promised land. Soon I spied the spires of the new church outlined against the twilit skies. A night watchman was waiting for me at the entrance holding a gas lantern. I followed him through portals and arches until we reached the stairs leading down to Gaudí's workshop. As I entered the crypt I felt my heart begin to race. A menagerie of fabulous creatures swayed in the shadows and at the centre of the workshop four skeletons were suspended from the vault above in a macabre ballet. Below them I found a small white-haired man with the bluest eyes I'd ever encountered – somehow he had the air of a person who has seen things other mortals can only dream of. He dropped a notepad on which he had been sketching and smiled at me. It was the smile of a child, full of magic and mystery.

'Moscardó will have told you that I'm a raving madman who never speaks Spanish. The truth is, I do speak Spanish, but only when it pisses somebody off. What I don't speak is a word of English, and on Saturday I'm boarding a ship bound for New York. I understand that you speak it, young man? English, I mean.'

That night I felt like the luckiest man in the universe as I shared Gaudí's conversation and half of his dinner, just a handful of nuts and some lettuce leaves sprinkled with a hint of olive oil. When we had finished, Gaudí poured two glasses of water and looked at me with his penetrating stare.

'Do you know what a skyscraper is?'

For want of any personal experience in the matter, I dusted off various notions we had received in class about the Chicago School, steel-reinforced concrete and the invention of the moment, the Otis elevator.

'Nonsense,' Gaudí cut in. 'A skyscraper is simply a cathedral for people who, instead of believing in God, believe in money.'

It was thus that I learned Gaudí had received an offer from a fabulously wealthy tycoon to design and build a skyscraper in the heart of Manhattan, and that my role was to be his interpreter during a meeting that was to take place between the architect and his mysterious client nine days later, at the Waldorf-Astoria.

*

I spent the next three days secluded in my room perusing a pile of English grammar books and dictionaries that I had borrowed in haste from the college library. On Friday we took the train to Calais, whence we would cross the English Channel to Southampton to board the *Lusitania*. As soon as we boarded the ship, Gaudí retired to his cabin, overwhelmed by homesickness. He wouldn't emerge until the following day, when I found him at dusk, seated at the bow of the ship watching the sun bleed over a horizon of sapphire and copper.

'Now, *that* is real architecture,' he muttered. 'Mist and light. If you really want to learn, Miranda, you have to observe nature. All the answers lie within.'

For me, the crossing of the Atlantic became a blinding crash course in itself. Every afternoon we walked around the deck discussing blueprints, techniques and the secrets of the trade. Lacking better company, and perhaps aware of the almost religious devotion he inspired in me, Gaudí offered his friendship and showed me the sketches he had dreamed up for his skyscraper, a Wagnerian needle of stone and light that, in my humble opinion, could easily become the most prodigious structure ever created by man – were it ever built.

Gaudí's ideas were breathtaking, yet I could not help but

notice that there was no warmth or even a shadow of interest in his voice whenever he talked about the project. It seemed obvious to me that his heart was elsewhere. The night before our arrival I dared ask the question that had been gnawing at me since we set sail.

'Master,' I ventured hesitantly, 'why do you want to embark on an endeavour that could take you away from your home and your work at the Sagrada Familia for months, even years?'

Gaudí smiled, sadly.

'Sometimes, to do the Lord's work you have to shake the hand of the devil.'

He then told me that if he agreed to build this Babel in the heart of New York, his client would underwrite the completion of the Sagrada Familia. I still remember his words. *God is patient, but I won't live forever . . .*

*

We arrived in New York as the sun set. A storm was brewing and a malevolent mist slithered between the spires of Manhattan, the metropolis trapped beneath scarlet skies that pulsated with lightning and the smell of sulphur. A black carriage was waiting for us at the Chelsea pier and carried us through darkening canyons of stone towards the centre of the island. Spirals of steam rose from the cobblestones, and trams, carriages and pedestrians swarmed furiously across the infernal hive of a city built with layer upon layer of grandiose mansions. Gaudí beheld the spectacle with sombre eyes. The clouds were pierced by swords of blood-tinted light as we turned into Fifth Avenue and saw the silhouette of the grand Waldorf-Astoria looming ahead, a mausoleum of gables and towers erected on 34th Street at the site where, twenty years later, the Empire State Building would rise from the ashes of the grandest hotel the city had ever seen.

The manager of the Waldorf greeted us in person at the door, informing us that our client would see us later that evening. I was translating as he spoke, whispering to Gaudí, who simply nodded. We were escorted to a luxurious room on the sixth floor from which we could see the storm clouds massing over the city. Moments later, rain began to pelt the windows. I gave the bellboy a handsome tip and thereby learned that our client lived in a suite occupying the entire top floor and that, to the bellboy's knowledge, this person had never emerged from their quarters. When I asked what kind of person he was and what he looked like, the boy departed in a hurry, leaving us to witness the gathering storm in silence.

*

When the time for our appointment came, Gaudí stood up and gave me an anguished look. An elevator operator attired in red was waiting for us at the end of the corridor. As we ascended floor by floor in that steel cage, I noticed that Gaudí was growing increasingly pale and that he barely seemed capable of holding the portfolio containing his sketches, so I took it from him. The doors opened onto a spacious marble foyer leading to a long corridor that disappeared into shadows. As the elevator operator closed the doors behind us and the light from within faded away, I noticed the flame of a candle flickering in the hallway. It advanced towards us, held by a svelte figure dressed in white. Long, black hair framed the fairest face I had ever seen, with blue eyes that pierced the soul. Eyes that were identical to Gaudí's.

'Welcome to New York.'

Our client was a woman possessed of a disturbing beauty, almost painful to behold. A Victorian novelist would have described her as an angel, but I failed to perceive anything angelic about her presence. Her movements appeared feline, her smile vaguely reptilian. She took us to a dim drawing room in which the curtains seemed to catch fire with each burst of lighting. We sat down. One by one, Gaudí produced his sketches while I translated his words. An hour, or an eternity, later, the lady fixed her eyes on me and, licking her carmine lips, intimated that I should now leave her alone with Gaudí. I looked at the master, hesitant. He nodded slowly.

Against my better judgement, I obeyed and left the room, walking down the corridor towards the foyer, where the elevator doors were already beginning to open. Once inside, I looked back for a second. The woman was leaning over Gaudí and, taking his face in her hands with infinite tenderness, she kissed him on the lips. Just then a flare of lightning ignited the shadows and, for a split second, it seemed as if the person holding my master's face was no lady, but a dark, cadaverous figure with a great black dog seated at its feet. The last thing I saw before the elevator doors closed were the tears on Gaudí's cheeks.

*

When I got back to the room I lay on the bed, invaded by a growing sense of nausea. In a matter of minutes, I fell into a deep and blinding sleep. When the first light of dawn caressed my face, I woke up with a start and rushed to my master's chamber. The bed was still made and there was no sign of Gaudí. I went down to the reception desk to ask if anybody knew his whereabouts. One of the doormen told me he'd seen a man who looked like my master leaving the hotel a few minutes earlier.

'I asked him if he wanted a cab, but he didn't seem to notice me. He crossed Fifth Avenue without looking where he was going and a tram almost hit him. I called after him, but he just kept on walking . . .'

I could not explain exactly why, but I had a feeling I knew where I would find him.

'Is there a church around here?' I asked.

Following the doorman's instructions, I walked north to St Patrick's Cathedral. It was very early in the morning and the church was deserted. I stood on the threshold and caught sight of the master, kneeling in the aisle by the front pew. I walked down the aisle and took a seat at his side. He turned to look at me. His face seemed to have aged twenty years in one night, transformed by that absent air that would accompany him until the last of his days.

'You should watch out for the trams, Master.'

He nodded.

'That's what everybody keeps telling me.'

He made the sign of the cross, stood up and then sat down beside me, his eyes lost in the altar.

'Who was that woman, Master?'

He looked at me, bemused. I understood then that only I had seen the lady in white. I did not dare imagine what the master had seen, but I was positive about one thing: they both shared the same gaze.

That evening we took the boat back home. We stood at the stern of the ship and watched the lights of New York evaporate on the horizon. Then, once we had reached the open sea and were being lashed by a cold wind, Gaudí took the portfolio containing his sketches and threw it into the ocean.

'Master! Why?' I asked, horrified. 'What about the funds for the Sagrada Familia?'

Gaudí took a deep breath, his hand shaking as he gripped the rail and faced the cold wind blowing in from the North Atlantic.

'God is patient, and I cannot afford the price that is asked of me,' he whispered.

During the trip home, I would ask him many times about that price, and the identity of his client. Many times he would smile at me wearily and simply shake his head. Days later, en route to Barcelona, I had to face the fact that my services as an interpreter would no longer be needed. I spent the last few hours on the train from Paris brooding, fearful of my return to the routine of student life, away from the master. Gaudí seemed to sense my sadness and, before he bid me farewell at the station, he embraced me and told me I could visit him at his study anytime I wanted.

*

The day after our arrival I returned to the School of Architecture, where Moscardó was waiting to interrogate me.

'So?' he said.

'Nothing much,' I offered. 'We went to Manchester to visit a factory that makes steel rivets, but after three days Gaudí said he wanted to come back home because the British only serve boiled beef and hate the Virgin Mary.'

Moscardó stared without blinking. I shrugged.

'That's about it.'

He chuckled.

'Crazy as a cuckoo,' he muttered to himself, deeply disappointed.

*

Months later, during one of my many visits to the Sagrada Familia building site, I found myself staring at one of the new sculptures on the pediment. I would have recognised that face anywhere. The lady in white. Her figure, intertwined in a whirl of snakes, invoked an angel with pointed wings, luminous and cruel. I stayed there for a long time, until the sun faded and a shroud of darkness crept over the stone, and watched as her face sank into the shadows, smiling at me.

*

Gaudí and I never talked about what had happened in New York. Whenever I brought up the subject, he would smile and silently shake his head. I knew that the trip would always be our secret. Years went by and I became a passable architect, but hardly a successor to Gaudí. With his recommendation I obtained a position at the studio of Hector Guimard in Paris. It was there, almost two decades after that night in Manhattan, that I received the news of Gaudí's death. A tram had run him over on the Gran Vía as he returned to the Sagrada Familia after going to confession at his favourite church in the Gothic quarter of the old town. Passers-by had left him there bleeding for hours, thinking him a beggar. By the time his apprentices found him a day later, agonising in an asylum for the homeless, it was too late.

I took the first train to Barcelona, just in time to catch the funeral procession that would escort him on his last trip to the crypt of the Sagrada Familia, where I had met him and where he would be buried. That same day I sent a telegram to Hector Guimard in Paris announcing that I would not be returning. At dusk I retraced my steps to the church where I had first met Gaudí. Over the years the city had expanded around the site and the spires of my master's cathedral rose above it, reaching towards a sky splattered with stars. I closed my eyes, and for a second I could picture it finished, as Gaudí himself must have seen it in his mind.

I knew then I would dedicate my life to continuing my

master's work, realising that sooner or later I too would hand on the responsibility to others, and in time they would do the same. Because although God is patient, Gaudí, wherever he may be, is still waiting.

TWO-MINUTE APOCALYPSE

Written in English by Carlos Ruiz Zafón

The day the world ended I was standing at the corner of 5th and 57th checking my phone when a redhead with eyes of silver turned to me and said:

'Have you noticed how the smarter phones get, the dumber people become?'

She looked like a bride of Dracula fresh from a Goth shopping spree next door.

'Can I help you, miss?'

She said the world was coming to an end. Heavenly Legal had issued a malfunction recall and she was a fallen angel sent from below to ensure poor souls like mine found their way into the tenth circle of hell in an orderly fashion.

'I thought there were only nine circles down there,' I objected.

'We had to add one for all of those who've lived their lives as if they were going to live forever.'

I never took my medication seriously, but one look into those silver-dollar eyes and I knew she spoke the truth. Sensing my despair, she announced that since I had not worked in the financial sector I was to be granted three wishes before the big bang recanted and the universe imploded back into a cheerio.

'Pick wisely.'

I gave it some thought.

'I want to know the meaning of life, I want to know where I

can find the best chocolate ice cream ever and I want to fall in love,' I declared.

'The answer to your first two wishes is the same.'

As for the third, she gave me a kiss that tasted of all the truth in the world and made me want to be a decent man. We went for a goodbye walk in the Park and then we crossed the street and took the elevator to the top of the venerable Gothic-spired hotel to watch the world go in style.

'I love you,' I said.

'I know.'

We stood there, hand in hand, glancing at a furious tide of crimson clouds shrouding the skies, and I cried, happy at last.

Extract from

THE SHADOW OF
THE WIND

Translated by Lucia Graves

THE CEMETERY OF
FORGOTTEN BOOKS

I still remember the day my father took me to the Cemetery of Forgotten Books for the first time. It was the early summer of 1945, and we walked through the streets of a Barcelona trapped beneath ashen skies as dawn poured over Rambla de Santa Monica in a wreath of liquid copper.

'Daniel, you mustn't tell anyone what you're about to see today,' my father warned. 'Not even your friend Tomás. No one.

'Not even Mummy?'

My father sighed, hiding behind the sad smile that followed him like a shadow all through his life.

'Of course you can tell her,' he answered, heavy-hearted. 'We keep no secrets from her. You can tell her everything.'

Shortly after the Civil War, an outbreak of cholera had taken my mother away. We buried her in Montjuïc on my fourth birthday. The only thing I can recall is that it rained all day and all night, and that when I asked my father whether heaven was crying, he couldn't bring himself to reply. Six years later my mother's absence remained in the air around us, a deafening silence that I had not yet learned to stifle with words. My father and I lived in a modest apartment on Calle Santa Ana, a stone's throw from the church square. The apartment was directly above the bookshop, a legacy from my grandfather, that specialised in rare collectors' editions and second hand books – an enchanted bazaar, which my father hoped would one day be mine. I was raised among books, making invisible friends in pages that seemed cast from dust and whose smell I carry on my hands to this day. As a child I learned to fall asleep talking to my mother in the darkness of my bedroom, telling her about the day's events, my adventures at school, and the things I had been taught. I couldn't hear her voice or feel her touch, but her radiance and her warmth haunted every corner of our home, and I believed, with the innocence of those who can still count their age on their ten fingers, that if I closed my eyes and spoke to her, she would be able to hear me wherever she was. Sometimes my father would listen to me from the dining room, crying in silence.

On that June morning, I woke up screaming at first light. My heart was pounding in my chest as if my very soul was trying to escape. My father hurried into my room and held me in his arms, trying to calm me.

'I can't remember her face. I can't remember Mummy's face,' I muttered, breathless.

My father held me tight.

'Don't worry, Daniel. I'll remember for both of us.'

We looked at each other in the half-light, searching for words that didn't exist. For the first time, I realised my father was growing old. He stood up and drew the curtains to let in the pale glint of dawn.

'Come, Daniel, get dressed. I want to show you something,' he said.

'Now? At five o'clock in the morning?'

'Some things can only be seen in the shadows,' my father said, flashing a mysterious smile probably borrowed from the pages of one of his worn Alexandre Dumas romances.

Night watchmen still lingered in the misty streets when we stepped out of the front door. The lamps along the Ramblas marked out an avenue in the early morning haze as the city awoke, like a watercolour slowly coming to life. When we reached Calle Arco del Teatro, we continued through its arch toward the Raval quarter, entering a vault of blue haze. I followed my father through that narrow lane, more of a scar than a street, until the glimmer of the Ramblas faded behind us. The brightness of dawn filtered down from balconies and cornices in streaks of slanting light that dissolved before touching the ground. At last my father stopped in front of a large door of carved wood, blackened by time and humidity. Before us loomed what to my eyes seemed the carcass of a palace, a place of echoes and shadows.

'Daniel, you mustn't tell anyone what you're about to see today. Not even your friend Tomás. No one.'

A smallish man with vulturine features framed by thick grey hair opened the door. His impenetrable aquiline gaze rested on mine.

'Good morning, Isaac. This is my son, Daniel,' my father announced. 'He'll be eleven soon, and one day the shop will be his. It's time he knew this place.'

The man called Isaac nodded and invited us in. A blue-tinted gloom obscured the sinuous contours of a marble staircase and a gallery of frescoes peopled with angels and fabulous creatures. We followed our host through a palatial corridor and arrived at a sprawling round hall where a spiralling basilica of shadows was pierced by shafts of light from a high glass dome above us. A labyrinth of passageways and crammed bookshelves rose from base to pinnacle like a beehive, woven with tunnels, steps, platforms and bridges that presaged an immense library of seemingly impossible geometry. I looked at my father, stunned. He smiled at me and winked.

'Welcome to the Cemetery of Forgotten Books, Daniel.'

Scattered among the library's corridors and platforms I could make out about a dozen human figures. Some of them turned to greet me from afar, and I recognised the faces of various colleagues of my father's, fellows of the second hand booksellers' guild. To my ten-year-old eyes, they looked like a brotherhood of alchemists in furtive study. My father knelt next to me and, with his eyes fixed on mine, addressed me in the hushed voice he reserved for promises and secrets.

'This is a place of mystery, Daniel, a sanctuary. Every book, every volume you see here, has a soul. The soul of the person who wrote it and of those who read it and lived and dreamed with it. Every time a book changes hands, every time someone runs his eyes down its pages, its spirit grows and strengthens. This place was already ancient when my father brought me here for the first time, many years ago. Perhaps as old as the city itself. Nobody knows for certain how long it has existed, or who created it. I will tell you what my father told me, though. When a library disappears, or a bookshop closes down, when a book is consigned to oblivion, those of us who know this place, its guardians, make sure that it gets here. In this place, books no longer remembered by anyone, books that are lost in time, live forever, waiting for the day when they will reach a new reader's hands. In the shop we buy and sell them, but in truth books have no owner. Every book you see here has been somebody's best friend. Now they only have us, Daniel. Do you think you'll be able to keep such a secret?'

My gaze was lost in the immensity of the place and its sorcery of light. I nodded, and my father smiled.

'And do you know the best thing about it?' he asked.

I shook my head.

'According to tradition, the first time someone visits this place, he must choose a book, whichever he wants, and adopt it, making sure that it will never disappear, that it will always stay alive. It's a very important promise. For life,' explained my father. 'Today it's your turn.'

For almost half an hour, I wandered within the winding labyrinth, breathing in the smell of old paper and dust. I let my hand brush across the avenues of exposed spines, musing over what my choice would be. Among the titles faded by age, I could make out words in familiar languages and others I couldn't identify. I roamed through galleries filled with hundreds, thousands of volumes. After a while it occurred to me that between the covers of each of those books lay a boundless universe waiting to be discovered, while beyond those walls, in the outside world, people allowed life to pass by in afternoons of football and radio soaps, content to do little more than gaze at their navels. It might have been that notion, or just chance, or its more flamboyant relative, destiny, but at that precise moment, I knew I had already chosen the book I was going to adopt, or that was going to adopt me. It stood out timidly on one corner of a shelf, bound in wine-coloured leather. The gold letters of its title gleamed in the light bleeding from the dome above. I drew near and caressed them with the tips of my fingers, reading to myself.

The Shadow of the Wind
JULIÁN CARAX

I had never heard of the title or the author, but I didn't care. The decision had been taken. I took the book down with great care and leafed through the pages, letting them flutter. Once liberated from its prison on the shelf, it shed a cloud of golden dust. Pleased with my choice, I tucked it under my arm and retraced my steps through the labyrinth, a smile on my lips. Perhaps the bewitching atmosphere of the place had got the better of me, but I felt sure that *The Shadow of the Wind* had been waiting there for me for years, probably since before I was born.

That afternoon, back in the apartment on Calle Santa Ana, I barricaded myself in my room to read the first few lines. Before I knew what was happening, I had fallen right into it. The novel told the story of a man in search of his real father, whom he had never known and whose existence was only revealed to him by his mother on her deathbed. The story of that quest became a ghostly odyssey in which the protagonist struggled to recover his lost youth, and in which the shadow of a cursed love slowly surfaced to haunt him until his dying breath. As it unfolded, the structure of the story began to remind me of one of those Russian dolls that contain innumerable diminishing replicas of themselves inside. Step by step the narrative split into a thousand stories, as if it had entered a gallery of mirrors, its identity fragmented into endless reflections. The minutes and hours glided by as in a dream. When the cathedral bells tolled midnight, I barely heard them. Under the warm light cast by the reading lamp, I was plunged into a new world of images and sensations peopled by characters who seemed as real to me as my surroundings. Page after page I let the spell of the story and its world take me over, until the breath of dawn touched my window and my tired eyes slid over the last page. I lay in the bluish half-light with the book on my chest and listened to the murmur of the sleeping city. My eyes began to close, but I resisted. I did not want to lose the story's spell or bid farewell to its characters just yet.

Once, in my father's bookshop, I heard a regular customer say that few things leave a deeper mark on a reader than the first book that finds its way into his heart. Those first images, the echo of words we think we have left behind, accompany us throughout our lives and sculpt a place in our memory to which, sooner or later – no matter how many books we read, how many worlds we discover, or how much we learn or forget – we will return. For me those enchanted pages will always be the ones I found among the passageways of the Cemetery of Forgotten Books.

ENTER THE WORLD OF THE CEMETERY OF FORGOTTEN BOOKS . . .

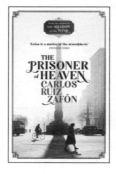
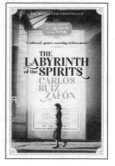

In the bestselling Barcelona-based cycle of novels which began with *The Shadow of the Wind*

Find out more at carlosruizzafon.co.uk